MW00794947

HAUNTINGS AND
OTHER FANTASTIC TALES

broadview editions
series editor: L.W. Conolly

HAUNTINGS AND OTHER FANTASTIC TALES

Vernon Lee

edited by Catherine Maxwell and Patricia Pulham

broadview editions

©2006 Catherine Maxwell and Patricia Pulham

All rights reserved. The use of any part of this publication reproduced, transmitted in any form or by any means, electronic, mechanical, photocopying, recording, or otherwise, or stored in a retrieval system, without prior written consent of the publisher—or in the case of photocopying, a licence from Access Copyright (Canadian Copyright Licensing Agency), One Yonge Street, Suite 1900, Toronto, Ontario M5E 1E5—is an infringement of the copyright law.

Library and Archives Canada Cataloguing in Publication

Lee, Vernon, 1856–1935.
  Hauntings and other fantastic tales / Vernon Lee ; edited by Catherine Maxwell and Patricia Pulham.

(Broadview editions)
Includes bibliographical references.
ISBN 1-55111-578-6

  1. Fantasy fiction, English.   I. Maxwell, Catherine, 1962-   II. Pulham, Patricia, 1959-   III. Title.   IV. Series.

PR5115.P2H69 2006   823'.8   C2006-900632-6

Broadview Editions
The Broadview Editions series represents the ever-changing canon of literature in English by bringing together texts long regarded as classics with valuable lesser-known works.

Advisory editor for this volume: Eugene Benson

Broadview Press is an independent, international publishing house, incorporated in 1985. Broadview believes in shared ownership, both with its employees and with the general public; since the year 2000 Broadview shares have traded publicly on the Toronto Venture Exchange under the symbol BDP.

We welcome comments and suggestions regarding any aspect of our publications—please feel free to contact us at the addresses below or at broadview@broadviewpress.com.

North America
Post Office Box 1243, Peterborough, Ontario, Canada K9J 7H5
3576 California Road, Post Office Box 1015, Orchard Park, NY, USA 14127
Tel: (705) 743-8990; Fax: (705) 743-8353;
email: customerservice@broadviewpress.com

UK, Ireland, and continental Europe
NBN International, Estover Road, Plymouth PL6 7PY UK
Tel: 44 (0) 1752 202300   Fax: 44 (0) 1752 202330
email: enquiries@nbninternational.com

Australia and New Zealand
UNIREPS, University of New South Wales
Sydney, NSW, 2052 Australia
Tel: 61 2 9664 0999; Fax: 61 2 9664 5420
email: info.press@unsw.edu.au

www.broadviewpress.com

Typesetting and assembly: True to Type Inc., Mississauga, Canada.

PRINTED IN CANADA

Contents

Acknowledgements

In preparing this edition we have benefited from the kind assistance of a number of people. We would like to thank Stefano Evangelista, Franca Basta, and Mike Edwards for help with the translation of German, Italian, and Latin phrases, and Terry Pulham for his work in checking many of the typescripts. Stefano Evangelista also helpfully identified the quotation from Goethe's *Roman Elegies* in "Amour Dure," while Margaret Stetz provided the date of death for Lee's dedicatee Margaret Brooke. We would also like to acknowledge Patricia Burdick, the Librarian of Colby College, which holds Lee's copyright, for permission to publish this selection of her short stories and other prose.

Introduction

Vernon Lee, described by Maurice Baring as "by far the cleverest person I have ever met in my life,"[1] first appeared on the British literary scene at the age of 24 with a critical work, *Studies of the Eighteenth Century in Italy* (1880), promptly acclaimed for its elegant style and breadth of erudition. With this passport to literary and artistic circles that included such prominent figures as Robert Browning, William Michael Rossetti, Walter Pater, Oscar Wilde, and Henry James, Lee quickly established herself as a force to be reckoned with, following up her early triumph with a succession of essay and story collections, many of which reflected her cosmopolitan continental outlook and, in particular, her love and deep knowledge of Italy, her adopted homeland. In a writing career that spanned 53 years she won international renown, producing 43 major works that reflected her wide-ranging interests in fiction, aesthetics, philosophy, history, and travel writing. More recently, Lee has emerged as one of the leading writers whose work bridged the gap between late-Victorian aestheticism and early modernist writing, earning the interest of scholars who recognise that literary modernism owes more to its predecessors than its practitioners cared to admit. To modern readers she offers the satisfying spectacle of the economically independent woman of letters, apparently more or less free to say, write, and do as she pleased. This freedom may, however, have been partly responsible for her loss of popularity in the early twentieth century when she seems to have lost her audience as she turned increasingly to more philosophical concerns. Moreover, she saw a further decline in her readership due to the unpopularity of the pacifist stance she adopted during World War I. However, there were other factors involved: her work was unstrategically disseminated, often published in

---

1 "Vernon Lee" was the pseudonym of Violet Paget (1856-1935), who adopted the name in 1875 when publishing her first articles because, as she later remarked in 1878, "no one reads a women's writing on art, history or aesthetics with anything but mitigated contempt" (*Vernon Lee's Letters*, 59). She was known to her friends as "Vernon." Maurice Baring (1874-1945), British diplomat, linguist, and author was a friend of Vernon Lee and the dedicatee of her short story collection *For Maurice* (1927). See his *Lost Lectures of the Fruit of Experience* (London: Peter Davies, 1932) 68.

several periodicals before being offered to book publishers, and the essay style in which she specialised began to seem outmoded in the changing literary climate of the early twentieth century. More generally, Lee's strong personality and strongly held opinions seem to have aroused the hostility of a number of male writers and thinkers: the historian John Addington Symonds (1840-93) resented her failure to accept his corrections, the philosopher Bertrand Russell (1872-1970) appeared jealous of her sway over younger women, the cartoonist Max Beerbohm (1872-1956) nastily caricatured her as a busybody who picked fights with male luminaries, and the art historian and critic Bernard Berenson (1865-1959) accused her of plagiarising his ideas. In addition, the up-and-coming generation of writers, unable or unwilling to acknowledge their indebtedness, claimed to find her work stylistically fusty and irrelevant. Thus the advent of modernism, and the establishment of a predominantly male literary canon, assisted her literary demise, and it is only now that Lee's contribution to English literature and to the development of modernist writing is being fully acknowledged.

A revival of interest in Vernon Lee over the last 20 years or so has resulted in an increasing flow of essays, articles, and, more recently, monographs, which have, with the addition of an international conference devoted to discussion of her life and works, begun to give this considerable if long-neglected woman writer the attention she deserves.[1] Clearly, for her work to reach a new generation of readers, new editions are needed. Lee's stories have always been among the most popular and accessible of her works and have regularly been reprinted in anthologies. However, modern collections of her stories, although obtainable, are unedited, providing little or no context for the work, and, more importantly, providing no guidance in the way of annotation to the dense allusiveness of Lee's writing—those many references to European art and literature, to myth, history, and geography that so enrich an understanding of her fiction. This collection aims to provide that context and help readers gain a better appreciation of the way in which Lee's wide range of reference contributes to her meaning. Learning, for example, something of the troubled lives of the famous Renaissance women mentioned in "Amour Dure," such as Lucrezia Borgia and Bianca Cappello, helps the reader respond to Lee's Medea da Carpi not merely as an enig-

---

1   "Vernon Lee: Literary Revenant," held at the Institute of English Studies, Senate House, London University, 10 June 2003.

matic *femme fatale* but as a brilliant woman trapped in history, while knowledge of Lee's use of the "Gods in Exile" theme employed in "Dionea" significantly increases the impact of the tale.

In putting together this collection we have chosen to reprint *Hauntings*, Lee's first and most famous collection of supernatural tales, which she was working on during the 1880s and published in 1890.[1] Three of these stories are set in Italy, Lee's preferred setting for the supernatural, and one in an English country house. Three of the stories feature descendants of the *femmes fatales* made famous in nineteenth-century art and literature by men, and Appendices A and C reproduce key British sources from well-known texts by Algernon Charles Swinburne and Walter Pater, which Lee evidently draws on in her construction of this type. However, Lee's enigmatic, elusive yet compelling women transcend the often reductive misogynist limitations of this type as they defy being fixed and defined by those around them, even seeming to cross the boundaries of time and space. They have an ally in the strange male ghost who appears in the fourth tale, "A Wicked Voice," who, the text makes plain through its references to Baudelaire and Swinburne, is also related to the *femme fatale* and whose appeal and danger comes through a partial feminisation which makes his extraordinary voice seem indefinable: "there was no agreement on the subject of the voice. It was called by all sorts of names and described by all manner of incongruous adjectives; people went so far as to dispute whether the voice belonged to a man or to a woman; everyone had some new definition" (170). In extending and complicating definitions of gender and sexuality in these stories, Lee fuses femininity with the spectral to suggest something that resists simple categorisation and that leaves everything open and without resolution. This is accentuated by the fact that she uses male narrators, all of whom are thwarted or unfulfilled in a way that makes them susceptible to revenants and marks their projects with inconclusion.

In "Amour Dure" Spiridion Trepka, a young disaffected Polish historian, comes to Italy to write a history of Urbania, but soon finds himself taking an interest in Medea da Carpi, a fascinating

---

1   First editions of *Hauntings* are rare due to a warehouse fire that burnt most of the print run. *Hauntings* was subsequently republished in 1896 and 1906. Unless otherwise indicated, full publication details of primary and secondary works mentioned in the introduction are given in the Bibliography.

sixteenth-century political intriguer, and starts planning a revisionary history of her parallel to his official project. His diary records his growing obsession and his belief that she has begun to communicate with him. The story ends abruptly with Trepka's official and unofficial histories incomplete, his diary ambiguous, and the mystery of his strange romance and its consequences unresolved. "Dionea" features a beautiful but uncanny young woman, cast up on the local shore as a child and raised by nuns, whose idiosyncratic behaviour puts her at odds with the local community. She disturbs but also fascinates the elderly narrator, Dr. Alessandro de Rosis, who is writing a history of the gods in exile, and a visiting sculptor, Waldemar, who, initially disdainful of women as models, agrees to sculpt her. Unable to capture her beauty, which seems constantly to outstrip his efforts, he becomes increasingly obsessed, eventually perishing in macabre circumstances while Dionea disappears. At the end of the story there is still a mystery about Dionea, her origins, involvement in the tragedy, and current whereabouts, and Waldemar's statue is unfinished as is De Rosis's mythological project, which, he has decided, lacks foundation. A similar lack of resolution also characterises "Oke of Okehurst" in which a young painter, recovering from a recent artistic failure, is engaged to paint the portrait of Alice Oke, wife of a country squire. While staying with the couple he finds himself frustrated and tantalised by his inability to capture the likeness of the elusive Alice. He also watches Alice frustrate and tease her adoring and vulnerable husband with her tales of her romance with the ghost of a Caroline poet. In the end, events conspire to prevent the completion of the painting. Finally, in "A Wicked Voice" the young Norwegian composer Magnus, who has come to Venice to finish his Wagnerian opera *Ogier the Dane*, insults the memory of Zaffirino, a famous eighteenth-century singer, and then finds himself unable to complete his opera when he is overwhelmed and then possessed by Zaffirino's voice.

Through the struggles of these male narrators to frame or put into words the spectral femininity that allures and thwarts them, Lee suggests among other things the elusiveness of creativity and of a certain kind of imaginative impulse. This is a major theme in the essay "Faustus and Helena: Notes on the Supernatural in Art" (Appendix D), first published as an article in 1880 and then collected in *Belcaro* the following year. In this essay Lee explores what seems to her to be a "hostility" (295) between the supernatural and art, for although both are dependent on the imagination, she proposes that art depends on "distinct and palpable forms" (295) while the supernatural is based on uncertainty. As she puts it: "the supernatural is necessarily essentially vague, while art is necessarily distinct: give shape to the vague and it ceases to exist." The essay contends that once art sets about trying to "paint, or model, or narrate the supernatural," the supernatural "[becomes] the natural" (296): "paint us that vagueness, mould into shape that darkness, modulate into chords that silence—tell us the character and history of those vague beings....What do we obtain? A picture, a piece of music, a story but the ghost is gone" (310). The supernatural is thus characterised by the imaginative work of suggestion rather than definition. Lee was certainly aware of the inherent difficulties of writing a supernatural tale, anxious that the textual bodying-out of her stories might in some way deprive them of their power. In the preface to "Oke of Okehurst," she addresses her dedicatee Count Peter Boutourline, reminding him of when he first heard her tell it to him at Florence: "You thought it a fantastic tale, you lover of fantastic things, and urged me to write it out at once, although I protested that, in such matters, to write is to exorcise, to dispel the charm; and that print-ers' ink chases away the ghosts that may pleasantly haunt us, as efficaciously as gallons of holy water" (105).

The imaginative suggestiveness of the supernatural, which makes one find a crude sketch more haunting than a finished masterpiece, finds its way into Lee's stories where ghostly projec-tions are cued or triggered by blurring, breaks, gaps, fissures, ruins, relics, and fragments. The Preface to *Hauntings* intimates that her ghosts are born out of suggestions, mental oddments, mnemonic bits and pieces: "They are things of imagination, born there, bred there, sprung from the strange confused heaps, half-rubbish, half-treasure, which lie in our fancy, heaps of half-faded recollections, of fragmentary vivid impressions, litter of multi-coloured tatters" (39). Two of Lee's narratives—"Amour Dure" and "Dionea"—indeed have a somewhat fragmentary appear-ance in that they are pieced together out of letters and diary entries, but the narrators of all the *Hauntings* stories seem alive to suggestion, to cues and associations that trigger imaginative recreation. Disappointed by Rome, Trepka discovers in Urbania a place already formed by art, streets peopled by characters who look as if they were painted by Signorelli or Raphael, and of whom he writes: "I do not talk much to these people. I fear my illusions being dispelled"(43). Later, as a witness at an olive pressing that features "vague figures working at pulleys and hurdles," he notices how it all "looks, to my fancy, like some scene of the Inquisition"(62). His impressions, recorded in the form of diary entries, will, he thinks, console him with their imaginative reconstruction when he returns to Berlin: "These scraps will help ... to bring to my mind ... these happy Italian days"(44). De Rosis in "Dionea" describes the way in which natural effects and phenomena can so combine as to suggest to sensitive imaginations the presence of numinous presences. The painter in "Oke of Okehurst" reports himself "very susceptible" to the "imaginative impression"(112) of the house Okehurst, especially "the yellow room, where the very air, with its scent of heady flowers and old perfumed stuffs, seemed redolent of ghosts" (142), while Magnus in "A Wicked Voice," examining Zaffirino's portrait, finds himself recalling *femmes fatales* described by Swinburne and Baudelaire and, responding to a subconscious cue, brings about his fateful encounter with Zaffirino at Mistrà.

Myth, history, and the past prove fertile sources for the suggestive fragments and relics around which these spectral fancies form. Appendix A, Walter Pater's translation of a key passage from Heinrich Heine's serio-comic "The Gods in Exile"—a shaping force for "Dionea,"—along with the poems by Eugene Lee-Hamilton, Lee's half-brother, and her friend Agnes Mary Frances Robinson in Appendices E and H, reminds us of how the mythic return, whether in the form of a person or artifact, can temporarily disturb or irradiate the present with an exotic beauty and power that rouses desire, fear, and a sad awareness of latter-day lacks and deficiencies. In her later research on art appreciation with her friend Kit Anstruther-Thomson, Lee became famous for promoting an aesthetics of empathy, but this empathetic tendency is already clearly visible in her attitude towards past scenes or persons, as when in an essay of 1892, "In Praise of Old Houses," she writes of "the sense of being companioned by the past, being in a place warmed for our living by the lives of others."[1] Lee's narrators in *Hauntings* all show this heightened awareness of the past or something of her own sensitivity to atmosphere, to the *genius loci* or spirit of place. This sensitivity, so characteristic of her travel writings, means that she is always conscious of the hidden accretions or layers of history that have built up around a particular locale. The late short essay "Out of Venice

---

1 "In Praise of Old Houses," originally published in *Longman's Magazine* 20 (1892), and then reprinted in *Limbo and Other Essays* (1897) where this quotation occurs on p. 29.

at Last" (Appendix I) provides an interesting example of how, in Venice, Lee finds the weight or pressure of this accumulated history of associations excessive in its burden on her consciousness: "Venice is always too much and too much so ... I cannot cope with it, it submerges me" (340). Readers may also recall how in George Eliot's *Middlemarch* (1871-72) similar symptoms overtake Dorothea on her disappointing honeymoon when she is oppressed by the "stupendous fragmentariness" of Rome.[1] The sense of panic, of being overwhelmed by the past, which is present in both Eliot's and Lee's texts, connected perhaps to a return of the repressed, strengthens the link with Lee's earlier Venetian story "A Wicked Voice" in which the highly strung Magnus is confronted by the excessive and voluptuous voice of the androgynous Zaffirino, which he finds at once attractive and repellent. This story also has a possible source in "The Mandolin" (Appendix F), a poem by Eugene Lee-Hamilton that Lee particularly admired and that also explores the theme of a revenge made through insistent ghostly music. Although Lee had published an earlier version of this story in 1881 as "A Culture Ghost: or, Winthrop's Adventure" a year before the publication of her half-brother's poem, the motif of a phantasmal musical revenge does not come into this version, while the later "A Wicked Voice" seems to be clearly marked by Lee-Hamilton's monologue. Moreover, when Magnus in "A Wicked Voice" hears the music, it is introduced on one occasion by "little, sharp, metallic, detached notes, like those of a mandoline"(164) and on another again by "chords, metallic sharp, rather like the tone of a mandoline" (178). Lee-Hamilton's skilfully executed dramatic monologue shows his own interest in reviving a voice from a particular historical period, while another kind of historical empathy can be seen in the extract from Mary Robinson's "The Ladies of Milan" (Appendix G), which bears comparison with "Amour Dure." Like Lee's narrator Spiridion Trepka, Robinson uses an art object, in this case a sculpture of Beatrice d'Este, as a means of communicating with the past and providing another, more sympathetic, view of a woman conventionally seen as "the adored and evil wife of Lodovico il Moro" (334).

In addition to the tales from *Hauntings*, we have chosen three other stories to represent Lee's best work: "Prince Alberic and the Snake Lady" and "A Wedding Chest," taken from the collection

---

1 George Eliot, *Middlemarch*, ed. W.J. Harvey (Harmondsworth: Penguin, 1965) 224.

Pope Jacynth and Other Fantastic Tales (1904), and "The Virgin of
the Seven Daggers," taken from *For Maurice* (1927). "Prince
Alberic and the Snake Lady," first published in the avant garde
fin-de-siècle journal the *Yellow Book* in 1896, a story in the fairy tale
genre, uses an elaborate and sensuous aesthetic style similar to
that used by Oscar Wilde in his fairy tales. Like Wilde, Lee uses
the form of the fairy story as a means of camouflaging ideas which
readers might otherwise reject if presented in unadorned prose.
The story, which some critics have seen as a lesbian fable, certainly seems to trace a sexual rite of passage.[1] In addition to using
the fairy tale motif of an ugly creature who is transformed when
made the object of affection, Lee, who was widely read in European literature, may also be drawing on Théophile Gautier's witty
and risqué short story "Omphale: The Tapestry in Love" (1834)[2]
in which the youthful hero, sleeping in an old room hung with a
tapestry featuring the alluring Omphale, the seductress of Hercules, finds that she comes to life and initiates him into sexual
pleasure. This comes to an end when his uncle, the owner of the
tapestry and, it is implied, a previous recipient of its charms, con-
fiscates it and puts it in the attic. In Lee's story, the tattered tapestry of the snake lady is confiscated by Prince Alberic's grandfather, the Duke of Luna, who detests snakes, and replaced with a
modern one of Susanna and the Elders, presumably with the idea
that its voyeuristic heterosexuality is suitable for a growing boy.
Alberic, however, destroys the replacement tapestry and is exiled
to the Castle of Sparkling Waters where he meets his godmother,
the lady from the tapestry. Again, the mysterious and beautiful
snake lady seems to be Lee's reworking of the *femme fatale*
common to much decadent literature authored by men, in which
serpentine traits indicate woman's sexually dangerous nature (see
Appendix A). Lee's portrayal of the tender, nurturing snake lady
suggests rather that it is her serpentine traits that expose her to
male inconstancy, cruelty, and prejudice.

---

1 See the articles by Vicinus and Hotchkiss listed in the Bibliography.
2 Originally published in *Journal des gens du monde* 9 (7 Feb 1834) as
   "Omphale, ou la tapisserie amoureuse" (Omphale, or The Tapestry in
   Love), and subsequently retitled "Omphale: histoire rococo." The story
   appears as "Omphale: A Rococo Story," in *The Works of Théophile
   Gautier*, tr. F.C. de Sumichrast, 24 vols (London: G.G. Harrap, 1900-
   03) 21, 269-85, and as "The Adolescent" in Théophile Gautier, *My
   Fantoms*, selected, translated and with a postcript by Richard Holmes
   (London: Quartet Books, 1976) 1-12.

In spite of its fairy tale appearance "Prince Alberic and the Snake Lady" is full of allusions to authentic historical and political referents, indicating that Lee had planned its setting and chronology with great care. The same feeling for historical authenticity can be seen in "A Wedding Chest," the other tale from *Pope Jacynth*, even though this story, which emulates the narrative of a Renaissance chronicle, has its own wholly distinct style. In "A Wedding Chest" the chronicler lavishes attention on material objects and events while remaining far less communicative about characters' subjectivity and motives. His interest lies far more with handsome villain Troilo Baglioni and the brooding painter Desiderio than with the unfortunate Maddalena who is the object of rivalry between the two men. In spite of his condemnation of Troilo's evil deeds, the chronicler nonetheless seems to find him attractive and there is far more space devoted to his appearance than there is to Maddalena's. Throughout the story we never have any real insight into the nature of Maddalena's own wishes and desires as she is turned from a lovely dutiful maiden into a beautiful fetishized corpse. Yet although this story, unlike all the others we have chosen, cannot be classed as supernatural, the blank space that it so signally and suggestively writes in for Maddalena among the elaborate descriptions of the wedding chest and the funeral rites cannot help but draw attention to that which is missing—the woman herself—whose erased consciousness becomes a kind of phantom that haunts the text. Both this tale and "Prince Alberic" contain disturbing images of a woman's naked mutilated body, reminding us that Lee's stories frequently include images of violence made all the more shocking for their often abrupt intrusion into the text or their casual, matter-of-fact, and unanticipated deployment alongside passages of calm observation or even great beauty.

This unexpected violence is equally in evidence in "The Virgin of the Seven Daggers," first published in French as "La Madone aux sept glaives" in 1896, the English version of which appears in Lee's late collection of stories, *For Maurice* (1927). As Lee points out in her introduction to this story, her protagonist Don Juan Gusman del Pulgar, Count of Miramor, like his legendary counterpart, is a "conquering super-rake and super-ruffian" (246), known for his sexual exploits and for the ensuing conflicts with husbands and fathers that often end in murder. Don Juan's saving grace is his devotion to "Our Lady of the Seven Daggers of Grenada," whose representative on earth is a doll-like effigy attired in tawdry splendour. Sated by the pleasures of ordinary women, Don Juan seeks fulfilment in other-worldly realms and asks the Virgin to protect him as he ventures illegally into the Alhambra in search of a sleeping Infanta and her treasures, both of which he aims to take using necromantic means. However, success eludes him: his past sins return to haunt him, and his refusal to renounce his love for the Virgin in favour of the Infanta leads to bloodshed and misfortune. The closing half-frame of the tale features a quotation from an imaginary letter written by the foremost playwright of Spain's Golden Age, Don Pedro Calderón de la Barca (1600-81) in which he compares the story's Don Juan to his own Ludovico Enio, a character in his religious play, *El Purgatorio de San Patricio* (*The Purgatory of St Patrick*) (c. 1628), another Spanish villain who ultimately seeks salvation through unyielding faith. But Lee's Don Juan, clearly an *homme fatale*, is also a counterpart to those *femmes fatales* encountered in *Hauntings*—Medea, Dionea, and Alice Oke—and more interestingly, perhaps, a close relative of Zaffirino, the "lure-man" in the tale "A Wicked Voice" who uses his vocal prowess rather than his body to seduce. In "The Virgin of the Seven Daggers" we re-experience the oppressive weight of history in the subterranean passages of the Alhambra, a weight that is mirrored in a writing style that the critic Burdett Gardner once described as bearing "an unhealthy excess of color and jewelled ornament ... a style bedecked in ormolu,"[1] a decadent style which matches that of "Prince Alberic and the Snake Lady" published in the same year as the French version of the story. The sensitivity to historical excess that marks Lee's response to Venice in "Out of Venice at Last" also underlies the extravagant detail that characterises "The Virgin of the Seven Daggers." In her introduction, Lee writes of her "detestation" of the "Spanish cultus of death, damnation, tears and wounds" (245). Lee's tone, here, is playful, and she admits that she may have "cultivated animosity against that great Spanish art of the Catholic Revival" (246). Yet, in a private entry made in one of the Commonplace Books she kept, now held in the Special Collections of the Miller Library, Colby College, Waterville, Maine, her tone is very different, and fore-shadows that adopted in the later essay on Venice. Writing during her stay in Granada in January 1889 following a nervous illness, Lee's impression of the city, and of Spain in general, is a "gloomy" one: in the Spanish imagination she observes "a vio-

---

1 Burdett Gardner, *The Lesbian Imagination (Victorian Style): A Psychological and Critical Study of Vernon Lee*, 21.

lence, a thirst for the exaggerated, a desire, as it were to be bruised [and] stunned, or to bruise [and] stun others," and finds the Andalusian taste in religious decoration overwhelming. In their churches she discovers "gold foil enough to make your eyes ache [and] ... spirals, garlands enough to make [your] head spin."[1] Like Venice, Granada is "too much."

Given this aversion to the superfluous, and Lee's expressed preference for the undefined, the suggested, the ghostly, it is ironic that in the view of many in her own lifetime and beyond, Vernon Lee was herself considered "too much." In a letter to Gardner, Bernard Berenson recalls, "She was the most inveterate talker I have ever known in my life" and he judges her profusion of writings in a corresponding light stating, "It's just the same thing as her talk. It wasn't her industry. She just showed a lack of self-control."[2] Her friend and executor, Irene Cooper Willis, though more restrained, has a similar view. While acknowledging Lee's brilliance, writing to Gardner in the 1950s she notes that Lee "is little read now and I understand why—too discursive, too long winded and erudite"[3] and in a letter written to Violet Dickinson in July 1909 Virginia Woolf complains, "My head spins with [Vernon Lee] whom I have to review. What a woman! Like a garrulous baby."[4] Others, however, evidently enjoyed her company and admired her intellectual dexterity. Of her conversation, Aldous Huxley wrote: "She had read everything in most European languages; but her talk was not merely erudite, it was extremely witty."[5] In a rather more poetic vein, Edith Wharton considered Lee's conversation "the best of its day," and described her talk as having "the opalescent play of a northerly sky."[6]

Lee, it seems, always elicited polarised opinions but for a long period following World War I, aside from occasional articles by her and reviews of her work, she scarcely featured at all in journals, literary reference books, or in the critical forum. By 1954

1 *Commonplace Book*, ns. 4, Special Collections, Miller Library, Colby College, Waterville, Maine, U.S.A. Lee evidently made extensive use of the notes made in Granada in the opening pages of "The Virgin of the Seven Daggers" (249-50).
2 Quoted in Gardner, 60.
3 Ibid., 50.
4 Nigel Nicolson and Joanne Trautmann (eds.), *The Letters of Virginia Woolf*, 6 vols (New York: Harcourt, Brace, Jovanovich, 1976) I, 400.
5 Quoted in Richard Cary, "Aldous Huxley, Vernon Lee and the Genius Loci," *Colby Library Quarterly* 5 (June 1960): 128-40.
6 Edith Wharton, *A Backward Glance* (London: Century, 1987) 133.

Gardner finds that she is "unmentioned in the *Cambridge History of English Literature* and in the *Oxford University Annals of English Literature*" of the period, and that in the *Oxford Companion to English Literature* she merits only the inclusion of her name and dates, and the entry "English essayist and novelist."[1] Some of the likely reasons for this neglect are provided in the opening paragraphs of this introduction, but Vernon Lee did not completely disappear from view. Instead in the 1920s, 1930s and 1940s she was doomed to what some might consider a worse fate. Despite producing such works as *Satan the Waster: A Philosophical War Trilogy* (1920), *The Handling of Words and Other Studies in Literary Psychology* (1923), and *Music and Its Lovers* (1932), which are the subject of current critical attention, she was often reduced to the part of "bit-player" in the dramas of other people's lives, mentioned in a number of autobiographies: Maurice Baring's *The Puppet Show of Memory* (1922), Edith Wharton's *A Backward Glance* (1932), and Dame Ethel Smyth's *As Time Went On* (1936) and *What Happened Next* (1940). The fault may, in part, have been her own. Replying to Gardner's request to write a biography of Vernon Lee, Irene Cooper Willis replies: "In her testamentary instructions to me she prohibited absolutely any biography and added 'my life is my own and I leave that to nobody.'"[2] In her will, Lee also asked that her correspondence should not be read "except privately" until 1980.[3] Fifty copies of an expurgated selection of these letters were, however, privately printed with Cooper Willis's permission in 1937 and circulated among friends.

In the absence of an authorised biography, and limited access to the full content of her letters, what has remained of Lee is a kind of caricature as damaging as that Beerbohm drew on the title page of his copy of *Gospels of Anarchy* (1908), and labelled "Poor dear dreadful little lady."[4] Central to this are Richard Cary's article "Vernon Lee's Vignettes of Literary Acquaintances," published in the *Colby Library Quarterly* in September 1970, and, in particular, Gardner's book *The Lesbian Imagination (Victorian Style): A Psychological and Critical Study of "Vernon Lee,"* written originally as a doctoral dissertation in 1954, before being published by Garland in 1987 in the wake of growing interest. Cary quotes numerous extracts from Lee's private letters out of context and makes com-

---

1 Gardner, 44-45.
2 Quoted in Gardner, 49.
3 Ibid., 50.
4 Quoted in Peter Gunn, *Vernon Lee: Violet Paget 1856-1935*, 3.

ments as acidic as those he attributes to Lee. "To be fair to Vernon Lee," he writes, "it must be recorded that she lays about impartially, friend or foe. She has a grim pride of her self-centrism. 'I *am* hard and I *am* cold,' she says to her executrix [Irene Cooper Willis]; '*I can do without anyone,*' she assures her most devoted crony."[1] However, what Cary chooses to omit casts a very different light on Lee. In the same letter, before acknowledging her lack of unconditional sympathy, Lee tells Cooper Willis: "Loving them [people] in the way you speak of, the way of being willing to do anything for them, is *intolerable* for me. I *cannot* like, or love, at the expense of having my skin rubbed off."[2] Lee's apparent aloofness is not based, as Cary suggests, on insensitivity, but on a heightened sensitivity whose only defence is emotional withdrawal. Arguably, Gardner's book has had an even wider impact. As a full-length study of Lee's works, it is often, along with Phyllis F. Mannocchi's and Carl Markgraf's bibliographies,[3] among the first critical material studied by the fledgling Lee scholar, but one feels that it has not always been read with due caution and scepticism. Denied the opportunity of writing Lee's biography using her personal papers, Gardner's thesis looks at Lee's "lesbian imagination" from a Freudian perspective that he embeds in a framework of biographical detail, developing an image of Lee from her published work and the printed or personal reminiscences of those who knew her. While not technically a biography, it nevertheless works in much the same way, and it represents Lee via a process of "re-membering," of pulling together distinct parts, for its own ends, to create a picture of a fascinating, cold, mannish woman and destructive lesbian "monster." Another major starting point for students of Lee is Peter Gunn's *Vernon Lee: Violet Paget 1856-1935*, published in 1964, and more recently, Vineta Colby's *Vernon Lee: A Literary Biography* (2003). Both of these are more compassionate studies, but they are also literary biographies and, as such, despite their best efforts, continue to interweave the writer's life with her work. While interesting insights may be gained from doing so, a difficulty in Lee's case has been the tendency to dismiss or unfairly judge the work because it is sometimes read in the light of unsympathetic constructions of Lee's private and literary personae. Another

---

1 Richard Cary, "Vernon Lee's Vignettes of Literary Acquaintances," 179-80.
2 Quoted in Gunn, 203.
3 See Phyllis F. Mannocchi, "Vernon Lee: A Reintroduction and Primary Bibliography" and Carl Markgraf, "Vernon Lee: A Commentary and Annotated Bibliography."

related problem is that Vernon Lee is simply difficult to categorise. She wrote on a vast range of subjects and her work spanned two very different literary periods. As Colby writes: "In the end Vernon Lee fits into no single category. She was too late to be a Victorian, too early to be a Modernist. She was a nonmilitant feminist, a sexually repressed lesbian, an aesthete, a cautious socialist, a secular humanist. In short, she was protean."[1] Cruel caricatures and reductive evaluations (or often, in Lee's case, devaluations) of such an author's writings provide a way of containing that which seems elusive and uncontainable and it certainly appears that for a while no one knew quite what to do with this "protean" author.

In 1952, Cooper Willis transferred the Vernon Lee collection in her possession to the library at Colby College, Maine. It consists of letters, as well as books, manuscripts (published and unpublished), articles, photographs, and miscellaneous memorabilia. As a direct result of this gift, the November 1952 edition of the *Colby Library Quarterly* was devoted to the collection and included the following articles: Elizabeth F. Libbey, "The Vernon Lee Papers," Carl J. Weber, "The Date of Miss Jewett's Letter to Vernon Lee," "An Interim Bibliography of Vernon Lee," "Letters from Gosse and Benson," "Mr Wells and Vernon Lee," and "A List of Those Who Wrote Letters to Vernon Lee." It seems that Lee's importance for readers at the time was contingent upon her acquaintance with other authors and this is reflected in many of the articles about her written in the 1950s, 1960s, and early 1970s, most of which revisited her friendships with well-known figures such as Henry James, Karl Hillebrand, Paul Bourget, Aldous Huxley, Carlo Placci, and John Singer Sargent.[2] However, it is in the

---

1   Vineta Colby, *Vernon Lee: A Literary Biography*, xii. It is still a matter of debate whether Vernon Lee's attraction to women had physical expression. In *Intimate Friends: Women Who Loved Women* (2004), Martha Vicinus provides details which suggest that Lee's relationship with Mary Robinson had a physical dimension. See, for example, p. 234.

2   See Carl J. Weber, "Henry James and His Tiger-Cat"; Perley L. Leighton, "'To My Friend, Karl Hillebrand': The Dedication in *Ottilie* and Its Aftermath," *Colby Library Quarterly* 3 (Nov 1953): 185-89; Gordon W. Smith, trans. and ed. "Letters from Paul Bourget to Vernon Lee," *Colby Library Quarterly* 3 (Aug 1954): 237-44; Sybille Pantazzi, "Carlo Placci and Vernon Lee: Their Letters and Their Friends," *English Miscellany* (Rome), 12 (1961): 97-122; Richard Cary, "Aldous Huxley, Vernon Lee, and the Genius Loci," *Colby Library Quarterly* 5 (June 1960): 128-40; Richard Ormond, "John Singer Sargent and Vernon Lee," *Colby Library Quarterly* 9 (1970): 154-78.

1970s that one detects a growing shift in Lee criticism: Vineta Colby considered Vernon Lee in the context of nineteenth-century aestheticism in her book *The Singular Anomaly: Women Novelists of the Nineteenth Century* (1970), and in the same year Leonée Ormond published an article on Lee's critique of the aesthetic movement, her first novel, *Miss Brown* (1884). In 1980, the prohibition on the reading of Lee's private correspondence (housed at Colby College) was lifted and, whether it was this factor, or the re-examination of works by marginalised female writers fostered by Second Wave feminist criticism, it is clear that Lee was back in the academic consciousness.

From the 1980s onwards almost every year has seen a number of articles published on different aspects of Lee's work: her writings on aestheticism, on pacifism, and on her fiction—most particularly on *Miss Brown* and her supernatural tales. By this time it was not only the *Colby Library Quarterly* that was interested in running articles on Lee. Adeline Tintner's "Fiction is the Best Revenge: Portraits of Henry James by Four Women Writers" was published in the journal *Turn of the Century Women* (1985), Phyllis Mannocchi's "Vernon Lee and Kit Anstruther-Thomson: A Study of Love and Collaboration between Romantic Friends" appeared in a *Women's Studies* issue in 1986, and the *Lamar Journal of the Humanities* published Peter Christensen's "'A Wicked Voice': Vernon Lee's Artist Parable" in 1989. In France Jean de Palacio's "Y a-t-il une écriture feminine de la Décadence? (à propos d'une nouvelle de Vernon Lee)" appeared in the journal *Romantisme: Revue du Dix-Nouvième Siècle* in 1983, and in Denmark, in 1988, Merete Licht's essay "Henry James's Portrait of a Lady: Vernon Lee in *The Princess Cassamassima*" was published in *A Literary Miscellany Presented to Eric Jacobsen*. The 1990s saw a broadening in Lee criticism. She begins to appear more often in studies of the Decadent and Aesthetic movement, and there is an engagement with a wider range of her work. As well as being the subject of numerous articles, Lee is discussed in Diana Basham's *The Trial of Woman* (1992), in *Rituals of Disintegration* (1993) by Edwin F. Block Jr., and in Susan Navarette's study *The Shape of Fear* (1998). By the late 1990s and early 2000s she also features in essays in edited collections such as *Victorian Sexual Dissidence* (edited by Richard Dellamora, 1999), *Women and British Aestheticism* (edited by Talia Schaffer and Kathy Alexis Psomiades, 2000), *Athena's Shuttle* (edited by Franco Marucci and Emma Sdegno, 2000), *Brittania, Italia, Germania* (edited by Carol Richardson and Graham Smith, 2001), *Feminist Forerun-*

ners (edited by Ann Heilmann, 2003), *Unfolding the South* (edited by Alison Chapman and Jane Stabler, 2003), *The Victorians and the Eighteenth Century* (edited by Francis O'Gorman and Kathleen Turner, 2004), and *Marketing the Author* (edited by Marysa Demoor, 2004). In addition to these are Colby's monograph, Christa Zorn's *Vernon Lee: Aesthetics, History, and the Victorian Female Intellectual* published in 2003, and Mary Patricia Kane's short study, *Spurious Ghosts: The Fantastic Tales of Vernon Lee* (2004).

Looking at this collection of critical work, one might think that it was no longer necessary, as required in the special Lee issue of the *Colby Library Quarterly* of 1952, to answer the question "Who Was Vernon Lee?"[1] Yet some, it appears, still believe this to be the case and it is worth considering just how much things have changed in the ensuing fifty years. Twelve years after Colby College's acquisition of the collection, Peter Gunn notes in the preface to his literary biography of Lee:

> More than a quarter of a century has elapsed since Vernon Lee's death in 1935. To many of those now living she is a shadowy figure, at the most perhaps only a vaguely remembered name; a name, however, which recalls to an older generation a literary craftsman and polemicist of undoubted importance in her day—but it is the more precise nature of this importance which now eludes our memory.[2]

In Gunn's opening we find that the intervening period between 1952 and 1964 had made apparently little difference to Lee's fame in academic circles. One might expect a very different preface to Vineta Colby's literary biography of Lee published in 2003. Yet the book opens in a comparable way. Colby writes: "It is a small company who read Vernon Lee today. It is an even smaller one who read her with delight for her quirky prose, her flashes of brilliance, her bold and stubborn spirit, and her grasp of the culture of a Europe that no longer exists."[3] Similarly, in her book, Christa Zorn acknowledges that "Vernon Lee, today [is] one of the most underread and underrated critics from the period

---

1   Burdett Gardner, "Who Was Vernon Lee?" *Colby Library Quarterly* 3 (Nov 1952): 120-22.

2   Gunn, ix.

3   Colby, xi.

between 1880 and 1920."[1] Gunn's opening, written in 1964, is perhaps understandable. Vineta Colby's insistence that it is a "small company" who read Vernon Lee today is a little more puzzling. Whilst it is certainly true, as Zorn notes, that Vernon Lee remains "underread and underrated," it is equally true that this is more due to the difficulty in obtaining editions of Lee's works, than to ignorance of the author herself. The attendance of delegates from America, England, France, Germany, and Italy at the Vernon Lee conference held in London in 2003 was testament to this and borne out by the range of articles and longer works written by academics from many of these countries.[2] It seems that the resurgence in Lee studies has been simultaneous internationally.

Lee's fantastic tales have long been at the forefront of this critical interest, perhaps because they lend themselves to interpretation within a variety of contexts including those that have a bearing on the contents of this edition: history, decadence, aestheticism, feminism, and queer studies. However, it is in the fields of gender and sexuality that her supernatural stories have drawn most attention. In her literary biography of Lee, Vineta Colby, while happy to discuss Lee's romantic friendships with other women, resists queer interpretations of her tales. She writes "To read them as unconscious revelations of her inner self—of her sexual frustration and repressed lesbianism ... is unrewarding."[3] Yet she concedes "To the extent that all works of the creative imagination reflect in some degree the psyche of their creators, they are of course self-revealing."[4] One fully understands her concerns when one considers the crude Freudian analysis Gardner applies to Lee's oeuvre in *The Lesbian Imagination*, but times have moved on, and the correlation between Lee's own desires and the sexual tensions that inform her works have been the subject of critical examination by Martha Vicinus and Kathy Alexis Psomiadies, among others, who have proved that such analyses can be handled with sensitivity and success.[5]

---

1   Christa Zorn, *Vernon Lee: Aesthetics, History and the Victorian Female Intellectual*, xv.
2   A collection of critical essays arising from this conference will be published by Palgrave Macmillan in 2006.
3   Colby, 226.
4   Ibid., 226.
5   See Martha Vicinus, "The Adolescent Boy: Fin-de-Siècle Femme Fatale?"; Kathy Alexis Psomiades, "'Still Burning from this Strangling Embrace': Vernon Lee on Desire and Aesthetics."

Whatever one's interest in Lee's supernatural tales, their power consolidates their contribution to the genre. In response to receipt of a volume of her fantastic stories, Henry James thanked Lee for her gift. In his letter he writes:

> The ingenious tales ... are *there*—diffused through my intellectual being and within reach of my introspective—or introactive—hand. (My organism will strike you as mixed, as well as my metaphor—and what I mainly mean is that I *possess* the eminently psychical stories as well as the material volume).[1]

As Adeline Tintner has observed, James's *possession* of and perhaps *possession* by Lee's stories revived his interest in the supernatural tale despite the assertion in his letter to Lee that "The supernatural story, the subject wrought in fantasy, is not the *class* of fiction I myself most cherish."[2] In her comparison of "Oke of Okehurst" with James's "The Way it Came," Tintner contrasts Lee's style with that of the "superior" male writer commenting that, "Whereas Vernon Lee's tale is long, artificial, redundant and overdrawn, James's tale is such a concise masterpiece that he made almost no changes in his revision for the New York Edition."[3] Tintner's remark is an all-too-familiar denigration of Lee's work. Vernon Lee has long been described as a literary follower, rather than a leader, a precocious student taking lessons from her "masters" Walter Pater and Henry James. Those who read this collection will decide for themselves whether Lee deserves to be considered as a "master" in her own right. In a manuscript collection of essays and notes entitled *Lore of the Ego*, there is a piece dated 8 August 1932 which bears the heading: "Je suis venue trop tôt dans un monde trop jeune."[4] In it Lee laments

1   Henry James, *Henry James: Letters*, ed. Leon Edel, 4 vols (Cambridge: Harvard UP, 1974-84) 3, 276.
2   Adeline R. Tintner, "Vernon Lee's 'Oke of Okehurst; Or the Phantom-Lover' and James's 'The Way It Came'," p. 355; Henry James, *Letters*, 3, 277.
3   Adeline R. Tintner, "Vernon Lee's 'Oke of Okehurst; Or the Phantom-Lover' and James's 'The Way It Came'," 356.
4   Vernon Lee, "Je suis venue trop tôt dans un monde trop jeune," (Translation: I came too late into a world too young) in *Lore of the Ego*, manuscript collection, Miller Library, Colby College, Waterville, Maine, USA.

"I am now quite convinced that my intellectual maturity has come too late" and regrets that her age and her deafness prevent her from "all possibility of personal contact with the generation to which I ought to have belonged." Like the revenants who people her stories, Vernon Lee has returned once more: let us make our time, and the future her own.

Vernon Lee: A Brief Chronology

1856   14 October: Violet Paget born in Boulogne-sur-Mer, France, to Matilda (née Adams), former wife of Captain James Lee-Hamilton (deceased), and Henry Ferguson Paget.

1862   Visits England for the first time, spending summer with parents on the Isle of Wight.

1866   The Paget family becomes acquainted with the Fitzwilliam Sargents of Philadelphia in Nice, South of France. Vernon Lee's first meeting with John Singer Sargent.

1868   The Pagets and the Sargents spend the winter in Rome together. The Pagets introduced to American literary and artistic circles.

1870   First publication, 'Les aventures d'une pièce de monnaie', published in *La Famille*, a Lausanne periodical. June: Violet visits her half-brother, the poet Eugene Lee-Hamilton (child of Matilda Paget's first marriage), in Paris.

1873   First signs of Eugene Lee-Hamilton's debilitating illness. The Pagets settle in Florence.

1878   Meets Mme. Annie Meyer in Florence with whom she forms her first passionate friendship.

1880   *Studies of the Eighteenth Century in Italy*; *Tuscan Fairy Tales*. Sends copy of *Studies* to John Addington Symonds. Mary Robinson visits "Casa Paget" at 12 Via Solferino, Florence.

1881   *Belcaro: Being Essays on Sundry Aesthetical Questions*. Visits Mary in London. Meets Edmund Gosse, William Rossetti, William Morris, Robert Browning, Oscar Wilde, and Walter Pater among others. John Singer Sargent paints her portrait.

1882   The Pagets move from Via Solferino to 5 Via Garibaldi, Florence.

1883   *The Prince of the Hundred Soups*; *Ottilie: An Eighteenth-Century Idyll*. Stays in London with Bella Duffy. Visits G.F. Watts's studio and Sir Frederick Leighton's home, Leighton House, in Kensington.

1884   *Euphorion: Being Studies of the Antique and the Mediæval in the Renaissance*; *The Countess of Albany*; *Miss Brown*.

Satirical content of *Miss Brown* offends members of her social circle.

1886   *Baldwin: Being Dialogues on Views and Aspirations*; *A Phantom Lover: A Fantastic Story* (reprinted as "Oke of Okehurst" in *Hauntings,* 1890).

1887   *Juvenilia: Being a Second Series of Essays on Sundry Æsthetical Questions.* August: Mary Robinson becomes engaged to James Darmesteter; meets Clementina (Kit) Anstruther-Thomson. Suffers attack of neurasthenia.

1888   Kit visits Vernon Lee in Florence. Lee still unwell. August: Mary Robinson marries James Darmesteter. November: Lee travels with Evelyn Wimbush to Tangiers and Spain for her health.

1889   The Pagets lease Villa Il Palmerino in Maiano, in the hills above Florence.

1890   *Hauntings: Fantastic Stories.*

1892   *Vanitas: Polite Stories.* William James visits Vernon Lee at Il Palmerino.

1893   *Althea: A Second Book of Dialogues on Aspirations and Duties.* Introduced to George Bernard Shaw. Meets Ethel Smyth at a dinner party at Windsor Castle and Maurice Baring in Florence.

1894   July: Walter Pater dies. November: death of father, Henry Ferguson Paget.

1895   *Renaissance Fancies and Studies.*

1896   March: Matilda Paget dies; Eugene Lee-Hamilton leaves Il Palmerino for America.

1897   *Limbo, and Other Essays.* August: receives letter from Bernard Berenson accusing her and Kit of plagiarism, resulting in long-term feud.

1898   Eugene Lee-Hamilton marries the novelist, Annie Holdsworth. Kit leaves Il Palmerino to nurse another friend, Mrs. Christian Head.

1899   *Genius Loci: Notes on Places.* Kit spends six months of the year with Lee; six with Mrs. Head.

1900   Mary Darmesteter (née Robinson) marries Emile Duclaux. Final break with Kit.

1903   *Ariadne in Mantua*; *Penelope Brandling.* Lee's niece, Persis, daughter of Eugene Lee-Hamilton and Annie Holdsworth, is born.

1904   *Pope Jacynth, and Other Fantastic Tales*; *Hortus Vitae: Essays on the Gardening of Life.* Begins friendship with

H.G. Wells. March: meets Edith Wharton who visits her at Il Palmerino. October: Persis dies.

1905   *The Enchanted Woods, and Other Essays.*

1906   *The Spirit of Rome.* Lee buys Il Palmerino.

1907   September: Eugene Lee-Hamilton dies. Lee travels to Greece and Egypt.

1908   *The Sentimental Traveller; Gospels of Anarchy.*

1909   *Laurus Nobilis: Chapters on Art and Life.*

1911   Meets Irene Cooper Willis, who later becomes her executor. Lee opposes the Italo-Turkish war.

1912   *Vital Lies; Beauty and Ugliness.*

1913   *The Beautiful.*

1914   *Louis Norbert: A Two-Fold Romance; The Tower of Mirrors.* August: World War I begins. Lee is unable to return to Italy after summer in England. Her pacifism loses her friends and publishers. Accused of pro-German sympathies.

1915   *The Ballet of the Nations: A Present-Day Morality.* Becomes a member of the Union of Democratic Control.

1920   *Satan the Waster: A Philosophical War Trilogy.* Returns to Florence. Reconciled with Bernard Berenson.

1921   Death of Clementina (Kit) Anstruther-Thomson.

1923   *The Handling of Words.*

1924   *Art and Man* (written with Clementina Anstruther-Thomson). September 20: University of Durham confers on Lee the degree of Doctor of Letters.

1925   *The Golden Keys, and Other Essays on the Genius Loci; Proteus: or the Future of Intelligence.* Death of John Singer Sargent.

1926   *The Poet's Eye.*

1927   *For Maurice: Five Unlikely Stories.*

1932   *Music and Its Lovers.*

1934   Last visit to England. Taken ill and returns to Italy.

1935   13 February: dies at Il Palmerino. Buried in the Allori cemetery in Florence.

A Note on the Texts

For *Hauntings: Fantastic Stories*, we have used the first edition of 1890 as the definitive text for these stories, this being also the text reissued in the subsequent editions of 1896 and 1906. For "Prince Alberic and the Snake Lady" and "A Wedding Chest" from *Pope Jacynth and other Fantastic Tales*, we have used the second edition of 1907 as there was no loanable first edition available to us. However, the text appears to be identical to the earlier 1904 edition we consulted in the British Library. For "The Virgin of the Seven Daggers," we have used *For Maurice: Five Unlikely Stories* (1927). Obvious printers' errors have been silently corrected throughout.

Hauntings and Other Fantastic Tales

Hauntings: Fantastic Stories

To Flora Priestley and Arthur Lemon[1] are dedicated "Dionea," "Amour Dure," and these pages of introduction and apology.

Preface[2]

WE were talking last evening—as the blue moon-mist poured in through the old-fashioned grated window, and mingled with our yellow lamplight at table—we were talking of a certain castle whose heir is initiated (as folk tell) on his twenty-first birthday to the knowledge of a secret so terrible as to overshadow his subsequent life. It struck us, discussing idly the various mysteries and terrors that may lie behind this fact or this fable, that no doom or horror conceivable and to be defined in words could ever adequately solve this riddle; that no reality of dreadfulness could seem aught but paltry, bearable, and easy to face in comparison with this vague we know not what.

And this leads me to say, that it seems to me that the supernatural, in order to call forth those sensations, terrible to our ancestors and terrible but delicious to ourselves, sceptical posterity, must necessarily, and with but a few exceptions, remain enwrapped in mystery. Indeed, 'tis the mystery that touches us, the vague shroud of moonbeams that hangs about the haunting lady, the glint on the warrior's breastplate, the click of his unseen spurs, while the figure itself wanders forth, scarcely outlined, scarcely separated from the surrounding trees; or walks, and sucked back, ever and anon, into the flickering shadows.

A number of ingenious persons of our day, desirous of a

---

1 Flora Priestley (1859-1944) was a close friend of the painter John Singer Sargent (1856-1925) who did several portraits of her. He introduced her to Vernon Lee and the two women probably met in the early 1880s and then again in Paris where Priestley was studying painting at the Académie Julien. They remained lifelong friends. Arthur D. Lemon (1850-1912), whom Lee also seems to have met in the early 1880s, was born on the Isle of Man but grew up in Rome; he was a notable painter of equine subjects and pastoral scenes. His work includes many rural and landscape paintings of Tuscany. Lee wrote an introduction to the catalogue of the memorial exhibition of his works, held at the Goupil Gallery, 1913.

2 Text taken from *Hauntings: Fantastic Stories* (London: W. Heinemann, 1890) vii-xi.

pocket-superstition, as men of yore were greedy of a pocket-saint to carry about in gold and enamel, a number of highly reasoning men of semi-science have returned to the notion of our fathers, that ghosts have an existence outside our own fancy and emotion; and have culled from the experience of some Jemima Jackson, who fifty years ago, being nine years of age, saw her maiden aunt appear six months after decease, abundant proof of this fact. One feels glad to think the maiden aunt should have walked about after death, if it afforded her any satisfaction, poor soul! but one is struck by the extreme uninterestingness of this lady's appearance in the spirit, corresponding perhaps to her want of charm while in the flesh. Altogether one quite agrees, having duly perused the collection of evidence on the subject, with the wisdom of these modern ghost-experts, when they affirm that you can always tell a genuine ghost-story by the circumstance of its being about a nobody, its having no point or picturesqueness, and being, generally speaking, flat, stale, and unprofitable.

A genuine ghost-story! But then they are not genuine ghost-stories, those tales that tingle through our additional sense, the sense of the supernatural, and fill places, nay whole epochs, with their strange perfume of witchgarden flowers.

No, alas! neither the story of the murdered King of Denmark (murdered people, I am told, usually stay quiet, as a scientific fact), nor of that weird woman who saw King James the Poet three times with his shroud wrapped ever higher; nor the tale of the finger of the bronze Venus closing over the wedding-ring, whether told by Morris in verse patterned like some tapestry, or by Mérimée in terror of cynical reality, or droned by the original mediæval professional storyteller, none of these are genuine ghost-stories.[1] They exist, these ghosts, only in our minds, in the minds of those dead folk; they have never stumbled and fumbled

---

1 In Shakespeare's *Hamlet* (first printed 1603), the eponymous hero, the Prince of Denmark, encounters the ghost of his father (Old Hamlet) who has been murdered by his brother (young Hamlet's uncle) Claudius. James I of Scotland (1394-1437), a man of cultivation and a poet, was repeatedly warned of his impending death by an old Highland woman whom he ignored. He was assassinated on 20 February 1437 by Sir Robert Graham. The story is told in the poem "The King's Tragedy" (1881) by Dante Gabriel Rossetti. For the statue of Venus and the wedding-ring, see William Morris, "The Ring given to Venus" in his *The Earthly Paradise* (1868-70), and Prosper Mérimée's story "Venus d'Ille"(1837). Lee adapts this tale in her own story "St Eudæmon and his Orange-Tree" in *Pope Jacynth & Other Fantastic Tales* (1904).

about, with Jemima Jackson's maiden aunt, among the arm-chairs and rep sofas of reality.

They are things of the imagination, born there, bred there, sprung from the strange confused heaps, half-rubbish, half-treasure, which lie in our fancy, heaps of half-faded recollections, of fragmentary vivid impressions, litter of multi-coloured tatters, and faded herbs and flowers, whence arises that odour (we all know it), musty and damp, but penetratingly sweet and intoxicatingly heady, which hangs in the air when the ghost has swept through the unopened door, and the flickering flames of candle and fire start up once more after waning.

The genuine ghost? And is not this he, or she, this one born of ourselves, of the weird places we have seen, the strange stories we have heard—this one, and not the aunt of Miss Jemima Jackson? For what use, I entreat you to tell me, is that respectable spinster's vision? Was she worth seeing, that aunt of hers, or would she, if followed, have led the way to any interesting brimstone or any endurable beatitude?

The supernatural can open the caves of Jamschid and scale the ladder of Jacob:[1] what use has it got if it land us in Islington or Shepherd's Bush? It is well known that Dr. Faustus, having been offered any ghost he chose, boldly selected, for Mephistopheles to convey, no less a person than Helena of Troy.[2] Imagine if the familiar fiend had summoned up some Miss Jemima Jackson's Aunt of Antiquity!

That is the thing—the Past, the more or less remote Past, of which the prose is clean obliterated by distance—that is the place to get our ghosts from. Indeed we live ourselves, we educated folk of modern times, on the borderland of the Past, in houses looking down on its troubadours' orchards and Greek folks' pillared courtyards; and a legion of ghosts, very vague and changeful, are perpetually to and fro, fetching and carrying for us between it and the Present.

Hence, my four little tales are of no genuine ghosts in the sci-

---

1 Jamschid (normally Jamshid) was a legendary king of Persia. Takt-e-Jamschid or "Throne of Jamschid" (also known as Persepolis) was the ancient capital city of the Persian Empire. In Genesis 28. 11-16, Jacob has a vision of a ladder with its feet on earth and its top in heaven with the angels ascending and descending.

2 See Christopher Marlowe's *Doctor Faustus* (1604, 1616), Act 5, Scene 1. Lee discusses this incident in Marlowe's play in her essay "Faustus and Helena: Notes on the Supernatural in Art" (Appendix D).

entific sense; they tell of no hauntings such as could be con-
tributed by the Society for Psychical Research,[1] of no spectres
that can be caught in definite places and made to dictate judicial
evidence. My ghosts are what you call spurious ghosts (according
to me the only genuine ones), of whom I can affirm only one
thing, that they haunted certain brains, and have haunted, among
others, my own and my friends'—yours, dear Arthur Lemon,
along the dim twilit tracks, among the high growing bracken and
the spectral pines, of the south country; and yours, amidst the
mist of moonbeams and olive-branches, dear Flora Priestley,
while the moonlit sea moaned and rattled against the mouldering
walls of the house whence Shelley set sail for eternity.[2]

VERNON LEE.

MAIANO, *near* FLORENCE,
June 1889.

---

1 The Society for Psychical Research (SPR) was founded in 1882 by a
   distinguished group of Cambridge scholars that included Lee's friend
   Edward Gurney. It was the first group to examine allegedly paranormal
   phenomena in a scientific and unbiased way. In her *Letters* (p. 176), Lee
   reports attending a meeting of the SPR in July 1885 which she found "a
   very dull business."
2 In 1888 Lee and her friend Kit Anstruther-Thomson visited Lerici
   where, joined by Flora Priestley, they stayed next door to Casa Magni,
   last home of the English Romantic poet Percy Bysshe Shelley (b. 1792)
   who drowned in the Bay of Lerici in 1822.

Amour Dure:
Passages from the Diary of Spiridion Trepka[1]

PART I

Urbania, August 20th, 1885.—I had longed, these years and years, to be in Italy, to come face to face with the Past; and was this Italy, was this the Past? I could have cried, yes cried, for disappointment when I first wandered about Rome, with an invitation to dine at the German Embassy in my pocket, and three or four Berlin and Munich Vandals at my heels, telling me where the best beer and sauerkraut could be had, and what the last article by Grimm or Mommsen was about.[2]

Is this folly? Is it falsehood? Am I not myself a product of modern, northern civilisation; is not my coming to Italy due to this very modern scientific vandalism, which has given me a travelling scholarship because I have written a book like all those other atrocious books of erudition and art-criticism? Nay, am I not here at Urbania[3] on the express understanding that, in a certain number of months, I shall produce just another such

---

1 "Amour Dure" was first published in *Murray's Magazine* 1 (1887) 49ff; 188ff. It was then republished in *Hauntings: Fantastic Stories* (London: William Heinemann, 1890) 3-58, from which this text is taken. During the early 1880s Lee was working on a full-length "Renaissance novel" *Medea da Carpi*, but was unable to secure a publisher. To her amusement Blackwood turned it down in July 1885 "because he thinks it a pity to put the historical facts into a fictitious frame! Isn't that a joke!" (*Letters*, 183). She eventually cut the narrative down for publication in the new periodical *Murray's Magazine*.

2 The Vandals were an ancient Germanic people who invaded Western Europe and in AD 455 sacked Rome. They were noted for their love of plunder and booty. Spiridion Trepka comments here acidly on what he regards as a philistine German colonisation of Rome. He also seems to despise the "scientific vandalism" and pedantry of contemporary German scholarship. Hermann Grimm (1828-1901), German writer and historian, early art historical theorist, Michelangelo scholar, Professor of Art at the University of Berlin, 1872-1901; Christian Matthias Theodor Mommsen (1817-1903), German writer and historian, famous for his *The History of Rome*, taught at Friedrich Wilhelm University, Berlin.

3 There is a small mediaeval city of Urbania in the Alpine foothills of the Italian Marches and named after Pope Urban VIII in 1636, but Lee's Urbania seems to be a fictional place.

book? Dost thou imagine, thou miserable Spiridion, thou Pole grown into the semblance of a German pedant,[1] doctor of philosophy, professor even, author of a prize essay on the despots of the fifteenth century, dost thou imagine that thou, with thy ministerial letters and proof-sheets in thy black professorial coat-pocket, canst ever come in spirit into the presence of the Past?

Too true, alas! But let me forget it, at least, every now and then; as I forgot it this afternoon, while the white bullocks dragged my gig slowly winding along interminable valleys, crawling along interminable hill-sides, with the invisible droning torrent far below, and only the bare grey and reddish peaks all around, up to this town of Urbania, forgotten of mankind, towered and battlemented on the high Apennine ridge. Sigillo, Penna, Fossombrone, Mercatello, Montemurlo[2]—each single village name, as the driver pointed it out, brought to my mind the recollection of some battle or some great act of treachery of former days. And as the huge mountains shut out the setting sun, and the valleys filled with bluish shadow and mist, only a band of threatening smoke-red remaining behind the towers and cupolas of the city on its mountain-top, and the sound of church bells floated across the precipice from Urbania, I almost expected, at every turning of the road, that a troop of horsemen, with beaked helmets and clawed shoes, would emerge, with armour glittering and pennons waving in the sunset. And then, not two hours ago, entering the town at dusk, passing along the deserted streets, with only a smoky light here and there under a shrine or in front of a fruit-stall, or a fire reddening the blackness of a smithy; passing beneath the battlements and turrets of the palace.... Ah, that was Italy, it was the Past!

---

1 Spiridion is from Posen, originally known as Wielpolska (literally "Greater Poland"), a province of Poland which was the historical centre of origin of the Polish nation in the tenth century, and which, in 1793, was taken over by Prussia. Renamed "Southern Prussia" it then came to be known by the name of its capital town, Poznan (German Posen). During the nineteenth century German colonisation of the province increased significantly. As a Pole, Spiridion is uncomfortable with his acquired German identity. Lee's father, Henry Ferguson Paget, spent a large part of his youth in Warsaw, Poland, and eventually had to flee the country due to his involvement in the Polish revolutionary uprisings of 1846.

2 The Apennines are a mountain range running down the length of Italy. Sigillo, Penna, Fossombrone, Mercatello are the names of towns or villages in Umbria while Montemurlo is a town located in Tuscany.

August 21*st.*—And this is the Present! Four letters of introduction to deliver, and an hour's polite conversation to endure with the Vice-Prefect, the Syndic, the Director of the Archives, and the good man to whom my friend Max had sent me for lodgings....

August 22nd-27*th.*—Spent the greater part of the day in the Archives, and the greater part of my time there in being bored to extinction by the Director thereof, who to-day spouted Æneas Sylvius' Commentaries[1] for three-quarters of an hour without taking breath. From this sort of martyrdom (what are the sensations of a former racehorse being driven in a cab? If you can conceive them, they are those of a Pole turned Prussian professor) I take refuge in long rambles through the town. This town is a handful of tall black houses huddled on to the top of an Alp, long narrow lanes trickling down its sides, like the slides we made on hillocks in our boyhood, and in the middle the superb red brick structure, turreted and battlemented, of Duke Ottobuono's palace, from whose windows you look down upon a sea, a kind of whirlpool, of melancholy grey mountains. Then there are the people, dark, bushy-bearded men, riding about like brigands, wrapped in green-lined cloaks upon their shaggy pack-mules; or loitering about, great, brawny, low-headed youngsters, like the parti-coloured bravos in Signorelli's frescoes; the beautiful boys, like so many young Raphaels, with eyes like the eyes of bullocks, and the huge women, Madonnas or St. Elizabeths,[2] as the case may be, with their clogs firmly poised on their toes and their brass pitchers on their heads, as they go up and down the steep black alleys. I do not talk much to these people; I fear my illusions being dispelled. At the corner of a street, opposite Francesco di Giorgio's beautiful little portico, is a great blue and red advertisement, representing an angel descending to crown Elias Howe, on account of his sewing-machines;[3] and the clerks of the Vice-Prefecture, who dine at the place where I get my dinner, yell politics, Minghetti, Cairoli, Tunis, ironclads, &c., at each other,

1 Æneas Sylvius Piccolomini (1405-64), afterwards Pope Pius II, poet, orator, and interpreter of antiquity.
2 Luca Signorelli (c. 1441/50-1523) is best known for his apocalyptic fresco cycle in Orvieto Cathedral. Raphael or Raffaello Sanzio (1483-1520), one of the great High Renaissance painters. In Renaissance art St. Elizabeth, the mother of John the Baptist, is often portrayed with her relative, the Madonna or Virgin Mary.
3 Francesco di Giorgio Martini (1439-1501), Italian, architect, painter, and sculptor; Elias Howe (1818-67), American inventor of the sewing machine.

and sing snatches of *La Fille de Mme. Angot*,[1] which I imagine they have been performing here recently.

No; talking to the natives is evidently a dangerous experiment. Except indeed, perhaps, to my good landlord, Signor Notaro Porri, who is just as learned, and takes considerably less snuff (or rather brushes it off his coat more often) than the Director of the Archives. I forgot to jot down (and I feel I must jot down, in the vain belief that some day these scraps will help, like a withered twig of olive or a three-wicked Tuscan lamp on my table, to bring to my mind, in that hateful Babylon of Berlin, these happy Italian days)—I forgot to record that I am lodging in the house of a dealer in antiquities. My window looks up the principal street to where the little column with Mercury on the top rises in the midst of the awnings and porticoes of the market-place. Bending over the chipped ewers and tubs full of sweet basil, clove pinks, and marigolds, I can just see a corner of the palace turret, and the vague ultramarine of the hills beyond. The house, whose back goes sharp down into the ravine, is a queer up-and-down black place, whitewashed rooms, hung with the Raphaels and Francias and Peruginos,[2] whom mine host regularly carries to the chief inn whenever a stranger is expected; and surrounded by old carved chairs, sofas of the Empire, embossed and gilded wedding-chests, and the cupboards which contain bits of old damask and embroidered altar-cloths scenting the place with the smell of old incense and mustiness; all of which are presided over by Signor Porri's three maiden sisters—Sora Serafina, Sora Lodovica, and Sora Adalgisa—the three Fates in person, even to the distaffs and their black cats.[3]

---

1 Marco Minghetti (1819-86), Italian economist and statesman; Benedetto Cairoli (1825-89), Italian statesman and devoted supporter of the Risorgimento. He resigned from government after his failure to foresee the French occupation of Tunis, North Africa (which Italy had also been interested in), on 11 May 1881, an occupation which lasted till 1956. Ironclads are warships: ships sheathed in thick iron plate for protection; *La Fille de Mme Angot* (1872), a light opera by Alexandre Lecocq.

2 Raphaels (see above); Francesco Francia (c. 1450-1517/18), Italian painter influenced by Raphael; Perugino (c. 1445/50-1523), painter and teacher of Raphael.

3 In classical mythology the Parcae, or Fates, the three daughters of Themis (goddess of Necessity), preside over the fortunes of human life in their symbolic spinning. Life is woven by Clotho, measured by Lachesis, and finally the thread of life is cut by Atropos.

Sor Asdrubale, as they call my landlord, is also a notary. He regrets the Pontifical Government, having had a cousin who was a Cardinal's train-bearer, and believes that if only you lay a table for two, light four candles made of dead men's fat, and perform certain rites about which he is not very precise, you can, on Christmas Eve and similar nights, summon up San Pasquale Baylon,[1] who will write you the winning numbers of the lottery upon the smoked back of a plate, if you have previously slapped him on both cheeks and repeated three Ave Marias. The difficulty consists in obtaining the dead men's fat for the candles, and also in slapping the saint before he have time to vanish.

"If it were not for that," says Sor Asdrubale, "the Government would have had to suppress the lottery ages ago—eh!"

Sept. 9th.—This history of Urbania is not without its romance, although that romance (as usual) has been overlooked by our Dryasdusts.[2] Even before coming here I felt attracted by the strange figure of a woman, which appeared from out of the dry pages of Gualterio's and Padre de Sanctis' histories of this place.[3] This woman is Medea, daughter of Galeazzo IV. Malatesta, Lord of Carpi, wife first of Pierluigi Orsini, Duke of Stimigliano, and subsequently of Guidalfonso II., Duke of Urbania, predecessor of the great Duke Robert II.[4]

This woman's history and character remind one of that of

---

1   San Pasquale Baylon: Spanish saint (died 1592), also referred to in "Prince Alberic and the Snake Lady," who attained outstanding holiness in leading the uneventful life of a laybrother. He was canonised in 1690.

2   A Dryasdust is a dull pedantic speaker or writer, named after Dr. Jonas Dryasdust, a fictitious character to whom Sir Walter Scott dedicated some of his novels.

3   Raffaello Gualterio and Padre de Sanctis are fictional historians as is the later-mentioned Don Arcangelo Zappi.

4   Carpi is a town in the province of Modena in central Italy but was ruled by the Pios, not the Malatesti, who were the ruling family in Rimini and controlled a number of other cities in the Romagna and the Marca d'Ancona until 1500. The Malastesti were prominent in the history of Italy in the fourteenth and fifteenth centuries and many of them were well-known for their crimes and cruelty. The town of Stimigliano in the Lazio region in central Italy was the dominion of the Orsini family from 1368-1605 when it returned to the government of the Pope. The Orsini were one of the most ancient and distinguished families of the Roman nobility and played a key part in the history of Italy, especially in Rome and the papal states.

Bianca Cappello, and at the same time of Lucrezia Borgia.[1] Born in 1556, she was affianced at the age of twelve to a cousin, a Malatesta of the Rimini family. This family having greatly gone down in the world, her engagement was broken, and she was betrothed a year later to a member of the Pico family,[2] and married to him by proxy at the age of fourteen. But this match not satisfying her own or her father's ambition, the marriage by proxy was, upon some pretext, declared null, and the suit encouraged of the Duke of Stimigliano, a great Umbrian feudatory of the Orsini family. But the bridegroom, Giovanfrancesco Pico, refused to submit, pleaded his case before the Pope, and tried to carry off by force his bride, with whom he was madly in love, as the lady was most lovely and of most cheerful and amiable manner, says an old anonymous chronicle. Pico waylaid her litter as she was going to a villa of her father's, and carried her to his castle near Mirandola, where he respectfully pressed his suit; insisting that he had a right to consider her as his wife. But the lady escaped by letting herself into the moat by a rope of sheets, and Giovanfrancesco Pico was discovered stabbed in the chest, by the hand of Madonna Medea da Carpi. He was a handsome youth only eighteen years old.

The Pico having been settled, and the marriage with him declared null by the Pope, Medea da Carpi was solemnly married

---

1   Bianca Cappello (1548-87), grand duchess of Tuscany, daughter of Bartolommeo Cappello and a member of the richest and noblest Venetian families. Famed for her beauty, she eloped and married a young Florentine clerk but afterwards became the mistress, then wife, of Francesco de' Medici, grand Duke of Tuscany, and was hated by her brother-in law Cardinal Ferdinand as an interloper. Lucrezia Borgia (1480-1519), illegitimate daughter of the Spanish Cardinal Rodrigo Borgia, afterwards Pope Alexander VI, famed for her beauty and depravity, although modern scholarship has suggested that her reputation may be based more on rumour than historical truth. She was married three times, in the last instance to Alfonso d'Este, afterwards Duke of Ferrara. In Ferrara she involved herself in the literary and cultivated life of the court. She died in childbirth aged 39. See also the extract from the "The Ladies of Milan" by Lee's friend, A. Mary F. Robinson (Appendix G).

2   Lee imagines Medea betrothed to a member of the Pico family who were Lords of Mirandola in the Duchy of Modena where they had a castle. The philosopher Pico della Mirandola (1463-94) is their most famous scion.

to the Duke of Stimigliano, and went to live upon his domains near Rome.

Two years later, Pierluigi Orsini was stabbed by one of his grooms at his castle of Stimigliano, near Orvieto; and suspicion fell upon his widow, more especially as, immediately after the event, she caused the murderer to be cut down by two servants in her own chamber; but not before he had declared that she had induced him to assassinate his master by a promise of her love. Things became so hot for Medea da Carpi that she fled to Urbania and threw herself at the feet of Duke Guidalfonso II., declaring that she had caused the groom to be killed merely to avenge her good fame, which he had slandered, and that she was absolutely guiltless of the death of her husband. The marvellous beauty of the widowed Duchess of Stimigliano, who was only nineteen, entirely turned the head of the Duke of Urbania. He affected implicit belief in her innocence, refused to give her up to the Orsinis, kinsmen of her late husband, and assigned to her magnificent apartments in the left wing of the palace, among which the room containing the famous fireplace ornamented with marble Cupids on a blue ground. Guidalfonso fell madly in love with his beautiful guest. Hitherto timid and domestic in character, he began publicly to neglect his wife, Maddalena Varano of Camerino,[1] with whom, although childless, he had hitherto lived on excellent terms; he not only treated with contempt the admonitions of his advisers and of his suzerain the Pope, but went so far as to take measures to repudiate his wife, on the score of quite imaginary ill-conduct. The Duchess Maddalena, unable to bear this treatment, fled to the convent of the barefooted sisters at Pesaro,[2] where she pined away, while Medea da Carpi reigned in her place at Urbania, embroiling Duke Guidalfonso in quarrels both with the powerful Orsinis, who continued to accuse her of Stimigliano's murder, and with the Varanos, kinsmen of the injured Duchess Maddalena; until at length, in the year 1576, the Duke of Urbania, having become suddenly, and not without suspicious circumstances, a widower, publicly married Medea da Carpi two days after the decease of his unhappy wife. No child was born of this marriage; but such was the infatuation of Duke Guidalfonso, that the new Duchess induced him to settle the inheritance of the Duchy (having, with great difficulty, obtained the consent of the Pope) on the boy Bar-

---

1 A large part of Camerino, a town in the Marca d'Ancona, was built under the benign rule of the da Varano family from 1200-1539.
2 A sea-side town in the Italian Marches.

tolommeo, her son by Stimigliano, but whom the Orsinis refused to acknowledge as such, declaring him to be the child of that Giovanfrancesco Pico to whom Medea had been married by proxy, and whom, in defence, as she had said, of her honour, she had assassinated; and this investiture of the Duchy of Urbania on to a stranger and a bastard was at the expense of the obvious rights of the Cardinal Robert, Guidalfonso's younger brother.

In May 1579 Duke Guidalfonso died suddenly and mysteriously, Medea having forbidden all access to his chamber, lest, on his deathbed, he might repent and reinstate his brother in his rights. The Duchess immediately caused her son, Bartolommeo Orsini, to be proclaimed Duke of Urbania, and herself regent; and, with the help of two or three unscrupulous young men, particularly a certain Captain Oliverotto da Narni,[1] who was rumoured to be her lover, seized the reins of government with extraordinary and terrible vigour, marching an army against the Varanos and Orsinis, who were defeated at Sigillo, and ruthlessly exterminating every person who dared question the lawfulness of the succession; while, all the time, Cardinal Robert, who had flung aside his priest's garb and vows, went about in Rome, Tuscany, Venice—nay, even to the Emperor and the King of Spain, imploring help against the usurper. In a few months he had turned the tide of sympathy against the Duchess-Regent; the Pope solemnly declared the investiture of Bartolommeo Orsini worthless, and published the accession of Robert II., Duke of Urbania and Count of Montemurlo; the Grand Duke of Tuscany and the Venetians secretly promised assistance, but only if Robert were able to assert his rights by main force. Little by little, one town after the other of the Duchy went over to Robert, and Medea da Carpi found herself surrounded in the mountain citadel of Urbania like a scorpion surrounded by flames. (This simile is not mine, but belongs to Raffaello Gualterio, historiographer to Robert II.) But, unlike the scorpion, Medea refused to commit suicide. It is perfectly marvellous how, without money or allies, she could so long keep her enemies at bay; and Gualterio attributes this to those fatal fascinations which had brought Pico and Stimigliano to their deaths, which had turned the once honest Guidalfonso into a villain, and which were such that, of all

---

1   A mediaeval town in Perugia. Oliverotto is perhaps a descendent of butcher's boy-turned-famous-*condottiere*, the general Erasmo da Narni (1370-1443), immortalized in 1447 by the sculptor Donatello in a famous equestrian statue in Padua.

her lovers, not one but preferred dying for her, even after he had been treated with ingratitude and ousted by a rival; a faculty which Messer Raffaello Gualterio clearly attributed to hellish connivance.

At last the ex-Cardinal Robert succeeded, and triumphantly entered Urbania in November 1579. His accession was marked by moderation and clemency. Not a man was put to death, save Oliverotto da Narni, who threw himself on the new Duke, tried to stab him as he alighted at the palace, and who was cut down by the Duke's men, crying, "Orsini, Orsini! Medea, Medea! Long live Duke Bartolommeo!" with his dying breath, although it is said that the Duchess had treated him with ignominy. The little Bartolommeo was sent to Rome to the Orsinis; the Duchess, respectfully confined in the left wing of the palace.

It is said that she haughtily requested to see the new Duke, but that he shook his head, and, in his priest's fashion, quoted a verse about Ulysses and the Sirens; and it is remarkable that he persistently refused to see her, abruptly leaving his chamber one day that she had entered it by stealth. After a few months a conspiracy was discovered to murder Duke Robert, which had obviously been set on foot by Medea. But the young man, one Marcantonio Frangipani of Rome,[1] denied, even under the severest torture, any complicity of hers; so that Duke Robert, who wished to do nothing violent, merely transferred the Duchess from his villa at Sant' Elmo to the convent of the Clarisse in town,[2] where she was guarded and watched in the closest manner. It seemed impossible that Medea should intrigue any further, for she certainly saw and could be seen by no one. Yet she contrived to send a letter and her portrait to one Prinzivalle degli Ordelaffi, a youth, only nineteen years old, of noble Romagnole family,[3] and who was betrothed to one of the most beautiful girls of Urbania. He immediately broke off his engagement, and, shortly afterwards, attempted to shoot Duke Robert with a holster-pistol as he knelt at mass on the festival of Easter Day. This time Duke Robert was deter-

---

1 The Frangipani were a wealthy Roman family who influenced the papacy and empire in the eleventh to thirteenth centuries.
2 The Clarisse, also known as the Poor Clares or the Order of Poor Ladies, are a Roman Catholic Franciscan order of contemplative nuns founded by St. Clare of Assisi (c. 1194-1253).
3 The noble Ordelaffi family ruled the town of Forlì in the Romagna region for most of the fourteenth and fifteenth centuries.

mined to obtain proofs against Medea. Prinzivalle degli Ordelaffi was kept some days without food, then submitted to the
most violent tortures, and finally condemned. When he was
going to be flayed with red-hot pincers and quartered by
horses, he was told that he might obtain the grace of immediate death by confessing the complicity of the Duchess; and the
confessor and nuns of the convent, which stood in the place of
execution outside Porta San Romano, pressed Medea to save
the wretch, whose screams reached her, by confessing her own
guilt. Medea asked permission to go to a balcony, where she
could see Prinzivalle and be seen by him. She looked on coldly,
then threw down her embroidered kerchief to the poor
mangled creature. He asked the executioner to wipe his mouth
with it, kissed it, and cried out that Medea was innocent. Then,
after several hours of torments, he died. This was too much for
the patience even of Duke Robert. Seeing that as long as
Medea lived his life would be in perpetual danger, but unwilling to cause a scandal (somewhat of the priest-nature remaining), he had Medea strangled in the convent, and, what is
remarkable, insisted that only women—two infanticides to
whom he remitted their sentence—should be employed for the
deed.

"This clement prince," writes Don Arcangelo Zappi in his life
of him, published in 1725, "can be blamed only for one act of
cruelty, the more odious as he had himself, until released from his
vows by the Pope, been in holy orders. It is said that when he
caused the death of the infamous Medea da Carpi, his fear lest
her extraordinary charms should seduce any man was such, that
he not only employed women as executioners, but refused to
permit her a priest or monk, thus forcing her to die unshriven,
and refusing her the benefit of any penitence that may have
lurked in her adamantine heart."

Such is the story of Medea da Carpi, Duchess of Stimigliano
Orsini, and then wife of Duke Guidalfonso II. of Urbania. She
was put to death just two hundred and ninety-seven years ago,
December 1582, at the age of barely seven-and twenty, and
having, in the course of her short life, brought to a violent end
five of her lovers, from Giovanfrancesco Pico to Prinzivalle degli
Ordelaffi.

Sept. 20th.—A grand illumination of the town in honour of the
taking of Rome fifteen years ago. Except Sor Asdrubale, my landlord, who shakes his head at the Piedmontese, as he calls them,

the people here are all Italianissimi. The Popes kept them very much down since Urbania lapsed to the Holy See in 1645.[1]

Sept. 28th.—I have for some time been hunting for portraits of the Duchess Medea. Most of them, I imagine, must have been destroyed, perhaps by Duke Robert II.'s fear lest even after her death this terrible beauty should play him a trick. Three or four I have, however, been able to find—one a miniature in the Archives, said to be that which she sent to poor Prinzivalle degli Ordelaffi in order to turn his head; one a marble bust in the palace lumber-room; one in a large composition, possibly by Baroccio,[2] representing Cleopatra at the feet of Augustus.[3] Augustus is the idealised portrait of Robert II., round cropped head, nose a little awry, clipped beard and scar as usual, but in Roman dress. Cleopatra seems to me, for all her Oriental dress, and although she wears a black wig, to be meant for Medea da Carpi; she is kneeling, baring her breast for the victor to strike, but in reality to captivate him, and he turns away with an awkward gesture of loathing. None of these portraits seem very good, save the miniature, but that is an exquisite work, and with it, and the suggestions of the bust, it is easy to reconstruct the beauty of this terrible being. The type is that most admired by the late Renaissance, and, in some measure, immortalised by Jean Goujon and the French.[4] The face is a perfect oval, the forehead somewhat over-round, with minute curls, like a fleece, of bright auburn hair; the nose a trifle over-aquiline, and the cheek-bones a trifle too low; the eyes grey, large, prominent,

---

1 Italian unification was achieved on 20 September 1870 when Rome was removed from the Pope's sovereignty and proclaimed the capital of Italy. The Piedmont region was the springboard for Italy's unification, hence perhaps use of the term "Piedmontese" by Sor Asdrubale who is evidently not a supporter of unification, remaining loyal to the former Pontifical government. Italianissimi: "very pro-Italian."

2 Frederico Baroccio or Borroci (c. 1530-1612), Italian painter from Perugia, influenced by Raphael, Michelangelo, and Taddeo Zuccaro.

3 Cleopatra, Queen of Egypt (68-30 BC), was captured by Octavian (afterwards the Emperor Augustus) but failed to seduce him with her charms. She committed suicide rather than be taken back to Rome for a triumphal parade.

4 Jean Goujon (c. 1510-66), French Renaissance sculptor, noted for his elegant, elaborately draped figures, and whose unique style showed the influence of classical models. Compare this and the later portrait of Medea with those by Swinburne and Pater in Appendices A and C.

beneath exquisitely curved brows and lids just a little too tight at the corners; the mouth also, brilliantly red and most delicately designed, is a little too tight, the lips strained a trifle over the teeth. Tight eyelids and tight lips give a strange refinement, and, at the same time, an air of mystery, a somewhat sinister seductiveness; they seem to take, but not to give. The mouth with a kind of childish pout, looks as if it could bite or suck like a leech. The complexion is dazzlingly fair, the perfect transparent roset lily[1] of a red-haired beauty; the head, with hair elaborately curled and plaited close to it, and adorned with pearls, sits like that of the antique Arethusa[2] on a long, supple, swanlike neck. A curious, at first rather conventional, artificial-looking sort of beauty, voluptuous yet cold, which, the more it is contemplated, the more it troubles and haunts the mind. Round the lady's neck is a gold chain with little gold lozenges at intervals, on which is engraved the posy or pun (the fashion of French devices is common in those days), "Amour Dure—Dure Amour." The same posy is inscribed in the hollow of the bust, and, thanks to it, I have been able to identify the latter as Medea's portrait. I often examine these tragic portraits, wondering what this face, which led so many men to their death, may have been like when it spoke or smiled, what at the moment when Medea da Carpi fascinated her victims into love unto death—"Amour Dure—Dure Amour," as runs her device—love that lasts, cruel love—yes indeed, when one thinks of the fidelity and fate of her lovers.

Oct. 13th.—I have literally not had time to write a line of my diary all these days. My whole mornings have gone in those Archives, my afternoons taking long walks in this lovely autumn weather (the highest hills are just tipped with snow). My evenings go in writing that confounded account of the Palace of Urbania which Government requires, merely to keep me at work at something useless. Of my history I have not yet been able to write a word.... By the way, I must note down a curious circumstance mentioned in an anonymous MS. life of Duke Robert, which I fell upon to-day. When this prince had the equestrian statue of

---

1 Rose-coloured or roseate, referring to the faint pink tinge of Medea's skin.
2 The chaste water nymph Arethusa escaping the advances of Alpheus was turned into a spring by Artemis. By tradition Arethusa's spring or fountain is at Syracuse in Sicily, and old Sicilian coins often depict her head.

himself by Antonio Tassi, Gianbologna's pupil,[1] erected in the square of the *Corte*, he secretly caused to be made, says my anonymous MS., a silver statuette of his familiar genius or angel—"familiaris ejus angelus seu genius, quod a vulgo dicitur *idolino*"—which statuette or idol, after having been consecrated by the astrologers—"ab astrologis quibusdam ritibus sacrato"[2]— was placed in the cavity of the chest of the effigy by Tassi, in order, says the MS., that his soul might rest until the general Resurrection. This passage is curious, and to me somewhat puzzling; how could the soul of Duke Robert await the general Resurrection, when, as a Catholic, he ought to have believed that it must, as soon as separated from his body, go to Purgatory?[3] Or is there some semi-pagan superstition of the Renaissance (most strange, certainly, in a man who had been a Cardinal) connecting the soul with a guardian genius, who could be compelled, by magic rites ("ab astrologis sacrato," the MS. says of the little idol), to remain fixed to earth, so that the soul should sleep in the body until the Day of Judgment? I confess this story baffles me. I wonder whether such an idol ever existed, or exists nowadays, in the body of Tassi's bronze effigy?

Oct. 20th.—I have been seeing a good deal of late of the Vice-Prefect's son: an amiable young man with a love-sick face and a languid interest in Urbanian history and archæology, of which he is profoundly ignorant. This young man, who has lived at Siena and Lucca before his father was promoted here, wears extremely long and tight trousers, which almost preclude his bending his knees, a stick-up collar and an eyeglass, and a pair of fresh kid gloves stuck in the breast of his coat, speaks of Urbania as Ovid might have spoken of Pontus, and complains (as well he may) of the barbarism of the young men, the officials who dine at my inn and howl and sing like madmen, and the nobles who drive gigs,

---

1 Gianbologna, more usually Giambologna (1529-1608), also known as Giovanni da Bologna and Jean Boulogne, was a Flemish-born Italian Mannerist sculptor. Antonio Tassi appears to be Lee's invention.

2 *Corte*: "court" or "courtyard;" "familiaris ejus angelus seu genius, quod a vulgo dicitur *idolino*" (Latin): "of his familiar angel or genius, known in the vernacular as a little idol"; "ab astrologis quibusdam ritibus sacrato" (Latin): "consecrated by the astrologers with certain magical rites."

3 As a Roman Catholic, Duke Robert should believe that after death his soul will go to Purgatory: a place of temporary suffering or expiation in which the souls of the departed are cleansed from venial sins in readiness for the Day of Judgment.

showing almost as much throat as a lady at a ball. This person frequently entertains me with his *amori*,[1] past, present, and future; he evidently thinks me very odd for having none to entertain him with in return; he points out to me the pretty (or ugly) servant-girls and dressmakers as we walk in the street, sighs deeply or sings in falsetto behind every tolerably young-looking woman, and has finally taken me to the house of the lady of his heart, a great black-moustachioed countess, with a voice like a fish-crier; here, he says, I shall meet all the best company in Urbania and some beautiful women—ah, too beautiful, alas! I find three huge half-furnished rooms, with bare brick floors, petroleum lamps, and horribly bad pictures on bright washball-blue and gamboge walls, and in the midst of it all, every evening, a dozen ladies and gentlemen seated in a circle, vociferating at each other the same news a year old; the younger ladies in bright yellows and greens, fanning themselves while my teeth chatter, and having sweet things whispered behind their fans by officers with hair brushed up like a hedgehog. And these are the women my friend expects me to fall in love with! I vainly wait for tea or supper which does not come, and rush home, determined to leave alone the Urbanian *beau monde*.

It is quite true that I have no *amori*, although my friend does not believe it. When I came to Italy first, I looked out for romance; I sighed, like Goethe in Rome, for a window to open and a wondrous creature to appear, "welch mich versengend erquickt." Perhaps it is because Goethe was a German, accustomed to German *Fraus*,[2] and I am, after all, a Pole, accustomed to something very different from *Fraus*; but anyhow, for all my efforts, in Rome, Florence, and Siena, I never could find a woman to go mad about, either among the ladies, chattering bad French, or among the lower classes, as 'cute and cold as money-lenders; so I steer clear of Italian womankind, its shrill voice and gaudy toilettes. I am wedded to history, to the Past, to women like Lucrezia Borgia, Vittoria Accoramboni,[3] or that Medea da

---

1 Translation: "loves" or "romances."
2 Johann Wolfgang von Goethe (1749-1832), leading German writer. Trepka misremembers Goethe's first Roman elegy (1790), verse 6, which should read "das mich versengt und erquickt" which means literally "which scorches and refreshes me" or, in Trepka's version, "which scorches me, refreshes me." *Fraus* (German): "women."
3 Lucrezia Borgia (see above); Vittoria Accoramboni (1557-85), famous for her beauty, accomplishments, and tragic history. While engaged to

Carpi, for the present; some day I shall perhaps find a grand passion, a woman to play the Don Quixote[1] about, like the Pole that I am; a woman out of whose slipper to drink, and for whose pleasure to die; but not here! Few things strike me so much as the degeneracy of Italian women. What has become of the race of Faustinas, Marozias, Bianca Cappellos?[2] Where discover nowadays (I confess she haunts me) another Medea da Carpi? Were it only possible to meet a woman of that extreme distinction of beauty, of that terribleness of nature, even if only potential, I do believe I could love her, even to the Day of Judgment, like any Oliverotto da Narni, or Frangipani or Prinzivalle.

Oct. 27th.—Fine sentiments the above are for a professor, a learned man! I thought the young artists of Rome childish because they played practical jokes and yelled at night in the streets, returning from the Caffè Greco or the cellar in the Via Palombella; but am I not as childish to the full—I, melancholy wretch, whom they called Hamlet and the Knight of the Doleful Countenance?[3]

Nov. 5th.—I can't free myself from the thought of this Medea da Carpi. In my walks, my mornings in the Archives, my solitary evenings, I catch myself thinking over the woman. Am I turning novelist instead of historian? And still it seems to me that I under-

---

Francesco Peretti, she attracted the attention of the powerful Paolo Giordano Orsini, Duke of Bracciano, and her brother, wanting the better match, had her fiancé murdered. After her marriage to Orsini, she was the subject of much animosity and was even at one time imprisoned. Following the Duke's death in 1585 she was assassinated by one of his relatives in a dispute concerning property.

1 Hero of romance by Miguel de Cervantes (1547-1616), written to ridicule books of chivalry; hence a visionary full of lofty if impractical ideals.

2 Faustina the younger (AD 128-75), the wife of the Emperor Marcus Aurelius (AD 121-80), was charged by many ancient writers with adultery, treason, and even murder. She was beloved by her husband who deified her after her death. Marozia (c. 892-937), highly influential Italian noblewoman, former mistress to Pope Sergius II, who married three times to maintain political control and was eventually overthrown and imprisoned by Albert II of Spoleto, her son by her first marriage. For Bianca Cappello, see above.

3 Caffè Greco is the oldest café in Rome and the favourite haunt of many writers, artists, and composers. Via Palombella is a street in Rome near the Pantheon. Shakespeare's tragic hero Hamlet is famous for his melancholy; Don Quixote (see above) is known as the Knight of the Doleful Countenance.

stand her so well; so much better than my facts warrant. First, we must put aside all pedantic modern ideas of right and wrong. Right and wrong in a century of violence and treachery does not exist, least of all for creatures like Medea. Go preach right and wrong to a tigress, my dear sir! Yet is there in the world anything nobler than the huge creature, steel when she springs, velvet when she treads, as she stretches her supple body, or smooths her beautiful skin, or fastens her strong claws into her victim?

Yes; I can understand Medea. Fancy a woman of superlative beauty, of the highest courage and calmness, a woman of many resources, of genius, brought up by a petty princelet of a father, upon Tacitus and Sallust, and the tales of the great Malatestas, of Cæsar Borgia[1] and such-like!—a woman whose one passion is conquest and empire—fancy her, on the eve of being wedded to a man of the power of the Duke of Stimigliano, claimed, carried off by a small fry of a Pico, locked up in his hereditary brigand's castle, and having to receive the young fool's red-hot love as an honour and a necessity! The mere thought of any violence to such a nature is an abominable outrage; and if Pico chooses to embrace such a woman at the risk of meeting a sharp piece of steel in her arms, why, it is a fair bargain. Young hound—or, if you prefer, young hero—to think to treat a woman like this as if she were any village wench! Medea marries her Orsini. A marriage, let it be noted, between an old soldier of fifty and a girl of sixteen. Reflect what that means: it means that this imperious woman is soon treated like a chattel, made roughly to understand that her business is to give the Duke an heir, not advice; that she must never ask "wherefore this or that?" that she must courtesy before the Duke's counsellors, his captains, his mistresses; that, at the least suspicion of rebelliousness, she is subject to his foul words and blows; at the least suspicion of infidelity, to be strangled or starved to death, or thrown down an oubliette.[2] Suppose that she know that her husband has taken it into his head that she has looked too hard at this man or that,

1 Cornelius Tacitus (AD c. 56-117) Roman historian; Sallust (86-34 BC), Roman historian and politician; Malatestas (see above); Cæsar, more usually Caesare, Borgia (1476-1507), illegitimate son of the Spanish Cardinal Rodrigo Borgia, afterwards Pope Alexander VI, and a ruthless opportunistic statesman and military commander.
2 From the French *oublier*, "to forget": a dungeon or pit with an opening at the top into which prisoners could be dropped and forgotten, often found in mediaeval castles.

that one of his lieutenants or one of his women have whispered that, after all, the boy Bartolommeo might as soon be a Pico as an Orsini. Suppose she know that she must strike or be struck? Why, she strikes, or gets some one to strike for her. At what price? A promise of love, of love to a groom, the son of a serf! Why, the dog must be mad or drunk to believe such a thing possible; his very belief in anything so monstrous makes him worthy of death. And then he dares to blab! This is much worse than Pico. Medea is bound to defend her honour a second time; if she could stab Pico, she can certainly stab this fellow, or have him stabbed.

Hounded by her husband's kinsmen, she takes refuge at Urbania. The Duke, like every other man, falls wildly in love with Medea, and neglects his wife; let us even go so far as to say, breaks his wife's heart. Is this Medea's fault? Is it her fault that every stone that comes beneath her chariot-wheels is crushed? Certainly not. Do you suppose that a woman like Medea feels the smallest ill-will against a poor, craven Duchess Maddalena? Why, she ignores her very existence. To suppose Medea a cruel woman is as grotesque as to call her an immoral woman. Her fate is, sooner or later, to triumph over her enemies, at all events to make their victory almost a defeat; her magic faculty is to enslave all the men who come across her path; all those who see her, love her, become her slaves; and it is the destiny of all her slaves to perish. Her lovers, with the exception of Duke Guidalfonso, all come to an untimely end; and in this there is nothing unjust. The possession of a woman like Medea is a happiness too great for a mortal man; it would turn his head, make him forget even what he owed her; no man must survive long who conceives himself to have a right over her; it is a kind of sacrilege. And only death, the willingness to pay for such happiness by death, can at all make a man worthy of being her lover; he must be willing to love and suffer and die. This is the meaning of her device—"Amour Dure—Dure Amour." The love of Medea da Carpi cannot fade, but the lover can die; it is a constant and a cruel love.

Nov. 11th.—I was right, quite right in my idea. I have found— Oh, joy! I treated the Vice-Prefect's son to a dinner of five courses at the Trattoria La Stella d'Italia out of sheer jubilation—I have found in the Archives, unknown, of course, to the Director, a heap of letters—letters of Duke Robert about Medea da Carpi, letters of Medea herself! Yes, Medea's own handwriting—a round, scholarly character, full of abbreviations, with a Greek look about it, as befits a learned princess who could read Plato as well as Petrarch.[1] The letters are of little importance, mere drafts of business letters for her secretary to copy, during the time that she governed the poor weak Guidalfonso. But they are her letters, and I can imagine almost that there hangs about these mouldering pieces of paper a scent as of a woman's hair.

The few letters of Duke Robert show him in a new light. A cunning, cold, but craven priest. He trembles at the bare thought of Medea—"la pessima Medea"—worse than her namesake of Colchis,[2] as he calls her. His long clemency is a result of mere fear of laying violent hands upon her. He fears her as something almost supernatural; he would have enjoyed having had her burnt as a witch. After letter on letter, telling his crony, Cardinal Sanseverino, at Rome his various precautions during her lifetime— how he wears a jacket of mail under his coat; how he drinks only milk from a cow which he has milked in his presence; how he tries his dog with morsels of his food, lest it be poisoned; how he suspects the wax-candles because of their peculiar smell; how he fears riding out lest some one should frighten his horse and cause him to break his neck—after all this, and when Medea has been in her grave two years, he tells his correspondent of his fear of meeting the soul of Medea after his own death, and chuckles over the ingenious device (concocted by his astrologer and a certain Fra Gaudenzio, a Capuchin) by which he shall secure the absolute peace of his soul until that of the wicked Medea be finally "chained up in hell among the lakes of boiling pitch and the ice of Caina described by the immortal bard"—old pedant! Here, then, is the explanation of that silver image—*quod vulgo dicitur idolino*—which he caused to be soldered into his effigy by Tassi. As long as the image of his soul was attached to the image of his body, he should sleep awaiting the Day of Judgment, fully convinced that Medea's soul will then be properly tarred and feathered, while his—honest man!—will fly straight to Paradise. And to think that, two weeks ago, I believed this man to be a hero! Aha! my good Duke Robert, you shall be shown up in my

---

1 Plato (c. 429-347 BC), famous Greek philosopher, student of Socrates and author of many influential Dialogues. Francesco Petrarch (1304-74), leading Italian poet and humanist.
2 Translation: "the most evil Medea." In Greek myth Medea, a beautiful and clever sorceress, daughter of King Aeetes of Colchis, helps the hero Jason obtain the Golden Fleece in return for marriage. Her subsequent crimes include murdering her brother, her two children, Jason's second wife, and King Pelias of Iolcus.

history; and no amount of silver idolinos shall save you from being heartily laughed at!

Nov. 15th.—Strange! That idiot of a Prefect's son, who has heard me talk a hundred times of Medea da Carpi, suddenly recollects that, when he was a child at Urbania, his nurse used to threaten him with a visit from Madonna Medea, who rode in the sky on a black he-goat. My Duchess Medea turned into a bogey for naughty little boys!

Nov. 20th.—I have been going about with a Bavarian Professor of mediæval history, showing him all over the country. Among other places we went to Rocca Sant' Elmo, to see the former villa of the Dukes of Urbania, the villa where Medea was confined between the accession of Duke Robert and the conspiracy of Marcantonio Frangipani, which caused her removal to the nunnery immediately outside the town. A long ride up the desolate Apennine valleys, bleak beyond words just now with their thin fringe of oak scrub turned russet, thin patches of grass sered by the frost, the last few yellow leaves of the poplars by the torrents shaking and fluttering about in the chill Tramontana;[1] the mountain-tops are wrapped in thick grey cloud; to-morrow, if the wind continues, we shall see them round masses of snow against the cold blue sky. Sant' Elmo is a wretched hamlet high on the Apennine ridge, where the Italian vegetation is already replaced by that of the North. You ride for miles through leafless chestnut woods, the scent of the soaking brown leaves filling the air, the roar of the torrent, turbid with autumn rains, rising from the precipice below; then suddenly the leafless chestnut woods are replaced, as at Vallombrosa,[2] by a belt of black, dense fir plantations. Emerging from these, you come to an open space, frozen blasted meadows, the rocks of snow clad peak, the newly fallen snow, close above you; and in the midst, on a knoll, with a gnarled larch on either side, the ducal villa of Sant' Elmo, a big black stone box with a stone escutcheon, grated windows, and a double flight of steps in front. It is now let out to the proprietor of the neighbouring woods, who uses it for the storage of chestnuts, faggots, and charcoal from the neighbouring ovens. We tied our horses to the iron rings and entered: an old woman, with dishevelled hair, was alone in the house. The villa is a mere hunting-lodge, built by Ottobuono IV., the father of Dukes Guidalfonso

---

1 Cold north or north-east wind.
2 From the Latin *vallis umbrosa*, "shady valley": a forest summer resort in Tuscany, in the province of Florence.

and Robert, about 1530. Some of the rooms have at one time been frescoed and panelled with oak carvings, but all this has disappeared. Only, in one of the big rooms, there remains a large marble fireplace, similar to those in the palace at Urbania, beautifully carved with Cupids on a blue ground; a charming naked boy sustains a jar on either side, one containing clove pinks, the other roses. The room was filled with stacks of faggots.

We returned home late, my companion in excessively bad humour at the fruitlessness of the expedition. We were caught in the skirt of a snowstorm as we got into the chestnut woods. The sight of the snow falling gently, of the earth and bushes whitened all round, made me feel back at Posen, once more a child. I sang and shouted, to my companion's horror. This will be a bad point against me if reported at Berlin. A historian of twenty-four[1] who shouts and sings, and when another historian is cursing at the snow and the bad roads! All night I lay awake watching the embers of my wood fire, and thinking of Medea da Carpi mewed up, in winter, in that solitude of Sant' Elmo, the firs groaning, the torrent roaring, the snow falling all round; miles and miles away from human creatures. I fancied I saw it all, and that I, somehow, was Marcantonio Frangipani come to liberate her—or was it Prinzivalle degli Ordelaffi? I suppose it was because of the long ride, the unaccustomed pricking feeling of the snow in the air; or perhaps the punch which my professor insisted on drinking after dinner.

Nov. 23rd.—Thank goodness, that Bavarian professor has finally departed! Those days he spent here drove me nearly crazy. Talking over my work, I told him one day my views on Medea da Carpi; whereupon he condescended to answer that those were the usual tales due to the mythopœic (old idiot!) tendency of the Renaissance; that research would disprove the greater part of them, as it had disproved the stories current about the Borgias, &c.; that, moreover, such a woman as I made out was psychologically and physiologically impossible. Would that one could say as much of such professors as he and his fellows!

Nov. 24th.—I cannot get over my pleasure in being rid of that imbecile; I felt as if I could have throttled him every time he spoke of the Lady of my thoughts—for such she has become— *Metea*, as the animal called her!

---

1 Trepka, who tells us he has just published a scholarly book, is 24, the same age as Lee when she published her *Studies of the Eighteenth Century in Italy* (1880).

Nov. 30th.—I feel quite shaken at what has just happened; I am beginning to fear that that old pedant was right in saying that it was bad for me to live all alone in a strange country, that it would make me morbid. It is ridiculous that I should be put into such a state of excitement merely by the chance discovery of a portrait of a woman dead these three hundred years. With the case of my uncle Ladislas, and other suspicions of insanity in my family, I ought really to guard against such foolish excitement.

Yet the incident was really dramatic, uncanny. I could have sworn that I knew every picture in the palace here; and particularly every picture of Her. Anyhow, this morning, as I was leaving the Archives, I passed through one of the many small rooms—irregular-shaped closets—which fill up the ins and outs of this curious palace, turreted like a French château. I must have passed through that closet before, for the view was so familiar out of its window; just the particular bit of round tower in front, the cypress on the other side of the ravine, the belfry beyond, and the piece of the line of Monte Sant' Agata and the Leonessa, covered with snow, against the sky. I suppose there must be twin rooms, and that I had got into the wrong one; or rather, perhaps some shutter had been opened or curtain withdrawn. As I was passing, my eye was caught by a very beautiful old mirror-frame let into the brown and yellow inlaid wall. I approached, and looking at the frame, looked also, mechanically, into the glass. I gave a great start, and almost shrieked, I do believe—(it's lucky the Munich professor is safe out of Urbania!). Behind my own image stood another, a figure close to my shoulder, a face close to mine; and that figure, that face, hers! Medea da Carpi's! I turned sharp round, as white, I think, as the ghost I expected to see. On the wall opposite the mirror, just a pace or two behind where I had been standing, hung a portrait. And such a portrait!—Bronzino[1] never painted a grander one. Against a background of harsh, dark blue, there stands out the figure of the Duchess (for it is Medea, the real Medea, a thousand times more real, individual, and pow-

---

[1] Agnolo Bronzino (1503-72), Florentine, Court Painter to Cosimo I de' Medici, and one of the most important Mannerist portrait painters. His portraits have an icy elegance and clarity. His painting of Lucrezia di Panciatichi (c. 1450) who wears a gold necklace with the inscription "Amour Dure Sans Fin" ("Love lasts without end"), now in the Uffizi Gallery, Florence, is clearly the inspiration for the portrait of Medea, and also for the portrait in which Milly Theale recognises herself in Henry James's *The Wings of the Dove* (1902).

erful than in the other portraits), seated stiffly in a high-backed chair, sustained, as it were, almost rigid, by the stiff brocade of skirts and stomacher, stiffer for plaques of embroidered silver flowers and rows of seed pearl. The dress is, with its mixture of silver and pearl, of a strange dull red, a wicked poppy-juice colour, against which the flesh of the long, narrow hands with fringe-like fingers; of the long slender neck, and the face with bared forehead, looks white and hard, like alabaster. The face is the same as in the other portraits: the same rounded forehead, with the short fleece-like, yellowish-red curls; the same beautifully curved eyebrows, just barely marked; the same eyelids, a little tight across the eyes; the same lips, a little tight across the mouth; but with a purity of line, a dazzling splendour of skin, and intensity of look immeasurably superior to all the other portraits.

She looks out of the frame with a cold, level glance; yet the lips smile. One hand holds a dull-red rose; the other, long, narrow, tapering, plays with a thick rope of silk and gold and jewels hanging from the waist; round the throat, white as marble, partially confined in the tight dull-red bodice, hangs a gold collar, with the device on alternate enamelled medallions, "AMOUR DURE—DURE AMOUR."

On reflection, I see that I simply could never have been in that room or closet before; I must have mistaken the door. But, although the explanation is so simple, I still, after several hours, feel terribly shaken in all my being. If I grow so excitable I shall have to go to Rome at Christmas for a holiday. I feel as if some danger pursued me here (can it be fever?); and yet, and yet, I don't see how I shall ever tear myself away.

Dec. 10th.—I have made an effort, and accepted the Vice-Prefect's son's invitation to see the oil-making at a villa of theirs near the coast. The villa, or farm, is an old fortified, towered place, standing on a hillside among olive-trees and little osier-bushes, which look like a bright orange flame. The olives are squeezed in a tremendous black cellar, like a prison: you see, by the faint white daylight, and the smoky yellow flare of resin burning in pans, great white bullocks moving round a huge mill-stone; vague figures working at pulleys and handles: it looks, to my fancy, like some scene of the Inquisition.[1] The Cavaliere regaled me with his best wine and rusks. I took some long walks

---

1 Roman Catholic ecclesiastical tribunal set up in the thirteenth century to root out and suppress heresy, especially infamous in sixteenth-century Spain for its severities which included torture.

by the seaside; I had left Urbania wrapped in snow-clouds; down on the coast there was a bright sun; the sunshine, the sea, the bustle of the little port on the Adriatic seemed to do me good. I came back to Urbania another man. Sor Asdrubale, my landlord, poking about in slippers among the gilded chests, the Empire sofas,[1] the old cups and saucers and pictures which no one will buy, congratulated me upon the improvement in my looks. "You work too much," he says; "youth requires amusement, theatres, promenades, *amori*—it is time enough to be serious when one is bald"—and he took off his greasy red cap. Yes, I am better! and, as a result, I take to my work with delight again. I will cut them out still, those wiseacres at Berlin!

Dec. 14*th*.—I don't think I have ever felt so happy about my work. I see it all so well—that crafty, cowardly Duke Robert; that melancholy Duchess Maddalena; that weak, showy, would-be chivalrous Duke Guidalfonso; and above all, the splendid figure of Medea. I feel as if I were the greatest historian of the age; and, at the same time, as if I were a boy of twelve. It snowed yesterday for the first time in the city, for two good hours. When it had done, I actually went into the square and taught the ragamuffins to make a snow-man; no, a snow-woman; and I had the fancy to call her Medea. "La pessima Medea!" cried one of the boys— "the one who used to ride through the air on a goat?" "No, no," I said; "she was a beautiful lady, the Duchess of Urbania, the most beautiful woman that ever lived." I made her a crown of tinsel, and taught the boys to cry "Evviva, Medea!"[2] But one of them said, "She is a witch! She must be burnt!" At which they all rushed to fetch burning faggots and tow; in a minute the yelling demons had melted her down.

Dec. 15*th*.—What a goose I am, and to think I am twenty-four, and known in literature! In my long walks I have composed to a tune (I don't know what it is) which all the people are singing and whistling in the street at present, a poem in frightful Italian, beginning "Medea, mia dea," calling on her in the name of her various lovers. I go about humming between my teeth, "Why am I not Marcantonio? or Prinzivalle? or he of Narni? or the good Duke Alfonso? that I might be beloved by thee, Medea, mia dea," &c. &c. Awful rubbish! My landlord, I think, suspects that Medea

---

1 Style of furniture associated with the first French Empire (1804-15) which featured long straight lines and details from classical and ancient Egyptian art.
2 Translation: "Long live Medea!"

must be some lady I met while I was staying by the seaside. I am sure Sora Serafina, Sora Lodovica, and Sora Adalgisa—the three Parcæ or *Norns*,[1] as I call them—have some such notion. This afternoon, at dusk, while tidying my room, Sora Lodovica said to me, "How beautifully the Signorino has taken to singing!" I was scarcely aware that I had been vociferating, "Vieni, Medea, mia dea,"[2] while the old lady bobbed about making up my fire. I stopped; a nice reputation I shall get! I thought, and all this will somehow get to Rome, and thence to Berlin. Sora Lodovica was leaning out of the window, pulling in the iron hook of the shrine-lamp which marks Sor Asdrubale's house. As she was trimming the lamp previous to swinging it out again, she said in her odd, prudish little way, "You are wrong to stop singing, my son" (she varies between calling me Signor Professore and such terms of affection as "Nino," "Viscere mie,"[3] &c.); "you are wrong to stop singing, for there is a young lady there in the street who has actually stopped to listen to you."

I ran to the window. A woman, wrapped in a black shawl, was standing in an archway, looking up to the window.

"Eh, eh! the Signor Professore has admirers," said Sora Lodovica.

"Medea, mia dea!" I burst out as loud as I could, with a boy's pleasure in disconcerting the inquisitive passer-by. She turned suddenly round to go away, waving her hand at me; at that moment Sora Lodovica swung the shrine-lamp back into its place. A stream of light fell across the street. I felt myself grow quite cold; the face of the woman outside was that of Medea da Carpi!

What a fool I am, to be sure!

PART II

Dec. 17th.—I fear that my craze about Medea da Carpi has become well known, thanks to my silly talk and idiotic songs. That Vice-Prefect's son—or the assistant at the Archives, or perhaps some of the company at the Contessa's, is trying to play me a trick! But take care, my good ladies and gentlemen, I shall

---

1 In Norse mythology the Norns are the demi-goddesses of destiny.
2 Translation: "Come, Medea, my goddess."
3 "Nino", properly "Niño" (Spanish), "child"; "Viscere mie:" literally "my entrails," thus "my heart" or "my lifeblood."

pay you out in your own coin! Imagine my feelings when, this morning, I found on my desk a folded letter addressed to me in a curious handwriting which seemed strangely familiar to me, and which, after a moment, I recognised as that of the letters of Medea da Carpi at the Archives. It gave me a horrible shock. My next idea was that it must be a present from some one who knew my interest in Medea—a genuine letter of hers on which some idiot had written my address instead of putting it into an envelope. But it was addressed to me, written to me, no old letter; merely four lines, which ran as follows:—

"To spiridion.—A person who knows the interest you bear her will be at the Church of San Giovanni Decollato[1] this evening at nine. Look out, in the left aisle, for a lady wearing a black mantle, and holding a rose."

By this time I understood that I was the object of a conspiracy, the victim of a hoax. I turned the letter round and round. It was written on paper such as was made in the sixteenth century, and in an extraordinarily precise imitation of Medea da Carpi's characters. Who had written it? I thought over all the possible people. On the whole, it must be the Vice-Prefect's son, perhaps in combination with his lady-love, the Countess. They must have torn a blank page off some old letter; but that either of them should have had the ingenuity of inventing such a hoax, or the power of committing such a forgery, astounds me beyond measure. There is more in these people than I should have guessed. How pay them off? By taking no notice of the letter? Dignified, but dull. No, I will go; perhaps some one will be there, and I will mystify them in their turn. Or, if no one is there, how I shall crow over them for their imperfectly carried out plot! Perhaps this is some folly of the Cavalier Muzio's to bring me into the presence of some lady whom he destines to be the flame of my future. *amori*. That is likely enough. And it would be too idiotic and professorial to refuse such an invitation; the lady must be worth knowing who can forge sixteenth-century letters like this, for I am sure that languid swell Muzio never could. I will go! By Heaven! I'll pay them back in their own coin! It is now five— how long these days are!

Dec. 18*th*.—Am I mad? Or are there really ghosts? That adventure of last night has shaken me to the very depth of my soul.

---

1 Church of St. John the Baptist, (literally St John the Beheaded).

I went at nine, as the mysterious letter had bid me. It was bitterly cold, and the air full of fog and sleet; not a shop open, not a window unshuttered, not a creature visible; the narrow black streets, precipitous between their high walls and under their lofty archways, were only the blacker for the dull light of an oil-lamp here and there, with its flickering yellow reflection on the wet flags. San Giovanni Decollato is a little church, or rather oratory, which I have always hitherto seen shut up (as so many churches here are shut up except on great festivals); and situate behind the ducal palace, on a sharp ascent, and forming the bifurcation of two steep paved lanes. I have passed by the place a hundred times, and scarcely noticed the little church, except for the marble high relief over the door, showing the grizzly head of the Baptist in the charger, and for the iron cage close by, in which were formerly exposed the heads of criminals; the decapitated, or, as they call him here, decollated, John the Baptist, being apparently the patron of axe and block.

A few strides took me from my lodgings to San Giovanni Decollato. I confess I was excited; one is not twenty-four and a Pole for nothing. On getting to the kind of little platform at the bifurcation of the two precipitous streets, I found, to my surprise, that the windows of the church or oratory were not lighted, and that the door was locked! So this was the precious joke that had been played upon me; to send me on a bitter cold, sleety night, to a church which was shut up and had perhaps been shut up for years! I don't know what I couldn't have done in that moment of rage; I felt inclined to break open the church door, or to go and pull the Vice-Prefect's son out of bed (for I felt sure that the joke was his). I determined upon the latter course; and was walking towards his door, along the black alley to the left of the church, when I was suddenly stopped by the sound as of an organ close by; an organ, yes, quite plainly, and the voice of choristers and the drone of a litany. So the church was not shut, after all! I retraced my steps to the top of the lane. All was dark and in complete silence. Suddenly there came again a faint gust of organ and voices. I listened; it clearly came from the other lane, the one on the right-hand side. Was there, perhaps, another door there? I passed beneath the archway, and descended a little way in the direction whence the sounds seemed to come. But no door, no light, only the black walls, the black wet flags, with their faint yellow reflections of flickering oil-lamps; moreover, complete silence. I stopped a minute, and then the chant rose again; this time it seemed to me most certainly from the lane I had just left.

I went back—nothing. Thus backwards and forwards, the sounds always beckoning, as it were, one way, only to beckon me back, vainly, to the other.

At last I lost patience; and I felt a sort of creeping terror, which only a violent action could dispel. If the mysterious sounds came neither from the street to the right, nor from the street to the left, they could come only from the church. Half-maddened, I rushed up the two or three steps, and prepared to wrench the door open with a tremendous effort. To my amazement, it opened with the greatest ease. I entered, and the sounds of the litany met me louder than before, as I paused a moment between the outer door and the heavy leathern curtain. I raised the latter and crept in. The altar was brilliantly illuminated with tapers and garlands of chandeliers; this was evidently some evening service connected with Christmas. The nave and aisles were comparatively dark, and about half-full. I elbowed my way along the right aisle towards the altar. When my eyes had got accustomed to the unexpected light, I began to look round me, and with a beating heart. The idea that all this was a hoax, that I should meet merely some acquaintance of my friend the Cavaliere's, had somehow departed: I looked about. The people were all wrapped up, the men in big cloaks, the women in woollen veils and mantles. The body of the church was comparatively dark, and I could not make out anything very clearly, but it seemed to me, somehow, as if, under the cloaks and veils, these people were dressed in a rather extraordinary fashion. The man in front of me, I remarked, showed yellow stockings beneath his cloak; a woman, hard by, a red bodice, laced behind with gold tags. Could these be peasants from some remote part come for the Christmas festivities, or did the inhabitants of Urbania don some old-fashioned garb in honour of Christmas?

As I was wondering, my eye suddenly caught that of a woman standing in the opposite aisle, close to the altar, and in the full blaze of its lights. She was wrapped in black, but held, in a very conspicuous way, a red rose, an unknown luxury at this time of the year in a place like Urbania. She evidently saw me, and turning even more fully into the light, she loosened her heavy black cloak, displaying a dress of deep red, with gleams of silver and gold embroideries; she turned her face towards me; the full blaze of the chandeliers and tapers fell upon it. It was the face of Medea da Carpi! I dashed across the nave, pushing people roughly aside, or rather, it seemed to me, passing through impalpable bodies. But the lady turned and walked rapidly down the aisle towards the door. I followed close upon her, but somehow I could not get up with her. Once, at the curtain, she turned round again. She was within a few paces of me. Yes, it was Medea. Medea herself, no mistake, no delusion, no sham; the oval face, the lips tightened over the mouth, the eyelids tight over the corner of the eyes, the exquisite alabaster complexion! She raised the curtain and glided out. I followed; the curtain alone separated me from her. I saw the wooden door swing to behind her. One step ahead of me! I tore open the door; she must be on the steps, within reach of my arm!

I stood outside the church. All was empty, merely the wet pavement and the yellow reflections in the pools: a sudden cold seized me; I could not go on. I tried to re-enter the church; it was shut. I rushed home, my hair standing on end, and trembling in all my limbs, and remained for an hour like a maniac. Is it a delusion? Am I too going mad? O God, God! am I going mad?

Dec. 19th.—A brilliant, sunny day; all the black snow-slush has disappeared out of the town, off the bushes and trees. The snow-clad mountains sparkle against the bright blue sky. A Sunday, and Sunday weather; all the bells are ringing for the approach of Christmas. They are preparing for a kind of fair in the square with the colonnade, putting up booths filled with coloured cotton and woollen ware, bright shawls and kerchiefs, mirrors, ribbons, brilliant pewter lamps; the whole turn-out of the pedlar in "Winter's Tale."[1] The pork-shops are all garlanded with green and with paper flowers, the hams and cheeses stuck full of little flags and green twigs. I strolled out to see the cattle-fair outside the gate; a forest of interlacing horns, an ocean of lowing and stamping: hundreds of immense white bullocks, with horns a yard long and red tassels, packed close together on the little piazza d'armi under the city walls. Bah! why do I write this trash? What's the use of it all? While I am forcing myself to write about bells, and Christmas festivities, and cattle-fairs, one idea goes on like a bell within me: Medea, Medea! Have I really seen her, or am I mad?

Two hours later.—That Church of San Giovanni Decollato—so my landlord informs me—has not been made use of within the memory of man. Could it have been all a hallucination or a dream—perhaps a dream dreamed that night? I have been out

---

1 In Shakespeare's *A Winter's Tale* (first performed 1611), the thief and rogue Autolycus pretends to be a pedlar selling a whole host of things including ribbons, laces, fabrics, gloves, perfume, jewellery, songs, and ballads.

again to look at that church. There it is, at the bifurcation of the two steep lanes, with its bas-relief of the Baptist's head over the door. The door does look as if it had not been opened for years. I can see the cobwebs in the window-panes; it does look as if, as Sor Asdrubale says, only rats and spiders congregated within it. And yet—and yet; I have so clear a remembrance, so distinct a consciousness of it all. There was a picture of the daughter of Herodias dancing, upon the altar; I remember her white turban with a scarlet tuft of feathers, and Herod's blue caftan;[1] I remember the shape of the central chandelier; it swung round slowly, and one of the wax lights had got bent almost in two by the heat and draught.

Things, all these, which I may have seen elsewhere, stored unawares in my brain, and which may have come out, somehow, in a dream; I have heard physiologists allude to such things. I will go again: if the church be shut, why then it must have been a dream, a vision, the result of over-excitement. I must leave at once for Rome and see doctors, for I am afraid of going mad. If, on the other hand—pshaw! there *is no other hand* in such a case. Yet if there were—why then, I should really have seen Medea; I might see her again; speak to her. The mere thought sets my blood in a whirl, not with horror, but with ... I know not what to call it. The feeling terrifies me, but it is delicious. Idiot! There is some little coil of my brain, the twentieth of a hair's-breadth out of order—that's all!

Dec. 20th.—I have been again; I have heard the music; I have been inside the church; I have seen Her! I can no longer doubt my senses. Why should I? Those pedants say that the dead are dead, the past is past. For them, yes; but why for me?—why for a man who loves, who is consumed with the love of a woman?—a woman who, indeed—yes, let me finish the sentence. Why should there not be ghosts to such as can see them? Why should she not return to the earth, if she knows that it contains a man who thinks of, desires, only her?

A hallucination? Why, I saw her, as I see this paper that I write upon; standing there, in the full blaze of the altar. Why, I heard the rustle of her skirts, I smelt the scent of her hair, I raised the curtain which was shaking from her touch. Again I missed her.

---

1   See St. Mark 6. 14-29. Salome, daughter of Herodias, pleased King Herod with her dancing. He rashly promised her anything she desired and, primed by her mother, Herodias, she requested the head of the prophet John the Baptist.

But this time, as I rushed out into the empty moonlit street, I found upon the church steps a rose—the rose which I had seen in her hand the moment before—I felt it, smelt it; a rose, a real, living rose, dark red and only just plucked. I put it into water when I returned, after having kissed it, who knows how many times? I placed it on the top of the cupboard; I determined not to look at it for twenty-four hours lest it should be a delusion. But I must see it again; I must.... Good Heavens! this is horrible, horrible; if I had found a skeleton it could not have been worse! The rose, which last night seemed freshly plucked, full of colour and perfume, is brown, dry—a thing kept for centuries between the leaves of a book—it has crumbled into dust between my fingers. Horrible, horrible! But why so, pray? Did I not know that I was in love with a woman dead three hundred years? If I wanted fresh roses which bloomed yesterday, the Countess Fiammetta or any little sempstress in Urbania might have given them me. What if the rose has fallen to dust? If only I could hold Medea in my arms as I held it in my fingers, kiss her lips as I kissed its petals, should I not be satisfied if she too were to fall to dust the next moment, if I were to fall to dust myself?

Dec. 22nd, Eleven at night.—I have seen her once more!—almost spoken to her. I have been promised her love! Ah, Spiridion! you were right when you felt that you were not made for any earthly *amori*. At the usual hour I betook myself this evening to San Giovanni Decollato. A bright winter night; the high houses and belfries standing out against a deep blue heaven luminous, shimmering like steel with myriads of stars; the moon has not yet risen. There was no light in the windows; but, after a little effort, the door opened and I entered the church, the altar, as usual, brilliantly illuminated. It struck me suddenly that all this crowd of men and women standing all round, these priests chanting and moving about the altar, were dead—that they did not exist for any man save me. I touched, as if by accident, the hand of my neighbour; it was cold, like wet clay. He turned round, but did not seem to see me: his face was ashy, and his eyes staring, fixed, like those of a blind man or a corpse. I felt as if I must rush out. But at that moment my eye fell upon Her, standing as usual by the altar steps, wrapped in a black mantle, in the full blaze of the lights. She turned round; the light fell straight upon her face, the face with the delicate features, the eyelids and lips a little tight, the alabaster skin faintly tinged with pale pink. Our eyes met.

I pushed my way across the nave towards where she stood by the altar steps; she turned quickly down the aisle, and I after her.

Once or twice she lingered, and I thought I should overtake her; but again, when, not a second after the door had closed upon her, I stepped out into the street, she had vanished. On the church step lay something white. It was not a flower this time, but a letter. I rushed back to the church to read it; but the church was fast shut, as if it had not been opened for years. I could not see by the flickering shrine-lamps—I rushed home, lit my lamp, pulled the letter from my breast. I have it before me. The handwriting is hers; the same as in the Archives, the same as in that first letter:—

"To SPIRIDION.—Let thy courage be equal to thy love, and thy love shall be rewarded. On the night preceding Christmas, take a hatchet and saw; cut boldly into the body of the bronze rider who stands in the Corte, on the left side, near the waist. Saw open the body, and within it thou wilt find the silver effigy of a winged genius. Take it out, hack it into a hundred pieces, and fling them in all directions, so that the winds may sweep them away. That night she whom thou lovest will come to reward thy fidelity."

On the brownish wax is the device—

"AMOUR DURE—DURE AMOUR."

Dec. 23rd.—So it is true! I was reserved for something wonderful in this world. I have at last found that after which my soul has been straining. Ambition, love of art, love of Italy, these things which have occupied my spirit, and have yet left me continually unsatisfied, these were none of them my real destiny. I have sought for life, thirsting for it as a man in the desert thirsts for a well; but the life of the senses of other youths, the life of the intellect of other men, have never slaked that thirst. Shall life for me mean the love of a dead woman? We smile at what we choose to call the superstition of the past, forgetting that all our vaunted science of to-day may seem just such another superstition to the men of the future; but why should the present be right and the past wrong? The men who painted the pictures and built the palaces of three hundred years ago were certainly of as delicate fibre, of as keen reason, as ourselves, who merely print calico and build locomotives. What makes me think this, is that I have been calculating my nativity by help of an old book belonging to Sor

Asdrubale—and see, my horoscope tallies almost exactly with that of Medea da Carpi, as given by a chronicler. May this explain? No, no; all is explained by the fact that the first time I read of this woman's career, the first time I saw her portrait, I loved her, though I hid my love to myself in the garb of historical interest. Historical interest indeed!

I have got the hatchet and the saw. I bought the saw of a poor joiner, in a village some miles off; he did not understand at first what I meant, and I think he thought me mad; perhaps I am. But if madness means the happiness of one's life, what of it? The hatchet I saw lying in a timber-yard, where they prepare the great trunks of the fir-trees which grow high on the Apennines of Sant' Elmo. There was no one in the yard, and I could not resist the temptation; I handled the thing, tried its edge, and stole it. This is the first time in my life that I have been a thief; why did I not go into a shop and buy a hatchet? I don't know; I seemed unable to resist the sight of the shining blade. What I am going to do is, I suppose, an act of vandalism; and certainly I have no right to spoil the property of this city of Urbania. But I wish no harm either to the statue or the city; if I could plaster up the bronze, I would do so willingly. But I must obey Her; I must avenge Her; I must get at that silver image which Robert of Montemurlo had made and consecrated in order that his cowardly soul might sleep in peace, and not encounter that of the being whom he dreaded most in the world. Aha! Duke Robert, you forced her to die unshriven, and you stuck the image of your soul into the image of your body, thinking thereby that, while she suffered the tortures of Hell, you would rest in peace, until your well-scoured little soul might fly straight up to Paradise;—you were afraid of Her when both of you should be dead, and thought yourself very clever to have prepared for all emergencies! Not so, Serene Highness. You too shall taste what it is to wander after death, and to meet the dead whom one has injured.

What an interminable day! But I shall see her again to-night.

Eleven o'clock.—No; the church was fast closed; the spell had ceased. Until to-morrow I shall not see her. But to-morrow! Ah, Medea! did any of thy lovers love thee as I do?

Twenty-four hours more till the moment of happiness—the moment for which I seem to have been waiting all my life. And after that, what next? Yes, I see it plainer every minute; after that, nothing more. All those who loved Medea da Carpi, who loved and who served her, died: Giovanfrancesco Pico, her first husband, whom she left stabbed in the castle from which she fled;

Stimigliano, who died of poison; the groom who gave him the poison, cut down by her orders; Oliverotto da Narni, Marcantonio Frangipani, and that poor boy of the Ordelaffi, who had never even looked upon her face, and whose only reward was that handkerchief with which the hangman wiped the sweat off his face, when he was one mass of broken limbs and torn flesh: all had to die, and I shall die also.

The love of such a woman is enough, and is fatal—"Amour Dure," as her device says. I shall die also. But why not? Would it be possible to live in order to love another woman? Nay, would it be possible to drag on a life like this one after the happiness of to-morrow? Impossible; the others died, and I must die. I always felt that I should not live long; a gipsy in Poland told me once that I had in my hand the cut-line which signifies a violent death. I might have ended in a duel with some brother-student, or in a railway accident. No, no; my death will not be of that sort! Death—and is not she also dead? What strange vistas does such a thought not open! Then the others—Pico, the Groom, Stimigliano, Oliverotto, Frangipani, Prinzivalle degli Ordelaffi— will they all be *there*? But she shall love me best—me by whom she has been loved after she has been three hundred years in the grave!

Dec. 24th.—I have made all my arrangements. To-night at eleven I slip out; Sor Asdrubale and his sisters will be sound asleep. I have questioned them; their fear of rheumatism prevents their attending midnight mass. Luckily there are no churches between this and the Corte; whatever movement Christmas night may entail will be a good way off. The Vice-Prefect's rooms are on the other side of the palace; the rest of the square is taken up with state-rooms, archives, and empty stables and coach-houses of the palace. Besides, I shall be quick at my work.

I have tried my saw on a stout bronze vase I bought of Sor Asdrubale; and the bronze of the statue, hollow and worn away by rust (I have even noticed holes), cannot resist very much, especially after a blow with the sharp hatchet. I have put my papers in order, for the benefit of the Government which has sent me hither. I am sorry to have defrauded them of their "History of Urbania." To pass the endless day and calm the fever of impatience, I have just taken a long walk. This is the coldest day we have had. The bright sun does not warm in the least, but seems only to increase the impression of cold, to make the snow on the mountains glitter, the blue air to sparkle like steel. The few people who are out are muffled to the nose, and carry earthenware braziers beneath their cloaks; long icicles hang from the fountain with the figure of Mercury upon it; one can imagine the wolves trooping down through the dry scrub and beleaguering this town. Somehow this cold makes me feel wonderfully calm—it seems to bring back to me my boyhood.

As I walked up the rough, steep, paved alleys, slippery with frost, and with their vista of snow mountains against the sky, and passed by the church steps strewn with box and laurel, with the faint smell of incense coming out, there returned to me—I know not why—the recollection, almost the sensation, of those Christmas Eves long ago at Posen and Breslau,[1] when I walked as a child along the wide streets, peeping into the windows where they were beginning to light the tapers of the Christmas-trees, and wondering whether I too, on returning home, should be let into a wonderful room all blazing with lights and gilded nuts and glass beads. They are hanging the last strings of those blue and red metallic beads, fastening on the last gilded and silvered walnuts on the trees out there at home in the North; they are lighting the blue and red tapers; the wax is beginning to run on to the beautiful spruce green branches; the children are waiting with beating hearts behind the door, to be told that the Christ-Child has been. And I, for what am I waiting? I don't know; all seems a dream; everything vague and unsubstantial about me, as if time had ceased, nothing could happen, my own desires and hopes were all dead, myself absorbed into I know not what passive dreamland. Do I long for to-night? Do I dread it? Will to-night ever come? Do I feel anything, does anything exist all round me? I sit and seem to see that street at Posen, the wide street with the windows illuminated by the Christmas lights, the green fir-branches grazing the window-panes.

Christmas Eve, Midnight.—I have done it. I slipped out noiselessly. Sor Asdrubale and his sisters were fast asleep. I feared I had waked them, for my hatchet fell as I was passing through the principal room where my landlord keeps his curiosities for sale; it struck against some old armour which he has been piecing. I heard him exclaim, half in his sleep; and blew out my light and

---

1 Posen (see above); Breslau, name given by Frederick II the Great of Prussia in 1741 to what is now once more Wroclaw, one of the oldest and most beautiful cities in Poland and the economic and cultural capital of lower Silesia in south-western Poland. The description of recollections of Christmas has a similarity with Lee's essay "Christkindchen" in *Juvenilia* (1887).

hid in the stairs. He came out in his dressing-gown, but finding no one, went back to bed again. "Some cat, no doubt!" he said. I closed the house door softly behind me. The sky had become stormy since the afternoon, luminous with the full moon, but strewn with grey and buff-coloured vapours; every now and then the moon disappeared entirely. Not a creature abroad; the tall gaunt houses staring in the moonlight.

I know not why, I took a roundabout way to the Corte, past one or two church doors, whence issued the faint flicker of midnight mass. For a moment I felt a temptation to enter one of them; but something seemed to restrain me. I caught snatches of the Christmas hymn. I felt myself beginning to be unnerved, and hastened towards the Corte. As I passed under the portico at San Francesco I heard steps behind me; it seemed to me that I was followed. I stopped to let the other pass. As he approached his pace flagged; he passed close by me and murmured, "Do not go: I am Giovanfrancesco Pico." I turned round; he was gone. A coldness numbed me; but I hastened on.

Behind the cathedral apse, in a narrow lane, I saw a man leaning against a wall. The moonlight was full upon him; it seemed to me that his face, with a thin pointed beard, was streaming with blood. I quickened my pace; but as I grazed by him he whispered, "Do not obey her; return home: I am Marcantonio Frangipani." My teeth chattered, but I hurried along the narrow lane, with the moonlight blue upon the white walls.

At last I saw the Corte before me: the square was flooded with moonlight, the windows of the palace seemed brightly illuminated, and the statue of Duke Robert, shimmering green, seemed advancing towards me on its horse. I came into the shadow. I had to pass beneath an archway. There started a figure as if out of the wall, and barred my passage with his outstretched cloaked arm. I tried to pass. He seized me by the arm, and his grasp was like a weight of ice. "You shall not pass!" he cried, and, as the moon came out once more, I saw his face, ghastly white and bound with an embroidered kerchief; he seemed almost a child. "You shall not pass!" he cried; "you shall not have her! She is mine, and mine alone! I am Prinzivalle degli Ordelaffi." I felt his ice-cold clutch, but with my other arm I laid about me wildly with the hatchet which I carried beneath my cloak. The hatchet struck the wall and rang upon the stone. He had vanished.

I hurried on. I did it. I cut open the bronze; I sawed it into a wider gash. I tore out the silver image, and hacked it into innumerable pieces. As I scattered the last fragments about, the moon was suddenly veiled; a great wind arose, howling down the square; it seemed to me that the earth shook. I threw down the hatchet and the saw, and fled home. I felt pursued, as if by the tramp of hundreds of invisible horsemen.

Now I am calm. It is midnight; another moment and she will be here! Patience, my heart! I hear it beating loud. I trust that no one will accuse poor Sor Asdrubale. I will write a letter to the authorities to declare his innocence should anything happen.... One! the clock in the palace tower has just struck.... "I hereby certify that, should anything happen this night to me, Spiridion Trepka, no one but myself is to be held ..." A step on the staircase! It is she! it is she! At last, Medea, Medea! Ah! AMOUR DURE—DURE AMOUR!

NOTE.—Here ends the diary of the late Spiridion Trepka. The chief newspapers of the province of Umbria informed the public that, on Christmas morning of the year 1885, the bronze equestrian statue of Robert II. had been found grievously mutilated; and that Professor Spiridion Trepka of Posen, in the German Empire, had been discovered dead of a stab in the region of the heart, given by an unknown hand.

Dionea[1]

From the Letters of Doctor Alessandro De Rosis to the Lady Evelyn Savelli, Princess of Sabina.

MONTEMIRTO LIGURE,[2] *June* 29, 1873.
I TAKE immediate advantage of the generous offer of your Excellency (allow an old Republican[3] who has held you on his knees to address you by that title sometimes, 'tis so appropriate) to help our poor people. I never expected to come a-begging so soon. For the olive crop has been unusually plenteous. We semi-Genoese don't pick the olives unripe, like our Tuscan neighbours, but let them grow big and black, when the young fellows go into the trees with long reeds and shake them down on the grass for the women to collect—a pretty sight which your Excellency must see some day: the grey trees with the brown, barefoot lads craning, balanced in the branches, and the turquoise sea as background just beneath.... That sea of ours—it is all along of it that I wish to ask for money. Looking up from my desk, I see the sea through the window, deep below and beyond the olive woods, bluish-green in the sunshine and veined with violet under the cloud-bars, like one of your Ravenna mosaics spread out as pavement for the world: a wicked sea, wicked in its loveliness, wickeder than your grey northern ones, and from which must have arisen in times gone by (when Phœnicians or Greeks built the temples at Lerici and Porto Venere) a baleful goddess of beauty, a Venus Verticordia,[4] but in

---

1 "Dionea" was first published in *Hauntings: Fantastic Stories* (London: William Heinemann, 1890) 61-103, from which this text is taken. Lee's interest in Venus-Aphrodite, goddess of love and desire, was shared with her brother the poet Eugene Lee-Hamilton (see Appendix H). See also the poem by her close friend, the poet A. Mary F. Robinson in Appendix E.

2 Montemirto means "myrtle mountain," a significant detail in that myrtle is a shrub dedicated to Venus-Aphrodite. This fictional village is situated in the Gulf of La Spezia. Nearby authentic places mentioned by de Rosis include Porto Venere, Lerici, Sarzana, and the islands of Palmaria and Tino.

3 De Rosis has been involved in the recent fierce political struggle for a unified republican Italy. Italy was finally unified in September 1870, but under the monarchy in the person of King Victor Emmanuel. It did not become a Republic until after World War II.

4 Literally "Venus-Turner-of-Hearts," title traditionally given to Venus signifying her ability to turn the hearts of women and girls to virtue, but occasionally used ironically as in Dante Gabriel Rossetti's sensual picture (1864-68) of the same name.

the bad sense of the word, overwhelming men's lives in sudden darkness like that squall of last week.

To come to the point. I want you, dear Lady Evelyn, to promise me some money, a great deal of money, as much as would buy you a little mannish cloth frock—for the complete bringing-up, until years of discretion, of a young stranger whom the sea has laid upon our shore. Our people, kind as they are, are very poor, and overburdened with children; besides, they have got a certain repugnance for this poor little waif, cast up by that dreadful storm, and who is doubtless a heathen, for she had no little crosses or scapulars[1] on, like proper Christian children. So, being unable to get any of our women to adopt the child, and having an old bachelor's terror of my housekeeper, I have bethought me of certain nuns, holy women, who teach little girls to say their prayers and make lace close by here; and of your dear Excellency to pay for the whole business.

Poor little brown mite! She was picked up after the storm (such a set-out of ship-models and votive candles as that storm must have brought the Madonna at Porto Venere![2]) on a strip of sand between the rocks of our castle: the thing was really miraculous, for this coast is like a shark's jaw, and the bits of sand are tiny and far between. She was lashed to a plank, swaddled up close in outlandish garments; and when they brought her to me they thought she must certainly be dead: a little girl of four or five, decidedly pretty, and as brown as a berry, who, when she came to, shook her head to show she understood no kind of Italian, and jabbered some half-intelligible Eastern jabber, a few Greek words embedded in I know not what; the Superior of the College De Propagandâ Fidē[3] would be puzzled to know. The child appears to be the only survivor from a ship which must have gone down in the great squall, and whose timbers have been strewing the bay for some days past; no one at Spezia or in any of our ports knows anything about her, but she was seen, apparently making for Porto Venere, by some of our sardine-fishers: a big, lumbering craft, with eyes painted on each side of the prow, which, as you know, is a peculiarity of Greek boats. She was sighted for the last time off the island of Palmaria, entering, with

---

1 Cloth badge of affiliation to a Catholic religious order.
2 Fourteenth-century white marble statue of the Madonna attributed to Mina da Fiesole and the protectress of the fishing port of Porto Venere.
3 The Pontifical Urban College for the Propagation of Faith is a Roman seminary founded in 1627 by Pope Urban VII.

all sails spread, right into the thick of the storm-darkness. No bodies, strangely enough, have been washed ashore.

July 10.

I have received the money, dear Donna Evelina. There was tremendous excitement down at San Massimo when the carrier came in with a registered letter, and I was sent for, in presence of all the village authorities, to sign my name on the postal register.

The child has already been settled some days with the nuns; such dear little nuns (nuns always go straight to the heart of an old priest-hater and conspirator against the Pope, you know), dressed in brown robes and close, white caps, with an immense round straw-hat flapping behind their heads like a nimbus: they are called Sisters of the Stigmata, and have a convent and school at San Massimo, a little way inland, with an untidy garden full of lavender and cherry-trees. Your *protégée* has already half set the convent, the village, the Episcopal See,[1] the Order of St. Francis, by the ears. First, because nobody could make out whether or not she had been christened. The question was a grave one, for it appears (as your uncle-in-law, the Cardinal, will tell you) that it is almost equally undesirable to be christened twice over as not to be christened at all. The first danger was finally decided upon as the less terrible; but the child, they say, had evidently been baptized before, and knew that the operation ought not to be repeated, for she kicked and plunged and yelled like twenty little devils, and positively would not let the holy water touch her. The Mother Superior, who always took for granted that the baptism had taken place before, says that the child was quite right, and that Heaven was trying to prevent a sacrilege; but the priest and the barber's wife, who had to hold her, think the occurrence fearful, and suspect the little girl of being a Protestant. Then the question of the name. Pinned to her clothes—striped Eastern things, and that kind of crinkled silk stuff they weave in Crete and Cyprus[2]—was a piece of parchment, a scapular we thought at first, but which was found to contain only the name Διονεα— Dionea, as they pronounce it here. The question was, Could such a name be fitly borne by a young lady at the Convent of the Stigmata? Half the population here have names as unchristian quite—Norma, Odoacer, Archimedes—my housemaid is called

---

1 Area under jurisdiction of a particular bishop.
2 The principal seat of worship for Aphrodite is Paphos in southern Cyprus.

Themis—but Dionea seemed to scandalise every one, perhaps because these good folk had a mysterious instinct that the name is derived from Dione,[1] one of the loves of Father Zeus, and mother of no less a lady than the goddess Venus. The child was very near being called Maria, although there are already twenty-three other Marias, Mariettas, Mariuccias, and so forth at the convent. But the sister-book-keeper, who apparently detests monotony, bethought her to look out Dionea first in the Calendar,[2] which proved useless; and then in a big vellum-bound book, printed at Venice in 1625, called "Flos Sanctorum, or Lives of the Saints, by Father Ribadeneira, S.J.,[3] with the addition of such Saints as have no assigned place in the Almanack, otherwise called the Movable or Extravagant Saints." The zeal of Sister Anna Maddalena has been rewarded, for there, among the Extravagant Saints, sure enough, with a border of palm-branches and hour-glasses, stands the name of Saint Dionea, Virgin and Martyr, a lady of Antioch, put to death by the Emperor Decius.[4] I know your Excellency's taste for historical information, so I forward this item. But I fear, dear Lady Evelyn, I fear that the heavenly patroness of your little sea-waif was a much more extravagant saint than that.

December 21, 1879.

Many thanks, dear Donna Evelina, for the money for Dionea's schooling. Indeed, it was not wanted yet: the accomplishments of young ladies are taught at a very moderate rate at Montemirto: and as to clothes, which you mention, a pair of wooden clogs, with pretty red tips, costs sixty-five centimes, and ought to last three years, if the owner is careful to carry them on her head in a neat parcel when out walking, and to put them on again only on entering the village. The Mother Superior is greatly overcome by your Excellency's munificence towards the convent, and much perturbed at being unable to send you a specimen of your *protégée*'s

---

1 In Homer's *Iliad* Dione is the mother of Aphrodite by Zeus. In Hesiod's *Theogony*, Aphrodite springs from the foam (*aphros* in Greek) that gathered about the severed genitals of Uranus when his son Cronus threw them into the sea.
2 The Catholic calendar of the saints.
3 Pedro de Ribadeneira (1526-1611), Jesuit and hagiologist, famous for his book of saints' lives, the *Flos Sanctorum* (1599-1610).
4 Gaius Messius Quintus Decius (reigned AD 249-251), soldier-emperor noted for his harsh persecution of Christians.

skill, exemplified in an embroidered pocket-handkerchief or a pair of mittens; but the fact is that poor Dionea *has* no skill. "We will pray to the Madonna and St. Francis to make her more worthy," remarked the Superior. Perhaps, however, your Excellency, who is, I fear but a Pagan woman (for all the Savelli Popes and St. Andrew Savelli's miracles),[1] and insufficiently appreciative of embroidered pocket-handkerchiefs, will be quite as satisfied to hear that Dionea, instead of skill, has got the prettiest face of any little girl in Montemirto. She is tall, for her age (she is eleven) quite wonderfully well proportioned and extremely strong: of all the convent-full, she is the only one for whom I have never been called in. The features are very regular, the hair black, and despite all the good Sisters' efforts to keep it smooth like a Chinaman's, beautifully curly. I am glad she should be pretty, for she will more easily find a husband; and also because it seems fitting that your *protégée* should be beautiful. Unfortunately her character is not so satisfactory: she hates learning, sewing, washing up the dishes, all equally. I am sorry to say she shows no natural piety. Her companions detest her, and the nuns, although they admit that she is not exactly naughty, seem to feel her as a dreadful thorn in the flesh. She spends hours and hours on the terrace overlooking the sea (her great desire, she confided to me, is to get to the sea—to *get back to the sea*, as she expressed it), and lying in the garden, under the big myrtle-bushes, and, in spring and summer, under the rose-hedge. The nuns say that rose-hedge and that myrtle-bush are growing a great deal too big, one would think from Dionea's lying under them; the fact, I suppose, has drawn attention to them. "That child makes all the useless weeds grow," remarked Sister Reparata. Another of Dionea's amusements is playing with pigeons.[2] The number of pigeons she collects about her is quite amazing; you would never have thought that San Massimo or the neighbouring hills contained as many. They flutter down like snowflakes, and strut and swell themselves out, and furl and unfurl their tails, and peck with little sharp movements of their silly, sensual heads and a little throb and gurgle in their throats, while Dionea lies stretched out full length in the sun, putting out her lips, which they come to kiss, and uttering strange, cooing sounds; or hopping about, flapping her arms slowly like wings, and raising her little head with much the same odd gesture

---

1 Prominent and influential Italian noble family of illustrious ancestry.
2 Roses are Aphrodite's signature blossom while doves or white pigeons are her birds.

as they;—'tis a lovely sight, a thing fit for one of your painters, Burne Jones or Tadema,[1] with the myrtle-bushes all round, the bright, white-washed convent walls behind, the white marble chapel steps (all steps are marble in this Carrara country),[2] and the enamel blue sea through the ilex-branches beyond. But the good Sisters abominate these pigeons, who, it appears, are messy little creatures, and they complain that, were it not that the Reverend Director likes a pigeon in his pot on a holiday, they could not stand the bother of perpetually sweeping the chapel steps and the kitchen threshold all along of those dirty birds....

August 6, 1882.

Do not tempt me, dearest Excellency, with your invitations to Rome. I should not be happy there, and do but little honour to your friendship. My many years of exile, of wanderings in northern countries, have made me a little bit into a northern man: I cannot quite get on with my own fellow-countrymen, except with the good peasants and fishermen all round. Besides—forgive the vanity of an old man, who has learned to make triple acrostic sonnets to cheat the days and months at Theresienstadt and Spielberg—I have suffered too much for Italy to endure patiently the sight of little parliamentary cabals and municipal wranglings, although they also are necessary in this day as conspiracies and battles were in mine.[3] I am not fit for your roomful of ministers and learned men and pretty women: the former would think me an ignoramus, and the latter—what would afflict me much more—a pedant.... Rather, if your Excellency really wants to show yourself and your children to your father's old *protégé* of Mazzinian times,[4] find a few days to come here next spring. You shall have some very bare rooms with

---

1   Sir Edward Coley Burne Jones (1833-98), English painter associated with the Pre-Raphaelites whose romantic visionary works are important to British Aestheticism; Sir Laurence Alma Tadema (1836-1912), of Dutch origin but lived in England, famous for his exotic or languorous paintings of Hellenic women.

2   Carrara, a city in the Massa Carrara province of Tuscany, is famous for its fine white or blue-grey marble.

3   De Rosis indicates that at an earlier stage in his life his political allegiances forced him into exile. Theresienstadt, a tiny eighteenth-century walled town in Bohemia (now Terezin, in Czechoslavakia), and Spielberg, a village in Austria.

4   Giuseppe Mazzini (1805-72), exiled Italian political revolutionary, writer, and intellectual, founder of the "Young Italy" movement, and the key figure behind the demand for a unified democratic Italian Republic.

brick floors and white curtains opening out on my terrace; and a dinner of all manner of fish and milk (the white garlic flowers shall be mown away from under the olives lest my cow should eat it) and eggs cooked in herbs plucked in the hedges. Your boys can go and see the big ironclads at Spezia; and you shall come with me up our lanes fringed with delicate ferns and overhung by big olives, and into the fields where the cherry-trees shed their blossoms on to the budding vines, the fig-trees stretching out their little green gloves, where the goats nibble perched on their hind legs, and the cows low in the huts of reeds; and there rise from the ravines, with the gurgle of the brooks, from the cliffs with the boom of the surf, the voices of unseen boys and girls, singing about love and flowers and death, just as in the days of Theocritus, whom your learned Excellency does well to read. Has your Excellency ever read Longus, a Greek pastoral novelist? He is a trifle free, a trifle nude for us readers of Zola; but the old French of Amyot[1] has a wonderful charm, and he gives one an idea, as no one else does, how folk lived in such valleys, by such sea-boards, as these in the days when daisy-chains and garlands of roses were still hung on the olive-trees for the nymphs of the grove; when across the bay, at the end of the narrow neck of blue sea, there clung to the marble rocks not a church of Saint Laurence, with the sculptured martyr on his grid-iron, but the temple of Venus, protecting her harbour.... Yes, dear Lady Evelyn, you have guessed aright. Your old friend has returned to his sins, and is scribbling once more. But no longer at verses or political pamphlets. I am enthralled by a tragic history, the history of the fall of the Pagan Gods.... Have you ever read of their wanderings and disguises, in my friend Heine's little book?[2]

And if you come to Montemirto, you shall see also your *protégée*, of whom you ask for news. It has just missed being disastrous. Poor Dionea! I fear that early voyage tied to the spar did no good to her wits, poor little waif! There has been a fearful row; and it has required all my influence, and all the awfulness of your

---

1   Theocritus (fl. c. 270 BC), Classical Greek poet born in Syracuse, regarded as the originator of pastoral poetry; Longus, author of the mid-third-century Greek pastoral romance *Daphnis and Chloe*; Émile Zola (1840-1902), leading French naturalistic novelist; Jacques Amyot (1513-93), Bishop of Auxerre and man of letters, translated Plutrach's lives into French and was responsible for a translation of *Daphnis and Chloe* (1559).
2   Heinrich Heine (1797/9-1856), author of "The Gods in Exile." See the passage translated by Walter Pater in the extract from "Pico della Mirandula" in Appendix B.

Excellency's name, and the Papacy, and the Holy Roman Empire, to prevent her expulsion by the Sisters of the Stigmata. It appears that this mad creature very nearly committed a sacrilege: she was discovered handling in a suspicious manner the Madonna's gala frock and her best veil of *pizzo di Cantù*,[1] a gift of the late Marchioness Violante Vigalena of Fornovo. One of the orphans, Zaira Barsanti, whom they call the Rossaccia, even pretends to have surprised Dionea as she was about to adorn her wicked little person with these sacred garments; and, on another occasion, when Dionea had been sent to pass some oil and sawdust over the chapel floor (it was the eve of Easter of the Roses),[2] to have discovered her seated on the edge of the altar, in the very place of the Most Holy Sacrament. I was sent for in hot haste, and had to assist at an ecclesiastical council in the convent parlour, where Dionea appeared, rather out of place, an amazing little beauty, dark, lithe, with an odd, ferocious gleam in her eyes, and a still odder smile, tortuous, serpentine, like that of Leonardo da Vinci's women,[3] among the plaster images of St. Francis, and the glazed and framed samplers before the little statue of the Virgin, which wears in summer a kind of mosquito-curtain to guard it from the flies, who, as you know, are creatures of Satan.[4]

Speaking of Satan, does your Excellency know that on the inside of our little convent door, just above the little perforated plate of metal (like the rose of a watering-pot) through which the Sister-portress peeps and talks, is pasted a printed form, an arrangement of holy names and texts in triangles, and the stigmatised hands of St. Francis, and a variety of other devices, for the purpose, as is explained in a special notice, of baffling the Evil One, and preventing his entrance into that building? Had you seen Dionea, and the stolid, contemptuous way in which she took, without attempting to refute, the various shocking allega-

---

1 Lace celebrated for its intricate designs of meandering trails and curls and made in Cantù, a town north of Milan.

2 In the Catholic liturgical tradition, the Sundays after Easter have different titles. The Sunday which falls within the octave of Ascension is known at Rome as *Pascha rosarum* (or *rosatum*) since in the ancient church of the Pantheon rose-leaves were thrown from the rotunda into the church.

3 Leonardo da Vinci (1452-1519), Florentine artist whose most famous work is the mysterious *Mona Lisa*. Dionea unites the enigma of the Mona Lisa with the serpentine qualities of the *femme fatale* as described by Swinburne and Pater in Appendices A and C.

4 Beelzebub, a Hebrew name for Satan, means "Lord of the Flies."

tions against her, your Excellency would have reflected, as I did, that the door in question must have been accidentally absent from the premises, perhaps at the joiner's for repair, the day that your *protégée* first penetrated into the convent. The ecclesiastical tribunal, consisting of the Mother Superior, three Sisters, the Capuchin Director, and your humble servant (who vainly attempted to be Devil's advocate), sentenced Dionea, among other things, to make the sign of the cross twenty-six times on the bare floor with her tongue. Poor little child! One might almost expect that, as happened when Dame Venus scratched her hand on the thorn-bush, red roses should sprout up between the fissures of the dirty old bricks.

October 14, 1883.

You ask whether, now that the Sisters let Dionea go and do half a day's service now and then in the village, and that Dionea is a grown-up creature, she does not set the place by the ears with her beauty. The people here are quite aware of its existence. She is already dubbed *La bella Dionea*; but that does not bring her any nearer getting a husband, although your Excellency's generous offer of a wedding-portion is well known throughout the district of San Massimo and Montemirto. None of our boys, peasants or fishermen, seem to hang on her steps; and if they turn round to stare and whisper as she goes by straight and dainty in her wooden clogs, with the pitcher of water or the basket of linen on her beautiful crisp dark head, it is, I remark, with an expression rather of fear than of love. The women, on their side, make horns with their fingers as she passes,[1] and as they sit by her side in the convent chapel; but that seems natural. My housekeeper tells me that down in the village she is regarded as possessing the evil eye and bringing love misery. "You mean," I said, "that a glance from her is too much for our lads' peace of mind." Veneranda shook her head, and explained, with the deference and contempt with which she always mentions any of her countryfolk's superstitions to me, that the matter is different: it's not with her they are in love (they would be afraid of her eye), but whereever she goes the young people must needs fall in love with each other, and usually where it is far from desirable. "You know Sora Luisa, the blacksmith's widow? Well, Dionea did a *half-service* for her last month, to prepare for the

---

1 The *mano cornuto* or "horned hand" is a traditional Italian hand-gesture to avert the evil eye. Horn-shaped amulets are still worn in Italy to avert the evil eye.

wedding of Luisa's daughter. Well, now, the girl must say, forsooth! that she won't have Pieriho of Lerici any longer, but will have that raggamuffin Wooden Pipe from Solaro, or go into a convent. And the girl changed her mind the very day that Dionea had come into the house. Then there is the wife of Pippo, the coffee-house keeper; they say she is carrying on with one of the coastguards, and Dionea helped her to do her washing six weeks ago. The son of Sor Temistocle has just cut off a finger to avoid the conscription, because he is mad about his cousin and afraid of being taken for a soldier; and it is a fact that some of the shirts which were made for him at the Stigmata had been sewn by Dionea;" ... and thus a perfect string of love misfortunes, enough to make a little "Decameron,"[1] I assure you, and all laid to Dionea's account. Certain it is that the people of San Massimo are terribly afraid of Dionea....

July 17, 1884.

Dionea's strange influence seems to be extending in a terrible way. I am almost beginning to think that our folk are correct in their fear of the young witch. I used to think, as physician to a convent, that nothing was more erroneous than all the romancings of Diderot and Schubert[2] (your Excellency sang me his "Young Nun" once: do you recollect, just before your marriage?), and that no more humdrum creature existed than one of our little nuns, with their pink baby faces under their tight white caps. It appeared the romancing was more correct than the prose. Unknown things have sprung up in these good Sisters' hearts, as unknown flowers have sprung up among the myrtle-bushes and the rose-hedge which Dionea lies under. Did I ever mention to you a certain little Sister Giuliana, who professed only two years ago?—a funny rose and white little creature presiding over the infirmary, as prosaic a little saint as ever kissed a crucifix or scoured a saucepan. Well, Sister Giuliana has disappeared, and the same day has disappeared also a sailor-boy from the port.

August 20, 1884.

The case of Sister Giuliana seems to have been but the beginning of an extraordinary love epidemic at the Convent of the

---

1 Famous collection of tales by Giovanni Boccaccio (1313-75).
2 Denis Diderot (1713-84), French philosopher, dramatist, and critic, and author of the sensationalist novel *The Nun*. Franz Schubert (1797-1828), Viennese composer, famous for his songs (*lieder*), which include the "Young Nun."

Stigmata: the elder schoolgirls have to be kept under lock and key lest they should talk over the wall in the moonlight, or steal out to the little hunchback who writes love-letters at a penny a-piece, beautiful flourishes and all, under the portico by the Fishmarket. I wonder does that wicked little Dionea, whom no one pays court to, smile (her lips like a Cupid's bow or a tiny snake's curves) as she calls the pigeons down around her, or lies fondling the cats under the myrtle-bush, when she sees the pupils going about with swollen, red eyes; the poor little nuns taking fresh penances on the cold chapel flags; and hears the long-drawn guttural vowels, *amore* and *morte* and *mio bene*,[1] which rise up of an evening, with the boom of the surf and the scent of the lemon-flowers, as the young men wander up and down, arm-in-arm, twanging their guitars along the moonlit lanes under the olives?

October 20, 1885.

A terrible, terrible thing has happened! I write to your Excellency with hands all a-tremble; and yet I *must* write, I must speak, or else I shall cry out. Did I ever mention to you Father Domenico of Casoria, the confessor of our Convent of the Stigmata? A young man, tall, emaciated with fasts and vigils, but handsome like the monk playing the virginal in Giorgione's "Concert,"[2] and under his brown serge still the most stalwart fellow of the country all round? One has heard of men struggling with the tempter. Well, well, Father Domenico had struggled as hard as any of the Anchorites recorded by St. Jerome,[3] and he had conquered. I never knew anything comparable to the angelic serenity of gentleness of this victorious soul. I don't like monks, but I loved Father Domenico. I might have been his father, easily, yet I always felt a certain shyness and awe of him; and yet men have accounted me a clean-lived man in my generation; but I felt, whenever I approached him, a poor worldly creature, debased by

---

1   *Amore*: "Love (or darling)," *morte*: "death," *mio bene*: "my precious" (literally, "my good").

2   Giorgione (c. 1476/8-1510), Venetian painter, said by Vasari to be, with Leonardo, one of the founders of modern painting. *The Concert* memorably praised by Walter Pater in 1877 in an essay thereafter republished in the third edition of *The Renaissance* in 1888, is now normally attributed to Titian.

3   St. Jerome (c. 342-420), scholar, theologian, and translator, spent several years living as an anchorite or Christian hermit in the desert of Chalcis, Syria, and also wrote a biography of St Paul of Thebes, another anchorite.

the knowledge of so many mean and ugly things. Of late Father Domenico had seemed to me less calm than usual: his eyes had grown strangely bright, and red spots had formed on his salient cheekbones. One day last week, taking his hand, I felt his pulse flutter, and all his strength as it were, liquefy under my touch. "You are ill," I said. "You have fever, Father Domenico. You have been overdoing yourself—some new privation, some new penance. Take care and do not tempt Heaven; remember the flesh is weak." Father Domenico withdrew his hand quickly. "Do not say that," he cried; "the flesh is strong!" and turned away his face. His eyes were glistening and he shook all over. "Some quinine," I ordered. But I felt it was no case for quinine. Prayers might be more useful, and could I have given them he should not have wanted. Last night I was suddenly sent for to Father Domenico's monastery above Montemirto: they told me he was ill. I ran up through the dim twilight of moonbeams and olives with a sinking heart. Something told me my monk was dead. He was lying in a little low whitewashed room; they had carried him there from his own cell in hopes he might still be alive. The windows were wide open; they framed some olive-branches, glistening in the moonlight, and far below, a strip of moonlit sea. When I told them that he was really dead, they brought some tapers and lit them at his head and feet, and placed a crucifix between his hands. "The Lord has been pleased to call our poor brother to Him," said the Superior. "A case of apoplexy, my dear Doctor—a case of apoplexy. You will make out the certificate for the authorities." I made out the certificate. It was weak of me. But, after all, why make a scandal? He certainly had no wish to injure the poor monks.

Next day I found the little nuns all in tears. They were gathering flowers to send as a last gift to their confessor. In the convent garden I found Dionea, standing by the side of a big basket of roses, one of the white pigeons perched on her shoulder.

"So," she said, "he has killed himself with charcoal, poor Padre Domenico!"[1]

Something in her tone, her eyes, shocked me.

"God has called to Himself one of His most faithful servants," I said gravely.

Standing opposite this girl, magnificent, radiant in her beauty, before the rose-hedge, with the white pigeons furling and unfurl-

---

1 Inhaling charcoal fumes: a method of asphyxiation used by Lee's friend, the poet Amy Levy, who committed suicide in 1889.

ing, strutting and pecking all round, I seemed to see suddenly the whitewashed room of last night, the big crucifix, that poor thin face under the yellow waxlight. I felt glad for Father Domenico; his battle was over.

"Take this to Father Domenico from me," said Dionea, breaking off a twig of myrtle starred over with white blossom; and raising her head with that smile like the twist of a young snake, she sang out in a high guttural voice a strange chaunt, consisting of the word *Amor—amor—amor*. I took the branch of myrtle and threw it in her face.

January 3, 1886.

It will be difficult to find a place for Dionea, and in this neighbourhood well-nigh impossible. The people associate her somehow with the death of Father Domenico, which has confirmed her reputation of having the evil eye. She left the convent (being now seventeen) some two months back, and is at present gaining her bread working with the masons at our notary's new house at Lerici: the work is hard, but our women often do it, and it is magnificent to see Dionea, in her short white skirt and tight white bodice, mixing the smoking lime with her beautiful strong arms; or, an empty sack drawn over her head and shoulders, walking majestically up the cliff, up the scaffoldings with her load of bricks.... I am, however, very anxious to get Dionea out of the neighbourhood, because I cannot help dreading the annoyances to which her reputation for the evil eye exposes her, and even some explosion of rage if ever she should lose the indifferent contempt with which she treats them. I hear that one of the rich men of our part of the world, a certain Sor Agostino of Sarzana, who owns a whole flank of marble mountain, is looking out for a maid for his daughter, who is about to be married; kind people and patriarchal in their riches, the old man still sitting down to table with all his servants; and his nephew, who is going to be his son-in-law, a splendid young fellow, who has worked like Jacob,[1] in the quarry and at the saw-mill, for love of his pretty cousin. That whole house is so good, simple, and peaceful, that I hope it may tame down even Dionea. If I do not succeed in getting Dionea this place (and all your Excellency's illustriousness and all my poor eloquence will be needed to counteract the sinister reports

---

1   In the Biblical Old Testament (Genesis 30. 20-30), Jacob, future father of the twelve tribes of Israel, labours for fourteen years to secure his wife Rachel.

attaching to our poor little waif), it will be best to accept your suggestion of taking the girl into your household at Rome, since you are curious to see what you call our baleful beauty. I am amused, and a little indignant at what you say about your footmen being handsome: Don Juan[1] himself, my dear Lady Evelyn, would be cowed by Dionea....

May 29, 1886.

Here is Dionea back upon our hands once more! but I cannot send her to your Excellency. Is it from living among these peasants and fishing-folk, or is it because, as people pretend, a sceptic is always superstitious? I could not muster courage to send you Dionea, although your boys are still in sailor-clothes and your uncle, the Cardinal, is eighty-four; and as to the Prince, why, he bears the most potent amulet against Dionea's terrible powers in your own dear capricious person. Seriously, there is something eerie in this coincidence. Poor Dionea! I feel sorry for her, exposed to the passion of a once patriarchally respectable old man. I feel even more abashed at the incredible audacity, I should almost say sacrilegious madness, of the vile old creature. But still the coincidence is strange and uncomfortable. Last week the lightning struck a huge olive in the orchard of Sor Agostino's house above Sarzana. Under the olive was Sor Agostino himself, who was killed on the spot; and opposite, not twenty paces off, drawing water from the well, unhurt and calm, was Dionea. It was the end of a sultry afternoon: I was on a terrace in one of those villages of ours, jammed, like some hardy bush, in the gash of a hill-side. I saw the storm rush down the valley, a sudden blackness, and then, like a curse, a flash, a tremendous crash, re-echoed by a dozen hills. "I told him," Dionea said very quietly, when she came to stay with me the next day (for Sor Agostino's family would not have her for another half-minute), "that if he did not leave me alone Heaven would send him an accident."

July 15, 1886.

My book? Oh, dear Donna Evelina, do not make me blush by talking of my book! Do not make an old man, respectable, a Government functionary (communal physician of the district of San Massimo and Montemirto Ligure), confess that he is but a lazy

---

1 Legendary fictitious libertine first given literary personality by the Spanish dramatist Tirso de Molina in his play *The Seducer of Seville* (1630).

unprofitable dreamer, collecting materials as a child picks hips out of a hedge, only to throw them away, liking them merely for the little occupation of scratching his hands and standing on tiptoe, for their pretty redness.... You remember what Balzac says about projecting any piece of work?—"*C'est fumer des cigarettes enchantées.*"[1] ... Well, well! The data obtainable about the ancient gods in their days of adversity are few and far between: a quotation here and there from the Fathers; two or three legends; Venus reappearing; the persecutions of Apollo in Styria; Proserpina going, in Chaucer, to reign over the fairies; a few obscure religious persecutions in the Middle Ages on the score of Paganism; some strange rites practised till lately in the depths of a Breton forest near Lannion.[2] ... As to Tannhäuser, he was a real knight, and a sorry one, and a real Minnesinger not of the best. Your Excellency will find some of his poems in Von der Hagen's four immense volumes, but I recommend you to take your notions of Ritter Tannhäuser's poetry rather from Wagner.[3] Certain it is that the Pagan divinities lasted much longer than we suspect, sometimes in their own nakedness, sometimes in the stolen garb of the Madonna or the saints. Who knows whether they do not exist to this day? And, indeed, is it possible they should not? For the awfulness of the deep woods, with their filtered green light, the creak of the swaying, solitary reeds, exists, and is Pan;[4] and the

---

1 Honoré de Balzac (1799-1850), French novelist and author of the compendious *Comédie Humaine*. The quotation is from Balzac's novel *La Cousine Bette* (1846). Translation: "It's like smoking enchanted cigarettes."

2 Styria, in the southeast of Austria, is the country's second biggest province. (On Apollo in Styria, see Appendix B); In Geoffrey Chaucer's "The Merchant's Tale," Pluto and Proserpina are not classical deities but King and Queen of the fairies. Lannion is a small historic town in Brittany.

3 Tannhäuser was a German Minnesinger or lyric poet of the thirteenth century and the protagonist in the legend of the knight who spends seven years with Venus in the Venusberg. This legend was the subject of an opera by Richard Wagner, first performed in 1845. Friedrich Heinrich Von der Hagen (1780-1856), German philologist, known for his research in Old German literature, published between 1838-56 his four-volume collection the *Minnesinger*.

4 Pan, in form half-man, half-goat, is the god of woods and fields, flocks and shepherds, and plays his reed pipe. This passage on suggestion is very similar to one in Lee's earlier essay "Faustus and Helena" (Appendix D).

blue, starry May night exists, the sough of the waves, the warm wind carrying the sweetness of the lemon-blossoms, the bitterness of the myrtle on our rocks, the distant chaunt of the boys cleaning out their nets, of the girls sickling the grass under the olives, *Amor—amor—amor*, and all this is the great goddess Venus. And opposite to me, as I write, between the branches of the ilexes, across the blue sea, streaked like a Ravenna mosaic with purple and green, shimmer the white houses and walls, the steeple and towers, an enchanted Fata Morgana[1] city, of dim Porto Venere; ... and I mumble to myself the verse of Catullus, but addressing a greater and more terrible goddess than he did:— "Procul a mea sit furor omnis, Hera, domo; alios age incitatos, alios age rabidos."[2]

March 25, 1887.

Yes; I will do everything in my power for your friends. Are you well-bred folk as well bred as we, Republican *bourgeois*, with the coarse hands (though you once told me mine were psychic hands when the mania of palmistry had not yet been succeeded by that of the Reconciliation between Church and State), I wonder, that you should apologise, you whose father fed me and housed me and clothed me in my exile, for giving me the horrid trouble of hunting for lodgings? It is like you, dear Donna Evelina, to have sent me photographs of my future friend Waldemar's statue.... I have no love for modern sculpture, for all the hours I have spent in Gibson's and Dupré's studio:[3] 'tis a dead art we should do better to bury. But your Waldemar has something of the old spirit: he seems to feel the divineness of the mere body, the spirituality of a limpid stream of mere physical life. But why among these

---

1 Named after the fairy enchantress Morgan le Fay who could change shape at will, a fata morgana is a complex mirage created by layers of alternating warm and cool air, which sometimes produces the illusion of a castle half in the air and half in the sea.

2 Gaius Valerius Catullus (c. 84-54 BC), Roman poet. De Rosis quotes from the last two lines of one of his most famous poems (Poem 63) addressed to Cybele, the great Eastern Mother goddess: "May all your furies, mistress, all fall far from my house./Make other men mad, but have mercy on me!" In Lee's original text a semi-colon was erroneously placed after "alios." De Rosis misremembers *era* (mistress) as "Hera."

3 John Gibson (1790-1866), English Neoclassical sculptor who lived in Rome from 1817, most celebrated for his *Tinted Venus*, now in Liverpool. Jules Dupré (1811-89), French, leading member of the Barbizon School of Romantic landscape painting.

statues only men and boys, athletes and fauns? Why only the bust of that thin, delicate-lipped little Madonna wife of his? Why no wide-shouldered Amazon or broad-flanked Aphrodite?

April 10, 1887.

You ask me how poor Dionea is getting on. Not as your Excellency and I ought to have expected when we placed her with the good Sisters of the Stigmata: although I wager that, fantastic and capricious as you are, you would be better pleased (hiding it carefully from that grave side of you which bestows devout little books and carbolic acid upon the indigent) that your *protégée* should be a witch than a serving-maid, a maker of philters rather than a knitter of stockings and sewer of shirts.

A maker of philters. Roughly speaking, that is Dionea's profession. She lives upon the money which I dole out to her (with many useless objurgations) on behalf of your Excellency; and her ostensible employment is mending nets, collecting olives, carrying bricks, and other miscellaneous jobs; but her real status is that of village sorceress. You think our peasants are sceptical? Perhaps they do not believe in thought-reading, mesmerism, and ghosts, like you, dear Lady Evelyn. But they believe very firmly in the evil eye, in magic, and in love-potions. Every one has his little story of this or that which happened to his brother or cousin or neighbour. My stable-boy and male factotum's brother-in-law, living some years ago in Corsica, was seized with a longing for a dance with his beloved at one of those balls which our peasants give in the winter, when the snow makes leisure in the mountains. A wizard anointed him for money, and straightway he turned into a black cat, and in three bounds was over the seas, at the door of his uncle's cottage, and among the dancers. He caught his beloved by the skirt to draw her attention; but she replied with a kick which sent him squealing back to Corsica. When he returned in summer he refused to marry the lady, and carried his left arm in a sling. "You broke it when I came to the Veglia!"[1] he said, and all seemed explained. Another lad, returning from working in the vineyards near Marseilles, was walking up to his native village, high in our hills, one moonlight night. He heard sounds of fiddle and fife from a roadside barn, and saw yellow light from its chinks; and then entering, he found many women dancing, old and young, and among them his affianced. He tried to snatch her

1   Alpe Veglia, a glacial large natural basin surrounded by mountains, in the Piedmontese Alps in Northern Italy.

round the waist for a waltz (they play *Mme. Angot*[1] at our rustic balls), but the girl was unclutchable, and whispered, "Go; for these are witches, who will kill thee; and I am a witch also. Alas! I shall go to hell when I die."

I could tell your Excellency dozens of such stories. But love-philters are among the commonest things to sell and buy. Do you remember the sad little story of Cervantes' Licentiate, who, instead of a love-potion, drank a philter which made him think he was made of glass, fit emblem of a poor mad poet?[2] ... It is love-philters that Dionea prepares. No; do not misunderstand; they do not give love of her, still less her love. Your seller of love-charms is as cold as ice, as pure as snow. The priest has crusaded against her, and stones have flown at her as she went by from dissatisfied lovers; and the very children, paddling in the sea and making mud-pies in the sand, have put out forefinger and little finger and screamed, "Witch, witch! ugly witch!" as she passed with basket or brick load; but Dionea has only smiled, that snake-like, amused smile, but more ominous than of yore. The other day I determined to seek her and argue with her on the subject of her evil trade. Dionea has a certain regard for me; not, I fancy, a result of gratitude, but rather the recognition of a certain admiration and awe which she inspires in your Excellency's foolish old servant. She has taken up her abode in a deserted hut, built of dried reeds and thatch, such as they keep cows in, among the olives on the cliffs. She was not there, but about the hut pecked some white pigeons, and from it, startling me foolishly with its unexpected sound, came the eerie bleat of her pet goat.... Among the olives it was twilight already, with streakings of faded rose in the sky, and faded rose, like long trails of petals, on the distant sea. I clambered down among the myrtle-bushes and came to a little semicircle of yellow sand, between two high and jagged rocks, the place where the sea had deposited Dionea after the wreck. She was seated there on the sand, her bare foot dabbling in the waves; she had twisted a wreath of myrtle and wild roses on her black, crisp hair. Near her was one of our prettiest girls, the Lena of Sor Tullio the blacksmith, with ashy, terrified face under her flowered kerchief. I determined to speak to the child, but without startling her now, for she is a nervous, hysteric little thing. So I sat on the rocks, screened by the myrtle-bushes,

---

1 *La Fille de Mme Angot* (1872), a light opera by Alexandre Lecocq.
2 Miguel de Cervantes (1547-1616), Spanish novelist, and author of *Don Quixote* (Part 1, 1605; Part 2, 1615).

waiting till the girl had gone. Dionea, seated listless on the sands, leaned over the sea and took some of its water in the hollow of her hand. "Here," she said to the Lena of Sor Tullio, "fill your bottle with this and give it to drink to Tommasino the Rosebud." Then she set to singing:—

"Love is salt, like sea-water—I drink and I die of thirst.... Water! water! Yet the more I drink, the more I burn. Love! thou art bitter as the seaweed."

April 20, 1887.

Your friends are settled here, dear Lady Evelyn. The house is built in what was once a Genoese fort, growing like a grey spiked aloes out of the marble rocks of our bay; rock and wall (the walls existed long before Genoa was ever heard of) grown almost into a homogeneous mass, delicate grey, stained with black and yellow lichen, and dotted here and there with myrtle-shoots and crimson snapdragon. In what was once the highest enclosure of the fort, where your friend Gertrude watches the maids hanging out the fine white sheets and pillow-cases to dry (a bit of the North, of Hermann and Dorothea[1] transferred to the South), a great twisted fig-tree juts out like an eccentric gurgoyle over the sea, and drops its ripe fruit into the deep blue pools. There is but scant furniture in the house, but a great oleander overhangs it, presently to burst into pink splendour; and on all the window-sills, even that of the kitchen (such a background of shining brass saucepans Waldemar's wife has made of it!) are pipkins and tubs full of trailing carnations, and tufts of sweet basil and thyme and mignonette. She pleases me most, your Gertrude, although you foretold I should prefer the husband; with her thin white face, a Memling[2] Madonna finished by some Tuscan sculptor, and her long, delicate white hands ever busy, like those of a mediæval lady, with some delicate piece of work; and the strange blue, more limpid than the sky and deeper than the sea, of her rarely lifted glance.

---

1 *Hermann und Dorothea* (1797), an idyllic poem by Johann Wolfgang von Goethe (1749-1832), in which the heroine fleeing from the turmoil caused by the French revolution settles in a German village and falls in love with the son of a wealthy burgher.

2 Hans Memling (c. 1430/40-94), German-born painter who lived in Bruges. His Netherlandish paintings portray gentle pious devotional scenes. Gertrude is clearly intended as a type of chaste, controlled Northern womanhood, contrasting with the Southern Dionea's dangerous sensuality.

It is in her company that I like Waldemar best; I prefer to the genius that infinitely tender and respectful, I would not say *lover*—yet I have no other word—of his pale wife. He seems to me, when with her, like some fierce, generous, wild thing from the woods, like the lion of Una,[1] tame and submissive to this saint.... This is really very beautiful on the part of that big lion Waldemar, with his odd eyes, as of some wild animal—odd, and, your Excellency remarks, not without a gleam of latent ferocity. I think that hereby hangs the explanation of his never doing any but male figures: the female figure, he says (and your Excellency must hold him responsible, not me, for such profanity), is almost inevitably inferior in strength and beauty; woman is not form, but expression, and therefore suits painting, but not sculpture. The point of a woman is not her body, but (and here his eyes rested very tenderly upon the thin white profile of his wife) her soul. "Still," I answered, "the ancients, who understood such matters, did manufacture some tolerable female statues: the Fates of the Parthenon, the Phidian Pallas, the Venus of Milo."[2] ...

"Ah! yes," exclaimed Waldemar, smiling, with that savage gleam of his eyes; "but those are not women, and the people who made them have left us the tales of Endymion, Adonis, Anchises:[3] a goddess might sit for them." ...

May 5, 1887.

Has it ever struck your Excellency in one of your La Rochefoucauld[4] fits (in Lent say, after too many balls) that not merely maternal but conjugal unselfishness may be a very selfish thing? There! you toss your little head at my words; yet I wager I

---

1 Female character representing Truth and the One True Faith and protected by a lion in the unfinished allegorical epic poem *The Faerie Queen* by Edmund Spenser (1552-99).

2 The Fates of the Parthenon are three beautiful draped headless figures originally sited on the Eastern pediment of the Parthenon and now in the British Museum. The Parthenon also originally housed a gigantic statue of Pallas Athena by the celebrated Greek sculptor Phidias which no longer survives. The antique statue of the Venus of Milo, now in the Louvre, Paris, was discovered in 1820, on the Aegean island of Melos.

3 In classical mythology handsome young men loved by goddesses. Endymion, a shepherd, was beloved by the moon-goddess Selene, while Adonis and Anchises were beloved by Aphrodite.

4 François La Rochefoucauld (1613-80), French author and moralist, best known for his maxims—laconic epigrams expressing a harsh or paradoxical truth.

have heard you say that *other* women may think it right to humour their husbands, but as to you, the Prince must learn that a wife's duty is as much to chasten her husband's whims as to satisfy them. I really do feel indignant that such a snow-white saint should wish another woman to part with all instincts of modesty merely because that other woman would be a good model for her husband; really it is intolerable. "Leave the girl alone," Waldemar said, laughing. "What do I want with the unæsthetic sex, as Schopenhauer[1] calls it?" But Gertrude has set her heart on his doing a female figure; it seems that folk have twitted him with never having produced one. She has long been on the look-out for a model for him. It is odd to see this pale, demure, diaphanous creature, not the more earthly for approaching motherhood, scanning the girls of our village with the eyes of a slave-dealer.

"If you insist on speaking to Dionea," I said, "I shall insist on speaking to her at the same time, to urge her to refuse your proposal." But Waldemar's pale wife was indifferent to all my speeches about modesty being a poor girl's only dowry. "She will do for a Venus," she merely answered.

We went up to the cliffs together, after some sharp words, Waldemar's wife hanging on my arm as we slowly clambered up the stony path among the olives. We found Dionea at the door of her hut, making faggots of myrtle-branches. She listened sullenly to Gertrude's offer and explanations; indifferently to my admonitions not to accept. The thought of stripping for the view of a man, which would send a shudder through our most brazen village girls, seemed not to startle her, immaculate and savage as she is accounted. She did not answer, but sat under the olives, looking vaguely across the sea. At that moment Waldemar came up to us; he had followed with the intention of putting an end to these wranglings.

"Gertrude," he said, "do leave her alone. I have found a model—a fisher-boy, whom I much prefer to any woman."

Dionea raised her head with that serpentine smile. "I will come," she said.

Waldemar stood silent; his eyes were fixed on her, where she stood under the olives, her white shift loose about her splendid

---

1 Arthur Schopenhauer (1788-1860), German philosopher, whose writings include the misogynist essay "On Women" (1851) in which he opines that not only are women physically ugly but also that they lack any genuine aesthetic sensibility.

throat, her shining feet bare in the grass. Vaguely, as if not knowing what he said, he asked her name. She answered that her name was Dionea; for the rest, she was an Innocentina, that is to say, a foundling; then she began to sing:—

> "Flower of the myrtle!
> My father is the starry sky;
> The mother that made me is the sea."[1]

June 22, 1887.

I confess I was an old fool to have grudged Waldemar his model. As I watch him gradually building up his statue, watch the goddess gradually emerging from the clay heap, I ask myself—and the case might trouble a more subtle moralist than me—whether a village girl, an obscure, useless life within the bounds of what we choose to call right and wrong, can be weighed against the possession by mankind of a great work of art, a Venus immortally beautiful? Still, I am glad that the two alternatives need not be weighed against each other. Nothing can equal the kindness of Gertrude, now that Dionea has consented to sit to her husband; the girl is ostensibly merely a servant like any other; and, lest any report of her real functions should get abroad and discredit her at San Massimo or Montemirto, she is to be taken to Rome, where no one will be the wiser, and where, by the way, your Excellency will have an opportunity of comparing Waldemar's goddess of love with our little orphan of the Convent of the Stigmata. What reassures me still more is the curious attitude of Waldemar towards the girl. I could never have believed that an artist could regard a woman so utterly as a mere inanimate thing, a form to copy, like a tree or flower. Truly he carries out his theory that sculpture knows only the body, and the body scarcely considered as human. The way in which he speaks to Dionea after hours of the most rapt contemplation of her is almost brutal in its coldness. And yet to hear him exclaim, "How beautiful she is! Good God, how beautiful!" No love of mere woman was ever so violent as this love of woman's mere shape.

---

1 Dionea sings a *stornello*, a three-line Tuscan song whose first line always runs "Flower of the ——." (Lee's friend, the poet A. Mary F. Robinson, also experimented with this song-form.) Dionea's song with its allusions to the myrtle and the elements seems to hint at her origins.

You asked me once, dearest Excellency, whether there survived among our people (you had evidently added a volume on folk-lore to that heap of half-cut, dog's-eared books that litter about among the Chineseries and mediæval brocades of your rooms) any trace of Pagan myths. I explained to you then that all our fairy mythology, classic gods, and demons and heroes, teemed with fairies, ogres, and princes. Last night I had a curious proof of this. Going to see the Waldemar, I found Dionea seated under the oleander at the top of the old Genoese fort, telling stories to the two little blonde children who were making the falling pink blossoms into necklaces at her feet; the pigeons, Dionea's white pigeons, which never leave her, strutting and pecking among the basil pots, and the white gulls flying round the rocks overhead. This is what I heard.... "And the three fairies said to the youngest son of the King, to the one who had been brought up as a shepherd, 'Take this apple, and give it to her among us who is most beautiful.' And the first fairy said, 'If thou give it to me thou shalt be Emperor of Rome, and have purple clothes, and have a gold crown and gold armour, and horses and courtiers;' and the second said, 'If thou give it to me thou shalt be Pope, and wear a mitre, and have the keys of heaven and hell; and the third fairy said, 'Give the apple to me, for I will give thee the most beautiful lady to wife.' And the youngest son of the King sat in the green meadow and thought about it a little, and then said, 'What use is there in being Emperor or Pope? Give me the beautiful lady to wife, since I am young myself.' And he gave the apple to the third of the three fairies." ...[1]

Dionea droned out the story in her half-Genoese dialect, her eyes looking far away across the blue sea, dotted with sails like white sea-gulls, that strange serpentine smile on her lips.

"Who told thee that fable?" I asked.

She took a handful of oleander-blossoms from the ground, and throwing them in the air, answered listlessly, as she watched

---

1 Dionea's fairytale is an adaptation of the Greek mythological tale of the Judgement of Paris in which Hera, Athena, and Aphrodite all contend for a golden apple inscribed "for the most beautiful" and appeal to Paris, the son of Priam, King of Troy, to settle the dispute. Each goddess tries to sway Paris with a gift, and he accepts Aphrodite's promise of the most beautiful woman in the world, abducts Helen of Sparta from her husband Menelaus, and so starts the Trojan War.

the little shower of rosy petals descend on her black hair and pale breast—

"Who knows?"

July 6, 1887.

How strange is the power of art! Has Waldemar's statue shown me the real Dionea, or has Dionea really grown more strangely beautiful than before? Your Excellency will laugh; but when I meet her I cast down my eyes after the first glimpse of her loveliness; not with the shyness of a ridiculous old pursuer of the Eternal Feminine,[1] but with a sort of religious awe—the feeling with which, as a child kneeling by my mother's side, I looked down on the church flags when the Mass bell told the elevation of the Host.... Do you remember the story of Zeuxis and the ladies of Crotona, five of the fairest not being too much for his Juno?[2] Do you remember—you, who have read everything—all the bosh of our writers about the Ideal in Art? Why, here is a girl who disproves all this nonsense in a minute; she is far, far more beautiful than Waldemar's statue of her. He said so angrily, only yesterday, when his wife took me into his studio (he has made a studio of the long-desecrated chapel of the old Genoese fort, itself, they say, occupying the site of the temple of Venus).

As he spoke that odd spark of ferocity dilated in his eyes, and seizing the largest of his modelling tools, he obliterated at one swoop the whole exquisite face. Poor Gertrude turned ashy white, and a convulsion passed over her face....

July 15.

I wish I could make Gertrude understand, and yet I could never, never bring myself to say a word. As a matter of fact, what is there to be said? Surely she knows best that her husband will never love any woman but herself. Yet ill, nervous as she is, I quite understand that she must loathe this unceasing talk of Dionea, of the superiority of the model over the statue. Cursed statue! I wish it were finished, or else that it had never been begun.

---

1   Famous saying from the closing lines of Goethe's *Faust* (Part 2, 1832): "The eternal feminine leads us upward."
2   De Rosis mistakes Juno for Helen. Zeuxis, Greek painter (fifth to the fourth centuries BC), famously created a painting of Helen of Troy by combining the best physical characteristics of five beautiful women models from the town of Croton or Crotona.

This morning Waldemar came to me. He seemed strangely agitated: I guessed he had something to tell me, and yet I could never ask. Was it cowardice on my part? He sat in my shuttered room, the sunshine making pools on the red bricks and tremulous stars on the ceiling, talking of many things at random, and mechanically turning over the manuscript, the heap of notes of my poor, never-finished book on the Exiled Gods. Then he rose, and walking nervously round my study, talking disconnectedly about his work, his eye suddenly fell upon a little altar, one of my few antiquities, a little block of marble with a carved garland and rams' heads, and a half-effaced inscription dedicating it to Venus, the mother of Love.

"It was found," I explained, "in the ruins of the temple, somewhere on the site of your studio: so, at least, the man said from whom I bought it."

Waldemar looked at it long. "So," he said, "this little cavity was to burn the incense in; or rather, I suppose, since it has two little gutters running into it, for collecting the blood of the victim? Well, well! they were wiser in that day, to wring the neck of a pigeon or burn a pinch of incense than to eat their own hearts out, as we do, all along of Dame Venus;" and he laughed, and left me with that odd ferocious lighting-up of his face. Presently there came a knock at my door. It was Waldemar. "Doctor," he said very quietly, "will you do me a favour? Lend me your little Venus altar—only for a few days, only till the day after to-morrow. I want to copy the design of it for the pedestal of my statue: it is appropriate." I sent the altar to him: the lad who carried it told me that Waldemar had set it up in the studio, and calling for a flask of wine, poured out two glasses. One he had given to my messenger for his pains; of the other he had drunk a mouthful, and thrown the rest over the altar, saying some unknown words.[1] "It must be some German habit," said my servant. What odd fancies this man has!

You ask me, dearest Excellency, to send you some sheets of my book: you want to know what I have discovered. Alas! dear Donna Evelina, I have discovered, I fear, that there is nothing to discover; that Apollo was never in Styria; that Chaucer, when he called the Queen of the Fairies Proserpine, meant nothing more

---

1 Waldemar apparently offers a libation of wine in honour of Venus.

than an eighteenth century poet when he called Dolly or Betty Cynthia or Amaryllis; that the lady who damned poor Tannhäuser was not Venus, but a mere little Suabian[1] mountain sprite; in fact, that poetry is only the invention of poets, and that that rogue, Heinrich Heine, is entirely responsible for the existence of *Dieux en Exil*.... My poor manuscript can only tell you what St. Augustine, Tertullian,[2] and sundry morose old Bishops thought about the loves of Father Zeus and the miracles of the Lady Isis,[3] none of which is much worth your attention.... Reality, my dear Lady Evelyn, is always prosaic: at least when investigated into by bald old gentlemen like me.

And yet, it does not look so. The world, at times, seems to be playing at being poetic, mysterious, full of wonder and romance. I am writing, as usual, by my window, the moonlight brighter in its whiteness than my mean little yellow-shining lamp. From the mysterious greyness, the olive groves and lanes beneath my terrace, rises a confused quaver of frogs, and buzz and whirr of insects: something, in sound, like the vague trails of countless stars, the galaxies on galaxies blurred into mere blue shimmer by the moon, which rides slowly across the highest heaven. The olive twigs glisten in the rays: the flowers of the pomegranate and oleander are only veiled as with bluish mist in their scarlet and rose. In the sea is another sea, of molten, rippled silver, or a magic causeway leading to the shining vague offing, the luminous pale sky-line, where the islands of Palmaria and Tino float like unsubstantial, shadowy dolphins. The roofs of Montemirto glimmer among the black, pointing cypresses: farther below, at the end of that half-moon of land, is San Massimo: the Genoese fort inhabited by our friends is profiled black against the sky. All is dark: our fisher-folk go to bed early; Gertrude and the little ones are asleep: they at least are, for I can imagine Gertrude lying awake, the moonbeams on her thin Madonna face, smiling as she thinks of the little ones around her, of the other tiny thing that will soon lie on her breast.... There is a light in the old desecrated chapel, the thing that was once the temple of Venus, they say, and is now

---

1 More usually "Swabian." Swabia is a former mediaeval German duchy in the lands now forming southwestern Germany, including Baden-Wüttemberg (the Black Forest), parts of western Bavaria, and northern Switzerland.

2 St. Augustine (354-430), Tertullian (c. 160-220), theologians and Church Fathers.

3 Isis, major ancient Egyptian goddess, honoured as the source of life.

Waldemar's workshop, its broken roof mended with reeds and thatch. Waldemar has stolen in, no doubt to see his statue again. But he will return, more peaceful for the peacefulness of the night, to his sleeping wife and children. God bless and watch over them! Good-night, dearest Excellency.

July 26.

I have your Excellency's telegram in answer to mine. Many thanks for sending the Prince. I await his coming with feverish longing; it is still something to look forward to. All does not seem over. And yet what can he do?

The children are safe: we fetched them out of their bed and brought them up here. They are still a little shaken by the fire, the bustle, and by finding themselves in a strange house; also, they want to know where their mother is; but they have found a tame cat, and I hear them chirping on the stairs.

It was only the roof of the studio, the reeds and thatch, that burned, and a few old pieces of timber. Waldemar must have set fire to it with great care; he had brought armfuls of faggots of dry myrtle and heather from the bakehouse close by, and thrown into the blaze quantities of pine-cones, and of some resin, I know not what, that smelt like incense. When we made our way, early this morning, through the smouldering studio, we were stifled with a hot church-like perfume: my brain swam, and I suddenly remembered going into St. Peter's[1] on Easter Day as a child.

It happened last night, while I was writing to you. Gertrude had gone to bed, leaving her husband in the studio. About eleven the maids heard him come out and call to Dionea to get up and come and sit to him. He had had this craze once before, of seeing her and his statue by an artificial light: you remember he had theories about the way in which the ancients lit up the statues in their temples. Gertrude, the servants say, was heard creeping downstairs a little later.

Do you see it? I have seen nothing else these hours, which have seemed weeks and months. He had placed Dionea on the big marble block behind the altar, a great curtain of dull red brocade—you know that Venetian brocade with the gold pomegranate pattern—behind her, like a Madonna of Van Eyck's.[2] He

---

1   St. Peter's Basilica, Rome, in the Vatican state, the largest church in the world and centre for Catholicism.

2   Jan van Eyck (d. 1441), major artist of the early Netherlandish school. A number of his Madonnas are posed against rich brocade backgrounds, an example being his *Madonna By the Fountain* of 1439.

showed her to me once before like this, the whiteness of her neck and breast, the whiteness of the drapery round her flanks, toned to the colour of old marble by the light of the resin burning in pans all round.... Before Dionea was the altar—the altar of Venus which he had borrowed from me. He must have collected all the roses about it, and thrown the incense upon the embers when Gertrude suddenly entered. And then, and then ...

We found her lying across the altar, her pale hair among the ashes of the incense, her blood—she had but little to give, poor white ghost!—trickling among the carved garlands and rams' heads, blackening the heaped-up roses. The body of Waldemar was found at the foot of the castle cliff. Had he hoped, by setting the place on fire, to bury himself among its ruins, or had he not rather wished to complete in this way the sacrifice, to make the whole temple an immense votive pyre? It looked like one, as we hurried down the hills to San Massimo: the whole hillside, dry grass, myrtle, and heather, all burning, the pale short flames waving against the blue moonlit sky, and the old fortress outlined black against the blaze.

August 30.

Of Dionea I can tell you nothing certain. We speak of her as little as we can. Some say they have seen her, on stormy nights, wandering among the cliffs: but a sailor-boy assures me, by all the holy things, that the day after the burning of the Castle Chapel—we never call it anything else—he met at dawn, off the island of Palmaria, beyond the Strait of Porto Venere, a Greek boat, with eyes painted on the prow, going full sail to sea, the men singing as she went. And against the mast, a robe of purple and gold about her, and a myrtle-wreath on her head, leaned Dionea, singing words in an unknown tongue, the white pigeons circling around her.

Oke of Okehurst; Or, The Phantom Lover[1]

To Count Peter Boutourline,
At Tagantcha,
Government of Kiew, Russia[2]

MY DEAR BOUTOURLINE,—Do you remember my telling you, one afternoon that you sat upon the hearthstool at Florence, the story of Mrs. Oke of Okehurst?

You thought it a fantastic tale, you lover of fantastic things, and urged me to write it out at once, although I protested that, in such matters, to write is to exorcise, to dispel the charm; and that printers' ink chases away the ghosts that may pleasantly haunt us, as efficaciously as gallons of holy water.

But if, as I suspect, you will now put down any charm that story may have possessed to the way in which we had been working ourselves up, that firelight evening, with all manner of fantastic stuff—if, as I fear, the story of Mrs. Oke of Okehurst will strike you as stale and unprofitable—the sight of this little book will serve at least to remind you, in the middle of your Russian summer, that there is such a season as winter, such a place as Florence, and such a person as your friend,

Vernon Lee.

KENSINGTON, *July* 1886.

I

THAT sketch up there with the boy's cap? Yes; that's the same woman. I wonder whether you could guess who she was. A sin-

---

1 Published earlier in novella form by William Blackwood in 1886 as *A Phantom Lover: A Fantastic Story,* this text is taken from Vernon Lee, *Hauntings and Other Fantastic Stories* (London: Heinemann, 1890) 109-91.

2 Count Peter Boutourline was a minor Russian poet and friend of Vernon Lee. He appears as the young Russian, Boris, one of the speakers in her book *Althea: A Second Book of Dialogues on Aspirations and Duties* (1894). Lee also acknowledges his help in the introduction to *The Countess of Albany* (1884)—Boutourline's grandfather and great-aunt having been among the Countess of Albany's friends; Kiew (Kiev): the capital of the Ukraine situated on the Dnipo river.

gular being, is she not? The most marvellous creature, quite, that I have ever met: a wonderful elegance, exotic, far-fetched, poignant; an artificial perverse sort of grace and research in every outline and movement and arrangement of head and neck, and hands and fingers. Here are a lot of pencil-sketches I made while I was preparing to paint her portrait. Yes; there's nothing but her in the whole sketch-book. Mere scratches, but they may give some idea of her marvellous, fantastic kind of grace. Here she is leaning over the staircase, and here sitting in the swing. Here she is walking quickly out of the room. That's her head. You see she isn't really handsome; her forehead is too big, and her nose too short. This gives no idea of her. It was altogether a question of movement. Look at the strange cheeks, hollow and rather flat; well, when she smiled she had the most marvellous dimples here. There was something exquisite and uncanny about it. Yes; I began the picture, but it was never finished. I did the husband first. I wonder who has his likeness now? Help me to move these pictures away from the wall. Thanks. This is her portrait; a huge wreck. I don't suppose you can make much of it; it is merely blocked in, and seems quite mad. You see my idea was to make her leaning against a wall—there was one hung with yellow that seemed almost brown—so as to bring out the silhouette.

It was very singular I should have chosen that particular wall. It does look rather insane in this condition, but I like it; it has something of her. I would frame it and hang it up, only people would ask questions. Yes; you have guessed quite right—it is Mrs. Oke of Okehurst.[1] I forgot you had relations in that part of the country; besides, I suppose the newspapers were full of it at the

---

1 Okehurst, the setting for this story, is reputedly based on Goddington, a seventeenth-century manor house set in an oak-studded park in Ashford, Kent. In 1885, Vernon Lee and Mary Robinson visited the poet Alfred Austin at Swinford Old Manor, a dower house built on the Goddington estate. The character of Alice Oke is most probably based on Janey Sevilla, Lady Archibald Campbell (c. 1846-1923), the daughter of James Henry Callander of Craigforth, Stirlingshire, and Ardkinglass, Argyllshire. The artist, James Abbot McNeill Whistler (1834-1903), painted several portraits of her, the most famous being *Arrangement in Black; The Lady in the Yellow Buskin* (Philadelphia Museum of Art). She and her husband put on plays in the open air at Coombe Hill Farm and, around July 1884, Whistler painted Lady Campbell as Orlando in Shakespeare's play *As You Like It* (Hunterian Art Gallery, Glasgow).

time. You didn't know that it all took place under my eyes? I can scarcely believe now that it did: it all seems so distant, vivid but unreal, like a thing of my own invention. It really was much stranger than any one guessed. People could no more understand it than they could understand her. I doubt whether any one ever understood Alice Oke besides myself. You mustn't think me unfeeling. She was a marvellous, weird, exquisite creature, but one couldn't feel sorry for her. I felt much sorrier for the wretched creature of a husband. It seemed such an appropriate end for her; I fancy she would have liked it could she have known. Ah! I shall never have another chance of painting such a portrait as I wanted. She seemed sent me from heaven or the other place. You have never heard the story in detail? Well, I don't usually mention it, because people are so brutally stupid or sentimental; but I'll tell it you. Let me see. It's too dark to paint any more to-day, so I can tell it you now. Wait; I must turn her face to the wall. Ah, she was a marvellous creature!

II

YOU remember, three years ago, my telling you I had let myself in for painting a couple of Kentish squireen? I really could not understand what had possessed me to say yes to that man. A friend of mine had brought him one day to my studio—Mr. Oke of Okehurst, that was the name on his card. He was a very tall, very well-made, very good-looking young man, with a beautiful fair complexion, beautiful fair moustache, and beautifully fitting clothes; absolutely like a hundred other young men you can see any day in the Park, and absolutely uninteresting from the crown of his head to the tip of his boots. Mr. Oke, who had been a lieutenant in the Blues[1] before his marriage, was evidently extremely uncomfortable on finding himself in a studio. He felt misgivings about a man who could wear a velvet coat in town, but at the same time he was nervously anxious not to treat me in the very

---

1   William Oke's regiment was that now known as The Royal Horse Guards which began life as the Parliamentarian Cavalry Regiment whose soldiers wore dark blue coats. The regiment was re-organized in 1661 as a royal regiment led by the Earl of Oxford, Aubrey de Vere, whose own personal livery was also blue and the regiment quickly became known by the nickname "The Blues" which still partly lives on to the present day.

least like a tradesman. He walked round my place, looked at everything with the most scrupulous attention, stammered out a few complimentary phrases, and then, looking at his friend for assistance, tried to come to the point, but failed. The point, which the friend kindly explained, was that Mr. Oke was desirous to know whether my engagements would allow of my painting him and his wife, and what my terms would be. The poor man blushed perfectly crimson during this explanation, as if he had come with the most improper proposal; and I noticed—the only interesting thing about him—a very odd nervous frown between his eyebrows, a perfect double gash,—a thing which usually means something abnormal: a mad-doctor of my acquaintance calls it the maniac-frown. When I had answered, he suddenly burst out into rather confused explanations: his wife—Mrs. Oke—had seen some of my—pictures—paintings—portraits—at the—the—what d'you call it?—Academy. She had—in short, they had made a very great impression upon her. Mrs. Oke had a great taste for art; she was, in short, extremely desirous of having her portrait and his painted by me, *etcetera*.

"My wife," he suddenly added, "is a remarkable woman. I don't know whether you will think her handsome,—she isn't exactly, you know. But she's awfully strange," and Mr. Oke of Okehurst gave a little sigh and frowned that curious frown, as if so long a speech and so decided an expression of opinion had cost him a great deal.

It was a rather unfortunate moment in my career. A very influential sitter of mine—you remember the fat lady with the crimson curtain behind her?—had come to the conclusion or been persuaded that I had painted her old and vulgar, which, in fact, she was. Her whole clique had turned against me, the newspapers had taken up the matter, and for the moment I was considered as a painter to whose brushes no woman would trust her reputation. Things were going badly. So I snapped but too gladly at Mr. Oke's offer, and settled to go down to Okehurst at the end of a fortnight.[1] But the door had scarcely closed upon my future sitter when I began to regret my rashness; and my disgust at the thought of wasting a whole summer upon the portrait of a totally

---

1   Although it was Whistler who painted Lady Archibald Campbell, the artist in this story may be based on Lee's friend, John Singer Sargent (1856-1925), whose provocative portrait of Madame Pierre Gautreau (*Madame X*) caused an outrage when exhibited in the Paris Salon of 1884.

uninteresting Kentish squire, and his doubtless equally uninteresting wife, grew greater and greater as the time for execution approached. I remember so well the frightful temper in which I got into the train for Kent, and the even more frightful temper in which I got out of it at the little station nearest to Okehurst. It was pouring floods. I felt a comfortable fury at the thought that my canvases would get nicely wetted before Mr. Oke's coachman had packed them on the top of the waggonette. It was just what served me right for coming to this confounded place to paint these confounded people. We drove off in the steady downpour. The roads were a mass of yellow mud; the endless flat grazing-grounds under the oak-trees, after having been burnt to cinders in a long drought, were turned into a hideous brown sop; the country seemed intolerably monotonous.

My spirits sank lower and lower. I began to meditate upon the modern Gothic country-house, with the usual amount of Morris furniture, Liberty rugs, and Mudie novels, to which I was doubtless being taken.[1] My fancy pictured very vividly the five or six little Okes—that man certainly must have at least five children— the aunts, and sisters-in-law, and cousins; the eternal routine of afternoon tea and lawn-tennis; above all, it pictured Mrs. Oke, the bouncing, well-informed, model house-keeper, electioneering, charity-organising young lady, whom such an individual as Mr. Oke would regard in the light of a remarkable woman. And my spirit sank within me, and I cursed my avarice in accepting the commission, my spiritlessness in not throwing it over while yet there was time. We had meanwhile driven into a large park, or rather a long succession of grazing-grounds, dotted about with large oaks, under which the sheep were huddled together for shelter from the rain. In the distance, blurred by the sheets of rain, was a line of low hills, with a jagged fringe of bluish firs and a solitary windmill. It must be a good mile and a half since we had passed a house, and there was none to be seen in the dis-

---

1 William Morris (1834-96), British painter, poet, and political publisher who became known as a designer of wall coverings, stained glass, carpets, tapestries, and furniture; Liberty, a now famous department store in Regent Street, London, that was fashionable in the late nineteenth century and popular with followers of the Aesthetic movement. It opened in 1875 selling ornaments, fabrics, rugs, and objets d'art from Japan and the East; Mudie novels: Charles Edward Mudie (1818-90) was a British bookseller and publisher who established a circulating library that became popular in the nineteenth century and made expensive three-volume novels accessible to a wide reading public.

tance—nothing but the undulation of sere grass, sopped brown beneath the huge blackish oak-trees, and whence arose, from all sides, a vague disconsolate bleating. At last the road made a sudden bend, and disclosed what was evidently the home of my sitter. It was not what I had expected. In a dip in the ground a large red-brick house, with the rounded gables and high chimney-stacks of the time of James I.,—a forlorn, vast place, set in the midst of the pasture-land, with no trace of garden before it, and only a few large trees indicating the possibility of one to the back; no lawn either, but on the other side of the sandy dip, which suggested a filled-up moat, a huge oak, short, hollow, with wreathing, blasted, black branches, upon which only a handful of leaves shook in the rain. It was not at all what I had pictured to myself the home of Mr. Oke of Okehurst.

My host received me in the hall, a large place, panelled and carved, hung round with portraits up to its curious ceiling—vaulted and ribbed like the inside of a ship's hull. He looked even more blond and pink and white, more absolutely mediocre in his tweed suit; and also, I thought, even more good-natured and duller. He took me into his study, a room hung round with whips and fishing-tackle in place of books, while my things were being carried upstairs. It was very damp, and a fire was smouldering. He gave the embers a nervous kick with his foot, and said, as he offered me a cigar—

"You must excuse my not introducing you at once to Mrs. Oke. My wife—in short, I believe my wife is asleep."

"Is Mrs. Oke unwell?" I asked, a sudden hope flashing across me that I might be off the whole matter.

"Oh no! Alice is quite well; at least, quite as well as she usually is. My wife," he added, after a minute, and in a very decided tone, "does not enjoy very good health—a nervous constitution. Oh no! not at all ill, nothing at all serious, you know. Only nervous, the doctors say; mustn't be worried or excited, the doctors say; requires lots of repose,—that sort of thing."

There was a dead pause. This man depressed me, I knew not why. He had a listless, puzzled look, very much out of keeping with his evident admirable health and strength.

"I suppose you are a great sportsman?" I asked from sheer despair, nodding in the direction of the whips and guns and fishing-rods.

"Oh no! not now. I was once. I have given up all that," he answered, standing with his back to the fire, and staring at the polar bear beneath his feet. "I—I have no time for all that now," he added, as if an explanation were due. "A married man—you know. Would you like to come up to your rooms?" he suddenly interrupted himself. "I have had one arranged for you to paint in. My wife said you would prefer a north light. If that one doesn't suit, you can have your choice of any other."

I followed him out of the study, through the vast entrance-hall. In less than a minute I was no longer thinking of Mr. and Mrs. Oke and the boredom of doing their likeness; I was simply overcome by the beauty of this house, which I had pictured modern and philistine. It was, without exception, the most perfect example of an old English manor-house that I had ever seen; the most magnificent intrinsically, and the most admirably preserved. Out of the huge hall, with its immense fireplace of delicately carved and inlaid grey and black stone, and its rows of family portraits, reaching from the wainscoting to the oaken ceiling, vaulted and ribbed like a ship's hull, opened the wide, flat-stepped staircase, the parapet surmounted at intervals by heraldic monsters, the wall covered with oak carvings of coats-of-arms, leafage, and little mythological scenes, painted a faded red and blue, and picked out with tarnished gold, which harmonised with the tarnished blue and gold of the stamped leather that reached to the oak cornice, again delicately tinted and gilded. The beautifully damascened suits of court armour looked, without being at all rusty, as if no modern hand had ever touched them; the very rugs under foot were of sixteenth-century Persian make; the only things of to-day were the big bunches of flowers and ferns, arranged in majolica[1] dishes upon the landings. Everything was perfectly silent; only from below came the chimes, silvery like an Italian palace fountain, of an old-fashioned clock.

It seemed to me that I was being led through the palace of the Sleeping Beauty.

"What a magnificent house!" I exclaimed as I followed my host through a long corridor, also hung with leather, wainscoted with carvings, and furnished with big wedding coffers, and chairs that looked as if they came out of some Vandyck[2] portrait. In my mind was the strong impression that all this was natural, sponta-

---

1   Tin-glazed earthenware that is often richly coloured and decorated. The techniques used are commonly thought to have reached the height of perfection in Italy in the sixteenth century.
2   Sir Anthony Van Dyck (1599–1641), Flemish artist who was one of the most prolific portraitists of the seventeenth century, known for his paintings of the English court and European aristocracy.

neous—that it had about it nothing of the picturesqueness which swell studios have taught to rich and æsthetic houses. Mr. Oke misunderstood me.

"It is a nice old place," he said, "but it's too large for us. You see, my wife's health does not allow of our having many guests; and there are no children."

I thought I noticed a vague complaint in his voice; and he evidently was afraid there might have seemed something of the kind, for he added immediately—

"I don't care for children one jackstraw, you know, myself; can't understand how any one can, for my part."

If ever a man went out of his way to tell a lie, I said to myself, Mr. Oke of Okehurst was doing so at the present moment.

When he had left me in one of the two enormous rooms that were allotted to me, I threw myself into an arm-chair and tried to focus the extraordinary imaginative impression which this house had given me.

I am very susceptible to such impressions; and besides the sort of spasm of imaginative interest sometimes given to me by certain rare and eccentric personalities, I know nothing more subduing than the charm, quieter and less analytic, of any sort of complete and out-of-the-common-run sort of house. To sit in a room like the one I was sitting in, with the figures of the tapestry glimmering grey and lilac and purple in the twilight, the great bed, columned and curtained, looming in the middle, and the embers reddening beneath the overhanging mantelpiece of inlaid Italian stonework, a vague scent of rose-leaves and spices, put into the china bowls by the hands of ladies long since dead, while the clock downstairs sent up, every now and then, its faint silvery tune of forgotten days, filled the room;—to do this is a special kind of voluptuousness, peculiar and complex and indescribable, like the half-drunkenness of opium or haschisch, and which, to be conveyed to others in any sense as I feel it, would require a genius, subtle and heady, like that of Baudelaire.

After I had dressed for dinner I resumed my place in the arm-chair, and resumed also my reverie, letting all these impressions of the past—which seemed faded like the figures in the arras, but still warm like the embers in the fire-place, still sweet and subtle like the perfume of the dead rose-leaves and broken spices in the china bowls—permeate me and go to my head. Of Oke and Oke's wife I did not think; I seemed quite alone, isolated from the world, separated from it in this exotic enjoyment.

Gradually the embers grew paler; the figures in the tapestry more shadowy; the columned and curtained bed loomed out vaguer; the room seemed to fill with greyness; and my eyes wandered to the mullioned bow-window, beyond whose panes, between whose heavy stone-work, stretched a greyish-brown expanse of sere and sodden park grass, dotted with big oaks; while far off, behind a jagged fringe of dark Scotch firs, the wet sky was suffused with the blood-red of the sunset. Between the falling of the raindrops from the ivy outside, there came, fainter or sharper, the recurring bleating of the lambs separated from their mothers, a forlorn, quavering, eerie little cry.

I started up at a sudden rap at my door.

"Haven't you heard the gong for dinner?" asked Mr. Oke's voice.

I had completely forgotten his existence.

III

I FEEL that I cannot possibly reconstruct my earliest impressions of Mrs. Oke. My recollection of them would be entirely coloured by my subsequent knowledge of her; whence I conclude that I could not at first have experienced the strange interest and admiration which that extraordinary woman very soon excited in me. Interest and admiration, be it well understood, of a very unusual kind, as she was herself a very unusual kind of woman; and I, if you choose, am a rather unusual kind of man. But I can explain that better anon.

This much is certain, that I must have been immeasurably surprised at finding my hostess and future sitter so completely unlike everything I had anticipated. Or no—now I come to think of it, I scarcely felt surprised at all; or if I did, that shock of surprise could have lasted but an infinitesimal part of a minute. The fact is, that, having once seen Alice Oke in the reality, it was quite impossible to remember that one could have fancied her at all different: there was something so complete, so completely unlike every one else, in her personality, that she seemed always to have been present in one's consciousness, although present, perhaps, as an enigma.

Let me try and give you some notion of her: not that first impression, whatever it may have been, but the absolute reality of her as I gradually learned to see it. To begin with, I must repeat and reiterate over and over again, that she was, beyond all comparison, the most graceful and exquisite woman I have ever seen, but with a grace and an exquisiteness that had nothing to do with any preconceived notion or previous experience of what goes by these names: grace and exquisiteness recognised at once as perfect, but which were seen in her for the first, and probably, I do believe, for the last time. It is conceivable, is it not, that once in a thousand years there may arise a combination of lines, a system of movements, an outline, a gesture, which is new, unprecedented, and yet hits off exactly our desires for beauty and rareness? She was very tall; and I suppose people would have called her thin. I don't know, for I never thought about her as a body—bones, flesh, that sort of thing; but merely as a wonderful series of lines, and a wonderful strangeness of personality. Tall and slender, certainly, and with not one item of what makes up our notion of a well-built woman. She was as straight—I mean she had as little of what people call figure—as a bamboo; her shoulders were a trifle high, and she had a decided stoop; her arms and her shoulders she never once wore uncovered. But this bamboo figure of hers had a suppleness and a stateliness, a play of outline with every step she took, that I can't compare to anything else; there was in it something of the peacock and something also of the stag; but, above all, it was her own. I wish I could describe her. I wish, alas!—I wish, I wish, I have wished a hundred thousand times—I could paint her, as I see her now, if I shut my eyes—even if it were only a silhouette. There! I see her so plainly, walking slowly up and down a room, the slight highness of her shoulders just completing the exquisite arrangement of lines made by the straight supple back, the long exquisite neck, the head, with the hair cropped in short pale curls, always drooping a little, except when she would suddenly throw it back, and smile, not at me, nor at any one, nor at anything that had been said, but as if she alone had suddenly seen or heard something, with the strange dimple in her thin, pale cheeks, and the strange whiteness in her full, wide-opened eyes: the moment when she had something of the stag in her movement. But where is the use of talking about her? I don't believe, you know, that even the greatest painter can show what is the real beauty of a very beautiful woman in the ordinary sense: Titian's and Tintoretto's women must have been miles handsomer than they have made them.[1] Something—and that the very essence—

---

1 Tiziano Vecellio, known in England as "Titian" (c. 1477-1576), Italian Renaissance painter of the Venetian school; Jacopo Robusti, known an "Tintoretto" (c. 1518-94), Italian Renaissance artist, a Mannerist painter of the Venetian school.

always escapes, perhaps because real beauty is as much a thing in time—a thing like music, a succession, a series—as in space. Mind you, I am speaking of a woman beautiful in the conventional sense. Imagine, then, how much more so in the case of a woman like Alice Oke; and if the pencil and brush, imitating each line and tint, can't succeed, how is it possible to give even the vaguest notion with mere wretched words—words possessing only a wretched abstract meaning, an impotent conventional association? To make a long story short, Mrs. Oke of Okehurst was, in my opinion, to the highest degree exquisite and strange,—an exotic creature, whose charm you can no more describe than you could bring home the perfume of some newly discovered tropical flower by comparing it with the scent of a cabbage-rose or a lily.

That first dinner was gloomy enough. Mr. Oke—Oke of Okehurst, as the people down there called him—was horribly shy, consumed with a fear of making a fool of himself before me and his wife, I then thought. But that sort of shyness did not wear off; and I soon discovered that, although it was doubtless increased by the presence of a total stranger, it was inspired in Oke, not by me, but by his wife. He would look every now and then as if he were going to make a remark, and then evidently restrain himself, and remain silent. It was very curious to see this big, handsome, manly young fellow, who ought to have had any amount of success with women, suddenly stammer and grow crimson in the presence of his own wife. Nor was it the consciousness of stupidity; for when you got him alone, Oke, although always slow and timid, had a certain amount of ideas, and very defined political and social views, and a certain childlike earnestness and desire to attain certainty and truth which was rather touching. On the other hand, Oke's singular shyness was not, so far as I could see, the result of any kind of bullying on his wife's part. You can always detect, if you have any observation, the husband or the wife who is accustomed to be snubbed, to be corrected, by his or her better-half: there is a self-consciousness in both parties, a habit of watching and fault-finding, of being watched and found fault with. This was clearly not the case at Okehurst. Mrs. Oke evidently did not trouble herself about her husband in the very least; he might say or do any amount of silly things without rebuke or even notice; and he might have done so, had he chosen, ever since his wedding-day. You felt that at once. Mrs. Oke simply passed over his existence. I cannot say she paid much attention to any one's, even to mine. At first I thought it an affectation on her part—for there was something far-fetched in her whole appearance, something suggesting study, which might lead one to tax her with affectation at first; she was dressed in a strange way, not according to any established æsthetic eccentricity, but individually, strangely, as if in the clothes of an ancestress of the seventeenth century. Well, at first I thought it a kind of pose on her part, this mixture of extreme graciousness and utter indifference which she manifested towards me. She always seemed to be thinking of something else; and although she talked quite sufficiently, and with every sign of superior intelligence, she left the impression of having been as taciturn as her husband.

In the beginning, in the first few days of my stay at Okehurst, I imagined that Mrs. Oke was a highly superior sort of flirt; and that her absent manner, her look, while speaking to you, into an invisible distance, her curious irrelevant smile, were so many means of attracting and baffling adoration. I mistook it for the somewhat similar manners of certain foreign women—it is beyond English ones—which mean, to those who can understand, "pay court to me." But I soon found I was mistaken. Mrs. Oke had not the faintest desire that I should pay court to her; indeed she did not honour me with sufficient thought for that; and I, on my part, began to be too much interested in her from another point of view to dream of such a thing. I became aware, not merely that I had before me the most marvellously rare and exquisite and baffling subject for a portrait, but also one of the most peculiar and enigmatic of characters. Now that I look back upon it, I am tempted to think that the psychological peculiarity of that woman might be summed up in an exorbitant and absorbing interest in herself—a Narcissus attitude[1]—curiously complicated with a fantastic imagination, a sort of morbid day-dreaming, all turned inwards, and with no outer characteristic save a certain restlessness, a perverse desire to surprise and shock, to surprise and shock more particularly her husband, and thus be revenged for the intense boredom which his want of appreciation inflicted upon her.

I got to understand this much little by little, yet I did not seem to have really penetrated the something mysterious about Mrs. Oke. There was a waywardness, a strangeness, which I felt but could not explain—a something as difficult to define as the pecu-

---

1 In Greek mythology, Narcissus is a handsome youth punished for having broken a lover's heart by being made to fall in love with his own reflection in a pool. He eventually dies, either from excessive self-obsession or starvation.

liarity of her outward appearance, and perhaps very closely connected therewith. I became interested in Mrs. Oke as if I had been in love with her; and I was not in the least in love. I neither dreaded parting from her, nor felt any pleasure in her presence. I had not the smallest wish to please or to gain her notice. But I had her on the brain. I pursued her, her physical image, her psychological explanation, with a kind of passion which filled my days, and prevented my ever feeling dull. The Okes lived a remarkably solitary life. There were but few neighbours, of whom they saw but little; and they rarely had a guest in the house. Oke himself seemed every now and then seized with a sense of responsibility towards me. He would remark vaguely, during our walks and after-dinner chats, that I must find life at Okehurst horribly dull; his wife's health had accustomed him to solitude, and then also his wife thought the neighbours a bore. He never questioned his wife's judgment in these matters. He merely stated the case as if resignation were quite simple and inevitable; yet it seemed to me, sometimes, that this monotonous life of solitude, by the side of a woman who took no more heed of him than of a table or chair, was producing a vague depression and irritation in this young man, so evidently cut out for a cheerful, commonplace life. I often wondered how he could endure it at all, not having, as I had, the interest of a strange psychological riddle to solve, and of a great portrait to paint. He was, I found, extremely good,—the type of the perfectly conscientious young Englishman, the sort of man who ought to have been the Christian soldier kind of thing; devout, pure-minded, brave, incapable of any baseness, a little intellectually dense, and puzzled by all manner of moral scruples. The condition of his tenants and of his political party—he was a regular Kentish Tory—lay heavy on his mind. He spent hours every day in his study, doing the work of a land agent and a political whip, reading piles of reports and newspapers and agricultural treatises; and emerging for lunch with piles of letters in his hand, and that odd puzzled look in his good healthy face, that deep gash between his eyebrows, which my friend the mad-doctor calls the *maniac-frown*. It was with this expression of face that I should have liked to paint him; but I felt that he would not have liked it, that it was more fair to him to represent him in his mere wholesome pink and white and blond conventionality. I was perhaps rather unconscientious about the likeness of Mr. Oke; I felt satisfied to paint it no matter how, I mean as regards character, for my whole mind was swallowed up in thinking how I should paint Mrs. Oke, how I could best transport on to canvas that singular and enigmatic personality. I began with her husband, and told her frankly that I must have much longer to study her. Mr. Oke couldn't understand why it should be necessary to make a hundred and one pencil-sketches of his wife before even determining in what attitude to paint her; but I think he was rather pleased to have an opportunity of keeping me at Okehurst; my presence evidently broke the monotony of his life. Mrs. Oke seemed perfectly indifferent to my staying, as she was perfectly indifferent to my presence. Without being rude, I never saw a woman pay so little attention to a guest; she would talk with me sometimes by the hour, or rather let me talk to her, but she never seemed to be listening. She would lie back in a big seventeenth-century arm-chair while I played the piano, with that strange smile every now and then in her thin cheeks, that strange whiteness in her eyes; but it seemed a matter of indifference whether my music stopped or went on. In my portrait of her husband she did not take, or pretend to take, the very faintest interest; but that was nothing to me. I did not want Mrs. Oke to think me interesting; I merely wished to go on studying her.

The first time that Mrs. Oke seemed to become at all aware of my presence as distinguished from that of the chairs and tables, the dogs that lay in the porch, or the clergyman or lawyer or stray neighbour who was occasionally asked to dinner, was one day— I might have been there a week—when I chanced to remark to her upon the very singular resemblance that existed between herself and the portrait of a lady that hung in the hall with the ceiling like a ship's hull. The picture in question was a full length, neither very good nor very bad, probably done by some stray Italian of the early seventeenth century. It hung in a rather dark corner, facing the portrait, evidently painted to be its companion, of a dark man, with a somewhat unpleasant expression of resolution and efficiency, in a black Vandyck dress. The two were evidently man and wife; and in the corner of the woman's portrait were the words, "Alice Oke, daughter of Virgil Pomfret, Esq., and wife to Nicholas Oke of Okehurst," and the date 1626— "Nicholas Oke" being the name painted in the corner of the small portrait. The lady was really wonderfully like the present Mrs. Oke, at least so far as an indifferently painted portrait of the early days of Charles I. can be like a living woman of the nineteenth century. There were the same strange lines of figure and face, the same dimples in the thin cheeks, the same wide-opened eyes, the same vague eccentricity of expression, not destroyed even by the feeble painting and conventional manner of the time.

One could fancy that this woman had the same walk, the same beautiful line of nape of the neck and stooping head as her descendant; for I found that Mr. and Mrs. Oke, who were first cousins, were both descended from that Nicholas Oke and that Alice, daughter of Virgil Pomfret. But the resemblance was heightened by the fact that, as I soon saw, the present Mrs. Oke distinctly made herself up to look like her ancestress, dressing in garments that had a seventeenth-century look; nay, that were sometimes absolutely copied from this portrait.

"You think I am like her," answered Mrs. Oke dreamily to my remark, and her eyes wandered off to that unseen something, and the faint smile dimpled her thin cheeks.

"You are like her, and you know it. I may even say you wish to be like her, Mrs. Oke," I answered, laughing.

"Perhaps I do."

And she looked in the direction of her husband. I noticed that he had an expression of distinct annoyance besides that frown of his.

"Isn't it true that Mrs. Oke tries to look like that portrait?" I asked, with a perverse curiosity.

"Oh, fudge!" he exclaimed, rising from his chair and walking nervously to the window. "It's all nonsense, mere nonsense. I wish you wouldn't, Alice."

"Wouldn't what?" asked Mrs. Oke, with a sort of contemptuous indifference. "If I am like that Alice Oke, why I am; and I am very pleased any one should think so. She and her husband are just about the only two members of our family—our most flat, stale, and unprofitable family—that ever were in the least degree interesting."

Oke grew crimson, and frowned as if in pain.

"I don't see why you should abuse our family, Alice," he said. "Thank God, our people have always been honourable and upright men and women!"

"Excepting always Nicholas Oke and Alice his wife, daughter of Virgil Pomfret, Esq.," she answered, laughing, as he strode out into the park.

"How childish he is!" she exclaimed when we were alone. "He really minds, really feels disgraced by what our ancestors did two centuries and a half ago. I do believe William would have those two portraits taken down and burned if he weren't afraid of me and ashamed of the neighbours. And as it is, these two people really are the only two members of our family that ever were in the least interesting. I will tell you the story some day."

As it was, the story was told to me by Oke himself. The next day, as we were taking our morning walk, he suddenly broke a long silence, laying about him all the time at the sere grasses with the hooked stick that he carried, like the conscientious Kentishman he was, for the purpose of cutting down his and other folk's thistles.

"I fear you must have thought me very ill-mannered towards my wife yesterday," he said shyly; "and indeed I know I was."

Oke was one of those chivalrous beings to whom every woman, every wife—and his own most of all—appeared in the light of something holy. "But—but—I have a prejudice which my wife does not enter into, about raking up ugly things in one's own family. I suppose Alice thinks that it is so long ago that it has really got no connection with us; she thinks of it merely as a picturesque story. I daresay many people feel like that; in short, I am sure they do, otherwise there wouldnt be such lots of discreditable family traditions afloat. But I feel as if it were all one whether it was long ago or not; when it's a question of one's own people, I would rather have it forgotten. I can't understand how people can talk about murders in their families, and ghosts, and so forth."

"Have you any ghosts at Okehurst, by the way?" I asked. The place seemed as if it required some to complete it.

"I hope not," answered Oke gravely.

His gravity made me smile.

"Why, would you dislike it if there were?" I asked.

"If there are such things as ghosts," he replied, "I don't think they should be taken lightly. God would not permit them to be, except as a warning or a punishment."

We walked on some time in silence, I wondering at the strange type of this commonplace young man, and half wishing I could put something into my portrait that should be the equivalent of this curious unimaginative earnestness. Then Oke told me the story of those two pictures—told it me about as badly and hesitatingly as was possible for mortal man.

He and his wife were, as I have said, cousins, and therefore descended from the same old Kentish stock. The Okes of Okehurst could trace back to Norman, almost to Saxon times, far longer than any of the titled or better-known families of the neighbourhood. I saw that William Oke, in his heart, thoroughly looked down upon all his neighbours. "We have never done anything particular, or been anything particular—never held any office," he said; "but we have always been here, and apparently always done our duty. An ancestor of ours was killed in the Scotch wars, another at Agincourt[1]—mere honest captains." Well, early in the seventeenth century, the family had dwindled to a single member, Nicholas Oke, the same who had rebuilt Okehurst in its present shape. This Nicholas appears to have been somewhat different from the usual run of the family. He had, in his youth, sought adventures in America, and seems, generally speaking, to have been less of a nonentity than his ancestors. He married, when no longer very young, Alice, daughter of Virgil Pomfret, a beautiful young heiress from a neighbouring county. "It was the first time an Oke married a Pomfret," my host informed me, "and the last time. The Pomfrets were quite different sort of people—restless, self-seeking; one of them had been a favourite of Henry VIII." It was clear that William Oke had no feeling of having any Pomfret blood in his veins; he spoke of these people with an evident family dislike—the dislike of an Oke, one of the old, honourable, modest stock, which had quietly done its duty, for a family of fortune-seekers and Court minions. Well, there had come to live near Okehurst, in a little house recently inherited from an uncle, a certain Christopher Lovelock, a young gallant and poet, who was in momentary disgrace at Court for some love affair. This Lovelock had struck up a great friendship with his neighbours of Okehurst—too great a friendship, apparently, with the wife, either for her husband's taste or her own. Anyhow, one evening as he was riding home alone, Lovelock had been attacked and murdered, ostensibly by highwaymen, but as was afterwards rumoured, by Nicholas Oke, accompanied by his wife dressed as a groom. No legal evidence had been got, but the tradition had remained. "They used to tell it us when we were children," said my host, in a hoarse voice, "and to frighten my cousin—I mean my wife—and me with stories about Lovelock. It is merely a tradition, which I hope may die out, as I sincerely pray to heaven that it may be false." "Alice—Mrs. Oke—you see," he went on after some time, "doesn't feel about it as I do. Perhaps I am morbid. But I do dislike having the old story raked up."

And we said no more on the subject.

---

1   The Scottish wars of independence were fought against England in the thirteenth and fourteenth centuries; Agincourt: site of a famous battle fought and won by the English against the French in 1415 during The Hundred Years War.

IV

FROM that moment I began to assume a certain interest in the eyes of Mrs. Oke; or rather, I began to perceive that I had a means of securing her attention. Perhaps it was wrong of me to do so; and I have often reproached myself very seriously later on. But after all, how was I to guess that I was making mischief merely by chiming in, for the sake of the portrait I had undertaken, and of a very harmless psychological mania, with what was merely the fad, the little romantic affectation or eccentricity, of a scatter-brained and eccentric young woman? How in the world should I have dreamed that I was handling explosive substances? A man is surely not responsible if the people with whom he is forced to deal, and whom he deals with as with all the rest of the world, are quite different from all other human creatures.

So, if indeed I did at all conduce to mischief, I really cannot blame myself. I had met in Mrs. Oke an almost unique subject for a portrait-painter of my particular sort, and a most singular, *bizarre* personality. I could not possibly do my subject justice so long as I was kept at a distance, prevented from studying the real character of the woman. I required to put her into play. And I ask you whether any more innocent way of doing so could be found than talking to a woman, and letting her talk, about an absurd fancy she had for a couple of ancestors of hers of the time of Charles I., and a poet whom they had murdered?—particularly as I studiously respected the prejudices of my host, and refrained from mentioning the matter, and tried to restrain Mrs. Oke from doing so, in the presence of William Oke himself.

I had certainly guessed correctly. To resemble the Alice Oke of the year 1626 was the caprice, the mania, the pose, the whatever you may call it, of the Alice Oke of 1880; and to perceive this resemblance was the sure way of gaining her good graces. It was the most extraordinary craze, of all the extraordinary crazes of childless and idle women, that I had ever met; but it was more than that, it was admirably characteristic. It finished off the strange figure of Mrs. Oke, as I saw it in my imagination—this *bizarre* creature of enigmatic, far-fetched exquisiteness—that she should have no interest in the present, but only an eccentric passion in the past. It seemed to give the meaning to the absent look in her eyes, to her irrelevant and far-off smile. It was like the words to a weird piece of gipsy music, this that she, who was so different, so distant from all women of her own time, should try and identify herself with a woman of the past—that she should have a kind of flirtation—— But of this anon.

I told Mrs. Oke that I had learnt from her husband the outline of the tragedy, or mystery, whichever it was, of Alice Oke, daughter of Virgil Pomfret, and the poet Christopher Lovelock. That look of vague contempt, of a desire to shock, which I had noticed before, came into her beautiful, pale, diaphanous face.

"I suppose my husband was very shocked at the whole matter," she said— "told it you with as little detail as possible, and assured you very solemnly that he hoped the whole story might be a mere dreadful calumny? Poor Willie! I remember already when we were children, and I used to come with my mother to spend Christmas at Okehurst, and my cousin was down here for his holidays, how I used to horrify him by insisting upon dressing up in shawls and waterproofs, and playing the story of the wicked Mrs. Oke; and he always piously refused to do the part of Nicholas, when I wanted to have the scene on Cotes Common. I didn't know then that I was like the original Alice Oke; I found it out only after our marriage. You really think that I am?"

She certainly was, particularly at that moment, as she stood in a white Vandyck dress, with the green of the park-land rising up behind her, and the low sun catching her short locks and surrounding her head, her exquisitely bowed head, with a pale-yellow halo. But I confess I thought the original Alice Oke, siren and murderess though she might be, very uninteresting compared with this wayward and exquisite creature whom I had rashly promised myself to send down to posterity in all her unlikely wayward exquisiteness.

One morning while Mr. Oke was despatching his Saturday heap of Conservative manifestoes and rural decisions—he was justice of the peace in a most literal sense, penetrating into cottages and huts, defending the weak and admonishing the ill-conducted—one morning while I was making one of my many pencil-sketches (alas, they are all that remain to me now!) of my future sitter, Mrs. Oke gave me her version of the story of Alice Oke and Christopher Lovelock.

"Do you suppose there was anything between them?" I asked—"that she was ever in love with him? How do you explain the part which tradition ascribes to her in the supposed murder? One has heard of women and their lovers who have killed the husband; but a woman who combines with her husband to kill her lover, or at least the man who is in love with her—that is surely very singular." I was absorbed in my drawing, and really thinking very little of what I was saying.

"I don't know," she answered pensively, with that distant look in her eyes. "Alice Oke was very proud, I am sure. She may have loved the poet very much, and yet been indignant with him, hated having to love him. She may have felt that she had a right to rid herself of him, and to call upon her husband to help her to do so."

"Good heavens! what a fearful idea!" I exclaimed, half laughing. "Don't you think, after all, that Mr. Oke may be right in saying that it is easier and more comfortable to take the whole story as a pure invention?"

"I cannot take it as an invention," answered Mrs. Oke contemptuously, "because I happen to know that it is true."

"Indeed!" I answered, working away at my sketch, and enjoying putting this strange creature, as I said to myself, through her paces; "how is that?"

"How does one know that anything is true in this world?" she replied evasively; "because one does, because one feels it to be true, I suppose."

And, with that far-off look in her light eyes, she relapsed into silence.

"Have you ever read any of Lovelock's poetry?" she asked me suddenly the next day.

"Lovelock?" I answered, for I had forgotten the name. "Lovelock, who"—— But I stopped, remembering the prejudices of my host, who was seated next to me at table.

"Lovelock who was killed by Mr. Oke's and my ancestors."

And she looked full at her husband, as if in perverse enjoyment of the evident annoyance which it caused him.

"Alice," he entreated in a low voice, his whole face crimson, "for mercy's sake, don't talk about such things before the servants."

Mrs. Oke burst into a high, light, rather hysterical laugh, the laugh of a naughty child.

"The servants! Gracious heavens! do you suppose they haven't heard the story? Why, it's as well known as Okehurst itself in the neighbourhood. Don't they believe that Lovelock has been seen about the house? Haven't they all heard his footsteps in the big corridor? Haven't they, my dear Willie, noticed a thousand times that you never will stay a minute alone in the yellow drawing-room—that you run out of it, like a child, if I happen to leave you there for a minute?"

True! How was it I had not noticed that? or rather, that I only now remembered having noticed it? The yellow drawing-room was one of the most charming rooms in the house: a large, bright room, hung with yellow damask and panelled with carvings, that opened straight out on to the lawn, far superior to the room in which we habitually sat, which was comparatively gloomy. This time Mr. Oke struck me as really too childish. I felt an intense desire to badger him.

"The yellow drawing-room!" I exclaimed. "Does this interesting literary character haunt the yellow drawing-room? Do tell me about it. What happened there?"

Mr. Oke made a painful effort to laugh.

"Nothing ever happened there, so far as I know," he said, and rose from the table.

"Really?" I asked incredulously.

"Nothing did happen there," answered Mrs. Oke slowly, playing mechanically with a fork, and picking out the pattern of the tablecloth. "That is just the extraordinary circumstance, that, so far as any one knows, nothing ever did happen there; and yet that room has an evil reputation. No member of our family, they say, can bear to sit there alone for more than a minute. You see, William evidently cannot."

"Have you ever seen or heard anything strange there?" I asked of my host.

He shook his head. "Nothing," he answered curtly, and lit his cigar.

"I presume you have not," I asked, half laughing, of Mrs. Oke, "since you don't mind sitting in that room for hours alone? How do you explain this uncanny reputation, since nothing ever happened there?"

"Perhaps something is destined to happen there in the future," she answered, in her absent voice. And then she suddenly added, "Suppose you paint my portrait in that room?"

Mr. Oke suddenly turned round. He was very white, and looked as if he were going to say something, but desisted.

"Why do you worry Mr. Oke like that?" I asked, when he had gone into his smoking-room with his usual bundle of papers. "It is very cruel of you, Mrs. Oke. You ought to have more consideration for people who believe in such things, although you may not be able to put yourself in their frame of mind."

"Who tells you that I don't believe in *such things*, as you call them?" she answered abruptly.

"Come," she said, after a minute, "I want to show you why I believe in Christopher Lovelock. Come with me into the yellow room."

V

WHAT Mrs. Oke showed me in the yellow room was a large bundle of papers, some printed and some manuscript, but all of them brown with age, which she took out of an old Italian ebony inlaid cabinet. It took her some time to get them, as a complicated arrangement of double locks and false drawers had to be put in play; and while she was doing so, I looked round the room, in which I had been only three or four times before. It was certainly the most beautiful room in this beautiful house, and, as it seemed to me now, the most strange. It was long and low, with something that made you think of the cabin of a ship, with a great mullioned window that let in, as it were, a perspective of the brownish green park-land, dotted with oaks, and sloping upwards to the distant line of bluish firs against the horizon. The walls were hung with flowered damask, whose yellow, faded to brown, united with the reddish colour of the carved wainscoting and the carved oaken beams. For the rest, it reminded me more of an Italian room than an English one. The furniture was Tuscan of the early seventeenth century, inlaid and carved; there were a couple of faded allegorical pictures, by some Bolognese master, on the walls; and in a corner, among a stack of dwarf orange-trees, a little Italian harpsichord of exquisite curve and slenderness, with flowers and landscapes painted upon its cover. In a recess was a shelf of old books, mainly English and Italian poets of the Elizabethan time; and close by it, placed upon a carved wedding-chest, a large and beautiful melon-shaped lute. The panes of the mullioned window were open, and yet the air seemed heavy, with an indescribable heady perfume, not that of any growing flower, but like that of old stuff that should have lain for years among spices.

"It is a beautiful room!" I exclaimed. "I should awfully like to paint you in it;" but I had scarcely spoken the words when I felt I had done wrong. This woman's husband could not bear the room, and it seemed to me vaguely as if he were right in detesting it.

Mrs. Oke took no notice of my exclamation, but beckoned me to the table where she was standing sorting the papers.

"Look!" she said, "these are all poems by Christopher Lovelock;" and touching the yellow papers with delicate and reverent fingers, she commenced reading some of them out loud in a slow, half-audible voice. They were songs in the style of those of

Herrick, Waller, and Drayton,[1] complaining for the most part of the cruelty of a lady called Dryope,[2] in whose name was evidently concealed a reference to that of the mistress of Okehurst. The songs were graceful, and not without a certain faded passion; but I was thinking not of them, but of the woman who was reading them to me.

Mrs. Oke was standing with the brownish yellow wall as a background to her white brocade dress, which, in its stiff seventeenth-century make, seemed but to bring out more clearly the slightness, the exquisite suppleness, of her tall figure. She held the papers in one hand, and leaned the other, as if for support, on the inlaid cabinet by her side. Her voice, which was delicate, shadowy, like her person, had a curious throbbing cadence, as if she were reading the words of a melody, and restraining herself with difficulty from singing it; and as she read, her long slender throat throbbed slightly, and a faint redness came into her thin face. She evidently knew the verses by heart, and her eyes were mostly fixed with that distant smile in them, with which harmonised a constant tremulous little smile in her lips.

"That is how I would wish to paint her!" I exclaimed within myself; and scarcely noticed, what struck me on thinking over the scene, that this strange being read these verses as one might fancy a woman would read love-verses addressed to herself.

"Those are all written for Alice Oke—Alice the daughter of Virgil Pomfret," she said slowly, folding up the papers. "I found them at the bottom of this cabinet. Can you doubt of the reality of Christopher Lovelock now?"

The question was an illogical one, for to doubt of the existence of Christopher Lovelock was one thing, and to doubt of the mode of his death was another; but somehow I did feel convinced.

"Look!" she said, when she had replaced the poems, "I will

---

1 Robert Herrick (1591-1674), English cleric and poet, a disciple of Ben Jonson, who revived the spirit of classical lyric poetry. He produced one book, *Hesperides* (1648); Edmund Waller (1606-87), English poet whose adoption of smooth, regular versification prepared the way for the heroic couplet's emergence at the end of the seventeenth century as the dominant form of poetic expression; Michael Drayton (1563-1631), British poet, the first to write English odes in the manner of the Latin lyric poet, Horace.

2 In Greek mythology, Dryope was the daughter of Dryops or of Eurytus who metamorphoses into a black poplar tree.

show you something else." Among the flowers that stood on the upper storey of her writing-table—for I found that Mrs. Oke had a writing-table in the yellow room—stood, as on an altar, a small black carved frame, with a silk curtain drawn over it: the sort of thing behind which you would have expected to find a head of Christ or of the Virgin Mary. She drew the curtain and displayed a large-sized miniature, representing a young man, with auburn curls and a peaked auburn beard, dressed in black, but with lace about his neck, and large pear-shaped pearls in his ears: a wistful, melancholy face. Mrs. Oke took the miniature religiously off its stand, and showed me, written in faded characters upon the back, the name "Christopher Lovelock," and the date 1626.

"I found this in the secret drawer of that cabinet, together with the heap of poems," she said, taking the miniature out of my hand.

I was silent for a minute.

"Does—does Mr. Oke know that you have got it here?" I asked; and then wondered what in the world had impelled me to put such a question.

Mrs. Oke smiled that smile of contemptuous indifference. "I have never hidden it from any one. If my husband disliked my having it, he might have taken it away, I suppose. It belongs to him, since it was found in his house."

I did not answer, but walked mechanically towards the door. There was something heady and oppressive in this beautiful room; something, I thought, almost repulsive in this exquisite woman. She seemed to me, suddenly, perverse and dangerous.

I scarcely know why, but I neglected Mrs. Oke that afternoon. I went to Mr. Oke's study, and sat opposite to him smoking while he was engrossed in his accounts, his reports, and electioneering papers. On the table, above the heap of paper-bound volumes and pigeon-holed documents, was, as sole ornament of his den, a little photograph of his wife, done some years before. I don't know why, but as I sat and watched him, with his florid, honest, manly beauty, working away conscientiously, with that little perplexed frown of his, I felt intensely sorry for this man.

But this feeling did not last. There was no help for it: Oke was not as interesting as Mrs. Oke; and it required too great an effort to pump up sympathy for this normal, excellent, exemplary young squire, in the presence of so wonderful a creature as his wife. So I let myself go to the habit of allowing Mrs. Oke daily to talk over her strange craze, or rather of drawing her out about it. I confess that I derived a morbid and exquisite pleasure in doing so: it was so characteristic in her, so appropriate to the house! It completed her personality so perfectly, and made it so much easier to conceive a way of painting her. I made up my mind little by little, while working at William Oke's portrait (he proved a less easy subject than I had anticipated, and, despite his conscientious efforts, was a nervous, uncomfortable sitter, silent and brooding)—I made up my mind that I would paint Mrs. Oke standing by the cabinet in the yellow room, in the white Vandyck dress copied from the portrait of her ancestress. Mr. Oke might resent it, Mrs. Oke even might resent it; they might refuse to take the picture, to pay for it, to allow me to exhibit; they might force me to run my umbrella through the picture. No matter. That picture should be painted, if merely for the sake of having painted it; for I felt it was the only thing I could do, and that it would be far away my best work. I told neither of my resolution, but prepared sketch after sketch of Mrs. Oke, while continuing to paint her husband.

Mrs. Oke was a silent person, more silent even than her husband, for she did not feel bound, as he did, to attempt to entertain a guest or to show any interest in him. She seemed to spend her life—a curious, inactive, half-invalidish life, broken by sudden fits of childish cheerfulness—in an eternal day-dream, strolling about the house and grounds, arranging the quantities of flowers that always filled all the rooms, beginning to read and then throwing aside novels and books of poetry, of which she always had a large number; and, I believe, lying for hours, doing nothing, on a couch in that yellow drawing-room, which, with her sole exception, no member of the Oke family had ever been known to stay in alone. Little by little I began to suspect and to verify another eccentricity of this eccentric being, and to understand why there were stringent orders never to disturb her in that yellow room.

It had been a habit at Okehurst, as at one or two other English manor-houses, to keep a certain amount of the clothes of each generation, more particularly wedding-dresses. A certain carved oaken press, of which Mr. Oke once displayed the contents to me, was a perfect museum of costumes, male and female, from the early years of the seventeenth to the end of the eighteenth century—a thing to take away the breath of a *bric-a-brac* collector, an antiquary, or a *genre* painter.[1] Mr. Oke was none of these,

---

1 An artist who engaged in genre painting, which was inspired by seventeenth-century Dutch art and depicted interior scenes, or scenes from everyday life.

and therefore took but little interest in the collection, save in so far as it interested his family feeling. Still he seemed well acquainted with the contents of that press.

He was turning over the clothes for my benefit, when suddenly I noticed that he frowned. I know not what impelled me to say, "By the way, have you any dresses of that Mrs. Oke whom your wife resembles so much? Have you got that particular white dress she was painted in, perhaps?"

Oke of Okehurst flushed very red.

"We have it," he answered hesitatingly, "but—it isn't here at present—I can't find it. I suppose," he blurted out with an effort, "that Alice has got it. Mrs. Oke sometimes has the fancy of having some of these old things down. I suppose she takes ideas from them."

A sudden light dawned in my mind. The white dress in which I had seen Mrs. Oke in the yellow room, the day that she showed me Lovelock's verses, was not, as I had thought, a modern copy; it was the original dress of Alice Oke, the daughter of Virgil Pomfret—the dress in which, perhaps, Christopher Lovelock had seen her in that very room.

The idea gave me a delightful picturesque shudder. I said nothing. But I pictured to myself Mrs. Oke sitting in that yellow room—that room which no Oke of Okehurst save herself ventured to remain in alone, in the dress of her ancestress, confronting, as it were, that vague, haunting something that seemed to fill the place—that vague presence, it seemed to me, of the murdered cavalier poet.

Mrs. Oke, as I have said, was extremely silent, as a result of being extremely indifferent. She really did not care in the least about anything except her own ideas and day-dreams, except when, every now and then, she was seized with a sudden desire to shock the prejudices or superstitions of her husband. Very soon she got into the way of never talking to me at all, save about Alice and Nicholas Oke and Christopher Lovelock; and then, when the fit seized her, she would go on by the hour, never asking herself whether I was or was not equally interested in the strange craze that fascinated her. It so happened that I was. I loved to listen to her, going on discussing by the hour the merits of Lovelock's poems, and analysing her feelings and those of her two ancestors. It was quite wonderful to watch the exquisite, exotic creature in one of these moods, with the distant look in her grey eyes and the absent-looking smile in her thin cheeks, talking as if she had intimately known these people of the seventeenth century, discussing every minute mood of theirs, detailing every scene between them and their victim, talking of Alice, and Nicholas, and Lovelock as she might of her most intimate friends. Of Alice particularly, and of Lovelock. She seemed to know every word that Alice had spoken, every idea that had crossed her mind. It sometimes struck me as if she were telling me, speaking of herself in the third person, of her own feelings—as if I were listening to a woman's confidences, the recital of her doubts, scruples, and agonies about a living lover. For Mrs. Oke, who seemed the most self-absorbed of creatures in all other matters, and utterly incapable of understanding or sympathising with the feelings of other persons, entered completely and passionately into the feelings of this woman, this Alice, who, at some moments, seemed to be not another woman, but herself.

"But how could she do it—how could she kill the man she cared for?" I once asked her.

"Because she loved him more than the whole world!" she exclaimed, and rising suddenly from her chair, walked towards the window, covering her face with her hands.

I could see, from the movement of her neck, that she was sobbing. She did not turn round, but motioned me to go away.

"Don't let us talk any more about it," she said. "I am ill to-day, and silly."

I closed the door gently behind me. What mystery was there in this woman's life? This listlessness, this strange self-engrossment and stranger mania about people long dead, this indifference and desire to annoy towards her husband—did it all mean that Alice Oke had loved or still loved some one who was not the master of Okehurst? And his melancholy, his preoccupation, the something about him that told of a broken youth—did it mean that he knew it?

VI

THE following days Mrs. Oke was in a condition of quite unusual good spirits. Some visitors—distant relatives—were expected, and although she had expressed the utmost annoyance at the idea of their coming, she was now seized with a fit of housekeeping activity, and was perpetually about arranging things and giving orders, although all arrangements, as usual, had been made, and all orders given, by her husband.

William Oke was quite radiant.

"If only Alice were always well like this!" he exclaimed; "if only she would take, or could take, an interest in life, how different things would be! But," he added, as if fearful lest he should be supposed to accuse her in any way, "how can she, usually, with her wretched health? Still, it does make me awfully happy to see her like this."

I nodded. But I cannot say that I really acquiesced in his views. It seemed to me, particularly with the recollection of yesterday's extraordinary scene, that Mrs. Oke's high spirits were anything but normal. There was something in her unusual activity and still more unusual cheerfulness that was merely nervous and feverish; and I had, the whole day, the impression of dealing with a woman who was ill and who would very speedily collapse.

Mrs. Oke spent her day wandering from one room to another, and from the garden to the greenhouse, seeing whether all was in order, when, as a matter of fact, all was always in order at Oke-hurst. She did not give me any sitting, and not a word was spoken about Alice Oke or Christopher Lovelock. Indeed, to a casual observer, it might have seemed as if all that craze about Lovelock had completely departed, or never existed. About five o'clock, as I was strolling among the red-brick round-gabled outhouses— each with its armorial oak—and the old-fashioned spalliered kitchen and fruit garden, I saw Mrs. Oke standing, her hands full of York and Lancaster roses,[1] upon the steps facing the stables. A groom was currycombing a horse, and outside the coach-house was Mr. Oke's little high-wheeled cart.

"Let us have a drive!" suddenly exclaimed Mrs. Oke, on seeing me. "Look what a beautiful evening—and look at that dear little cart! It is so long since I have driven, and I feel as if I must drive again. Come with me. And you, harness Jim at once and come round to the door."

I was quite amazed; and still more so when the cart drove up before the door, and Mrs. Oke called to me to accompany her. She sent away the groom, and in a minute we were rolling along, at a tremendous pace, along the yellow-sand road, with the sere pasture-lands, the big oaks, on either side.

I could scarcely believe my senses. This woman, in her

---

1 Species of red and white striped rose (*Rosa Damascena*) symbolic of the unification of the dynastic houses of York and Lancaster that fought for the English throne in what came to be known as "The Wars of the Roses." During the conflict each house wore a badge of identification: York, a white rose, and Lancaster a red.

mannish little coat and hat, driving a powerful young horse with the utmost skill, and chattering like a school-girl of sixteen, could not be the delicate, morbid, exotic, hot-house creature, unable to walk or to do anything, who spent her days lying about on couches in the heavy atmosphere, redolent with strange scents and associations, of the yellow drawing-room. The movement of the light carriage, the cool draught, the very grind of the wheels upon the gravel, seemed to go to her head like wine.

"It is so long since I have done this sort of thing," she kept repeating; "so long, so long. Oh, don't you think it delightful, going at this pace, with the idea that any moment the horse may come down and we two be killed?" and she laughed her childish laugh, and turned her face, no longer pale, but flushed with the movement and the excitement, towards me.

The cart rolled on quicker and quicker, one gate after another swinging to behind us, as we flew up and down the little hills, across the pasture lands, through the little red-brick gabled villages, where the people came out to see us pass, past the rows of willows along the streams, and the dark-green compact hop-fields, with the blue and hazy tree-tops of the horizon getting bluer and more hazy as the yellow light began to graze the ground. At last we got to an open space, a high-lying piece of common-land, such as is rare in that ruthlessly utilised country of grazing-grounds and hop-gardens. Among the low hills of the Weald, it seemed quite preternaturally high up, giving a sense that its extent of flat heather and gorse, bound by distant firs, was really on the top of the world. The sun was setting just opposite, and its lights lay flat on the ground, staining it with the red and black of the heather, or rather turning it into the surface of a purple sea, canopied over by a bank of dark-purple clouds—the jet-like sparkle of the dry ling and gorse tipping the purple like sunlit wavelets. A cold wind swept in our faces.

"What is the name of this place?" I asked. It was the only bit of impressive scenery that I had met in the neighbourhood of Okehurst.

"It is called Cotes Common," answered Mrs. Oke, who had slackened the pace of the horse, and let the reins hang loose about his neck. "It was here that Christopher Lovelock was killed."

There was a moment's pause; and then she proceeded, tickling the flies from the horse's ears with the end of her whip, and looking straight into the sunset, which now rolled, a deep purple stream, across the heath to our feet—

"Lovelock was riding home one summer evening from Apple-dore, when, as he had got half-way across Cotes Common, some-where about here—for I have always heard them mention the pond in the old gravel-pits as about the place—he saw two men riding towards him, in whom he presently recognised Nicholas Oke of Okehurst accompanied by a groom. Oke of Okehurst hailed him; and Lovelock rode up to meet him. 'I am glad to have met you, Mr. Lovelock,' said Nicholas, 'because I have some important news for you;' and so saying, he brought his horse close to the one that Lovelock was riding, and suddenly turning round, fired off a pistol at his head. Lovelock had time to move, and the bullet, instead of striking him, went straight into the head of his horse, which fell beneath him. Lovelock, however, had fallen in such a way as to be able to extricate himself easily from his horse; and drawing his sword, he rushed upon Oke, and seized his horse by the bridle. Oke quickly jumped off and drew his sword; and in a minute, Lovelock, who was much the better swordsman of the two, was having the better of him. Lovelock had completely disarmed him, and got his sword at Oke's throat, crying out to him that if he would ask forgiveness he should be spared for the sake of their old friendship, when the groom sud-denly rode up from behind and shot Lovelock through the back. Lovelock fell, and Oke immediately tried to finish him with his sword, while the groom drew up and held the bridle of Oke's horse. At that moment the sunlight fell upon the groom's face, and Lovelock recognised Mrs. Oke. He cried out, 'Alice, Alice! it is you who have murdered me!' and died. Then Nicholas Oke sprang into his saddle and rode off with his wife, leaving Lovelock dead by the side of his fallen horse. Nicholas Oke had taken the precaution of removing Lovelock's purse and throwing it into the pond, so the murder was put down to certain highwaymen who were about in that part of the country. Alice Oke died many years afterwards, quite an old woman, in the reign of Charles II.; but Nicholas did not live very long, and shortly before his death got into a very strange condition, always brooding, and sometimes threatening to kill his wife. They say that in one of these fits, just shortly before his death, he told the whole story of the murder, and made a prophecy that when the head of his house and master of Okehurst should marry another Alice Oke, descended from himself and his wife, there should be an end of the Okes of Oke-hurst. You see, it seems to be coming true. We have no children, and I don't suppose we shall ever have any. I, at least, have never wished for them."

Mrs. Oke paused, and turned her face towards me with the absent smile in her thin cheeks: her eyes no longer had that distant look; they were strangely eager and fixed. I did not know what to answer; this woman positively frightened me. We remained for a moment in that same place, with the sunlight dying away in crimson ripples on the heather, gilding the yellow banks, the black waters of the pond, surrounded by thin rushes, and the yellow gravel-pits; while the wind blew in our faces and bent the ragged warped bluish tops of the firs. Then Mrs. Oke touched the horse, and off we went at a furious pace. We did not exchange a single word, I think, on the way home. Mrs. Oke sat with her eyes fixed on the reins, breaking the silence now and then only by a word to the horse, urging him to an even more furious pace. The people we met along the roads must have thought that the horse was running away, unless they noticed Mrs. Oke's calm manner and the look of excited enjoyment in her face. To me it seemed that I was in the hands of a mad-woman, and I quietly prepared myself for being upset or dashed against a cart. It had turned cold, and the draught was icy in our faces when we got within sight of the red gables and high chimney-stacks of Okehurst. Mr. Oke was standing before the door. On our approach I saw a look of relieved suspense, of keen pleasure come into his face.

He lifted his wife out of the cart in his strong arms with a kind of chivalrous tenderness.

"I am so glad to have you back, darling," he exclaimed—"so glad! I was delighted to hear you had gone out with the cart, but as you have not driven for so long, I was beginning to be frightfully anxious, dearest. Where have you been all this time?"

Mrs. Oke had quickly extricated herself from her husband, who had remained holding her, as one might hold a delicate child who has been causing anxiety. The gentleness and affection of the poor fellow had evidently not touched her—she seemed almost to recoil from it.

"I have taken him to Cotes Common," she said, with that perverse look which I had noticed before, as she pulled off her driving-gloves. "It is such a splendid old place."

Mr. Oke flushed as if he had bitten upon a sore tooth, and the double gash painted itself scarlet between his eyebrows.

Outside, the mists were beginning to rise, veiling the park-land dotted with big black oaks, and from which, in the watery moon-light, rose on all sides the eerie little cry of the lambs separated from their mothers. It was damp and cold, and I shivered.

VII

THE next day Okehurst was full of people, and Mrs. Oke, to my amazement, was doing the honours of it as if a house full of commonplace, noisy young creatures, bent upon flirting and tennis, were her usual idea of felicity.

The afternoon of the third day—they had come for an electioneering ball, and stayed three nights—the weather changed; it turned suddenly very cold and began to pour. Every one was sent indoors, and there was a general gloom suddenly over the company. Mrs. Oke seemed to have got sick of her guests, and was listlessly lying back on a couch, paying not the slightest attention to the chattering and piano-strumming in the room, when one of the guests suddenly proposed that they should play charades. He was a distant cousin of the Okes, a sort of fashionable artistic Bohemian, swelled out to intolerable conceit by the amateur-actor vogue of a season.

"It would be lovely in this marvellous old place," he cried, "just to dress up, and parade about, and feel as if we belonged to the past. I have heard you have a marvellous collection of old costumes, more or less ever since the days of Noah, somewhere, Cousin Bill."

The whole party exclaimed in joy at this proposal. William Oke looked puzzled for a moment, and glanced at his wife, who continued to lie listless on her sofa.

"There is a press full of clothes belonging to the family," he answered dubiously, apparently overwhelmed by the desire to please his guests; "but—but—I don't know whether it's quite respectful to dress up in the clothes of dead people."

"Oh, fiddlestick!" cried the cousin. "What do the dead people know about it? Besides," he added, with mock seriousness, "I assure you we shall behave in the most reverent way and feel quite solemn about it all, if only you will give us the key, old man."

Again Mr. Oke looked towards his wife, and again met only her vague, absent glance.

"Very well," he said, and led his guests upstairs.

An hour later the house was filled with the strangest crew and the strangest noises. I had entered, to a certain extent, into William Oke's feeling of unwillingness to let his ancestors' clothes and personality be taken in vain; but when the masquerade was complete, I must say that the effect was quite magnificent. A dozen youngish men and women—those who were staying in the

house and some neighbours who had come for lawn-tennis and
dinner—were rigged out, under the direction of the theatrical
cousin, in the contents of that oaken press: and I have never seen
a more beautiful sight than the panelled corridors, the carved and
escutcheoned staircase, the dim drawing-rooms with their faded
tapestries, the great hall with its vaulted and ribbed ceiling,
dotted about with groups or single figures that seemed to have
come straight from the past. Even William Oke, who, besides
myself and a few elderly people, was the only man not masquer-
aded, seemed delighted and fired by the sight. A certain schoolboy character suddenly came out in him; and finding that there
was no costume left for him, he rushed upstairs and presently
returned in the uniform he had worn before his marriage. I
thought I had really never seen so magnificent a specimen of the
handsome Englishman; he looked, despite all the modern associations of his costume, more genuinely old-world than all the rest,
a knight for the Black Prince or Sidney,[1] with his admirably
regular features and beautiful fair hair and complexion. After a
minute, even the elderly people had got costumes of some sort—
dominoes[2] arranged at the moment, and hoods and all manner of
disguises made out of pieces of old embroidery and Oriental
stuffs and furs; and very soon this rabble of masquers had
become, so to speak, completely drunk with its own amusement—with the childishness, and, if I may say so, the barbarism,
the vulgarity underlying the majority even of well-bred English
men and women—Mr. Oke himself doing the mountebank like a
schoolboy at Christmas.

"Where is Mrs. Oke? Where is Alice?" some one suddenly
asked.

Mrs. Oke had vanished. I could fully understand that to this
eccentric being, with her fantastic, imaginative, morbid passion
for the past, such a carnival as this must be positively revolting;
and, absolutely indifferent as she was to giving offence, I could
imagine how she would have retired, disgusted and outraged, to
dream her strange day-dreams in the yellow room.

But a moment later, as we were all noisily preparing to go in
to dinner, the door opened and a strange figure entered, stranger

1 Edward, the Black Prince, Prince of Wales (1343-76), who received his
   sobriquet because he wore black armour; Sir Philip Sidney (1554-86),
   English courtier, statesman, soldier, and poet.
2 Loose-hooded cloaks worn with a half mask as part of a masquerade
   costume.

than any of these others who were profaning the clothes of the dead: a boy, slight and tall, in a brown riding-coat, leathern belt, and big buff boots, a little grey cloak over one shoulder, a large grey hat slouched over the eyes, a dagger and pistol at the waist. It was Mrs. Oke, her eyes preternaturally bright, and her whole face lit up with a bold, perverse smile.

Every one exclaimed, and stood aside. Then there was a moment's silence, broken by faint applause. Even to a crew of noisy boys and girls playing the fool in the garments of men and women long dead and buried, there is something questionable in the sudden appearance of a young married woman, the mistress of the house, in a riding-coat and jack-boots; and Mrs. Oke's expression did not make the jest seem any the less questionable.

"What is that costume?" asked the theatrical cousin, who, after a second, had come to the conclusion that Mrs. Oke was merely a woman of marvellous talent whom he must try and secure for his amateur troop next season.

"It is the dress in which an ancestress of ours, my namesake Alice Oke, used to go out riding with her husband in the days of Charles I.," she answered, and took her seat at the head of the table. Involuntarily my eyes sought those of Oke of Okehurst. He, who blushed as easily as a girl of sixteen, was now as white as ashes, and I noticed that he pressed his hand almost convulsively to his mouth.

"Don't you recognise my dress, William?" asked Mrs. Oke, fixing her eyes upon him with a cruel smile.

He did not answer, and there was a moment's silence, which the theatrical cousin had the happy thought of breaking by jumping upon his seat and emptying off his glass with the exclamation—

"To the health of the two Alice Okes, of the past and the present!"

Mrs. Oke nodded, and with an expression I had never seen in her face before, answered in a loud and aggressive tone—

"To the health of the poet, Mr. Christopher Lovelock, if his ghost be honouring this house with its presence!"

I felt suddenly as if I were in a madhouse. Across the table, in the midst of this room full of noisy wretches, tricked out red, blue, purple, and parti-coloured, as men and women of the sixteenth, seventeenth, and eighteenth centuries, as improvised Turks and Eskimos, and dominoes, and clowns, with faces painted and corked and floured over, I seemed to see that sanguine sunset, washing like a sea of blood over the heather, to where, by the black pond and the wind-warped firs, there lay the body of Christopher Lovelock, with his dead horse near him, the yellow gravel and lilac ling soaked crimson all around; and above emerged, as out of the redness, the pale blond head covered with the grey hat, the absent eyes, and strange smile of Mrs. Oke. It seemed to me horrible, vulgar, abominable, as if I had got inside a madhouse.

VIII

FROM that moment I noticed a change in William Oke; or rather, a change that had probably been coming on for some time got to the stage of being noticeable.

I don't know whether he had any words with his wife about her masquerade of that unlucky evening. On the whole I decidedly think not. Oke was with every one a diffident and reserved man, and most of all so with his wife; besides, I can fancy that he would experience a positive impossibility of putting into words any strong feeling of disapprobation towards her, that his disgust would necessarily be silent. But be this as it may, I perceived very soon that the relations between my host and hostess had become exceedingly strained. Mrs. Oke, indeed, had never paid much attention to her husband, and seemed merely a trifle more indifferent to his presence than she had been before. But Oke himself, although he affected to address her at meals from a desire to conceal his feeling, and a fear of making the position disagreeable to me, very clearly could scarcely bear to speak to or even see his wife. The poor fellow's honest soul was quite brimful of pain, which he was determined not to allow to overflow, and which seemed to filter into his whole nature and poison it. This woman had shocked and pained him more than was possible to say, and yet it was evident that he could neither cease loving her nor commence comprehending her real nature. I sometimes felt, as we took our long walks through the monotonous country, across the oak-dotted grazing-grounds, and by the brink of the dull-green, serried hop-rows, talking at rare intervals about the value of the crops, the drainage of the estate, the village schools, the Primrose League,[1] and the iniquities of Mr. Gladstone,[2] while Oke of Okehurst carefully cut down every tall

---

1   A political organization founded in 1883 that worked to increase the popularity of traditional Conservative policies. The primrose was associated with Benjamin Disraeli, Lord Beaconsfield, who claimed it as his favourite flower.

2   William Gladstone (1809-98), British politician and Prime Minister.

thistle that caught his eye—I sometimes felt, I say, an intense and impotent desire to enlighten this man about his wife's character. I seemed to understand it so well, and to understand it well seemed to imply such a comfortable acquiescence; and it seemed so unfair that just he should be condemned to puzzle for ever over this enigma, and wear out his soul trying to comprehend what now seemed so plain to me. But how would it ever be possible to get this serious, conscientious, slow-brained representative of English simplicity and honesty and thoroughness to understand the mixture of self-engrossed vanity, of shallowness, of poetic vision, of love of morbid excitement, that walked this earth under the name of Alice Oke?

So Oke of Okehurst was condemned never to understand; but he was condemned also to suffer from his inability to do so. The poor fellow was constantly straining after an explanation of his wife's peculiarities; and although the effort was probably unconscious, it caused him a great deal of pain. The gash—the maniac-frown, as my friend calls it—between his eyebrows, seemed to have grown a permanent feature of his face.

Mrs. Oke, on her side, was making the very worst of the situation. Perhaps she resented her husband's tacit reproval of that masquerade night's freak, and determined to make him swallow more of the same stuff, for she clearly thought that one of William's peculiarities, and one for which she despised him, was that he could never be goaded into an outspoken expression of disapprobation; that from her he would swallow any amount of bitterness without complaining. At any rate she now adopted a perfect policy of teasing and shocking her husband about the murder of Lovelock. She was perpetually alluding to it in her conversation, discussing in his presence what had or had not been the feelings of the various actors in the tragedy of 1626, and insisting upon her resemblance and almost identity with the original Alice Oke. Something had suggested to her eccentric mind that it would be delightful to perform in the garden at Okehurst, under the huge ilexes and elms, a little masque[1] which she had discovered among Christopher Lovelock's works; and she began to scour the country and enter into vast correspondence for the purpose of effectuating this scheme. Letters arrived every other

---

1 A dramatic entertainment, often an elaborate morality play interspersing poetry and music, usually performed by masked players representing mythological or allegorical figures, that was popular in England in the sixteenth, and early seventeenth centuries.

day from the theatrical cousin, whose only objection was that Okehurst was too remote a locality for an entertainment in which he foresaw great glory to himself. And every now and then there would arrive some young gentleman or lady, whom Alice Oke had sent for to see whether they would do.

I saw very plainly that the performance would never take place, and that Mrs. Oke herself had no intention that it ever should. She was one of those creatures to whom realisation of a project is nothing, and who enjoy plan-making almost the more for knowing that all will stop short at the plan. Meanwhile, this perpetual talk about the pastoral, about Lovelock, this continual attitudinising as the wife of Nicholas Oke, had the further attraction to Mrs. Oke of putting her husband into a condition of frightful though suppressed irritation, which she enjoyed with the enjoyment of a perverse child. You must not think that I looked on indifferent, although I admit that this was a perfect treat to an amateur student of character like myself. I really did feel most sorry for poor Oke, and frequently quite indignant with his wife. I was several times on the point of begging her to have more consideration for him, even of suggesting that this kind of behaviour, particularly before a comparative stranger like me, was very poor taste. But there was something elusive about Mrs. Oke, which made it next to impossible to speak seriously with her; and besides, I was by no means sure that any interference on my part would not merely animate her perversity.

One evening a curious incident took place. We had just sat down to dinner, the Okes, the theatrical cousin, who was down for a couple of days, and three or four neighbours. It was dusk, and the yellow light of the candles mingled charmingly with the greyness of the evening. Mrs. Oke was not well, and had been remarkably quiet all day, more diaphanous, strange, and far-away than ever; and her husband seemed to have felt a sudden return of tenderness, almost of compassion, for this delicate, fragile creature. We had been talking of quite indifferent matters, when I saw Mr. Oke suddenly turn very white, and look fixedly for a moment at the window opposite to his seat.

"Who's that fellow looking in at the window, and making signs to you, Alice? Damn his impudence!" he cried, and jumping up, ran to the window, opened it, and passed out into the twilight. We all looked at each other in surprise; some of the party remarked upon the carelessness of servants in letting nasty-looking fellows hang about the kitchen, others told stories of tramps and burglars. Mrs. Oke did not speak; but I noticed the curious, distant-looking smile in her thin cheeks.

After a minute William Oke came in, his napkin in his hand. He shut the window behind him and silently resumed his place.

"Well, who was it?" we all asked.

"Nobody. I—I must have made a mistake," he answered, and turned crimson, while he busily peeled a pear.

"It was probably Lovelock," remarked Mrs. Oke, just as she might have said, "It was probably the gardener," but with that faint smile of pleasure still in her face. Except the theatrical cousin, who burst into a loud laugh, none of the company had ever heard Lovelock's name, and, doubtless imagining him to be some natural appanage[1] of the Oke family, groom or farmer, said nothing, so the subject dropped.

From that evening onwards things began to assume a different aspect. That incident was the beginning of a perfect system—a system of what? I scarcely know how to call it. A system of grim jokes on the part of Mrs. Oke, of superstitious fancies on the part of her husband—a system of mysterious persecutions on the part of some less earthly tenant of Okehurst. Well, yes, after all, why not? We have all heard of ghosts, had uncles, cousins, grandmothers, nurses, who have seen them; we are all a bit afraid of them at the bottom of our soul; so why shouldn't they be? I am too sceptical to believe in the impossibility of anything, for my part! Besides, when a man has lived throughout a summer in the same house with a woman like Mrs. Oke of Okehurst, he gets to believe in the possibility of a great many improbable things, I assure you, as a mere result of believing in her. And when you come to think of it, why not? That a weird creature, visibly not of this earth, a reincarnation of a woman who murdered her lover two centuries and a half ago, that such a creature should have the power of attracting about her (being altogether superior to earthly lovers) the man who loved her in that previous existence, whose love for her was his death—what is there astonishing in that? Mrs. Oke herself, I feel quite persuaded, believed or half believed it; indeed she very seriously admitted the possibility thereof, one day that I made the suggestion half in jest. At all events, it rather pleased me to think so; it fitted in so well with the woman's whole personality; it explained those hours and hours spent all alone in the yellow room, where the very air, with its scent of heady flowers and old perfumed stuffs, seemed redolent of ghosts. It explained that strange smile which was not for any of

---

1 A rightful, or customary, perquisite appropriate to one's station in life.

us, and yet was not merely for herself—that strange, far-off look in the wide pale eyes. I liked the idea, and I liked to tease, or rather to delight her with it. How should I know that the wretched husband would take such matters seriously?

He became day by day more silent and perplexed-looking; and, as a result, worked harder, and probably with less effect, at his land-improving schemes and political canvassing. It seemed to me that he was perpetually listening, watching, waiting for something to happen: a word spoken suddenly, the sharp opening of a door, would make him start, turn crimson, and almost tremble; the mention of Lovelock brought a helpless look, half a convulsion, like that of a man overcome by great heat, into his face. And his wife, so far from taking any interest in his altered looks, went on irritating him more and more. Every time that the poor fellow gave one of those starts of his, or turned crimson at the sudden sound of a footstep, Mrs. Oke would ask him, with her contemptuous indifference, whether he had seen Lovelock. I soon began to perceive that my host was getting perfectly ill. He would sit at meals never saying a word, with his eyes fixed scrutinisingly on his wife, as if vainly trying to solve some dreadful mystery; while his wife, ethereal, exquisite, went on talking in her listless way about the masque, about Lovelock, always about Lovelock. During our walks and rides, which we continued pretty regularly, he would start whenever in the roads or lanes surrounding Okehurst, or in its grounds, we perceived a figure in the distance. I have seen him tremble at what, on nearer approach, I could scarcely restrain my laughter on discovering to be some well-known farmer or neighbour or servant. Once, as we were returning home at dusk, he suddenly caught my arm and pointed across the oak-dotted pastures in the direction of the garden, then started off almost at a run, with his dog behind him, as if in pursuit of some intruder.

"Who was it?" I asked. And Mr. Oke merely shook his head mournfully. Sometimes in the early autumn twilights, when the white mists rose from the park-land, and the rooks formed long black lines on the palings, I almost fancied I saw him start at the very trees and bushes, the outlines of the distant oast-houses, with their conical roofs and projecting vanes, like gibing fingers in the half light.

"Your husband is ill," I once ventured to remark to Mrs. Oke, as she sat for the hundred-and-thirtieth of my preparatory sketches (I somehow could never get beyond preparatory sketches with her). She raised her beautiful, wide, pale eyes, making as she did so that exquisite curve of shoulders and neck and delicate pale head that I so vainly longed to reproduce.

"I don't see it," she answered quietly. "If he is, why doesn't he go up to town and see the doctor? It's merely one of his glum fits."

"You should not tease him about Lovelock," I added, very seriously. "He will get to believe in him."

"Why not? If he sees him, why he sees him. He would not be the only person that has done so;" and she smiled faintly and half perversely, as her eyes sought that usual distant indefinable something.

But Oke got worse. He was growing perfectly unstrung, like a hysterical woman. One evening that we were sitting alone in the smoking-room, he began unexpectedly a rambling discourse about his wife; how he had first known her when they were children, and they had gone to the same dancing-school near Portland Place; how her mother, his aunt-in-law, had brought her for Christmas to Okehurst while he was on his holidays; how finally, thirteen years ago, when he was twenty-three and she was eighteen, they had been married; how terribly he had suffered when they had been disappointed of their baby, and she had nearly died of the illness.

"I did not mind about the child, you know," he said in an excited voice; "although there will be an end of us now, and Okehurst will go to the Curtises. I minded only about Alice." It was next to inconceivable that this poor excited creature, speaking almost with tears in his voice and in his eyes, was the quiet, well-got-up, irreproachable young ex-Guardsman who had walked into my studio a couple of months before.

Oke was silent for a moment, looking fixedly at the rug at his feet, when he suddenly burst out in a scarce audible voice—

"If you knew how I cared for Alice—how I still care for her. I could kiss the ground she walks upon. I would give anything—my life any day—if only she would look for two minutes as if she liked me a little—as if she didn't utterly despise me;" and the poor fellow burst into a hysterical laugh, which was almost a sob. Then he suddenly began to laugh outright, exclaiming, with a sort of vulgarity of intonation which was extremely foreign to him—

"Damn it, old fellow, this *is* a queer world we live in!" and rang for more brandy and soda, which he was beginning, I noticed, to take pretty freely now, although he had been almost a blue-ribbon man[1]—as much so as is possible for a hospitable country gentleman—when I first arrived.

IX

IT became clear to me now that, incredible as it might seem, the thing that ailed William Oke was jealousy. He was simply madly in love with his wife, and madly jealous of her. Jealous—but of whom? He himself would probably have been quite unable to say. In the first place—to clear off any possible suspicion—certainly not of me. Besides the fact that Mrs. Oke took only just a very little more interest in me than in the butler or the upper-house-maid, I think that Oke himself was the sort of man whose imagination would recoil from realising any definite object of jealousy, even though jealousy might be killing him inch by inch. It remained a vague, permeating, continuous feeling—the feeling that he loved her, and she did not care a jackstraw about him, and that everything with which she came into contact was receiving some of that notice which was refused to him—every person, or thing, or tree, or stone: it was the recognition of that strange far-off look in Mrs. Oke's eyes, of that strange absent smile on Mrs. Oke's lips—eyes and lips that had no look and no smile for him.

Gradually his nervousness, his watchfulness, suspiciousness, tendency to start, took a definite shape. Mr. Oke was for ever alluding to steps or voices he had heard, to figures he had seen sneaking round the house. The sudden bark of one of the dogs would make him jump up. He cleaned and loaded very carefully all the guns and revolvers in his study, and even some of the old fowling-pieces and holster-pistols in the hall. The servants and tenants thought that Oke of Okehurst had been seized with a terror of tramps and burglars. Mrs. Oke smiled contemptuously at all these doings.

"My dear William," she said one day, "the persons who worry you have just as good a right to walk up and down the passages and staircase, and to hang about the house, as you or I. They were there, in all probability, long before either of us was born, and are greatly amused by your preposterous notions of privacy."

---

1   Members of a temperance movement called The Reform Club and Blue Ribbon Association, founded in Maine, U.S.A., and brought to England by William Noble in 1877, wore a blue ribbon in their coat lapels.

Mr. Oke laughed angrily. "I suppose you will tell me it is Love-lock—your eternal Lovelock—whose steps I hear on the gravel every night. I suppose he has as good a right to be here as you or I." And he strode out of the room.

"Lovelock—Lovelock! Why will she always go on like that about Lovelock?" Mr. Oke asked me that evening, suddenly staring me in the face.

I merely laughed.

"It's only because she has that play of his on the brain," I answered: "and because she thinks you superstitious, and likes to tease you."

"I don't understand," sighed Oke.

How could he? And if I had tried to make him do so, he would merely have thought I was insulting his wife, and have perhaps kicked me out of the room. So I made no attempt to explain psychological problems to him, and he asked me no more questions until once—— But I must first mention a curious incident that happened.

The incident was simply this. Returning one afternoon from our usual walk, Mr. Oke suddenly asked the servant whether any one had come. The answer was in the negative; but Oke did not seem satisfied. We had hardly sat down to dinner when he turned to his wife and asked, in a strange voice which I scarcely recognised as his own, who had called that afternoon.

"No one," answered Mrs. Oke; "at least to the best of my knowledge."

William Oke looked at her fixedly.

"No one?" he repeated, in a scrutinising tone; "no one, Alice?"

Mrs. Oke shook her head. "No one," she replied.

There was a pause.

"Who was it, then, that was walking with you near the pond, about five o'clock?" asked Oke slowly.

His wife lifted her eyes straight to his and answered contemptuously—

"No one was walking with me near the pond, at five o'clock or any other hour."

Mr. Oke turned purple, and made a curious hoarse noise like a man choking.

"I—I thought I saw you walking with a man this afternoon, Alice," he brought out with an effort; adding, for the sake of appearances before me, "I thought it might have been the curate come with that report for me."

Mrs. Oke smiled.

"I can only repeat that no living creature has been near me this afternoon," she said slowly. "If you saw any one with me, it must have been Lovelock, for there certainly was no one else."

And she gave a little sigh, like a person trying to reproduce in her mind some delightful but too evanescent impression.

I looked at my host; from crimson his face had turned perfectly livid, and he breathed as if some one were squeezing his windpipe.

No more was said about the matter. I vaguely felt that a great danger was threatening. To Oke or to Mrs. Oke? I could not tell which; but I was aware of an imperious inner call to avert some dreadful evil, to exert myself, to explain, to interpose. I determined to speak to Oke the following day, for I trusted him to give me a quiet hearing, and I did not trust Mrs. Oke. That woman would slip through my fingers like a snake if I attempted to grasp her elusive character.

I asked Oke whether he would take a walk with me the next afternoon, and he accepted to do so with a curious eagerness. We started about three o'clock. It was a stormy, chilly afternoon, with great balls of white clouds rolling rapidly in the cold blue sky, and occasional lurid gleams of sunlight, broad and yellow, which made the black ridge of the storm, gathered on the horizon, look blue-black like ink.

We walked quickly across the sere and sodden grass of the park, and on to the highroad that led over the low hills, I don't know why, in the direction of Cotes Common. Both of us were silent, for both of us had something to say, and did not know how to begin. For my part, I recognised the impossibility of starting the subject: an uncalled-for interference from me would merely indispose Mr. Oke, and make him doubly dense of comprehension. So, if Oke had something to say, which he evidently had, it was better to wait for him.

Oke, however, broke the silence only by pointing out to me the condition of the hops, as we passed one of his many hop-gardens. "It will be a poor year," he said, stopping short and looking intently before him—"no hops at all. No hops this autumn."

I looked at him. It was clear that he had no notion what he was saying. The dark-green bines were covered with fruit; and only yesterday he himself had informed me that he had not seen such a profusion of hops for many years.

I did not answer, and we walked on. A cart met us in a dip of the road, and the carter touched his hat and greeted Mr. Oke. But Oke took no heed; he did not seem to be aware of the man's presence.

The clouds were collecting all round; black domes, among which coursed the round grey masses of fleecy stuff.

"I think we shall be caught in a tremendous storm," I said; "hadn't we better be turning?" He nodded, and turned sharp round.

The sunlight lay in yellow patches under the oaks of the pasture-lands, and burnished the green hedges. The air was heavy and yet cold, and everything seemed preparing for a great storm. The rooks whirled in black clouds round the trees and the conical red caps of the oast-houses which give that country the look of being studded with turreted castles; then they descended—a black line—upon the fields, with what seemed an unearthly loudness of caw. And all round there arose a shrill quavering bleating of lambs and calling of sheep, while the wind began to catch the topmost branches of the trees.

Suddenly Mr. Oke broke the silence.

"I don't know you very well," he began hurriedly, and without turning his face towards me; "but I think you are honest, and you have seen a good deal of the world—much more than I. I want you to tell me—but truly, please—what do you think a man should do if"—— and he stopped for some minutes.

"Imagine," he went on quickly, "that a man cares a great deal—a very great deal for his wife, and that he finds out that she—well, that—that she is deceiving him. No—don't misunderstand me; I mean—that she is constantly surrounded by some one else and will not admit it—some one whom she hides away. Do you understand? Perhaps she does not know all the risk she is running, you know, but she will not draw back—she will not avow it to her husband"——

"My dear Oke," I interrupted, attempting to take the matter lightly, "these are questions that can't be solved in the abstract, or by people to whom the thing has not happened. And it certainly has not happened to you or me."

Oke took no notice of my interruption. "You see," he went on, "the man doesn't expect his wife to care much about him. It's not that; he isn't merely jealous, you know. But he feels that she is on the brink of dishonouring herself—because I don't think a woman can really dishonour her husband; dishonour is in our own hands, and depends only on our own acts. He ought to save her, do you see? He must, must save her, in one way or another. But if she will not listen to him, what can he do? Must he seek out the other one, and try and get him out of the way? You see it's all the fault of the other—not hers, not hers. If only she would trust in her husband, she would be safe. But that other one won't let her."

"Look here, Oke," I said boldly, but feeling rather frightened; "I know quite well what you are talking about. And I see you don't understand the matter in the very least. I do. I have watched you and watched Mrs. Oke these six weeks, and I see what is the matter. Will you listen to me?"

And taking his arm, I tried to explain to him my view of the situation—that his wife was merely eccentric, and a little theatrical and imaginative, and that she took a pleasure in teasing him. That he, on the other hand, was letting himself get into a morbid state; that he was ill, and ought to see a good doctor. I even offered to take him to town with me.

I poured out volumes of psychological explanations. I dissected Mrs. Oke's character twenty times over, and tried to show him that there was absolutely nothing at the bottom of his suspicions beyond an imaginative *pose* and a garden-play on the brain. I adduced twenty instances, mostly invented for the nonce, of ladies of my acquaintance who had suffered from similar fads. I pointed out to him that his wife ought to have an outlet for her imaginative and theatrical over-energy. I advised him to take her to London and plunge her into some set where every one should be more or less in a similar condition. I laughed at the notion of there being any hidden individual about the house. I explained to Oke that he was suffering from delusions, and called upon so conscientious and religious a man to take every step to rid himself of them, adding innumerable examples of people who had cured themselves of seeing visions and of brooding over morbid fancies. I struggled and wrestled, like Jacob with the angel,[1] and I really hoped I had made some impression. At first, indeed, I felt that not one of my words went into the man's brain—that, though silent, he was not listening. It seemed almost hopeless to present my views in such a light that he could grasp them. I felt as if I were expounding and arguing at a rock. But when I got on to the tack of his duty towards his wife and himself, and appealed to his moral and religious notions, I felt that I was making an impression.

---

1 In the Bible, Jacob, who sinned against his brother, is confronted by an angel. Afraid that God will punish him, Jacob wrestles with the angel and proves his faith by maintaining his belief in God while subjected to the pain the angel inflicts upon him. Accepting his contrition, the angel renames him "Israel" and his sins are forgiven (Genesis 32. 7-28).

"I daresay you are right," he said, taking my hand as we came in sight of the red gables of Okehurst, and speaking in a weak, tired, humble voice. "I don't understand you quite, but I am sure what you say is true. I daresay it is all that I'm seedy. I feel sometimes as if I were mad, and just fit to be locked up. But don't think I don't struggle against it. I do, I do continually, only sometimes it seems too strong for me. I pray God night and morning to give me the strength to overcome my suspicions, or to remove these dreadful thoughts from me. God knows, I know what a wretched creature I am, and how unfit to take care of that poor girl."

And Oke again pressed my hand. As we entered the garden, he turned to me once more.

"I am very, very grateful to you," he said, "and, indeed, I will do my best to try and be stronger. If only," he added, with a sigh, "if only Alice would give me a moment's breathing-time, and not go on day after day mocking me with her Lovelock."

X

I HAD begun Mrs. Oke's portrait, and she was giving me a sitting. She was unusually quiet that morning; but, it seemed to me, with the quietness of a woman who is expecting something, and she gave me the impression of being extremely happy. She had been reading, at my suggestion, the "Vita Nuova,"[1] which she did not know before, and the conversation came to roll upon that, and upon the question whether love so abstract and so enduring was a possibility. Such a discussion, which might have savoured of flirtation in the case of almost any other young and beautiful woman, became in the case of Mrs. Oke something quite different; it seemed distant, intangible, not of this earth, like her smile and the look in her eyes.

"Such love as that," she said, looking into the far distance of the oak-dotted park-land, "is very rare, but it can exist. It becomes a person's whole existence, his whole soul; and it can survive the death, not merely of the beloved, but of the lover. It is unextinguishable, and goes on in the spiritual world until it meet a reincarnation of the beloved; and when this happens, it jets out and draws to it all that may remain of that lover's soul, and takes shape and surrounds the beloved one once more."

---

1 Major work by the Italian poet, Dante Alighieri (1265-1321), completed around the year 1294 and composed of thirty-one poems linked by a prose narrative celebrating and debating the subject of love.

Mrs. Oke was speaking slowly, almost to herself, and I had never, I think, seen her look so strange and so beautiful, the stiff white dress bringing out but the more the exotic exquisiteness and incorporealness of her person.

I did not know what to answer, so I said half in jest—

"I fear you have been reading too much Buddhist literature, Mrs. Oke. There is something dreadfully esoteric in all you say."

She smiled contemptuously.

"I know people can't understand such matters," she replied, and was silent for some time. But, through her quietness and silence, I felt, as it were, the throb of a strange excitement in this woman, almost as if I had been holding her pulse.

Still, I was in hopes that things might be beginning to go better in consequence of my interference. Mrs. Oke had scarcely once alluded to Lovelock in the last two or three days; and Oke had been much more cheerful and natural since our conversation. He no longer seemed so worried; and once or twice I had caught in him a look of great gentleness and loving-kindness, almost of pity, as towards some young and very frail thing, as he sat opposite his wife.

But the end had come. After that sitting Mrs. Oke had complained of fatigue and retired to her room, and Oke had driven off on some business to the nearest town. I felt all alone in the big house, and after having worked a little at a sketch I was making in the park, I amused myself rambling about the house.

It was a warm, enervating, autumn afternoon: the kind of weather that brings the perfume out of everything, the damp ground and fallen leaves, the flowers in the jars, the old woodwork and stuffs; that seems to bring on to the surface of one's consciousness all manner of vague recollections and expectations, a something half pleasurable, half painful, that makes it impossible to do or to think. I was the prey of this particular, not at all unpleasurable, restlessness. I wandered up and down the corridors, stopping to look at the pictures, which I knew already in every detail, to follow the pattern of the carvings and old stuffs, to stare at the autumn flowers, arranged in magnificent masses of colour in the big china bowls and jars. I took up one book after another and threw it aside; then I sat down to the piano and began to play irrelevant fragments. I felt quite alone, although I had heard the grind of the wheels on the gravel, which meant that my host had returned. I was lazily turning over a book of verses —I remember it perfectly well, it was Morris's "Love is

Enough"[1]—in a corner of the drawing-room, when the door suddenly opened and William Oke showed himself. He did not enter, but beckoned to me to come out to him. There was something in his face that made me start up and follow him at once. He was extremely quiet, even stiff, not a muscle of his face moving, but very pale.

"I have something to show you," he said, leading me through the vaulted hall, hung round with ancestral pictures, into the gravelled space that looked like a filled-up moat, where stood the big blasted oak, with its twisted, pointing branches. I followed him on to the lawn, or rather the piece of park-land that ran up to the house. We walked quickly, he in front, without exchanging a word. Suddenly he stopped, just where there jutted out the bow-window of the yellow drawing-room, and I felt Oke's hand tight upon my arm.

"I have brought you here to see something," he whispered hoarsely; and he led me to the window.

I looked in. The room, compared with the out door, was rather dark; but against the yellow wall I saw Mrs. Oke sitting alone on a couch in her white dress, her head slightly thrown back, a large red rose in her hand.

"Do you believe now?" whispered Oke's voice hot at my ear. "Do you believe now? Was it all my fancy? But I will have him this time. I have locked the door inside, and, by God! he shan't escape."

The words were not out of Oke's mouth. I felt myself struggling with him silently outside that window. But he broke loose, pulled open the window, and leapt into the room, and I after him.

As I crossed the threshold, something flashed in my eyes; there was a loud report, a sharp cry, and the thud of a body on the ground.

Oke was standing in the middle of the room, with a faint smoke about him; and at his feet, sunk down from the sofa, with her blond head resting on its seat, lay Mrs. Oke, a pool of red forming in her white dress. Her mouth was convulsed, as if in that automatic shriek, but her wide-open white eyes seemed to smile vaguely and distantly.

---

1   Poem by William Morris (1873), in the form of a masque performed at the wedding celebration of a fictional emperor and empress in which a powerful king, tested by sickness and age, ultimately abandons his throne for the woman of his dreams.

I know nothing of time. It all seemed to be one second, but a second that lasted hours. Oke stared, then turned round and laughed.

"The damned rascal has given me the slip again!" he cried; and quickly unlocking the door, rushed out of the house with dreadful cries.

That is the end of the story. Oke tried to shoot himself that evening, but merely fractured his jaw, and died a few days later, raving. There were all sorts of legal inquiries, through which I went as through a dream; and whence it resulted that Mr. Oke had killed his wife in a fit of momentary madness. That was the end of Alice Oke. By the way, her maid brought me a locket which was found round her neck, all stained with blood. It contained some very dark auburn hair, not at all the colour of William Oke's. I am quite sure it was Lovelock's.

A Wicked Voice

To M.W.,[1]
In remembrance of the last song at Palazzo Barbaro,[2]
Chi ha inteso, intenda.[3]

THEY have been congratulating me again to-day upon being the
only composer of our days—of these days of deafening orchestral
effects and poetical quackery—who has despised the new-fangled
nonsense of Wagner,[4] and returned boldly to the traditions of
Handel and Gluck and the divine Mozart, to the supremacy of
melody and the respect of the human voice.[5]

O cursed human voice, violin of flesh and blood, fashioned
with the subtle tools, the cunning hands, of Satan! O execrable

---

1 Mary Wakefield, singer, daughter of a Cumberland banker. Vernon Lee
met her through Mrs. Humphrey Ward (the novelist) to whom Wakefield
was related by marriage.

2 Home of Daniel and Ariana Curtis from the 1880s. The Curtis family
were relations of the artist, John Singer Sargent. Sargent was a close
friend of Vernon Lee who, along with Henry James and Robert Browning, was among the many visitors received at the Palazzo Barbaro. James
later modelled Milly Theale's Venetian palazzo in *The Wings of the Dove*
(1902) on the Curtis home.

3 Translation (Italian): "he who has understood, will understand."

4 Richard Wagner (1813-83), German dramatic composer and theorist
whose operas include *The Flying Dutchman* (1843); a four opera cycle,
The Ring of the Nibelung (1869-76); and *Parsifal* (1882). Vernon Lee disliked Wagner's music and considered its emotional excess irrational and
self-destructive. She wrote on Wagner's music both directly and indirectly in a number of texts. See "Musical Expression and the Composers of the Eighteenth Century," *New Quarterly Magazine* 8 (1877):
186-202; "The Riddle of Music," *Quarterly Review* 204 (1906): 207-27;
"Beauty and Sanity," in *Laurus Nobilis: Chapters on Art and Life* (1909)
115-59; and *Music and Its Lovers* (1932).

5 George Friedrich Handel (1685-1759), German-born British composer.
He composed music for Italian operas including *Orlando* (1733) and
Alcina (1735), and his orchestral works include the famous piece, *Water
Music* (1717); Chistoph Willibald Gluck, later Ritter (knight) von Gluck
(1714-87), German opera composer whose famous works include *Orfeo
ed Euridice* (1762); Wolfgang Amadeus Mozart (1756-91), Austrian
composer of the Viennese classical school who wrote in all the musical
genres of his day. His operas include *The Marriage of Figaro* (1786), *Don
Giovanni* (1787), and *Così fan tutte* (1790).

art of singing, have you not wrought mischief enough in the past, degrading so much noble genius, corrupting the purity of Mozart, reducing Handel to a writer of high-class singing-exercises, and defrauding the world of the only inspiration worthy of Sophocles and Euripides,[1] the poetry of the great poet Gluck? Is it not enough to have dishonoured a whole century in idolatry of that wicked and contemptible wretch the singer, without persecuting an obscure young composer of our days, whose only wealth is his love of nobility in art, and perhaps some few grains of genius?

And then they compliment me upon the perfection with which I imitate the style of the great dead masters; or ask me very seriously whether, even if I could gain over the modern public to this bygone style of music, I could hope to find singers to perform it. Sometimes, when people talk as they have been talking to-day, and laugh when I declare myself a follower of Wagner, I burst into a paroxysm of unintelligible, childish rage, and exclaim, "We shall see that some day!"

Yes; some day we shall see! For, after all, may I not recover from this strangest of maladies? It is still possible that the day may come when all these things shall seem but an incredible nightmare; the day when *Ogier the Dane*[2] shall be completed, and men shall know whether I am a follower of the great master of the Future or the miserable singing-masters of the Past. I am but half-bewitched, since I am conscious of the spell that binds me. My old nurse, far off in Norway, used to tell me that were-wolves are ordinary men and women half their days, and that if, during that period, they become aware of their horrid transformation they may find the means to forestall it. May this not be the case with me? My reason, after all, is free, although my artistic inspiration be enslaved; and I can despise and loathe the music I am forced to compose, and the execrable power that forces me.

Nay, is it not because I have studied with the doggedness of hatred this corrupt and corrupting music of the Past, seeking for every little peculiarity of style and every biographical trifle merely

---

1   Sophocles (c. 496-406 BC), Greek tragedian whose plays include *Antigone*, *Electra*, and *Oedipus the King*; Euripides (c. 484-406 BC), Greek tragedian whose plays include *Medea* and *The Trojan Women*.
2   Legendary prince, reputedly the son of Geoffrey, king of Denmark who first appears in the French mediaeval epic poems known as *chansons de geste*. Known in Denmark as "Holge Danske," he is said to sleep in the mountain of Kronenberg until such time as Denmark should find itself in mortal danger, when he will rise again to protect the nation.

to display its vileness, is it not for this presumptuous courage that I have been overtaken by such mysterious, incredible vengeance?

And meanwhile, my only relief consists in going over and over again in my mind the tale of my miseries. This time I will write it, writing only to tear up, to throw the manuscript unread into the fire. And yet, who knows? As the last charred pages shall crackle and slowly sink into the red embers, perhaps the spell may be broken, and I may possess once more my long-lost liberty, my vanished genius.

It was a breathless evening under the full moon, that implacable full moon beneath which, even more than beneath the dreamy splendour of noon-tide, Venice seemed to swelter in the midst of the waters, exhaling, like some great lily, mysterious influences, which make the brain swim and the heart faint—a moral malaria, distilled, as I thought, from those languishing melodies, those cooing vocalisations which I had found in the musty music-books of a century ago. I see that moonlight evening as if it were present. I see my fellow-lodgers of that little artists' boarding-house. The table on which they lean after supper is strewn with bits of bread, with napkins rolled in tapestry rollers, spots of wine here and there, and at regular intervals chipped pepper-pots, stands of toothpicks, and heaps of those huge hard peaches which nature imitates from the marble-shops of Pisa. The whole *pension*[1]-full is assembled, and examining stupidly the engraving which the American etcher has just brought for me, knowing me to be mad about eighteenth century music and musicians, and having noticed, as he turned over the heaps of penny prints in the square of San Polo, that the portrait is that of a singer of those days.

Singer, thing of evil, stupid and wicked slave of the voice, of that instrument which was not invented by the human intellect, but begotten of the body, and which, instead of moving the soul, merely stirs up the dregs of our nature! For what is the voice but the Beast calling, awakening that other Beast sleeping in the depths of mankind, the Beast which all great art has ever sought to chain up, as the archangel chains up, in old pictures, the demon with his woman's face? How could the creature attached to this voice, its owner and its victim, the singer, the great, the real singer who once ruled over every heart, be otherwise than wicked and contemptible? But let me try and get on with my story.

---

1 Pensione, or Italian boarding-house.

I can see all my fellow-boarders, leaning on the table, contemplating the print, this effeminate beau, his hair curled into *ailes de pigeon*,[1] his sword passed through his embroidered pocket, seated under a triumphal arch somewhere among the clouds, surrounded by puffy Cupids and crowned with laurels by a bouncing goddess of fame. I hear again all the insipid exclamations, the insipid questions about this singer:—"When did he live? Was he very famous? Are you sure, Magnus, that this is really a portrait," &c. &c. And I hear my own voice, as if in the far distance, giving them all sorts of information, biographical and critical, out of a battered little volume called *The Theatre of Musical Glory; or, Opinions upon the most Famous Chapel-masters and Virtuosi of this Century*, by Father Prosdocimo Sabatelli, Barnalite, Professor of Eloquence at the College of Modena, and Member of the Arcadian Academy,[2] under the pastoral name of Evander Lilybæan, Venice, 1785, with the approbation of the Superiors. I tell them all how this singer, this Balthasar Cesari, was nicknamed Zaffirino[3] because of a sapphire engraved with cabalistic signs presented to him one evening by a masked stranger, in whom wise folk recognised that great cultivator of the human voice, the devil; how much more wonderful had been this Zaffirino's vocal gifts than those of any singer of ancient or modern times; how his brief life had been but a series of triumphs, petted by the greatest kings, sung by the most famous poets, and finally, adds Father Prosdocimo, "courted (if the grave Muse of history may incline her ear to the gossip of gallantry) by the most charming nymphs, even of the very highest quality."

My friends glance once more at the engraving; more insipid

---

1 Literally, "pigeon's wings": a hairstyle (usually a wig) worn by men, featuring tubular curls at the side of the head which sometimes continued round the back of the head without interruption.

2 Italian literary academy founded in Rome in 1690 to combat Marinism, the dominant Italian poetic style of the seventeenth century. The Arcadians sought a more natural, simple poetic style based on the classics and particularly on Greek and Roman pastoral poetry. Lee's early article "The Academy of the Arcadi" was published in *Fraser's Magazine* in June 1878, and reprinted in her first major work, *Studies of the Eighteenth Century in Italy*, in 1880.

3 Zaffirino (Italian for sapphire) appears to be based on the famous Italian castrato singer Farinelli (1705-82), whose real name was Carlo Broschi. Lee was fascinated by a portrait of Farinelli by the Italian artist, Corrado Giaquinto (1703-66), which she saw at what is now known as the Accademia Filarmonica in Bologna.

remarks are made; I am requested—especially by the American young ladies—to play or sing one of this Zaffirino's favourite songs—"For of course you know them, dear Maestro Magnus, you who have such a passion for all old music. Do be good, and sit down to the piano." I refuse, rudely enough, rolling the print in my fingers. How fearfully this cursed heat, these cursed moon-light nights, must have unstrung me! This Venice would certainly kill me in the long-run! Why, the sight of this idiotic engraving, the mere name of that coxcomb of a singer, have made my heart beat and my limbs turn to water like a love-sick hobbledehoy.

After my gruff refusal, the company begins to disperse; they prepare to go out, some to have a row on the lagoon, others to saunter before the *cafés* at St. Mark's; family discussions arise, gruntings of fathers, murmurs of mothers; peals of laughing from young girls and young men. And the moon, pouring in by the wide-open windows, turns this old palace ballroom, nowadays an inn dining-room, into a lagoon, scintillating, undulating like the other lagoon, the real one, which stretches out yonder furrowed by invisible gondolas betrayed by the red prow-lights. At last the whole lot of them are on the move. I shall be able to get some quiet in my room, and to work a little at my opera of *Ogier the Dane*. But no! Conversation revives, and, of all things, about that singer, that Zaffirino, whose absurd portrait I am crunching in my fingers.

The principal speaker is Count Alvise, an old Venetian with dyed whiskers, a great check tie fastened with two pins and a chain; a threadbare patrician who is dying to secure for his lanky son that pretty American girl, whose mother is intoxicated by all his mooning anecdotes about the past glories of Venice in general, and of his illus-trious family in particular. Why, in Heaven's name, must he pitch upon Zaffirino for his mooning, this old duffer of a patrician?

"Zaffirino,—ah yes, to be sure! Balthasar Cesari, called Zaf-firino," snuffles the voice of Count Alvise, who always repeats the last word of every sentence at least three times. "Yes, Zaffirino, to be sure! A famous singer of the days of my forefathers; yes, of my forefathers, dear lady!" Then a lot of rubbish about the former greatness of Venice, the glories of old music, the former Conser-vatoires, all mixed up with anecdotes of Rossini and Donizetti,[1]

---

1 Gioacchino Rossini (1792-1868), Italian composer noted for his operas, particularly his comic operas of which *The Barber of Seville* (1816) and *Semiramide* (1823) are among the most famous; Gaetano Donizetti (1797-1848), Italian composer of opera. Among his best-known works are *Lucia di Lammermoor* (1835) and *La favorite* (1840).

whom he pretends to have known intimately. Finally, a story, of course containing plenty about his illustrious family:—"My great grand-aunt, the Procuratessa Vendramin,[1] from whom we have inherited our estate of Mistrà, on the Brenta"[2]—a hopelessly muddled story, apparently, full of digressions, but of which that singer Zaffirino is the hero. The narrative, little by little, becomes more intelligible, or perhaps it is I who am giving it more attention.

"It seems," says the Count, "that there was one of his songs in particular which was called the 'Husbands' Air'"—*L'Aria dei Mariti*—because they didn't enjoy it quite as much as their better-halves.... My grand-aunt, Pisana Renier, married to the Procuratore Vendramin, was a patrician of the old school, of the style that was getting rare a hundred years ago. Her virtue and her pride rendered her unapproachable. Zaffirino, on his part, was in the habit of boasting that no woman had ever been able to resist his singing, which, it appears, had its foundation in fact—the ideal changes, my dear lady, the ideal changes a good deal from one century to another!—and that his first song could make any woman turn pale and lower her eyes, the second make her madly in love, while the third song could kill her off on the spot, kill her for love, there under his very eyes, if he only felt inclined. My grand-aunt Vendramin laughed when this story was told her, refused to go to hear this insolent dog, and added that it might be quite possible by the aid of spells and infernal pacts to kill a *gentildonna*,[3] but as to making her fall in love with a lackey— never! This answer was naturally reported to Zaffirino, who piqued himself upon always getting the better of any one who was wanting in deference to his voice. Like the ancient Romans, *parcere subjectis et debellare superbos*.[4] You American ladies, who are so learned, will appreciate this little quotation from the divine

---

1 The Vendramin family were prominent members of the Venetian aristocracy and lived in Ca' Vendramin Calergi, the palazzo in which the German composer, Richard Wagner, lived from 1882 to 1883 while completing the opera *Parsifal*, and in which he died on 13 February 1883.
2 The Brenta is one of the principal rivers of Italy which flows through the Trentino-Alto Adige and Veneto regions in the north-east of the country.
3 Translation (Italian): gentlewoman.
4 From Virgil (70-19 BC), *Aeneid* 6. 853. Translation (Latin): "spare the downtrodden, and destroy the haughty."

Virgil. While seeming to avoid the Procuratessa Vendramin, Zaffirino took the opportunity, one evening at a large assembly, to sing in her presence. He sang and sang and sang until the poor grand-aunt Pisana fell ill for love. The most skilful physicians were kept unable to explain the mysterious malady which was visibly killing the poor young lady; and the Procuratore Vendramin applied in vain to the most venerated Madonnas, and vainly promised an altar of silver, with massive gold candlesticks, to Saints Cosmas and Damian,[1] patrons of the art of healing. At last the brother-in-law of the Procuratessa, Monsignor Almorò Vendramin, Patriarch of Aquileia,[2] a prelate famous for the sanctity of his life, obtained in a vision of Saint Justina,[3] for whom he entertained a particular devotion, the information that the only thing which could benefit the strange illness of his sister-in-law was the voice of Zaffirino. Take notice that my poor grand-aunt had never condescended to such a revelation.

"The Procuratore was enchanted at this happy solution; and his lordship the Patriarch went to seek Zaffirino in person, and carried him in his own coach to the Villa of Mistrà, where the Procuratessa was residing. On being told what was about to happen, my poor grand-aunt went into fits of rage, which were succeeded immediately by equally violent fits of joy. However, she never forgot what was due to her great position. Although sick almost unto death, she had herself arrayed with the greatest pomp, caused her face to be painted, and put on all her diamonds: it would seem as if she were anxious to affirm her full dignity before this singer. Accordingly she received Zaffirino reclining on a sofa which had been placed in the great ballroom of the Villa of Mistrà, and beneath the princely canopy; for the Vendramins, who had intermarried with the house of Mantua,

---

1 Brothers, possibly twins, born in Arabia in the third century. They became eminent physicians who refused to take payment for their services. Being devout Christians, they were tortured and martyred for their faith.

2 A former city of the Roman Empire situated at the head of the Adriatic, on what is now the Austrian sea-coast, in the country of Goerz, at the confluence of the Anse and the Torre. For many centuries it was the seat of a famous Western patriarchate and, as such, plays an important part in the ecclesiastical history of the Holy See and Northern Italy.

3 Sister of Saint Aureus of Mainz (martyred AD 304) who, together with her brother, was murdered by the Huns while celebrating mass during the Liturgy of the Eucharist.

possessed imperial fiefs and were princes of the Holy Roman Empire. Zaffirino saluted her with the most profound respect, but not a word passed between them. Only, the singer inquired from the Procuratore whether the illustrious lady had received the Sacraments of the Church. Being told that the Procuratessa had herself asked to be given extreme unction from the hands of her brother-in-law, he declared his readiness to obey the orders of His Excellency, and sat down at once to the harpsichord.

"Never had he sung so divinely. At the end of the first song the Procuratessa Vendramin had already revived most extraordinarily; by the end of the second she appeared entirely cured and beaming with beauty and happiness; but at the third air—the *Aria dei Mariti*, no doubt—she began to change frightfully; she gave a dreadful cry, and fell into the convulsions of death. In a quarter of an hour she was dead! Zaffirino did not wait to see her die. Having finished his song, he withdrew instantly, took post-horses, and travelled day and night as far as Munich. People remarked that he had presented himself at Mistrà dressed in mourning, although he had mentioned no death among his relatives; also that he had prepared everything for his departure, as if fearing the wrath of so powerful a family. Then there was also the extraordinary question he had asked before beginning to sing, about the Procuratessa having confessed and received extreme unction.... No, thanks, my dear lady, no cigarettes for me. But if it does not distress you or your charming daughter, may I humbly beg permission to smoke a cigar?"

And Count Alvise, enchanted with his talent for narrative, and sure of having secured for his son the heart and the dollars of his fair audience, proceeds to light a candle, and at the candle one of those long black Italian cigars which require preliminary disinfection before smoking.

... If this state of things goes on I shall just have to ask the doctor for a bottle; this ridiculous beating of my heart and disgusting cold perspiration have increased steadily during Count Alvise's narrative. To keep myself in countenance among the various idiotic commentaries on this cock-and-bull story of a vocal coxcomb and a vapouring great lady, I begin to unroll the engraving, and to examine stupidly the portrait of Zaffirino, once so renowned, now so forgotten. A ridiculous ass, this singer, under his triumphal arch, with his stuffed Cupids and the great fat winged kitchenmaid crowning him with laurels. How flat and vapid and vulgar it is, to be sure, all this odious eighteenth century!

But he, personally, is not so utterly vapid as I had thought. That effeminate, fat face of his is almost beautiful, with an odd smile, brazen and cruel. I have seen faces like this, if not in real life, at least in my boyish romantic dreams, when I read Swinburne and Baudelaire, the faces of wicked, vindictive women.[1] Oh yes! he is decidedly a beautiful creature, this Zaffirino, and his voice must have had the same sort of beauty and the same expression of wickedness....

"Come on, Magnus," sound the voices of my fellow-boarders, "be a good fellow and sing us one of the old chap's songs; or at least something or other of that day, and we'll make believe it was the air with which he killed that poor lady."

"Oh yes! the *Aria dei Mariti*, the 'Husbands' Air,'" mumbles old Alvise, between the puffs at his impossible black cigar. "My poor grand-aunt, Pisana Vendramin; he went and killed her with those songs of his, with that *Aria dei Mariti*."

I feel senseless rage overcoming me. Is it that horrible palpitation (by the way, there is a Norwegian doctor, my fellow-countryman, at Venice just now) which is sending the blood to my brain and making me mad? The people round the piano, the furniture, everything together seems to get mixed and to turn into moving blobs of colour. I set to singing; the only thing which remains distinct before my eyes being the portrait of Zaffirino, on the edge of that boarding-house piano; the sensual, effeminate face, with its wicked, cynical smile, keeps appearing and disappearing as the print wavers about in the draught that makes the candles smoke and gutter. And I set to singing madly, singing I don't know what. Yes; I begin to identify it: 'tis the *Biondina in Gondoleta*,[2] the only song of the eighteenth century which is still remembered by the Venetian people. I sing it, mimicking every

---

1   Charles Baudelaire (1821-67), nineteenth-century French poet, translator, and critic of literature and art, best known for *Les Fleurs du mal* (*The Flowers of Evil*) (1857), a collection of controversial, dark, and sensual poetry. His work was deeply influential on the Aesthetic and Decadent movement that arose in the late nineteenth century. Algernon Charles Swinburne (1837-1909), English poet and critic known for his lyric prowess. His works include the collection *Poems and Ballads I* (1866), which covers a range of sexually-charged subjects and was influenced by Baudelaire's *Les Fleurs du mal*. Swinburne championed Baudelaire and introduced his poetry to an English audience. Both poets feature *femmes fatales* in some of their works. See Appendix A.

2   *The Blonde Girl in the Gondola*: eighteenth-century Venetian air attributed to Cavaliere Peruchini.

old-school grace; shakes, cadences, languishingly swelled and diminished notes, and adding all manner of buffooneries, until the audience, recovering from its surprise, begins to shake with laughing; until I begin to laugh myself, madly, frantically, between the phrases of the melody, my voice finally smothered in this dull, brutal laughter.... And then, to crown it all, I shake my fist at this long-dead singer, looking at me with his wicked woman's face, with his mocking, fatuous smile.

"Ah! you would like to be revenged on me also!" I exclaim. "You would like me to write you nice roulades and flourishes, another nice *Aria dei Mariti*, my fine Zaffirino!"

★ ★ ★ ★ ★

That night I dreamed a very strange dream. Even in the big half-furnished room the heat and closeness were stifling. The air seemed laden with the scent of all manner of white flowers, faint and heavy in their intolerable sweetness: tuberoses, gardenias, and jasmines drooping I know not where in neglected vases. The moonlight had transformed the marble floor around me into a shallow, shining pool. On account of the heat I had exchanged my bed for a big old-fashioned sofa of light wood, painted with little nosegays and sprigs, like an old silk; and I lay there, not attempting to sleep, and letting my thoughts go vaguely to my opera of *Ogier the Dane*, of which I had long finished writing the words, and for whose music I had hoped to find some inspiration in this strange Venice, floating, as it were, in the stagnant lagoon of the past. But Venice had merely put all my ideas into hopeless confusion; it was as if there arose out of its shallow waters a miasma of long-dead melodies, which sickened but intoxicated my soul. I lay on my sofa watching that pool of whitish light, which rose higher and higher, little trickles of light meeting it here and there, wherever the moon's rays struck upon some polished surface; while huge shadows waved to and fro in the draught of the open balcony.

I went over and over that old Norse story: how the Paladin, Ogier, one of the knights of Charlemagne, was decoyed during his homeward wanderings from the Holy Land by the arts of an enchantress, the same who had once held in bondage the great Emperor Cæsar and given him King Oberon for a son; how Ogier had tarried in that island only one day and one night, and yet, when he came home to his kingdom, he found all changed, his friends dead, his family dethroned, and not a man who knew his face; until at last, driven hither and thither like a beggar, a poor minstrel had taken compassion of his sufferings and given him all he could give—a song, the song of the prowess of a hero dead for hundreds of years, the Paladin Ogier the Dane.

The story of Ogier ran into a dream, as vivid as my waking thoughts had been vague. I was looking no longer at the pool of moonlight spreading round my couch, with its trickles of light and looming, waving shadows, but the frescoed walls of a great saloon. It was not, as I recognised in a second, the dining-room of that Venetian palace now turned into a boarding-house. It was a far larger room, a real ballroom, almost circular in its octagon shape, with eight huge white doors surrounded by stucco mould-ings, and, high on the vault of the ceiling, eight little galleries or recesses like boxes at a theatre, intended no doubt for musicians and spectators. The place was imperfectly lighted by only one of the eight chandeliers, which revolved slowly, like huge spiders, each on its long cord. But the light struck upon the gilt stuccoes opposite me, and on a large expanse of fresco, the sacrifice of Iphigenia, with Agamemnon and Achilles[1] in Roman helmets, lappets, and knee-breeches. It discovered also one of the oil panels let into the mouldings of the roof, a goddess in lemon and lilac draperies, foreshortened over a great green peacock. Round the room, where the light reached, I could make out big yellow satin sofas and heavy gilded consoles; in the shadow of a corner was what looked like a piano, and farther in the shade one of those big canopies which decorate the anterooms of Roman palaces. I looked about me, wondering where I was: a heavy, sweet smell, reminding me of the flavour of a peach, filled the place.

Little by little I began to perceive sounds; little, sharp, metallic, detached notes, like those of a mandoline;[2] and there was united to them a voice, very low and sweet, almost a whisper, which grew

---

1 Daughter of Agamemnon, leader of the Greek forces at Troy. Having offended Artemis, the hunter goddess, either by killing one of her sacred animals, or by boasting of his own hunting prowess (variations occur), Agamemnon must sacrifice Iphigenia to atone for his offence; Achilles, son of the mortal Peleus and the Nereid Thetis, one of the Greek heroes in the *Iliad* (c. 720 BC), Homer's epic poem about the Trojan War.
2 Small stringed musical instrument related to the lute. It evolved from the Renaissance mandola possibly as early as the fifteenth century, but remained obscure until the eighteenth century. It was built in several varieties in different Italian towns, the Neapolitan mandolin becoming the representative type. See Appendix F.

and grew and grew, until the whole place was filled with that exquisite vibrating note, of a strange, exotic, unique quality. The note went on, swelling and swelling. Suddenly there was a horrible piercing shriek, and the thud of a body on the floor, and all manner of smothered exclamations. There, close by the canopy, a light suddenly appeared; and I could see, among the dark figures moving to and fro in the room, a woman lying on the ground, surrounded by other women. Her blond hair, tangled, full of diamond-sparkles which cut through the half-darkness, was hanging dishevelled; the laces of her bodice had been cut, and her white breast shone among the sheen of jewelled brocade; her face was bent forwards, and a thin white arm trailed, like a broken limb, across the knees of one of the women who were endeavouring to lift her. There was a sudden splash of water against the floor, more confused exclamations, a hoarse, broken moan, and a gurgling, dreadful sound.... I awoke with a start and rushed to the window.

Outside, in the blue haze of the moon, the church and belfry of St. George loomed blue and hazy, with the black hull and rigging, the red lights, of a large steamer moored before them. From the lagoon rose a damp sea-breeze. What was it all? Ah! I began to understand: that story of old Count Alvise's, the death of his grand-aunt, Pisana Vendramin. Yes, it was about that I had been dreaming.

I returned to my room; I struck a light, and sat down to my writing-table. Sleep had become impossible. I tried to work at my opera. Once or twice I thought I had got hold of what I had looked for so long.... But as soon as I tried to lay hold of my theme, there arose in my mind the distant echo of that voice, of that long note swelled slowly by insensible degrees, that long note whose tone was so strong and so subtle.

* * * * *

There are in the life of an artist moments when, still unable to seize his own inspiration, or even clearly to discern it, he becomes aware of the approach of that long-invoked idea. A mingled joy and terror warn him that before another day, another hour have passed, the inspiration shall have crossed the threshold of his soul and flooded it with its rapture. All day I had felt the need of isolation and quiet, and at nightfall I went for a row on the most solitary part of the lagoon. All things seemed to tell that I was going to meet my inspiration, and I awaited its coming as a lover awaits his beloved.

I had stopped my gondola for a moment, and as I gently swayed to and fro on the water, all paved with moonbeams, it seemed to me that I was on the confines of an imaginary world. It lay close at hand, enveloped in luminous, pale blue mist, through which the moon had cut a wide and glistening path; out to sea, the little islands, like moored black boats, only accentuated the solitude of this region of moonbeams and wavelets; while the hum of the insects in orchards hard by merely added to the impression of untroubled silence. On some such seas, I thought, must the Paladin Ogier, have sailed when about to discover that during that sleep at the enchantress's knees centuries had elapsed and the heroic world had set, and the kingdom of prose had come.

While my gondola rocked stationary on that sea of moonbeams, I pondered over that twilight of the heroic world. In the soft rattle of the water on the hull I seemed to hear the rattle of all that armour, of all those swords swinging rusty on the walls, neglected by the degenerate sons of the great champions of old. I had long been in search of a theme which I called the theme of the "Prowess of Ogier;" it was to appear from time to time in the course of my opera, to develop at last into that song of the Minstrel, which reveals to the hero that he is one of a long-dead world. And at this moment I seemed to feel the presence of that theme. Yet an instant, and my mind would be overwhelmed by that savage music, heroic, funereal.

Suddenly there came across the lagoon, cleaving, chequering, and fretting the silence with a lacework of sound even as the moon was fretting and cleaving the water, a ripple of music, a voice breaking itself in a shower of little scales and cadences and trills.

I sank back upon my cushions. The vision of heroic days had vanished, and before my closed eyes there seemed to dance multitudes of little stars of light, chasing and interlacing like those sudden vocalisations.

"To shore! Quick!" I cried to the gondolier.

But the sounds had ceased; and there came from the orchards, with their mulberry-trees glistening in the moonlight, and their black swaying cypress-plumes, nothing save the confused hum, the monotonous chirp, of the crickets.

I looked around me: on one side empty dunes, orchards, and meadows, without house or steeple; on the other, the blue and misty sea, empty to where distant islets were profiled black on the horizon.

A faintness overcame me, and I felt myself dissolve. For all of a sudden a second ripple of voice swept over the lagoon, a shower of little notes, which seemed to form a little mocking laugh.

Then again all was still. This silence lasted so long that I fell once more to meditating on my opera. I lay in wait once more for the half-caught theme. But no. It was not that theme for which I was waiting and watching with baited breath. I realised my delusion when, on rounding the point of the Giudecca,[1] the murmur of a voice arose from the midst of the waters, a thread of sound slender as a moonbeam, scarce audible, but exquisite, which expanded slowly, insensibly, taking volume and body, taking flesh almost and fire, an ineffable quality, full, passionate, but veiled, as it were, in a subtle, downy wrapper. The note grew stronger and stronger, and warmer and more passionate, until it burst through that strange and charming veil, and emerged beaming, to break itself in the luminous facets of a wonderful shake, long, superb, triumphant.

There was a dead silence.

"Row to St. Mark's!" I exclaimed. "Quick!"

The gondola glided through the long, glittering track of moonbeams, and rent the great band of yellow, reflected light, mirroring the cupolas of St. Mark's, the lace-like pinnacles of the palace, and the slender pink belfry, which rose from the lit-up water to the pale and bluish evening sky.

In the larger of the two squares the military band was blaring through the last spirals of a *crescendo* of Rossini. The crowd was dispersing in this great open-air ballroom, and the sounds arose which invariably follow upon out-of-door music. A clatter of spoons and glasses, a rustle and grating of frocks and of chairs, and the click of scabbards on the pavement. I pushed my way among the fashionable youths contemplating the ladies while sucking the knob of their sticks; through the serried ranks of respectable families, marching arm in arm with their white frocked young ladies close in front. I took a seat before Florian's,[2] among the customers stretching themselves before departing, and the waiters hurrying to and fro, clattering their empty cups

---

1   The Giudecca Canal, about 400 m (about 1310 ft) wide, separates Giudecca Island, on the extreme south, from Venice proper.

2   Famous Venetian café, which was opened on 29 December 1720 by Floriano Francesconi under the name "Venezia Trionfante," ("Triumphant Venice.") It soon became known to its patrons as "Florian's" under which name it still exists today.

and trays. Two imitation Neapolitans were slipping their guitar and violin under their arm, ready to leave the place.

"Stop!" I cried to them; "don't go yet. Sing me something—sing *La Camesella* or *Funiculì, funiculà*[1]—no matter what, provided you make a row;" and as they screamed and scraped their utmost, I added, "But can't you sing louder, d—n you!—sing louder, do you understand?"

I felt the need of noise, of yells and false notes, of something vulgar and hideous to drive away that ghost-voice which was haunting me.

★ ★ ★ ★ ★

Again and again I told myself that it had been some silly prank of a romantic amateur, hidden in the gardens of the shore or gliding unperceived on the lagoon; and that the sorcery of moonlight and sea-mist had transfigured for my excited brain mere humdrum roulades out of exercises of Bordogni or Crescentini.[2]

But all the same I continued to be haunted by that voice. My work was interrupted ever and anon by the attempt to catch its imaginary echo; and the heroic harmonies of my Scandinavian legend were strangely interwoven with voluptuous phrases and florid cadences in which I seemed to hear again that same accursed voice.

To be haunted by singing-exercises! It seemed too ridiculous for a man who professedly despised the art of singing. And still, I preferred to believe in that childish amateur, amusing himself with warbling to the moon.

One day, while making these reflections the hundredth time over, my eyes chanced to light upon the portrait of Zaffirino, which my friend had pinned against the wall. I pulled it down and tore it into half a dozen shreds. Then, already ashamed of my folly, I watched the torn pieces float down from the window, wafted hither and thither by the sea-breeze. One scrap got caught

---

1   *La Camesella*: traditional Neapolitan folk song; *Funiculì, Funiculà*: popular song written by journalist Peppino Turco, and set to music by Luigi Denza in 1880, inspired by the inauguration of the first funicular at Mount Vesuvius.

2   Giulio Marco Bordogni (1789-1856), Italian performer equally famous as a dramatic tenor and a singing teacher at the Paris Conservatory; Girolamo Crescentini (1762-1848), famous castrato singer and vocal coach.

in a yellow blind below me; the others fell into the canal, and were speedily lost to sight in the dark water. I was overcome with shame. My heart beat like bursting. What a miserable, unnerved worm I had become in this cursed Venice, with its languishing moonlights, its atmosphere as of some stuffy boudoir, long unused, full of old stuffs and pot-pourri!

That night, however, things seemed to be going better. I was able to settle down to my opera, and even to work at it. In the intervals my thoughts returned, not without a certain pleasure, to those scattered fragments of the torn engraving fluttering down to the water. I was disturbed at my piano by the hoarse voices and the scraping of violins which rose from one of those music-boats that station at night under the hotels of the Grand Canal. The moon had set. Under my balcony the water stretched black into the distance, its darkness cut by the still darker outlines of the flotilla of gondolas in attendance on the music-boat, where the faces of the singers, and the guitars and violins, gleamed reddish under the unsteady light of the Chinese-lanterns.

"*Jammo, jammo; jammo, jammo jà*," sang the loud, hoarse voices; then a tremendous scrape and twang, and the yelled-out burden, "*Funiculì, funiculà; funiculì, funiculà; jammo, jammo, jammo, jammo, jammo jà*."[1]

Then came a few cries of "*Bis, Bis!*"[2] from a neighbouring hotel, a brief clapping of hands, the sound of a handful of coppers rattling into the boat, and the oar-stroke of some gondolier making ready to turn away.

"Sing the *Camesella*," ordered some voice with a foreign accent.

"No, no! *Santa Lucia*."[3]

"I want the *Camesella*."

"No! *Santa Lucia*. Hi! sing *Santa Lucia*—d'you hear?"

The musicians, under their green and yellow and red lamps, held a whispered consultation on the manner of conciliating these contradictory demands. Then, after a minute's hesitation, the violins began the prelude of that once famous air, which has remained popular in Venice—the words written, some hundred years ago, by the patrician Gritti, the music by an unknown composer—*La Biondina in Gondoleta*.

That cursed eighteenth century! It seemed a malignant fatal-

---

1 Translation (Neapolitan): "Let's go!"
2 Translation (Italian): "encore!"
3 Traditional Neapolitan folk song.

ity that made these brutes choose just this piece to interrupt me.

At last the long prelude came to an end; and above the cracked guitars and squeaking fiddles there arose, not the expected nasal chorus, but a single voice singing below its breath.

My arteries throbbed. How well I knew that voice! It was singing, as I have said, below its breath, yet none the less it sufficed to fill all that reach of the canal with its strange quality of tone, exquisite, far-fetched.

They were long-drawn-out notes, of intense but peculiar sweetness, a man's voice which had much of a woman's, but more even of a chorister's, but a chorister's voice without its limpidity and innocence; its youthfulness was veiled, muffled, as it were, in a sort of downy vagueness, as if a passion of tears withheld.

There was a burst of applause, and the old palaces re-echoed with the clapping. "Bravo, bravo! Thank you, thank you! Sing again—please, sing again. Who can it be?"

And then a bumping of hulls, a splashing of oars, and the oaths of gondoliers trying to push each other away, as the red prow-lamps of the gondolas pressed round the gaily lit singing-boat.

But no one stirred on board. It was to none of them that this applause was due. And while every one pressed on, and clapped and vociferated, one little red prow-lamp dropped away from the fleet; for a moment a single gondola stood forth black upon the black water, and then was lost in the night.

For several days the mysterious singer was the universal topic. The people of the music-boat swore that no one besides themselves had been on board, and that they knew as little as ourselves about the owner of that voice. The gondoliers, despite their descent from the spies of the old Republic, were equally unable to furnish any clue. No musical celebrity was known or suspected to be at Venice; and every one agreed that such a singer must be a European celebrity. The strangest thing in this strange business was, that even among those learned in music there was no agreement on the subject of this voice: it was called by all sorts of names and described by all manner of incongruous adjectives; people went so far as to dispute whether the voice belonged to a man or to a woman: every one had some new definition.

In all these musical discussions I, alone, brought forward no opinion. I felt a repugnance, an impossibility almost, of speaking about that voice; and the more or less commonplace conjectures of my friend had the invariable effect of sending me out of the room.

Meanwhile my work was becoming daily more difficult, and I soon passed from utter impotence to a state of inexplicable agitation. Every morning I arose with fine resolutions and grand projects of work; only to go to bed that night without having accomplished anything. I spent hours leaning on my balcony, or wandering through the network of lanes with their ribbon of blue sky, endeavouring vainly to expel the thought of that voice, or endeavouring in reality to reproduce it in my memory; for the more I tried to banish it from my thoughts, the more I grew to thirst for that extraordinary tone, for those mysteriously downy, veiled notes; and no sooner did I make an effort to work at my opera than my head was full of scraps of forgotten eighteenth century airs, of frivolous or languishing little phrases; and I fell to wondering with a bitter-sweet longing how those songs would have sounded if sung by that voice.

At length it became necessary to see a doctor, from whom, however, I carefully hid away all the stranger symptoms of my malady. The air of the lagoons, the great heat, he answered cheerfully, had pulled me down a little; a tonic and a month in the country, with plenty of riding and no work, would make me myself again. That old idler, Count Alvise, who had insisted on accompanying me to the physician's, immediately suggested that I should go and stay with his son, who was boring himself to death superintending the maize harvest on the mainland: he could promise me excellent air, plenty of horses, and all the peaceful surroundings and the delightful occupations of a rural life—"Be sensible, my dear Magnus, and just go quietly to Mistrà."

Mistrà—the name sent a shiver all down me.

I was about to decline the invitation, when a thought suddenly loomed vaguely in my mind.

"Yes, dear Count," I answered; "I accept your invitation with gratitude and pleasure. I will start to-morrow for Mistrà."

The next day found me at Padua,[1] on my way to the Villa of Mistrà. It seemed as if I had left an intolerable burden behind me. I was, for the first time since how long, quite light of heart. The tortuous, rough-paved streets, with their empty, gloomy

---

1 University city of northern Italy, now the economic centre of the Veneto region.

porticoes; the ill-plastered palaces, with closed, discoloured shutters; the little rambling square, with meagre trees and stubborn grass; the Venetian garden-houses reflecting their crumbling graces in the muddy canal; the gardens without gates and the gates without gardens, the avenues leading nowhere; and the population of blind and legless beggars, of whining sacristans, which issued as by magic from between the flag-stones and dust-heaps and weeds under the fierce August sun, all this dreariness merely amused and pleased me. My good spirits were heightened by a musical mass which I had the good fortune to hear at St. Anthony's.[1]

Never in all my days had I heard anything comparable, although Italy affords many strange things in the way of sacred music. Into the deep nasal chanting of the priests there had suddenly burst a chorus of children, singing absolutely independent of all time and tune; grunting of priests answered by squealing of boys, slow Gregorian modulation interrupted by jaunty barrel-organ pipings, an insane, insanely merry jumble of bellowing and barking, mewing and cackling and braying, such as would have enlivened a witches' meeting, or rather some mediæval Feast of Fools. And, to make the grotesqueness of such music still more fantastic and Hoffmannlike,[2] there was, besides, the magnificence of the piles of sculptured marbles and gilded bronzes, the tradition of the musical splendour for which St. Anthony's had been famous in days gone by. I had read in old travellers, Lalande and Burney,[3] that the Republic of St. Mark had squandered immense sums not merely on the monuments and decoration, but on the musical establishment of its great cathedral of Terra Firma. In the midst of this ineffable concert of impossible voices and instruments, I tried to imagine the voice of Guadagni, the soprano for whom Gluck had written *Che farò senza Euridice*, and the fiddle of Tartini, that Tartini with whom the devil had once

1 Basilica dedicated to St. Anthony, patron saint of Padua, who died there in AD 1231.
2 In the style of E.T.A. Hoffmann (1776-1822), German writer and composer, a major figure in German Romanticism renowned for his macabre imagination.
3 Joseph-Jérôme Le Français de Lalande (1732-1807), French astronomer and author of *Voyage d'un français en Italie* published in eight volumes; Dr. Charles Burney (1726-1814), British music historian and author of *General History of Music*, 4 vols (1776-89), which provided an account of European musical and intellectual life in the eighteenth century. His daughter was the novelist Frances (Fanny) Burney.

come and made music.[1] And the delight in anything so absolutely, barbarously, grotesquely, fantastically incongruous as such a performance in such a place was heightened by a sense of profanation: such were the successors of those wonderful musicians of that hated eighteenth century!

The whole thing had delighted me so much, so very much more than the most faultless performance could have done, that I determined to enjoy it once more; and towards vesper-time, after a cheerful dinner with two bagmen at the inn of the Golden Star, and a pipe over the rough sketch of a possible cantata upon the music which the devil made for Tartini, I turned my steps once more towards St. Anthony's.

The bells were ringing for sunset, and a muffled sound of organs seemed to issue from the huge, solitary church; I pushed my way under the heavy leathern curtain, expecting to be greeted by the grotesque performance of that morning.

I proved mistaken. Vespers must long have been over. A smell of stale incense, a crypt-like damp filled my mouth; it was already night in that vast cathedral. Out of the darkness glimmered the votive-lamps of the chapels, throwing wavering lights upon the red polished marble, the gilded railing, and chandeliers, and plaqueing with yellow the muscles of some sculptured figure. In a corner a burning taper put a halo about the head of a priest, burnishing his shining bald skull, his white surplice, and the open book before him. "Amen" he chanted; the book was closed with a snap, the light moved up the apse, some dark figures of women rose from their knees and passed quickly towards the door; a man saying his prayers before a chapel also got up, making a great clatter in dropping his stick.

The church was empty, and I expected every minute to be turned out by the sacristan making his evening round to close the doors. I was leaning against a pillar, looking into the greyness of the great arches, when the organ suddenly burst out into a series of chords, rolling through the echoes of the church: it seemed to be the conclusion of some service. And above the organ rose the notes of a voice; high, soft, enveloped in a kind of downiness, like a cloud of incense, and which ran through the mazes of a long

---

1   Gaetano Guadagni (1725-92), Italian singer, one of the famous castrati of the eighteenth century; famous aria from Gluck's opera, *Orfeo ed Euridice*; Giuseppe Tartini (1692-1770), Italian music theorist, composer, violinist, and teacher. In 1728 Tartini began a school for violin players in Padua.

cadence. The voice dropped into silence; with two thundering chords the organ closed in. All was silent. For a moment I stood leaning against one of the pillars of the nave: my hair was clammy, my knees sank beneath me, an enervating heat spread through my body; I tried to breathe more largely, to suck in the sounds with the incense-laden air. I was supremely happy, and yet as if I were dying; then suddenly a chill ran through me, and with it a vague panic. I turned away and hurried out into the open.

The evening sky lay pure and blue along the jagged line of roofs; the bats and swallows were wheeling about; and from the belfries all around, half-drowned by the deep bell of St. Anthony's, jangled the peal of the *Ave Maria*.[1]

★ ★ ★ ★ ★

"You really don't seem well," young Count Alvise had said the previous evening, as he welcomed me, in the light of a lantern held up by a peasant, in the weedy back-garden of the Villa of Mistrà. Everything had seemed to me like a dream: the jingle of the horse's bells driving in the dark from Padua, as the lantern swept the acacia-hedges with their wide yellow light; the grating of the wheels on the gravel; the supper-table, illumined by a single petroleum lamp for fear of attracting mosquitoes, where a broken old lackey, in an old stable jacket, handed round the dishes among the fumes of onion; Alvise's fat mother gabbling dialect in a shrill, benevolent voice behind the bullfights on her fan; the unshaven village priest, perpetually fidgeting with his glass and foot, and sticking one shoulder up above the other. And now, in the afternoon, I felt as if I had been in this long, rambling, tumble-down Villa of Mistrà—a villa three-quarters of which was given up to the storage of grain and garden tools, or to the exercise of rats, mice, scorpions, and centipedes—all my life; as if I had always sat there, in Count Alvise's study, among the pile of undusted books on agriculture, the sheaves of accounts, the samples of grain and silkworm seed, the ink-stains and the cigar-ends; as if I had never heard of anything save the cereal basis of Italian agriculture, the diseases of maize, the peronospora[2] of the

---

1 A peal rung to announce the Catholic 'Ave Maria', a prayer to the Blessed Virgin Mary which is part of the longer Angelus prayer.
2 Species of fungus causing a downy mildew in plants, especially in cool, humid regions.

vine, the breeds of bullocks, and the iniquities of farm labourers; with the blue cones of the Euganean hills closing in the green shimmer of plain outside the window.

After an early dinner, again with the screaming gabble of the fat old Countess, the fidgeting and shoulder-raising of the unshaven priest, the smell of fried oil and stewed onions, Count Alvise made me get into the cart beside him, and whirled me along among clouds of dust, between the endless glister of poplars, acacias, and maples, to one of his farms.

In the burning sun some twenty or thirty girls, in coloured skirts, laced bodices, and big straw-hats, were threshing the maize on the big red brick threshing-floor, while others were winnowing the grain in great sieves. Young Alvise III. (the old one was Alvise II.: every one is Alvise, that is to say, Lewis, in that family; the name is on the house, the carts, the barrows, the very pails) picked up the maize, touched it, tasted it, said something to the girls that made them laugh, and something to the head farmer that made him look very glum; and then led me into a huge stable, where some twenty or thirty white bullocks were stamping, switching their tails, hitting their horns against the mangers in the dark. Alvise III. patted each, called him by his name, gave him some salt or a turnip, and explained which was the Mantuan breed, which the Apulian, which the Romagnolo, and so on. Then he bade me jump into the trap, and off we went again through the dust, among the hedges and ditches, till we came to some more brick farm buildings with pinkish roofs smoking against the blue sky. Here there were more young women threshing and winnowing the maize, which made a great golden Danaë cloud;[1] more bullocks stamping and lowing in the cool darkness; more joking, fault-finding, explaining; and thus through five farms, until I seemed to see the rhythmical rising and falling of the flails against the hot sky, the shower of golden grains, the yellow dust from the winnowing-sieves on to the bricks, the switching of innumerable tails and plunging of innumerable horns, the glistening of huge white flanks and foreheads, whenever I closed my eyes.

---

1   In Greek mythology Danaë was the daughter of Acrisius. An oracle
     warned Acrisius that Danaë's son would someday kill him, so Acrisius
     shut Danaë in a bronze room, away from all male company. However,
     Zeus conceived a passion for Danaë, and came to her through the roof,
     in the form of a shower of gold that poured down into her lap. As a
     result she had a son, Perseus.

"A good day's work!" cried Count Alvise, stretching out his long legs with the tight trousers riding up over the Wellington boots. "Mamma, give us some aniseed-syrup after dinner; it is an excellent restorative and precaution against the fevers of this country."

"Oh! you've got fever in this part of the world, have you? Why, your father said the air was so good!"

"Nothing, nothing," soothed the old Countess. "The only thing to be dreaded are mosquitoes; take care to fasten your shutters before lighting the candle.

"Well," rejoined young Alvise, with an effort of conscience, "of course there *are* fevers. But they needn't hurt you. Only, don't go out into the garden at night, if you don't want to catch them. Papa told me that you have fancies for moonlight rambles. It won't do in this climate, my dear fellow; it won't do. If you must stalk about at night, being a genius, take a turn inside the house; you can get quite exercise enough."

After dinner the aniseed-syrup was produced, together with brandy and cigars, and they all sat in the long, narrow, half-furnished room on the first floor; the old Countess knitting a garment of uncertain shape and destination, the priest reading out the newspaper; Count Alvise puffing at his long, crooked cigar, and pulling the ears of a long, lean dog with a suspicion of mange and a stiff eye. From the dark garden outside rose the hum and whirr of countless insects, and the smell of the grapes which hung black against the starlit, blue sky, on the trellis. I went to the balcony. The garden lay dark beneath; against the twinkling horizon stood out the tall poplars. There was the sharp cry of an owl; the barking of a dog; a sudden whiff of warm, enervating perfume, a perfume that made me think of the taste of certain peaches, and suggested white, thick, wax-like petals. I seemed to have smelt that flower once before: it made me feel languid, almost faint.

"I am very tired," I said to Count Alvise. "See how feeble we city folk become!"

★ ★ ★ ★ ★

But, despite my fatigue, I found it quite impossible to sleep. The night seemed perfectly stifling. I had felt nothing like it at Venice. Despite the injunctions of the Countess I opened the solid wooden shutters, hermetically closed against mosquitoes, and looked out.

The moon had risen; and beneath it lay the big lawns, the rounded tree-tops, bathed in a blue, luminous mist, every leaf glistening and trembling in what seemed a heaving sea of light. Beneath the window was the long trellis, with the white shining piece of pavement under it. It was so bright that I could distinguish the green of the vine-leaves, the dull red of the catalpa-flowers.[1] There was in the air a vague scent of cut grass, of ripe American grapes, of that white flower (it must be white) which made me think of the taste of peaches all melting into the delicious freshness of falling dew. From the village church came the stroke of one: Heaven knows how long I had been vainly attempting to sleep. A shiver ran through me, and my head suddenly filled as with the fumes of some subtle wine; I remembered all those weedy embankments, those canals full of stagnant water, the yellow faces of the peasants; the word malaria returned to my mind. No matter! I remained leaning on the window, with a thirsty longing to plunge myself into this blue moon-mist, this dew and perfume and silence, which seemed to vibrate and quiver like the stars that strewed the depths of heaven.... What music, even Wagner's, or of that great singer of starry nights, the divine Schumann,[2] what music could ever compare with this great silence, with this great concert of voiceless things that sing within one's soul?

As I made this reflection, a note, high, vibrating, and sweet, rent the silence, which immediately closed around it. I leaned out of the window, my heart beating as though it must burst. After a brief space the silence was cloven once more by that note, as the darkness is cloven by a falling star or a firefly rising slowly like a rocket. But this time it was plain that the voice did not come, as I had imagined, from the garden, but from the house itself, from some corner of this rambling old villa of Mistrà.

Mistrà—Mistrà! The name rang in my ears, and I began at length to grasp its significance, which seems to have escaped me till then. "Yes," I said to myself, "it is quite natural." And with this odd impression of naturalness was mixed a feverish, impatient pleasure. It was as if I had come to Mistrà on purpose, and that I was about to meet the object of my long and weary hopes.

---

1 Product of large deciduous tree native to North America, eastern Asia, and the West Indies. Flowers appear in early summer, are usually white and resemble the foxglove.

2 Robert Schumann (1810-56), German Romantic composer renowned particularly for his piano music, songs, and orchestral music.

Grasping the lamp with its singed green shade, I gently opened the door and made my way through a series of long passages and of big, empty rooms, in which my steps re-echoed as in a church, and my light disturbed whole swarms of bats. I wandered at random, farther and farther from the inhabited part of the buildings.

This silence made me feel sick; I gasped as under a sudden disappointment.

All of a sudden there came a sound—chords, metallic, sharp, rather like the tone of a mandoline close to my ear. Yes, quite close: I was separated from the sounds only by a partition. I fumbled for a door; the unsteady light of my lamp was insufficient for my eyes, which were swimming like those of a drunkard. At last I found a latch, and, after a moment's hesitation, I lifted it and gently pushed open the door. At first I could not understand what manner of place I was in. It was dark all round me, but a brilliant light blinded me, a light coming from below and striking the opposite wall. It was as if I had entered a dark box in a half-lighted theatre. I was, in fact, in something of the kind, a sort of dark hole with a high balustrade, half-hidden by an up-drawn curtain. I remembered those little galleries or recesses for the use of musicians or lookers-on which exist under the ceiling of the ballrooms in certain old Italian palaces. Yes; it must have been one like that. Opposite me was a vaulted ceiling covered with gilt mouldings, which framed great time-blackened canvases; and lower down, in the light thrown up from below, stretched a wall covered with faded frescoes. Where had I seen that goddess in lilac and lemon draperies foreshortened over a big, green peacock? For she was familiar to me, and the stucco Tritons[1] also who twisted their tails round her gilded frame. And that fresco, with warriors in Roman cuirasses and green and blue lappets, and knee-breeches—where could I have seen them before? I asked myself these questions without experiencing any surprise. Moreover, I was very calm, as one is calm sometimes in extraordinary dreams—could I be dreaming?

I advanced gently and leaned over the balustrade. My eyes were met at first by the darkness above me, where, like gigantic spiders, the big chandeliers rotated slowly, hanging from the ceiling. Only one of them was lit, and its Murano-glass pendants, its carnations and roses, shone opalescent in the light of the gut-

---

1 In Greek mythology, mermen, demigods of the sea, who were represented as human down to the waist, with the tail of a fish.

tering wax. This chandelier lighted up the opposite wall and that piece of ceiling with the goddess and the green peacock; it illumined, but far less well, a corner of the huge room, where, in the shadow of a kind of canopy, a little group of people were crowding round a yellow satin sofa, of the same kind as those that lined the walls. On the sofa, half-screened from me by the surrounding persons, a woman was stretched out: the silver of her embroidered dress and the rays of her diamonds gleamed and shot forth as she moved uneasily. And immediately under the chandelier, in the full light, a man stooped over a harpsichord, his head bent slightly, as if collecting his thoughts before singing.

He struck a few chords and sang. Yes, sure enough, it was the voice, the voice that had so long been persecuting me! I recognised at once that delicate, voluptuous quality, strange, exquisite, sweet beyond words, but lacking all youth and clearness. That passion veiled in tears which had troubled my brain that night on the lagoon, and again on the Grand Canal singing the *Biondina*, and yet again, only two days since, in the deserted cathedral of Padua. But I recognised now what seemed to have been hidden from me till then, that this voice was what I cared most for in all the wide world.

The voice wound and unwound itself in long, languishing phrases, in rich, voluptuous *rifiorituras*,[1] all fretted with tiny scales and exquisite, crisp shakes; it stopped ever and anon, swaying as if panting in languid delight. And I felt my body melt even as wax in the sunshine, and it seemed to me that I too was turning fluid and vaporous, in order to mingle with these sounds as the moonbeams mingle with the dew.

Suddenly, from the dimly lighted corner by the canopy, came a little piteous wail; then another followed, and was lost in the singer's voice. During a long phrase on the harpsichord, sharp and tinkling, the singer turned his head towards the dais, and there came a plaintive little sob. But he, instead of stopping, struck a sharp chord; and with a thread of voice so hushed as to be scarcely audible, slid softly into a long *cadenza*.[2] At the same moment he threw his head backwards, and the light fell full upon the handsome, effeminate face, with its ashy pallor and big,

---

1 The literal meaning in Italian is "reflowering," but in a musical context, this suggests the ornamentation of notes as they are sung.

2 A solo passage before the final cadence, generally occurring in the first or last movement in the classical concerto. It suggests improvisation of the main themes and a display of the soloist's virtuosity.

black brows, of the singer Zaffirino. At the sight of that face, sensual and sullen, of that smile which was cruel and mocking like a bad woman's, I understood—I knew not why, by what process—that his singing *must* be cut short, that the accursed phrase *must* never be finished. I understood that I was before an assassin, that he was killing this woman, and killing me also, with his wicked voice.

I rushed down the narrow stair which led down from the box, pursued, as it were, by that exquisite voice, swelling, swelling by insensible degrees. I flung myself on the door which must be that of the big saloon. I could see its light between the panels. I bruised my hands in trying to wrench the latch. The door was fastened tight, and while I was struggling with that locked door I heard the voice swelling, swelling, rending asunder that downy veil which wrapped it, leaping forth clear, resplendent, like the sharp and glittering blade of a knife that seemed to enter deep into my breast. Then, once more, a wail, a death-groan, and that dreadful noise, that hideous gurgle of breath strangled by a rush of blood. And then a long shake, acute, brilliant, triumphant.

The door gave way beneath my weight, one half crashed in. I entered. I was blinded by a flood of blue moonlight. It poured in through four great windows, peaceful and diaphanous, a pale blue mist of moonlight, and turned the huge room into a kind of submarine cave, paved with moonbeams, full of shimmers, of pools of moonlight. It was as bright as at midday, but the brightness was cold, blue, vaporous, supernatural. The room was completely empty, like a great hay-loft. Only, there hung from the ceiling the ropes which had once supported a chandelier; and in a corner, among stacks of wood and heaps of Indian-corn, whence spread a sickly smell of damp and mildew, there stood a long, thin harpsichord, with spindle-legs, and its cover cracked from end to end.

I felt, all of a sudden, very calm. The one thing that mattered was the phrase that kept moving in my head, the phrase of that unfinished cadence which I had heard but an instant before I opened the harpsichord, and my fingers came down boldly upon its keys. A jingle-jangle of broken strings, laughable and dreadful, was the only answer.

Then an extraordinary fear overtook me. I clambered out of one of the windows; I rushed up the garden and wandered through the fields, among the canals and the embankments, until the moon had set and the dawn began to shiver, followed, pursued for ever by that jangle of broken strings.

People expressed much satisfaction at my recovery. It seems that one dies of those fevers.

Recovery? But have I recovered? I walk, and eat and drink and talk; I can even sleep. I live the life of other living creatures. But I am wasted by a strange and deadly disease. I can never lay hold of my own inspiration. My head is filled with music which is certainly by me, since I have never heard it before, but which still is not my own, which I despise and abhor: little, tripping flourishes and languishing phrases, and long-drawn, echoing cadences.

O wicked, wicked voice, violin of flesh and blood made by the Evil One's hand, may I not even execrate thee in peace; but is it necessary that, at the moment when I curse, the longing to hear thee again should parch my soul like hell-thirst? And since I have satiated thy lust for revenge, since thou hast withered my life and withered my genius, is it not time for pity? May I not hear one note, only one note of thine, O singer, O wicked and con-temptible wretch?

Prince Alberic and the Snake Lady[1]

To her Highness The Ranee of Saràwak

IN the year 1701, the Duchy of Luna became united to the Italian dominions of the Holy Roman Empire,[2] in consequence of the extinction of its famous ducal house in the persons of Duke Balthasar Maria and of his grandson Alberic, who should have

---

1 First published in the *Yellow Book* 10 (July 1896): 289-344, and subsequently collected in *Pope Jacynth and Other Fantastic Tales* (London: Grant Richards, 1904). This text is taken from the second edition (London: John Lane, The Bodley Head, 1907) 21-111. The dedicatee of this story is the Ranee of Sarawak, Lady Margaret Brooke (1849-1936), wife of Charles Brooke, the second Rajah of Sarawak. Sarawak was a large slice of the North Eastern coast of Borneo, now part of Malaysia, but originally part of the hereditary domains of the Sultan of Brunei. Margaret Brooke, author of *My Life in Sarawak* (1913) and *Good Morning and Good Night* (1934), later settled in England and was a friend to many literary figures including Algernon Charles Swinburne, Henry James, W.H. Hudson, and Oscar Wilde. Lee first met her in 1893 and they subsequently became good friends. Margaret Brooke visited Lee at her house, Il Palmerino, in Maiano, outside Florence.

2 The Holy Roman Empire designates a political entity that covered a large portion of Europe centred on Germany from 962-1806. At the time of Prince Alberic's death in 1700 (which is followed some months later by that of the Duke, his grandfather), the Holy Roman Emperor was Leopold I (born 1640), who reigned as Emperor from 1658-1705. 1701, specified as the date for the lapse of the duchy, is significant because it also marks the start of the War of Spanish Succession in Europe (1701-14), a conflict that arose out of the disputed succession to the Spanish throne after the death of the childless Charles II, last of the Spanish Hapsburgs, and involved various countries and powers laying claim to certain European territories. Lee's biographer Vineta Colby (p. 354) quotes a letter from Vernon Lee to Maurice Baring of 20 February 1906 telling him that in "Prince Alberic" she had boldly invented a state (i.e., Luna) "though I had Massa Carrara in mind." Massa Carrara is a province of Tuscany which embraces the two cities of Massa and Carrara, and was ruled from 1440 to 1741 by the Malaspinas and Cybo-Malaspinas, some of whom bear the first name Alberico.

have been third of the name. Under this dry historical fact lies hidden the strange story of Prince Alberic and the Snake Lady.

I

The first act of hostility of old Duke Balthasar towards the Snake Lady, in whose existence he did not, of course, believe, was connected with the arrival at Luna of certain tapestries after the designs of the famous Monsieur Le Brun, a present from his Most Christian Majesty King Lewis the XIV. These Gobelins, which represented the marriage of Alexander and Roxana,[1] were placed in the throne-room, and in the most gallant suite of chambers overlooking the great rockery garden, all of which had been completed by Duke Balthasar Maria in 1680; and, as a consequence, the already existing tapestries, silk hangings, and mirrors painted by Marius of the Flowers, were transferred into other apartments, thus occasioning a general re-hanging of the Red Palace at Luna. These magnificent operations, in which, as the court poets sang, Apollo and the Graces lent their services to their beloved patron, aroused in Duke Balthasar's mind a sudden curiosity to see what might be made of the rooms occupied by his grandson and heir, and which he had not entered since Prince Alberic's christening. He found the apartments in a shocking state of neglect, and the youthful prince unspeakably shy and rustic; and he determined to give him at once an establishment befitting his age, to look out presently for a princess worthy to be his wife, and, somewhat earlier, for a less illustrious but more agreeable lady to fashion his manners. Meanwhile, Duke Balthasar Maria gave orders to change the tapestry in Prince Alberic's chamber. This tapestry was of old and Gothic taste,[2] extremely worn, and represented Alberic the Blond and the Snake Lady Oriana, as described in the Chronicles of Archbishop Turpin and the

---

1 Charles Le Brun (1619-90), one of the great Baroque French painters and court painter to King Louis XIV (King of France, 1638-1715), was also the designer of allegorical tapestries produced for the court by the famous Gobelins manufactory. In 1660 Louis commissioned from him a tapestry series on the life of Alexander the Great.

2 The Snake Lady tapestry belongs to the first great period of tapestry-making known as the Gothic, which predates Renaissance and Gobelins tapestry work. Flanders was the centre for Gothic tapestry-making.

poems of Boiardo.[1] Duke Balthasar Maria was a prince of enlightened mind and delicate taste; the literature as well as the art of the dark ages found no grace in his sight; he reproved the folly of feeding the thoughts of youth on improbable events; besides, he disliked snakes and was afraid of the devil. So he ordered the tapestry to be removed and another, representing Susanna and the Elders,[2] to be put in its stead. But when Prince Alberic discovered the change, he cut Susanna and the Elders into strips with a knife he had stolen out of the ducal kitchens (no dangerous instruments being allowed to young princes before they were of an age to learn to fence) and refused to touch his food for three days.

The tapestry over which little Prince Alberic mourned so deeply had indeed been both tattered and Gothic. But for the boy it possessed an inexhaustible charm. It was quite full of things, and they were all delightful. The sorely-frayed borders consisted of wonderful garlands of leaves and fruits and flowers, tied at intervals with ribbons, although they seemed all to grow like tall narrow bushes, each from a big vase in the bottom corner, and made of all manner of different plants. There were bunches of spiky bays, and of acorned oak leaves; sheaves of lilies and heads

1 Turpin, Archbishop of Rheims, was a real-life personage of the time of Charlemagne (742-814), King of the Franks (768-814), who was crowned by the Pope as Holy Roman Emperor in 800. Turpin was the supposed author of a highly influential history of Charlemagne and the Frankish chief Orlando. This somewhat fantastic history, long accepted as genuine, helped inspire the great mediaeval and Renaissance romances about Charlemagne and Orlando, also known as Roland. Matteo Maria Boiardo, highly influential Italian poet and Count of Scandiano (c. 1434-94), is most famous for his epic poem *Orlando innamorata*, which tells of the love of Orlando (and Rinaldo) for Angelica. The poem is a precursor of the more famous *Orlando furioso* of Ludovico Ariosto (1474-1533). On Lee's interest in Boiardo, see her essay "The School of Boiardo" in *Euphorion* (1884). The story of Alberic the Blond and the Snake Lady does not occur in Turpin's Chronicles or in Boiardo.

2 The story of Susanna and the Elders is told in the Apocryphal book The History of Susanna, sometimes seen as a continuation of the book of Daniel (Daniel 13. 1-65). Susanna, a virtuous married woman, is spied on as she bathes by some lascivious elders who then make advances to her. When she repels them, they accuse her of adultery with a young man, but she is saved by a righteous youth named Daniel who asks that the Elders be examined separately and then points out the inconsistencies in their accounts.

of poppies, gourds, and apples and pears, and hazelnuts and mulberries, wheat ears, and beans, and pine tufts. And in each of these plants, of which those above named are only a very few, there were curious live creatures of some sort—various birds, big and little, butterflies on the lilies, snails, squirrels, mice, and rabbits, and even a hare, with such pointed ears, darting among the spruce fir. Alberic learned the names of most of these plants and creatures from his nurse, who had been a peasant, and he spent much ingenuity seeking for them in the palace gardens and terraces; but there were no live creatures there, except snails and toads, which the gardeners killed, and carp swimming about in the big tank, whom Alberic did not like, and who were not in the tapestry; and he had to supplement his nurse's information by that of the grooms and scullions, when he could visit them secretly. He was even promised a sight, one day, of a dead rabbit—the rabbit was the most fascinating of the inhabitants of the tapestry border—but he came to the kitchen too late, and saw it with its pretty fur pulled off, and looking so sad and naked that it made him cry. But Alberic had grown so accustomed to never quitting the Red Palace and its gardens, that he was usually satisfied with seeing the plants and animals in the tapestry, and looked forward to seeing the real things only when he should be grown up. 'When I am a man,' he would say to himself—for his nurse scolded him for saying it to her—'I will have a live rabbit of my own.'

The border of the tapestry interested Prince Alberic most when he was very little—indeed, his remembrance of it was older than that of the Red Palace, its terraces and gardens—but gradually he began to care more and more for the picture in the middle.

There were mountains, and the sea with ships; and these first made him care to go on to the topmost palace terrace and look at the real mountains and the sea beyond the roofs and gardens; and there were woods of all manner of tall trees, with clover and wild strawberries growing beneath them; and roads, and paths, and rivers, in and out; these were rather confused with the places where the tapestry was worn out, and with the patches and mendings thereof, but Alberic, in the course of time, contrived to make them all out, and knew exactly whence the river came which turned the big mill-wheel, and how many bends it made before coming to the fishing-nets; and how the horsemen must cross over the bridge, then wind behind the cliff with the chapel, and pass through the wood of pines in order to get from the castle in the left-hand corner nearest the bottom to the town, over which the sun was shining with all its beams, and a wind blowing with inflated cheeks on the right hand close to the top.

The centre of the tapestry was the most worn and discoloured; and it was for this reason perhaps that little Alberic scarcely noticed it for some years, his eye and mind led away by the bright red and yellow of the border of fruit and flowers, and the still vivid green and orange of the background landscape. Red, yellow, and orange, even green, had faded in the centre into pale blue and lilac; even the green had grown an odd dusty tint; and the figures seemed like ghosts, sometimes emerging then receding again into vagueness. Indeed, it was only as he grew bigger that Alberic began to see any figures at all; and then, for a long time he would lose sight of them. But little by little, when the light was strong, he could see them always; and even in the dark make them out with a little attention. Among the spruce firs and pines, and against a hedge of roses, on which there still lingered a remnant of redness, a knight had reined in his big white horse, and was putting one arm round the shoulder of a lady, who was leaning against the horse's flank. The knight was all dressed in armour—not at all like that of the equestrian statue of Duke Balthasar Maria in the square, but all made of plates, with plates also on the legs, instead of having them bare like Duke Balthasar's statue; and on his head he had no wig, but a helmet with big plumes. It seemed a more reasonable dress than the other, but probably Duke Balthasar was right to go to battle with bare legs and kilt and a wig, since he did so. The lady who was looking up into his face was dressed with a high collar and long sleeves, and on her head she wore a thick circular garland, from under which the hair fell about her shoulders. She was very lovely, Alberic got to think, particularly when, having climbed upon a chest of drawers, he saw that her hair was still full of threads of gold, some of them quite loose because the tapestry was so rubbed. The knight and his horse were of course very beautiful, and he liked the way in which the knight reined in the horse with one hand, and embraced the lady with the other arm. But Alberic got to love the lady most, although she was so very pale and faded, and almost the colour of the moonbeams through the palace windows in summer. Her dress was also so beautiful and unlike those of the ladies who got out of the coaches in the Court of Honour, and who had on hoops and no clothes at all on their upper part.[1] This lady, on the contrary, had that collar like a lily, and a beautiful gold chain, and patterns in gold (Alberic made them out little by little) all over her bodice. He got to want so much to see her skirt; it was probably very beautiful too, but it so happened that the inlaid chest of drawers before mentioned stood against the wall in that place, and on it a large ebony and ivory crucifix, which covered the lower part of the lady's body. Alberic often tried to lift off the crucifix, but it was a great deal too heavy, and there was not room on the chest of drawers to push it aside, so the lady's skirt and feet were invisible. But one day, when Alberic was eleven, his nurse suddenly took a fancy to having all the furniture shifted. It was time that the child should cease to sleep in her room, and plague her with his loud talking in his dreams. And she might as well have the handsome inlaid chest of drawers, and that nice pious crucifix for herself next door, in place of Alberic's little bed. So one morning there was a great shifting and dusting, and when Alberic came in from his walk on the terrace, there hung the tapestry entirely uncovered. He stood for a few minutes before it, riveted to the ground. Then he ran to his nurse, exclaiming: 'O, nurse, dear nurse, look—the lady——!'

For where the big crucifix had stood, the lower part of the beautiful pale lady with the gold-thread hair was now exposed. But instead of a skirt, she ended off in a big snake's tail, with scales of still most vivid (the tapestry not having faded there) green and gold.[2]

---

1   Seeing the ladies dressed in the French court style with hooped dresses and décolletage, Alberic comments indirectly on the trend for "dishabille" in the fashions of the second half of the seventeenth century when, among the fashion-conscious, ladies' necklines dropped considerably. Mistresses were often the most powerful women in society and the eroticism of dress reflects this.

2   Myth and legend portray various kinds of women who have snake-like attributes. Deriving from classical myth, the lamia, made famous in the 1820 poem by John Keats (1795-1821), is a vampiric creature with the head and breasts of a woman and body of a serpent who preys on human beings, especially small children. The more innocuous melusine, who derives from a French mediaeval legend, has the head and torso of a woman but from the waist down has a serpent's or fish's tail (in some cases two). Like the lamia in Keats's poem, she was able to assume a uniform human appearance for certain periods of time. Snake women, especially those that can temporarily change their shape, have long been portrayed as dangerously alluring or sexually provocative and have influenced the iconography of the classic *femme fatale* (see Swinburne's description in Appendix A). However, Lee's snake lady seems have more of a beneficent maternal eroticism.

The nurse turned round.

'Holy Virgin,' she cried, 'why, she's a serpent!' Then, noticing the boy's violent excitement, she added, 'You little ninny, it's only Duke Alberic the Blond, who was your ancestor, and the Snake Lady.'

Little Prince Alberic asked no questions feeling that he must not. Very strange it was, but he loved the beautiful lady with the thread of gold hair only the more because she ended off in the long twisting body of a snake. And that, no doubt, was why the knight was so very good to her.

II

For want of that tapestry, poor Alberic, having cut its successor to pieces, began to pine away. It had been his whole world; and now it was gone he discovered that he had no other. No one had ever cared for him except his nurse, who was very cross. Nothing had ever been taught him except the Latin catechism; he had nothing to make a pet of except the fat carp, supposed to be four hundred years old, in the tank; he had nothing to play with except a gala coral with bells by Benvenuto Cellini,[1] which Duke Balthasar Maria had sent him on his eighth birthday. He had never had anything except a Grandfather, and had never been outside the Red Palace.

Now, after the loss of the tapestry, the disappearance of the plants and flowers and birds and beasts on its borders, and the departure of the kind knight on the horse and the dear golden-haired Snake Lady, Alberic became aware that he had always hated both his grandfather and the Red Palace.

The whole world, indeed, were agreed that Duke Balthasar was the most magnanimous and fascinating of monarchs, and that the Red Palace of Luna was the most magnificent and delectable of residences.[2] But the knowledge of this universal opinion, and the

---

1 Benvenuto Cellini (1500-71), famous Florentine sculptor and gold-smith. The gala coral with bells is a combined teething device and rattle for babies, another indication of Duke Balthasar's lack of real interest in his grandson who, at eight, is far too old for such things.

2 The Red Palace evokes the Palazzo Ducale at Massa, also known as the Red Palace for its brilliant colouring, which was started by Alberico Cybo in 1557, transforming a previous Malaspina building. Finished in 1701, the palace is decorated with marbles, bronzes, statues, and paint-ings and contains a grotto representing Neptune's cave with the sea god's statue.

consequent sense of his own extreme unworthiness, merely exasperated Alberic's detestation, which, as it grew, came to identify the Duke and the Palace as the personification and visible manifestation of each other. He knew—oh, how well!—every time that he walked on the terrace or in the garden (at the hours when no-one else ever entered them) that he had always abominated the brilliant tomato-coloured plaster which gave the Palace its name: such a pleasant, gay colour, people would remark, particularly against the blue of the sky. Then there were the Twelve Cæsars[1]—they were the Twelve Cæsars, but multiplied over and over again—busts with flying draperies and spiky garlands, one over every first-floor window, hundreds of them, all fluttering and grimacing round the place. Alberic had always thought them uncanny; but now he positively avoided looking out of the window, lest his eye should catch the stucco eyeball of one of those Cæsars in the opposite wing of the building. But there was one thing more especially in the Red Palace, of which a bare glimpse had always filled the youthful Prince with terror, and which now kept recurring to his mind like a nightmare. This was no other than the famous grotto of the Court of Honour. Its roof was ingeniously inlaid with oyster-shells, forming elegant patterns, among which you could plainly distinguish some colossal satyrs; the sides were built of rockery, and in its depths, disposed in a most natural and tasteful manner, was a herd of lifesize animals all carved out of various precious marbles. On holidays the water was turned on, and spurted about in a gallant fashion. On such occasions persons of taste would flock to Luna from all parts of the world to enjoy the spectacle. But ever since his earliest infancy Prince Alberic had held this grotto in abhorrence. The oyster-shell satyrs on the roof frightened him into fits, particularly when the fountains were playing; and his terror of the marble animals was such that a bare allusion to the Porphyry Rhinoceros, the Giraffe of Cipollino, and the Verde Antique Monkeys,[2] set him screaming for an hour. The grotto, moreover, had become associated in his mind with the

1   The Twelve Caesars, the subject of a famous racy biography by Gaius Tranquillus Suetonius (AD 70-c.160), private secretary to the Emperor Hadrian, are, in chronological order: Julius Caesar, Augustus, Tiberius, Caligula, Claudius, Nero, Galba, Otho, Vitellius, Vepasian, Titus, Domitian.
2   Porphyry is a red or purplish coloured volcanic rock; cipollino or "onion skin" is a type of green marble streaked with white; verde antique is another impure marble composed of green serpentine streaked with white calcite.

other great glory of the Red Palace, to wit, the domed chapel in which Duke Balthasar Maria intended erecting monuments to his immediate ancestors, and in which he had already prepared a monument for himself. And the whole magnificent palace, grotto, chapel and all, had become mysteriously connected with Alberic's grandfather, owing to a particularly terrible dream. When the boy was eight years old, he was taken one day to seek his grandfather. It was the feast of St. Balthasar, one of the Three Wise Kings from the East, as is well known.[1] There had been firing of mortars and ringing of bells ever since daybreak. Alberic had his hair curled, was put into new clothes (his usual raiment being somewhat tattered), a large nosegay was placed in his hand, and he and his nurse were conveyed by complicated relays of lackeys and of pages up to the ducal apartments. Here, in a crowded outer room, he was separated from his nurse and received by a gaunt person in a long black robe like a sheath, and a long shovel hat, whom Alberic identified many years later as his father's Jesuit Confessor.[2] He smiled a long smile, discovering a prodigious number of teeth, in a manner which froze the child's blood; and lifting an embroidered curtain, pushed Alberic into his grandfather's presence. Duke Balthasar Maria, called in all Italy the Ever Young Prince, was at his toilet. He was wrapped in a green Chinese wrapper, embroidered with gold pagodas, and round his head was tied an orange scarf of delicate fabric. He was listening to the performance of some fiddlers, and of a lady dressed as a nymph, who was singing the birthday ode with many shrill trills and quavers; and meanwhile his face, in the hands of a valet, was being plastered with a variety of brilliant colours. In his green and gold wrapper and orange headdress, with the strange patches of vermilion and white on his cheeks, Duke Balthasar looked to the diseased fancy of his nephew as if he had been made of various precious metals, like the celebrated effigy he had erected of himself in the great burial-chapel. But, just as Alberic was mustering up courage and approaching his magnificent grandparent, his eye fell upon a sight so mysterious and terrible that he fled out of the ducal presence.

---

1 St. Balthasar: traditional name given to one of the Magi or Wise Kings from the East who visited the baby Jesus. Balthasar, who brought a gift of myrrh, is usually depicted as black and bearded. His feast day is 6 January.

2 The Roman Catholic order of Jesuits was the chief source of royal confessors (hearers of confessions) for kings and princes and those in authority throughout Europe. They often mixed their moral advice with political advice.

For through an open door he could see in an adjacent closet a man dressed in white, combing the long flowing locks of what he recognised as his grandfather's head, stuck on a short pole in the light of a window.[1]

That night Alberic had seen in his dreams the Ever Young Balthasar Maria descend from his niche in the burial-chapel; and, with his Roman lappets and corslet visible beneath the green bronze cloak embroidered with gold pagodas, march down the great staircase into the Court of Honour, and ascend to the empty place at the end of the rockery grotto (where, as a matter of fact, a statue of Neptune, by a pupil of Bernini,[2] was placed some months later), and there, raising his sceptre, receive the obeisance of all the marble animals—the Giraffe, the Rhinoceros, the Stag, the Peacock, and the Monkeys. And behold! suddenly his well-known features waxed dim, and beneath the great curly peruke there was a round blank thing—a barber's block!

Alberic, who was an intelligent child, had gradually learned to disentangle this dream from reality; but its grotesque terror never vanished from his mind, and became the core of all his feelings towards Duke Balthasar Maria and the Red Palace.

III

The news—which was kept back as long as possible—of the destruction of Susanna and the Elders threw Duke Balthasar Maria into a most violent rage with his grandson. The boy should be punished by exile, and exile to a terrible place; above all, to a place where there was no furniture to destroy. Taking due counsel with his Jesuit, his Jester, and his Dwarf, Duke Balthasar decided that in the whole Duchy of Luna there was no place more fitted for the purpose than the Castle of Sparkling Waters.

For the Castle of Sparkling Waters was little better than a ruin, and its sole inhabitants were a family of peasants. The original cradle of the House of Luna, and its principal bulwark against invasion, the castle had been ignominiously discarded and forsaken a couple of centuries before, when the dukes had built the

---

1   Alberic actually sees his grandfather's barber combing out one of his wigs.

2   Gianlorenzo Bernini (1598-1680), Tuscan sculptor and architect in the late mannerist style who moved to Rome in 1605 to work for Pope Paul V.

rectangular town in the plain; after which it had been used as a quarry for ready-cut stone, and the greater part carted off to rebuild the town of Luna, and even the central portion of the Red Palace. The castle was therefore reduced to its outer circuit of walls, enclosing vineyards and orange-gardens, instead of moats and yards and towers, and to the large gate tower, which had been kept, with one or two smaller buildings, for the housing of the farmer, his cattle, and his stores.

Thither the misguided young Prince was conveyed in a carefully shuttered coach and at a late hour of the evening, as was proper in the case of an offender at once so illustrious and so criminal. Nature, moreover, had clearly shared Duke Balthasar Maria's legitimate anger, and had done her best to increase the horror of this just though terrible sentence. For that particular night the long summer broke up in a storm of fearful violence; and Alberic entered the ruined castle amid the howling of wind, the rumble of thunder, and the rush of torrents of rain.

But the young Prince showed no fear or reluctance; he saluted with dignity and sweetness the farmer and his wife and family, and took possession of his attic, where the curtains of an antique and crazy four-poster shook in the draught of the unglazed window, as if he were taking possession of the gala chambers of a great palace. 'And so,' he merely remarked, looking round him with reserved satisfaction, 'I am now in the castle which was built by my ancestor and namesake, the Marquis Alberic the Blond.'

He looked not unworthy of such illustrious lineage, as he stood there in the flickering light of the pine-torch; tall for his age, slender and strong, with abundant golden hair falling about his very white face.

That first night at the Castle of Sparkling Waters, Alberic dreamed without end about his dear, lost tapestry. And when, in the radiant autumn morning, he descended to explore the place of his banishment and captivity, it seemed as if those dreams were still going on. Or had the tapestry been removed to this spot, and become a reality in which he himself was running about?

The gate tower in which he had slept was still intact and chivalrous. It had battlements, a drawbridge, a great escutcheon with the arms of Luna, just like the castle in the tapestry. Some vines, quite loaded with grapes, rose on the strong cords of their fibrous wood from the ground to the very roof of the town, exactly like those borders of leaves and fruit Alberic had loved so much. And, between the vines, all along the masonry, were strung long narrow ropes of maize, like garlands of gold. A plantation of orange-trees filled what had once been the moat; lemons were spalliered against the delicate pink brickwork. There were no lilies, indeed, but big carnations hung down from the tower windows, and a tall oleander, which Alberic mistook for a special sort of rose-tree, shed its blossoms on to the drawbridge. After the storm of the night, birds were singing all round; not indeed as they sang in spring, which Alberic, of course, did not know, but in a manner quite different from the canaries in the ducal aviaries at Luna. Moreover, other birds, wonderful white and gold creatures, some of them with brilliant tails and scarlet crests, were pecking and strutting and making curious noises in the yard. And—could it be true?—a little way further up the hill, for the castle walls climbed steeply from the seaboard, in the grass beneath the olive-trees, white creatures were running in and out—white creatures with pinkish lining to their ears, undoubtedly—as Alberic's nurse had taught him on the tapestry—undoubtedly *rabbits*.

Thus Alberic rambled on, from discovery to discovery, with the growing sense that he was in the tapestry, but that the tapestry had become the whole world. He climbed from terrace to terrace of the steep olive-yard, among the sage and fennel tufts, the long red walls of the castle winding ever higher on the hill. And on the very top of the hill was a high terrace surrounded by towers, and a white shining house with columns and windows, which seemed to drag him upwards.

It was, indeed, the citadel of the place, the very centre of the castle.

Alberic's heart beat strangely as he passed beneath the wide arch of delicate ivy-grown brick, and clambered up the rough-paved path to the topmost terrace. And there he actually forgot the tapestry. The terrace was laid out as a vineyard, the vines trellised on the top of stone columns; at one end stood a clump of trees, pines, and a big ilex and a walnut, whose shrivelled leaves already strewed the grass. To the back stood a tiny little house all built of shining marble, with two large rounded windows divided by delicate pillars, of the sort (as Alberic later learned) which people built in the barbarous days of the Goths. Among the vines, which formed a vast arbour, were growing, in open spaces, large orange and lemon trees, and pale pink roses. And in front of the house, under a great umbrella pine, was a well, with an arch over it and a bucket hanging to a chain.

Alberic wandered about in the vineyard, and then slowly mounted the marble staircase which flanked the white house.

There was no one in it. The two or three small upper chambers stood open, and on their blackened floor were heaped sacks, and faggots, and fodder, and all manner of coloured seeds. The unglazed windows stood open, framing in between their white pillars a piece of deep blue sea. For there, below, but seen over the tops of the olive-trees and the green leaves of the oranges and lemons, stretched the sea, deep blue, speckled with white sails, bounded by pale blue capes, and arched over by a dazzling pale blue sky. From the lower story there rose faint sounds of cattle, and a fresh, sweet smell as of grass and herbs and coolness, which Alberic had never known before. How long did Alberic stand at that window? He was startled by what he took to be steps close behind him, and a rustle as of silk. But the rooms were empty, and he could see nothing moving among the stacked up fodder and seeds. Still, the sounds seemed to recur, but now outside, and he thought he heard some one in a very low voice call his name. He descended into the vineyard; he walked round every tree and every shrub, and climbed upon the broken masses of rose-coloured masonry, crushing the scented ragwort and peppermint with which they were overgrown. But all was still and empty. Only, from far, far below, there rose a stave of peasant's song.

The great gold balls of oranges, and the delicate yellow lemons, stood out among their glossy green against the deep blue of the sea; the long bunches of grapes hung, filled with sunshine, like clusters of rubies and jacinths and topazes, from the trellis which patterned the pale blue sky. But Alberic felt not hunger, but sudden thirst, and mounted the three broken marble steps of the well. By its side was a long narrow trough of marble, such as stood in the court at Luna, and which, Alberic had been told, people had used as coffins in pagan times.[1] This one was evidently intended to receive water from the well, for it had a mark in the middle, with a spout; but it was quite dry and full of wild herbs, and even of pale, prickly roses. There were garlands carved upon it, and people with twisted snakes about them; and the carving was picked out with golden brown minute mosses. Alberic looked at it, for it pleased him greatly; and then he lowered the bucket into the deep well, and drank. The well was

---

1   A coffin of this kind, used as a cattle trough, is described by Lee in her essay "Ravenna and her Ghosts," first published in *Macmillan's Magazine* in September 1894, and then reprinted in *Limbo and Other Essays to Which is Now Added Ariadne in Mantua* (1908).

very, very deep. Its inner sides were covered, as far as you could see, with long delicate weeds like pale green hair, but this faded away in the darkness. At the bottom was a bright space, reflecting the sky, but looking like some subterranean country. Alberic, as he bent over, was startled by suddenly seeing what seemed a face filling up part of that shining circle; but he remembered it must be his own reflection, and felt ashamed. So, to give himself courage, he bent over again, and sang his own name to the image. But instead of his own boyish voice he was answered by wonderful tones, high and deep alternately, running through the notes of long, long cadence, as he had heard them on holidays at the Ducal Chapel at Luna.[1]

When he had slaked his thirst, Alberic was about to unchain the bucket, when there was a rustle hard by, and a sort of little hiss, and there rose from the carved trough, from among the weeds and roses, and glided on to the brick of the well, a long, green, glittering thing. Alberic recognised it to be a snake; only, he had no idea it had such a flat, strange little head, and such a long forked tongue, for the lady on the tapestry was a woman from the waist upwards. It sat on the opposite side of the well, moving its long neck in his direction, and fixing him with its small golden eyes. Then, slowly, it began to glide round the well circle towards him. Perhaps it wants to drink, thought Alberic, and tipped the bronze pitcher in his direction. But the creature glided past, and came around and rubbed itself against Alberic's hand. The boy was not afraid, for he knew nothing about snakes; but he started, for, on this hot day, the creature was icy cold. But then he felt sorry. 'It must be dreadful to be always so cold,' he said; 'come, try and get warm in my pocket.'

But the snake merely rubbed itself against his coat, and then disappeared back into the carved sarcophagus.

IV

Duke Balthasar Maria, as we have seen, was famous for his unfading youth, and much of his happiness and pride was due to this delightful peculiarity. Any comparison, therefore, which

---

1 The voice heard by Alberic resembles that of a castrato singer who would have been employed to sing in the Ducal Chapel at Luna. This practice would have been endorsed by the Vatican as women were not permitted to sing in church choirs in the Papal states.

might diminish it, was distasteful to the Ever Young sovereign of Luna; and when his son had died with mysterious suddenness, Duke Maria Balthasar Maria's grief had been tempered by the consolatory fact that he was now the youngest man at his own court. This very natural feeling explains why the Duke of Luna had put behind him for several years the fact of having a grandson, painful because implying that he was of an age to be a grandfather. He had done his best, and succeeded not badly, to forget Alberic while the latter abode under his own roof; and now that the boy had been sent away to a distance, he forgot him entirely for the space of several years.

But Balthasar Maria's three chief counsellors had no such reason for forgetfulness; and so, in turn, each unknown to the other, the Jesuit, the Dwarf, and the Jester sent spies to the Castle of Sparkling Waters, and even secretly visited that place in person. For by the coincidence of genius, the mind of each of these profound politicians had been illuminated by the same remarkable thought, to wit: that Duke Balthasar Maria, unnatural as it seemed, would some day have to die, and Prince Alberic, if still alive, become duke in his stead. Those were the times of subtle statecraft; and the Jesuit, the Dwarf, and the Jester were notable statesmen even in their day. So each of them had provided himself with a scheme, which, in order to be thoroughly artistic, was twofold and, so to speak, double-barrelled. Alberic might live or he might die, and therefore Alberic must be turned to profit in either case. If, to invert the chances, Alberic should die before coming to the throne, the Jesuit, the Dwarf, and the Jester had each privately determined to represent this death as purposely brought about by himself for the benefit of one of the three Powers which would claim the duchy in case of extinction of the male line. The Jesuit had chosen to attribute the murder to devotion to the Holy See; the Dwarf had preferred to appear active in favour of the King of Spain; and the Jester had decided that he would lay claim to the gratitude of the Emperor.[1] The very means

---

1 As Prince Alberic is later said to be 16 years old at this time, the year would be 1694. The Holy See, that is the Roman Catholic Church, supported by the Jesuit, would be ruled by Pope Innocent XII (reigned 1691-1700), the King of Spain, supported by the Dwarf, would be the childless Charles II (reigned 1665-1700, and whose death in 1700 would bring about the War of Spanish Succession), while the Holy Roman Emperor, supported by the Jester, would be Leopold I (reigned 1658-1705).

which each would pretend to have used had been thought out: poison in each case, only while the Dwarf had selected henbane, taken through a pair of perfumed gloves,[1] and the Jester pounded diamonds mixed in champagne, the Jesuit had modestly adhered to the humble cup of chocolate, which, whether real or fictitious, had always stood his order in such good stead. Thus did each of these wily courtiers dispose of Alberic in case he should die.

There remained the alternative of Alberic continuing to live; and for this the three rival statesmen were also prepared. If Alberic lived, it was obvious that he must be made to select one of the three as his sole minister, and banish, imprison, or put to death the other two. For this purpose it was necessary to secure his affection by gifts, until he should be old enough to understand that he had actually owed his life to the passionate loyalty of the Jesuit, or the Dwarf, or the Jester, each of whom had saved him from the atrocious enterprises of the other two counsellors of Balthasar Maria—nay, who knows? Perhaps from the malignity of Balthasar Maria himself?

In accordance with these subtle machinations, each of the three statesmen determined to outwit his rivals by sending young Alberic such things as would appeal most strongly to a poor young Prince living in banishment among peasants, and wholly unsupplied with pocket-money. The Jesuit expended a considerable sum on books, magnificently bound with the arms of Luna; the Dwarf prepared several suits of tasteful clothes; and the Jester selected, with infinite care, a horse of equal and perfect gentleness and mettle. And, unknown to one another, but much about the same period, each of the statesmen sent his present most secretly to Alberic. Imagine the astonishment and wrath of the Jesuit, the Dwarf, and the Jester, when each saw his messenger come back from Sparkling Waters with his gift returned, and the news that Prince Alberic was already supplied with a complete library, a handsome wardrobe, and not one, but two horses of the finest breed and training; nay, more unexpected still, that while returning the gifts to their respective donors, he had rewarded the messengers with splendid liberality.

The result of this amazing discovery was much the same in the

---

1 Henbane is a drug got from a poisonous and narcotic plant. Poisoned gloves were used as to assassinate Jeanne d'Albret, mother of Henri de Navarre, in Christopher Marlowe's *The Massacre at Paris*, and supposedly by the Marquise de Montespan in an effort to annihilate the mistress who had supplanted her in the affections of Louis XIV.

mind of the Jesuit, the Dwarf and the Jester. Each instantly suspected one or both of his rivals; then, on second thoughts, determined to change the present to one of the other items (horse, clothes, or books, as the case may be), little suspecting that each of them had been supplied already; and, on further reflection, began to doubt the reality of the whole business, to suspect connivance of the messengers, intended insult on the part of the Prince; and, therefore, decided to trust only to the evidence of his own eyes in the matter.

Accordingly, within the same few months, the Jesuit, the Dwarf, and the Jester, feigned grievous illness to their Ducal Master, and while everybody thought them safe in bed in the Red Palace at Luna, hurried, on horseback, or in a litter, or in a coach, to the Castle of Sparkling Waters.

The scene with the peasant and his family, young Alberic's host, was identical on the three occasions; and, as the farmer saw that each of these personages was willing to pay liberally for absolute secrecy, he very consistently swore to supply that desideratum to each of the three great functionaries. And similarly, in all three cases, it was deemed preferable to see the young Prince first from a hiding-place, before asking leave to pay their respects.

The Dwarf, who was the first in the field, was able to hide very conveniently in one of the cut velvet plumes which surmounted Alberic's four-post bedstead, and to observe the young Prince as he changed his apparel. But he scarcely recognised the Duke's grandson. Alberic was sixteen, but far taller and stronger than his age would warrant. His figure was at once manly and delicate, and full of grace and vigour of movement. His long hair, the colour of floss silk, fell in wavy curls, which seemed to imply almost a woman's care and coquetry. His hands also, though powerful, were, as the Dwarf took note, of princely form and whiteness. As to his garments, the open doors of his wardrobe displayed every variety that a young Prince could need; and, while the Dwarf was watching, he was exchanging a russet and purple hunting-dress, cut after the Hungarian fashion with cape and hood, and accompanied by a cap crowned with peacock's feathers, for a habit of white and silver, trimmed with Venetian lace, in which he intended to honour the wedding of one of the farmer's daughters. Never, in his most genuine youth, had Balthasar Maria, the ever young and handsome, been one-quarter as beautiful in person or as delicate in apparel as his grandson in exile among poor country folk.

The Jesuit, in his turn, came to verify his messenger's extraordinary statements. Through the gap between two rafters he was enabled to look down on to Prince Alberic in his study. Magnificently bound books lined the walls of the closet, and in their gaps hung valuable prints and maps. On the table were heaped several open volumes, among globes both terrestrial and celestial; and Alberic himself was leaning on the arm of a great chair, reciting the verses of Virgil in a most graceful chant. Never had the Jesuit seen a better-appointed study nor a more precocious young scholar.

As regards the Jester, he came at the very moment that Alberic was returning from a ride; and, having begun life as an acrobat, he was able to climb into a large ilex which commanded an excellent view of the Castle yard.

Alberic was mounted on a splendid jet-black barb, magnificently caparisoned in crimson and gold Spanish trappings.[1] His groom—for he had even a groom—was riding a horse only a shade less perfect: it was white and he was black—a splendid Negro such as only great princes own. When Alberic came in sight of the farmer's wife, who stood shelling peas on the doorstep, he waved his hat with infinite grace, caused his horse to caracole and rear three times in salutation, picked an apple up while cantering round the Castle yard, threw it in the air with his sword and cut it in two as it descended, and did a number of similar feats such as are taught only to the most brilliant cavaliers. Now, as he was going to dismount, a branch of the ilex cracked, the black barb reared, and Alberic, looking up, perceived the Jester moving in the tree.

'A wonderful parti-coloured bird!' he exclaimed, and seized the fowling-piece that hung to his saddle. But before he had time to fire the Jester had thrown himself down and alighted, making three somersaults, on the ground.

'My Lord,' said the Jester, 'you see before you a faithful subject who, braving the threats and traps of your enemies, and, I am bound to add, risking also your Highness's sovereign displeasure, has been determined to see his Prince once more, to have the supreme happiness of seeing him at last clad and equipped and mounted——'

'Enough!' interrupted Alberic sternly. 'You need say no more. You would have me believe that it is to you I owe my horses and

---

1 Breed of horse from Barbary, on the North coast of Africa.

books and clothes, even as the Dwarf and the Jesuit tried to make me believe about themselves last month. Know, then, that Alberic of Luna requires gifts from none of you. And now, most miserable counsellor of my unhappy grandfather, begone!'

The Jester checked his rage, and tried, all the way back to Luna, to get at some solution of this intolerable riddle. The Jesuit and the Dwarf—the scoundrels—had been trying *their* hand then! Perhaps, indeed, it was their blundering which had ruined his own perfectly-concocted scheme. But for their having come and claimed gratitude for gifts they had not made, Alberic would perhaps have believed that the Jester had not merely offered the horse which was refused, but had actually given the two which had been accepted, and the books and clothes (since there had been books and clothes given) into the bargain. But then, had not Alberic spoken as if he were perfectly sure from what quarter all his possessions had come? This reminded the Jester of the allusion to the Duke Balthasar Maria; Alberic had spoken of him as unhappy. Was it, could it be, possible that the treacherous old wretch had been keeping up relations with his grandson in secret, afraid—for he was a miserable old coward at bottom—both of the wrath of his three counsellors, and of the hatred of his grandson? Was it possible, thought the Jester, that not only the Jesuit and the Dwarf, but the Duke of Luna also, had been intriguing against him round young Prince Alberic? Balthasar Maria was quite capable of it; he might be enjoying the trick he was playing his three masters—for they were his masters; he might be preparing to turn suddenly upon them with his long neglected grandson like a sword to smite them. On the other hand, might this not be a mere mistaken supposition on the part of Prince Alberic, who, in his silly dignity, preferred to believe in the liberality of his ducal grandfather than in that of his grandfather's servants? Might the horses, and all the rest, not really be the gift of either the Dwarf or the Jesuit, although neither had got the credit for it? 'No, no,' exclaimed the Jester, for he hated his fellow-servants worse than his master, 'anything better than that! Rather a thousand times that it were the Duke himself who had outwitted them.'

Then, in his bitterness, having gone over the old arguments again and again, some additional circumstances returned to his memory. The black groom was deaf and dumb, and the peasants, it appeared, had been quite unable to extract any information from him. But he had arrived with those particular horses only a few months ago; a gift, the peasants had thought, from the old Duke of Luna. But Alberic, they had said, had possessed other horses before, which they had also taken for granted had come from the Red Palace. And the clothes and books had been accumulating, it appeared, ever since the Prince's arrival in his place of banishment. Since this was the case, the plot, whether on the part of the Jesuit or the Dwarf, or on that of the Duke himself, had been going on for years before the Jester had bestirred himself! Moreover, the Prince not only possessed horses, but he learned to ride, he not only had books, but he had learned to read, and even to read various tongues; and finally, the Prince was not only clad in princely garments, but he was every inch of him a Prince. He had then been consorting with other people than the peasants at Sparkling Waters. He must have been away— or—some one must have come. He had not been living in solitude.

But when—how—and above all, who?

And again the baffled Jester revolved the probabilities concerning the Dwarf, the Jesuit, and the Duke. It must be—it could be no other—it evidently could only be——.

'Ah!' exclaimed the unhappy diplomatist; 'if only one could believe in magic!'

And it suddenly struck him, with terror and mingled relief, 'Was it magic?'

But the Jester, like the Dwarf and the Jesuit, and the Duke of Luna himself, was altogether superior to such foolish beliefs.

V

The young Prince of Luna had never attempted to learn the story of Alberic the Blond and the Snake Lady. Children sometimes conceive an inexplicable shyness, almost a dread, of knowing more on some subject which is uppermost in their thoughts; and such had been the case of Duke Balthasar Maria's grandson. Ever since the memorable morning when the ebony crucifix had been removed from in front of the faded tapestry, and the whole figure of the Snake Lady had been for the first time revealed, scarcely a day had passed without their coming to the boy's mind: his nurse's words about his ancestors Alberic and the Snake Lady Oriana. But, even as he had asked no questions then, so he had asked no questions since; shrinking more and more from all further knowledge of the matter. He had never questioned his nurse; he had never questioned the peasants of Sparkling Waters, although the story, he felt quite sure, must be well known among the ruins of Alberic the Blond's own castle. Nay, stranger still, he had never mentioned the subject to his dear Godmother, to whom he had learned to open his heart about all things, and who had taught him all that he knew.

For the Duke's Jester had guessed rightly that, during these years at Sparkling Waters, the young Prince had not consorted solely with peasants. The very evening after his arrival, as he was sitting by the marble well in the vineyard, looking towards the sea, he had felt a hand placed lightly on his shoulder, and looked up into the face of a beautiful lady dressed in green.

'Do not be afraid,' she had said, smiling at his terror. 'I am not a ghost, but alive like you; and I am, though you do not know it, your Godmother. My dwelling is close to this castle, and I shall come every evening to play and talk with you, here by the little white palace with the pillars, where the fodder is stacked. Only, you must remember that I do so against the wishes of your grandfather and all his friends, and that if ever you mention me to any one, or allude in any way to our meetings, I shall be obliged to leave the neighbourhood, and you will never see me again. Some day when you are big you will learn why; till then you must take me on trust. And now what shall we play at?'

And thus his Godmother had come every evening at sunset, just for an hour and no more, and had taught the poor solitary little Prince to play (for he had never played) and to read, and to manage a horse, and, above all, to love: for, except the old tapestry in the Red Palace, he had never loved anything in the world.

Alberic told his dear Godmother everything, beginning with the story of the two pieces of tapestry, the one they had taken away and the one he had cut to pieces; and he asked her about all the things he had ever wanted to know, and she was always able to answer. Only about two things they were silent; she never told him her name nor where she lived, nor whether Duke Balthasar Maria knew her (the boy guessed that she had been a friend of his father's); and Alberic never revealed the fact that the tapestry had represented his ancestor and the beautiful Oriana; for, even to his dear Godmother, and most perhaps to her, he found it impossible even to mention Alberic the Blond and the Snake Lady.

But the story, or rather the name of the story he did not know, never loosened its hold on Alberic's mind. Little by little, as he grew up, it came to add to his life two friends, of whom he never told his Godmother. They were, to be sure, of such sort, however different, that a boy might find it difficult to speak about without feeling foolish. The first of the two friends was his own ancestor, Alberic the Blond; and the second that large tame grass snake whose acquaintance he had made the day after his arrival at the castle. About Alberic the Blond he knew indeed but little, save that he had reigned in Luna many hundreds of years ago, and that he had been a very brave and glorious Prince indeed, who had helped conquer the Holy Sepulchre with Godfrey and Tancred and the other heroes of Tasso.[1] But, perhaps in proportion to this vagueness, Alberic the Blond served to personify all the notions of chivalry which the boy learned from his Godmother, and those which bubbled up in his own breast. Nay, little by little the young Prince began to take his unknown ancestor as a model, and in a confused way, to identify himself with him. For was he not fair-haired too, and Prince of Luna, *Alberic*, third of the name, as the other had been first? Perhaps for this reason he could never speak of this ancestor with his Godmother. She might think it presumptuous and foolish; besides, she might perhaps tell him things about Alberic the Blond which would hurt him; the poor young Prince, who had compared the splendid reputation of his own grandfather with the miserable reality, had grown up precociously sceptical. As to the Snake, with whom he played every day in the grass, and who was his only companion during the many hours of his Godmother's absence, he would willingly have spoken of her, and had once been on the point of doing so, but he had noticed that the mere name of such creatures seemed to be odious to his Godmother. Whenever, in their readings, they came across any mention of serpents, his Godmother would exclaim, 'Let us skip that,' with a look of intense pain in her usually cheerful countenance. It was a pity, Alberic thought, that so lovely and dear a lady should feel such hatred towards any living creature, particularly towards a kind which, like his own tame grass snake, was perfectly harmless. But he loved her too much to dream of thwarting her; and he was very grateful to his tame snake for having the tact never to show herself at the hour of his Godmother's visits.

But to return to the story represented on the dear, faded tapestry in the Red Palace.

When Prince Alberic, unconscious to himself, was beginning

---

1 Godfrey of Bouillon or Boulogne (c. 1060-1100) is the lead protagonist in *Gerusalemme Liberata*, a classic epic poem of the First Crusade in 1099 by Torquato Tasso (1544-95), completed about 1576. Tancred (1076-1112) is one of his fellow noble crusaders.

to turn into a full-grown and gallant-looking youth, a change began to take place in him, and it was about the story of his ancestor and the Lady Oriana. He thought of it more than ever, and it began to haunt his dreams; only it was now a vaguely painful thought; and, while dreading still to know more, he began to experience a restless, miserable craving to know all. His curiosity was like a thorn in his flesh, working its way in and in; and it seemed something almost more than curiosity. And yet, he was still shy and frightened of the subject; nay, the greater his craving to know, the greater grew a strange certainty that the knowing would be accompanied by evil. So, although many people could have answered—the very peasants, the fishermen of the coast, and first and foremost, his Godmother—he let months pass before he asked the question.

It, and the answer, came of a sudden.

There came occasionally to Sparkling Waters an old man, who united in his tattered person the trades of mending crockery and reciting fairy tales. He would seat himself in summer, under the spreading fig-tree in the Castle yard, and in winter by the peasants' deep, black chimney, alternately boring holes in pipkins, or gluing plate edges, and singing, in a cracked nasal voice, but not without dignity and charm of manner, the stories of the King of Portugal's Cowherd, of the Feathers of the Griffin, or some of the many stanzas of *Orlando* or *Jerusalem Delivered* which he knew by heart.[1] Our young Prince had always avoided him, partly from a vague fear of a mention of his ancestor and the Snake Lady, and partly because of something vaguely sinister in the old man's eye. But now he awaited with impatience the vagrant's periodical return, and on one occasion summoned him to his own chamber.

'Sing me,' he commanded, 'the story of Alberic the Blond and the Snake Lady.'

The old man hesitated, and answered with a strange look—

'My Lord, I do not know it.'

A sudden feeling, such as the youth had never experienced before, seized hold of Alberic. He did not recognise himself. He saw and heard himself, as if it were some one else, nod first at some pieces of gold, of those his Godmother had given him, and

---

1 Griffins are fabulous creatures with an eagle's head and wings and a lion's body. Their feathers are supposed to cure blindness. For *Orlando*, see the note on Boiardo and Ariosto above; for *Jerusalem Delivered* (*Gerusalemme Liberata*), see note on Tasso. Alberic the Blond does not feature in this poem.

then at his fowling-piece hung on the wall; and as he did so he had a strange thought: 'I must be mad.' But he merely said, sternly—

'Old man, that is not true. Sing that story at once, if you value my money and your safety.'

The vagrant took his white-bearded chin in his hand, mused, and then, fumbling among the files and drills and pieces of wire in his tool-basket, which made a faint metallic accompaniment, he slowly began to chant the following stanzas:—

VI

Now listen, courteous Prince, to what befell your ancestor, the valorous Alberic, returning from the Holy Land.

Already a year had passed since the strongholds of Jerusalem had fallen beneath the blows of the faithful, and since the Sepulchre of Christ had been delivered from the worshippers of Macomet.[1] The great Godfrey was enthroned as its guardian, and the mighty barons, his companions, were wending their way homewards—Tancred, and Bohemund, and Reynold, and the rest.[2]

The valorous Alberic, the honour of Luna, after many perilous adventures, brought by the anger of the Wizard Macomet, whom he had offended, was shipwrecked on his homeward way, and cast, alone of all his great army, upon the rocky shore of an unknown island. He wandered long about, among woods and pleasant pastures, but without ever seeing any signs of habitation; nourishing himself solely on berries and clear water, and taking his rest in the green grass beneath the trees. At length, after some days of wandering, he came to a dense forest, the like of which he had never seen before, so deep was its shade and so tangled were its boughs. He broke the branches with his iron-gloved hand, and the air became filled with the croaking and screeching of dreadful night-birds. He pushed his way with shoulder and knee, tram-

---

1 Presumably the Prophet Mohammed, founder of Islam (c. 570-632).
2 After the capture of Jerusalem, Godfrey was made king of the city in 1099. Bohemund or Bohemond I, Prince of Antioch (c. 1056-1111) was a leader in the crusades and the uncle of Tancred. When Bohemond was captured by the Turks, Tancred took over as regent in his stead. Reynold is Rinaldo, a young crusader hero in Tasso's poem, in love with the sorceress Armida.

pling the broken leafage under foot, and the air was filled with the roaring of monstrous lions and tigers. He grasped his sharp double-edged sword and hewed through the interlaced branches, and the air was filled with the shrieks and sobs of a vanquished city. But the Knight of Luna went on, undaunted, cutting his way through the enchanted wood. And behold! As he issued thence, there was before him a lordly castle, as of some great Prince, situate in a pleasant meadow among running streams. And as Alberic approached, the portcullis was raised, and the drawbridge lowered; and there arose sounds of fifes and bugles, but nowhere could he descry any living wight[1] around. And Alberic entered the castle, and found therein guardrooms full of shining arms, and chambers spread with rich stuffs, and a banqueting-hall, with a great table laid and a chair of state at the end. And as he entered a concert of invisible voices and instruments greeted him sweetly, and called him by name, and bid him be welcome; but not a living soul did he see. So he sat him down at the table, and as he did so, invisible hands filled his cup and his plate, and ministered to him with delicacies of all sorts. Now when the good knight had eaten and drunken his fill, he drank to the health of his unknown host, declaring himself the servant thereof with his sword and heart. After which, weary with wandering, he prepared to take rest on the carpets which strewed the ground; but invisible hands unbuckled his armour, and clad him in silken robes, and led him to a couch all covered with rose-leaves. And when he had lain himself down, the concert of invisible singers and players put him to sleep with their melodies.

It was the hour of sunset when the valorous Baron awoke, and buckled on his armour, and hung on his thigh the great sword Brillamorte; and invisible hands helped him once more.

The Knight of Luna went all over the enchanted castle, and found all manner of rarities, treasures of precious stones, such as great kings possess, and stores of gold and silver vessels, and rich stuffs, and stables full of fiery coursers ready caparisoned; but never a human creature anywhere. And, wondering more and more, he went forth into the orchard, which lay within the castle walls. And such another orchard, sure, was never seen, since that in which the hero Hercules found the three golden apples and slew the great dragon. For you might see in this place fruit-trees of all kinds, apples and pears, and peaches and plums, and the goodly orange, which bore at the same time fruit and delicate and

---

1 Living being.

scented blossom. And all around were set hedges of roses, whose scent was even like heaven; and there were other flowers of all kinds, those into which the vain Narcissus turned through love of himself, and those which grew, they tell us, from the blood-drops of fair Venus's minion; and lilies of which that Messenger carried a sheaf who saluted the Meek Damsel, glorious above all womankind.[1] And in the trees sang innumerable birds; and others, of unknown breed, joined melody in hanging cages and aviaries. And in the orchard's midst was set a fountain, the most wonderful e'er made, its waters running in green channels among the flowered grass. For that fountain was made in the likeness of twin naked maidens, dancing together, and pouring water out of pitchers as they did so; and the maidens were of fine silver, and the pitchers of wrought gold, and the whole so cunningly contrived by magic art that the maidens really moved and danced with the waters they were pouring out—a wonderful work, most truly. And when the Knight of Luna had feasted his eyes upon this marvel, he saw among the grass, beneath a flowering almond-tree, a sepulchre of marble, cunningly carved and gilded, on which was written, 'Here is imprisoned the Fairy Oriana, most miserable of all fairies, condemned for no fault, but by envious powers to a dreadful fate,'—and as he read, the inscription changed and the sepulchre showed these words: 'O Knight of Luna, valorous Alberic, if thou wouldst show thy gratitude to the hapless mistress of this castle, summon up thy redoubtable courage, and, whatsoever creature issue from my marble heart, swear thou to kiss it three times on the mouth, that Oriana may be released.'

And Alberic drew his great sword, and on its hilt, shaped like a cross, he swore.

Then wouldst thou have heard a terrible sound of thunder, and seen the castle walls rock. But Alberic, nothing daunted, repeats in a loud voice, 'I swear,' and instantly that sepulchre's lid upheaves, and there issues thence and rises up a great green snake, wearing a golden crown, and raises itself and fawns

---

1 In Ovid's *Metamorphoses*, Book 3, the vain youth Narcissus falls in love with his own reflection, wastes away and dies, finally turning into the yellow and white narcissus flower. Venus' young lover, Adonis, slain by a wild boar, is transformed by her into the anemone. In Renaissance art the Angel Gabriel is often portrayed carrying a spray of white lilies signifying purity when he greets the Virgin Mary. Such lilies are often known by association as Madonna Lilies or Annunciation lilies.

towards the valorous Knight of Luna. And Alberic starts and recoils in terror. For rather, a thousand times, confront alone the armed hosts of all the heathen, than put his lips to that cold, creeping beast! And the serpent looks at Alberic with great gold eyes, and big tears issue thence, and it drops prostrate on the grass;[1] and Alberic summons courage and approaches; but when the serpent glides along his arm, a horror takes him, and he falls back, unable. And the tears stream from the snake's golden eyes, and moans come from its mouth.

And Alberic runs forward, and seizes the serpent in both arms, and lifts it up, and three times presses his warm lips against its cold and slippery skin, shutting his eyes in horror. And when the Knight of Luna opens them again, behold! O wonder! in his arms no longer a dreadful snake, but a damsel, richly dressed and beautiful beyond compare.

VII

Young Alberic sickened that very night, and lay for many days raging with fever. The peasant's wife and a good neighbouring priest nursed him unhelped, for when the messenger they sent arrived at Luna, Duke Balthasar was busy rehearsing a grand ballet in which he himself danced the part of Phoebus Apollo; and the ducal physician was therefore despatched to Sparkling Waters only when the young prince was already recovering.

Prince Alberic undoubtedly passed through a very bad illness, and went fairly out of his mind for fever and ague.

He raved so dreadfully in his delirium about enchanted tapestries and terrible grottoes, Twelve Cæsars with rolling eyeballs, barbers' blocks with perukes on them, monkeys of verde antique, and porphyry rhinoceroses, and all manner of hellish creatures, that the good priest began to suspect a case of demoniac possession, and caused candles to be kept lighted all day and all night, and holy water to be sprinkled, and a printed form of exorcism, absolutely sovereign in such trouble, to be nailed against the bed-

---

1   The trial of offering affection to an ugly creature which then turns into a beautiful human is common to fairy stories such as "Beauty and the Beast" and "The Frog Prince." Lee's biographer Vineta Colby suggests the influence of E.T.A. Hoffmann (1776-1822). In his "Der goldene Topf" ("The Golden Flower Pot") of 1814, the hero Anselm falls in love with Serpentina, an enchanted snake lady.

post. On the fourth day the young Prince fell into a profound sleep, from which he awaked in apparent possession of his faculties.

'Then you are not the Porphyry Rhinoceros?' he said, very slowly, as his eye fell upon the priest; 'and this is my own dear little room at Sparkling Waters, though I do not understand all those candles. I thought it was the great hall in the Red Palace, and that all those animals of precious marbles, and my grandfather, the Duke, in his bronze and gold robes, were beating me and my tame snake to death with harlequins' laths.[1] It was terrible. But now I see it was all fancy and delirium.'

The poor youth gave a sigh of relief, and feebly caressed the rugged old hand of the priest, which lay upon his counterpane. The Prince stayed for a long while motionless, but gradually a strange light came into his eyes and a smile on to his lips. Presently he made a sign that the peasants should leave the room, and taking once more the good priest's hand, he looked solemnly in his eyes, and spoke in an earnest voice. 'My father,' he said, 'I have seen and heard strange things in my sickness, and I cannot tell for certain now what belongs to the reality of my previous life, and what is merely the remembrance of delirium. On this I would fain be enlightened. Promise me, my father, to answer my questions truly, for this is a matter of the welfare of my soul, and therefore of your own.'

The priest nearly jumped on his chair. So he had been right. The demons had been trying to tamper with the poor young Prince, and now he was going to have a fine account of it all.

'My son,' he murmured, 'as I hope for the spiritual welfare of both of us, I promise to answer all your interrogations to the best of my powers. Speak without reticence.'

Alberic hesitated for a moment, and his eyes glanced from one long lit taper to the other.

'In that case,' he said slowly, 'let me conjure you, my father, to tell me whether or not there exists a certain tradition in my family, of the loves of my ancestor, Alberic the Blond, with a certain Snake Lady, and how he was unfaithful to her, and failed to disenchant her, and how a second Alberic, also my ancestor, loved this same Snake Lady, but failed before the ten years of fidelity were over, and became a monk.... Does such a story exist, or have I imagined it all during my sickness?'

---

1 Wooden flexible sword carried by a harlequin or clown character, and the originator of Mr. Punch's slap-stick.

'My son,' replied the good priest testily, for he was most horribly disappointed by this speech, 'it is scarce fitting that a young Prince but just escaped from the jaws of death—and, perhaps, even from the insidious onslaught of the Evil One—should give his mind to idle tales like these.'

'Call them what you choose,' answered the Prince gravely, 'but remember your promise, father. Answer me truly, and presume not to question my reasons.'

The priest started. What a hasty ass he had been! Why, these were probably the demons talking out of Alberic's mouth, causing him to ask silly irrelevant questions in order to prevent a good confession. Such were notoriously among their stock tricks! But he would outwit them. If only it were possible to summon up St. Paschal Baylon, that new fashionable saint who had been doing such wonders with devils lately! But St. Paschal Baylon required not only that you should say several rosaries, but that you should light four candles on a table and lay a supper for two; after that there was nothing he would not do.[1] So the priest hastily seized two candlesticks from the foot of the bed, and called to the peasant's wife to bring a clean napkin and plates and glasses; and meanwhile endeavoured to detain the demons by answering the poor Prince's foolish chatter, 'Your ancestors, the two Alberics—a tradition in your Serene family—yes, my Lord— there is such—let me see, how does this story go?—ah yes—this demon, I mean this Snake Lady was a— what they call a fairy— or witch, malefica or stryx is,[2] I believe, the proper Latin expression—who had been turned into a snake for her sins—good woman, woman, is it possible you cannot be a little quicker in bringing those plates for his Highness's supper? The Snake Lady—let me see—was to cease altogether being a snake if a cavalier remained faithful to her for ten years, and at any rate turned into a woman every time a cavalier was found who had the courage to give her a kiss as if she were not a snake—a disagreeable thing, besides being mortal sin. As I said just now, this enabled her to resume temporarily her human shape, which is said to have been fair enough; but how can one tell? I believe she

---

1 Spanish saint (died 1592), also referred to in "Amour Dure," who attained outstanding holiness in leading the uneventful life of a lay brother. He had been recently canonised in 1690.

2 A malefica is a witch taught by a demon. Her object is to inflict injury. A stryx is a witch who is transformed into a screech owl at night and who preys upon the blood of infants.

was allowed to change into a woman for an hour at sunset, in any case and without anybody kissing her, but only for an hour. A very unlikely story, my Lord, and not a very moral one, to my thinking!'

And the good priest spread the tablecloth over the table, wondering secretly when the plates and glasses for St. Paschal Baylon would make their appearance. If only the demon could be prevented from beating a retreat before all was ready! 'To return to the story about which Your Highness is pleased to inquire,' he continued, trying to gain time by pretending to humour the demon who was asking questions through the poor Prince's mouth, 'I can remember hearing a poem before I took orders—a foolish poem too, in a very poor style, if my memory is correct—that related the manner in which Alberic the Blond met this Snake Lady, and disenchanted her by performing the ceremony I have alluded to. The poem was frequently sung at fairs and similar resorts of the uneducated, and, as remarked, was a very inferior composition indeed. Alberic the Blond afterward came to his senses, it appears, and after abandoning the Snake Lady fulfilled his duty as a Prince, and married the Princess.... I cannot exactly remember what Princess, but it was a very suitable marriage, no doubt, from which Your Highness is of course descended.

'As regards the Marquis Alberic, second of the name, of whom it is accounted that he died in odour of sanctity (and indeed it is said that the facts concerning his beatification are being studied in the proper quarters), there is a mention in a life of Saint Fredevaldus, bishop and patron of Luna, printed at the beginning of the present century at Venice, with Approbation and Licence of the Authorities and Inquisition, a mention of the fact that this Marquis Alberic the second had contracted, having abandoned his lawful wife, a left-handed marriage[1] with this same Snake Lady (such evil creatures not being subject to natural death), she having induced him thereunto in hope of his proving faithful ten years, and by this means restoring her altogether to human shape. But a certain holy hermit, having got wind of this scandal, prayed to St. Fredevaldus as patron of Luna, whereupon St. Fredevaldus took pity on the Marquis Alberic's sins, and appeared to him in a vision at the end of the ninth year of his irregular connection with the Snake Lady, and touched his heart so thoroughly that he instantly forswore her company, and handing the Marquisate

---

1 An illicit or informal marriage.

over to his mother, abandoned the world and entered the order of St. Romwald,[1] in which he died, as remarked, in odour of sanctity, in consequence of which the present Duke, Your Highness's magnificent grandfather, is at the moment, as befits so pious a Prince, employing his influence with the Holy Father for the beatification of so glorious an ancestor. And now, my son,' added the good priest, suddenly changing his tone, for he had got the table ready, and lighted the candles, and only required to go through the preliminary invocation of St. Paschal Baylon—'and now, my son, let your curiosity trouble you no more, but endeavour to obtain some rest, and if possible——'

But the Prince interrupted him.

'One word more, good father,' he begged, fixing him with earnest eyes; is it known what has been the fate of the Snake Lady?'

The impudence of the demons made the priest quite angry, but he must not scare them before the arrival of St. Paschal, so he controlled himself, and answered slowly by gulps, between the lines of the invocation he was mumbling under his breath:

'My Lord—it results from the same life of St. Fredevaldus, that ... (in case of property lost, fire, flood, earthquake, plague) ... that the Snake Lady (thee we invoke, most holy Paschal Baylon!). The Snake Lady being of the nature of fairies, cannot die unless her head be severed from her trunk, and is still haunting the world, together with other evil spirits, in hopes that another member of the house of Luna (Thee we invoke, most holy Paschal Baylon!)—may succumb to her arts and be faithful to her for the ten years needful to her disenchantments—(most holy Paschal Baylon!—and most of all—on thee we call—for aid against the ...)——'

But before the priest could finish his invocation, a terrible shout came from the bed where the sick Prince was lying—

'O Oriana, Oriana!' cried Prince Alberic, sitting up in his bed with a look which terrified the priest as much as his voice. 'O Oriana, Oriana!' he repeated, and then fell back exhausted and broken.

'Bless my soul!' cried the priest, almost upsetting the table; 'why, the demon has already issued out of him! Who would have

1 Most likely St. Romuald (c. 950-1027), Italian Benedictine monk who founded many monasteries and hermitages, and principally the Camaldolese order of hermit monks, a small independent order of Benedictines.

guessed that St. Paschal Baylon performed his miracles as quick as that?'

VIII

Prince Alberic was awakened by the loud trill of a nightingale. The room was bathed in moonlight, in which tapers, left burning round the bed to ward off evil spirits, flickered yellow and ineffectual. Through the open casement came, with the scent of freshly-cut grass, a faint concert of nocturnal sounds: the silvery vibration of the cricket, the reedlike quavering notes of the leaf frogs, and, every now and then, the soft note of an owlet, seeming to stroke the silence as the downy wings growing out of the temples of the Sleep God might stroke the air. The nightingale had paused; and Alberic listened breathless for its next burst of song. At last, and when he expected it least, it came, liquid, loud, and triumphant; so near that it filled the room and thrilled through his marrow like an unison of Cremona viols.[1] It was singing on the pomegranate close outside, whose first buds must be opening into flame-coloured petals. For it was May. Alberic listened; and collected his thoughts, and understood. He arose and dressed, and his limbs seemed suddenly strong, and his mind strangely clear, as if his sickness had been but a dream. Again the nightingale trilled out, and again stopped. Alberic crept noiselessly out of his chamber, down the stairs and into the open. Opposite, the moon had just risen, immense and golden, and the pines and the cypresses of the hill, the furthest battlements of the castle walls, were printed upon it like delicate lace. It was so light that the roses were pink, and the pomegranate flower scarlet, and the lemons pale yellow, and the vines bright green, only differently coloured from how they looked by day, and as if washed over with silver. The orchard spread uphill, its twigs and separate leaves all glittering as if made of diamonds, and its tree-trunks and spalliers weaving strange black patterns of shadow. A little breeze shuddered up from the sea, bringing the scent of the irises grown for their root among the cornfields below. The nightingale was silent. But Prince Alberic did not stand waiting for its song. A spiral dance of fire-flies, rising and falling like a thin gold foun-

---

1 Cremona in Lombardy, Italy, produced during the sixteenth to eighteenth centuries the best violins made by the Amati, Stradivari, and Guarneri families.

tain, beckoned him upwards through the dewy grass. The circuit of castle walls, jagged and battlemented, and with tufts of trees profiled here and there against the resplendent blue pallor of the moonlight, seemed twined and knotted like huge snakes around the world.

Suddenly, again, the nightingale sang—a throbbing silver song. It was the same bird, Alberic felt sure; but it was in front of him now, and was calling him onwards. The fire-flies wove their golden dance a few steps in front, always a few steps in front, and drew him up-hill through the orchard.

As the ground became steeper, the long trellises, black and crooked seemed to twist and glide through the blue moonlit grass like black gliding snakes, and, at the top, its marble pillarets clear in the light, slumbered the little Gothic palace of white marble. From the solitary sentinel pine broke the song of the nightingale. This was the place. A breeze had risen, and from the shining moonlit sea, broken into causeways and flotillas of smooth and fretted silver, came a faint briny smell, mingling with that of the irises and blossoming lemons, with the scent of vague ripeness and freshness. The moon hung like a silver lantern over the orchard; the wood of the trellises patterned the blue luminous heaven; the vine-leaves seemed to swim, transparent, in the shining air. Over the circular well, in the high grass, the fireflies rose and fell like a thin fountain of gold. And, from the sentinel pine, the nightingale sang.

Prince Alberic leant against the brink of the well, by the trough carved with antique designs of serpent-bearing mænads. He was wonderfully calm, and his heart sang within him. It was, he knew, the hour and place of his fate.

The nightingale ceased: and the shrill song of the crickets was suspended. The silvery luminous world was silent.

A quiver came through the grass by the well, a rustle through the roses. And, on the well's brink, encircling its central blackness, glided the Snake.

'Oriana!' whispered Alberic. 'Oriana!' She paused, and stood almost erect. The Prince put out his hand, and she twisted round his arm, extending slowly her chilly coil to his wrist and fingers.

'Oriana!' whispered Prince Alberic again. And raising his hand to his face, he leaned down and pressed his lips on the little flat head of the serpent. And the nightingale sang. But a coldness seized his heart, the moon seemed suddenly extinguished, and he slipped away in unconsciousness.

When he awoke the moon was still high. The nightingale was

singing its loudest. He lay in the grass by the well, and his head rested on the knees of the most beautiful of ladies. She was dressed in cloth of silver which seemed woven of moon mists, and shimmering moonlit green grass. It was his own dear Godmother.

IX

When Duke Balthasar Maria had got through the rehearsals of the ballet called Daphne Transformed,[1] and finally danced his part of Phœbus Apollo to the infinite delight and glory of his subjects, he was greatly concerned, being benignly humoured, on learning that he had very nearly lost his grandson and heir. The Dwarf, the Jesuit, and the Jester, whom he delighted in pitting against one another, had severally accused each other of disrespectful remarks about the dancing of that ballet; so Duke Balthasar determined to disgrace all three together and inflict upon them the hated presence of Prince Alberic. It was, after all, very pleasant to possess a young grandson, whom one could take to one's bosom and employ in being insolent to one's own favourites. It was time, said Duke Balthasar, that Alberic should learn the habits of a court and take unto himself a suitable princess.

The young Prince accordingly was sent for from Sparkling Waters, and installed at Luna in a wing of the Red Palace, overlooking the Court of Honour, and commanding an excellent view of the great rockery, with the Verde Antique Apes and the Porphyry Rhinoceros. He found awaiting him on the great staircase a magnificent staff of servants, a master of the horse, a grand cook, a barber, a hairdresser and assistant, a fencing-master, and four fiddlers. Several lovely ladies of the Court, the principal ministers of the Crown, and the Jesuit, the Dwarf, and the Jester, were also ready to pay their respects. Prince Alberic threw himself out of the glass coach before they had time to open the door, and bowing coldly, ascended the staircase, carrying under his cloak what appeared to be a small wicker cage. The Jesuit, who was the soul of politeness, sprang forward and signed to an officer of the

---

1 In his *Metamorphoses*, Book 1, Ovid tells how the nymph Daphne is transformed into a laurel bush when pursued by the god Apollo. Balthasar Maria again emulates the Sun-King Louis XIV who also performed in a ballet as the sun god Phoebus Apollo.

household to relieve His Highness of this burden. But Alberic waved the man off; and the rumour went abroad that a hissing noise had issued from under the Prince's cloak, and like lightning, the head and forked tongue of a serpent.

Half an hour later the official spies had informed Duke Balthasar that his grandson and heir had brought from Sparkling Waters no apparent luggage save two swords, a fowling-piece, a volume of Virgil,[1] a branch of pomegranate blossom, and a tame grass snake.

Duke Balthasar did not like the idea of the grass snake; but wishing to annoy the Jester, the Dwarf, and the Jesuit, he merely smiled when they told him of it, and said: 'The dear boy! What a child he is! He probably, also, has a pet lamb, white as snow, and gentle as spring, mourning for him in his old home! How touching is the innocence of childhood! Heigho! I was just like that myself not so very long ago.' Whereupon the three favourites and the whole Court of Luna smiled and bowed and sighed: 'How lovely is the innocence of youth!' while the Duke fell to humming the well-known air, 'Thyrsis was a shepherd-boy,' of which the ducal fiddlers instantly struck up the ritornel.[2]

'But,' added Balthasar Maria, with that subtle blending of majesty and archness in which he excelled all living Princes, 'but it is now time that the Prince, my grandson, should learn'—here he put his hand on his sword and threw back slightly one curl of his jet-black peruke—'the stern exercises of Mars; and also, let us hope, the freaks and frolics of Venus.'[3]

Saying which, the old sinner pinched the cheek of a lady of the very highest quality, whose husband and father were instantly congratulated by the whole Court.

Prince Alberic was displayed next day to the people of Luna, standing on the balcony among a tremendous banging of mortars; while Duke Balthasar explained that he felt towards this youth all the fondness and responsibility of an elder brother. There was a grand ball, a gala opera, a review, a very high mass in the cathedral; the Dwarf, the Jesuit, and the Jester each separately offered his services to Alberic in case he wanted a loan of

---

1 Unspecified book of poetry by the classical poet Virgil (70-19 BC), author of the *Aeneid*, *Eclogues*, and *Georgics*.

2 "Thyrsis," a common name for a shepherd in pastoral poetry derived from classical precedents in Virgil (*Eclogues* 7) and Theocritus (*Idylls* 1). A ritornel is an instrumental refrain.

3 That is, military expertise and the art of love.

money, a love-letter carried, or in case even (expressed in more delicate terms) he might wish to poison his grandfather. Duke Balthasar Maria, on his side, summoned his ministers, and sent couriers, booted and liveried, to three great dukes of Italy, carrying each of them, in a morocco wallet emblazoned with the arms of Luna, an account of Prince Alberic's lineage and person, and a request for particulars of any marriageable princesses and dowries to be disposed of.

X

Prince Alberic did not give his grandfather that warm satisfaction which the old Duke had expected. Balthasar Maria, entirely bent upon annoying the three favourites, had said, and had finally believed that he intended to introduce his grandson to the delights and duties of life, and in the company of this beloved stripling, to dream that he, too, was a youth once more: a statement which the Court took with due deprecatory reverence, as the Duke was well known never to have ceased to be young.

But Alberic did not lend himself to so touching an idyll. He behaved, indeed, with the greatest decorum, and manifested the utmost respect for his grandfather. He was marvellously assiduous in the council chamber, and still more so in following the military exercises and learning the trade of a soldier. He surprised every one by his interest and intelligence in all affairs of state; he more than surprised the Court by his readiness to seek knowledge about the administration of the country and the condition of the people. He was a youth of excellent morals, courage, and diligence; but, there was no denying it, he had positively no conception of *sacrificing to the Graces*.[1] He sat out, as if he had been watching a review, the delicious operas and superb ballets which absorbed half the revenue of the duchy. He listened, without a smile of comprehension, to the witty innuendoes of the ducal table. But worst of all, he had absolutely no eyes, let alone a heart, for the fair sex. Now Balthasar Maria had assembled at Luna a perfect bevy of lovely nymphs, both ladies of the greatest birth, whose husbands received most honourable posts, military and civil, and young females of humbler extraction, though not less expensive habits, ranging from singers and

---

1 In Greek mythology the three Graces are the personification of grace and charm.

dancers to slave-girls of various colours, all dressed in their appropriate costume; a galaxy of beauty which was duly represented by the skill of celebrated painters on all the walls of the Red Palace, where you may still see their faded charms, habited as Diana, or Pallas, or in the spangles of Columbine, or the turbans of Sibyls.[1] These ladies were the object of Duke Balthasar's most munificently divided attentions; and in the delight of his new-born family affection, he had promised himself much tender interest in guiding the taste of his heir among such of these nymphs as had already received his own exquisite appreciation. Great, therefore, was the disappointment of the affectionate grandfather when his dream of companionship was dispelled, and it became hopeless to interest young Alberic in anything at Luna save despatches and cannons.

The Court, indeed found the means of consoling Duke Balthasar for this bitterness by extracting therefrom a brilliant comparison between the unfading grace, the vivacious, though majestic, character of the grandfather, and the gloomy and pedantic personality of the grandson. But, although Balthasar Maria would only smile at every new proof of Alberic's bearish obtuseness, and ejaculate in French, 'Poor child! he was born old, and I shall die young!' the reigning Prince of Luna grew vaguely to resent the peculiarities of his heir.

In this fashion things proceeded in the Red Palace at Luna, until Prince Alberic had attained his twenty-first year.

He was sent, in the interval, to visit the principal courts of Italy, and to inspect its chief curiosities, natural and historical, as befitted the heir to an illustrious state. He received the golden rose from the Pope in Rome; he witnessed the festivities of Ascension Day from the Doge's barge at Venice; he accompanied the Marquis of Montferrat to the camp under Turin; he witnessed the launching of a galley against the Barbary corsairs by the Knights of St. Stephen in the port of Leghorn, and a grand bullfight and burning of heretics given by the Spanish Viceroy at Palermo; and he was allowed to be present when the celebrated Dr. Borri turned two brass buckles into pure gold before the Archduke at

---

1 In classical mythology Diana (Artemis in the Greek pantheon) is the goddess of hunting and of the moon and Pallas Athene (Minerva in the Latin pantheon) the goddess of wisdom. Columbine is the mistress of Harlequin in Italian comedy. The Sibyls are the prophetesses and oracles of ancient classical times.

Milan.[1] On all of which occasions the heir-apparent of Luna bore himself with a dignity and discretion most singular in one so young. In the course of these journeys he was presented to several of the most promising heiresses in Italy, some of whom were of so tender age as to be displayed in jewelled swaddling clothes on brocade cushions; and a great many possible marriages were discussed behind his back. But Prince Alberic declared for his part that he had decided to lead a single life until the age of twenty eight or thirty, and that he would then require the assistance of no ambassadors or chancellors, but find for himself the future Duchess of Luna.

All this did not please Balthasar Maria, as indeed nothing else about his grandson did please him much. But, as the old Duke did not really relish the idea of a daughter-in-law at Luna, and as young Alberic's whimsicalities entailed no expense, and left him entirely free in his business and pleasure, he turned a deaf ear to the criticisms of his counsellors, and letting his grandson inspect fortifications, drill soldiers, pore over parchments, and mope in the wing of the palace, with no amusement save his repulsive tame snake, Balthasar Maria composed and practised various ballets, and began to turn his attention very seriously to the completion of the rockery grotto and of the sepulchral chapel, which,

---

1 A rose made of gold and blessed by the Pope in a special ceremony on the fourth Sunday in Lent and given to favoured churches, Catholic monarchs, or rulers as a mark of esteem. Annually on Ascension Day (i.e., forty days or the sixth Thursday after Easter) the Doge (chief magistrate of the Republic) blesses the City of Venice by symbolically wedding the Adriatic Sea as he drops a ring into the sea from his barge. The Marquisate of Montferrato in Piedmont, north-western Italy, was founded towards the end of the tenth century. Its possession during the sixteenth to the early eighteenth centuries was contested by the Gonzaga Dukes of Mantua and the House of Savoy. The sacred military order of St. Stephen was founded by Cosimo de' Medici in Pisa in 1561 and approved by Pope Pius IV, principally to defend the shipping of Christian nations against pirates, liberate Christians from the slavery of the Turks, and defend the Church and the Catholic faith. Barbary corsairs were Muslim pirates from North Africa who terrorised shipping principally in the sixteenth century. Leghorn is Livorno, a city and seaport in Tuscany, Italy. Sicily had been part of the kingdom of Spain since 1479, and Palermo, its principal city, was the seat of the Spanish Viceroy. Giuseppe Francesco Borri (1627-95) was an Italian adventurer and alchemist who died imprisoned in Castel S. Angelo by Pope Innocent XII.

besides the Red Palace itself, were the chief monuments of his glorious reign.

It was the growing desire to witness the fulfilment of these magnanimous projects which led the Duke of Luna into unexpected conflict with his grandson. The wonderful enterprises above-mentioned involved immense expenses, and had periodically been suspended for lack of funds. The collection of animals in the rockery was very far from complete. A camelopard of spotted alabaster, an elephant of Sardinian jasper, and the entire families of a cow and sheep, all of correspondingly rich marbles, were urgently required to fill up the corners. Moreover, the supply of water was at present so small that the fountains were dry save for a couple of hours on the very greatest holidays; and it was necessary for the perfect naturalness of this ingenious work that an aqueduct twenty miles long should pour perennial streams from a high mountain lake into the grotto of the Red Palace.

The question of the sepulchral chapel was, if possible, even more urgent, for, after every new ballet, Duke Balthasar went through a fit of contrition, during which he fixed his thoughts on death; and the possibilities of untimely release, and of burial in an unfinished mausoleum, filled him with terrors. It is true that Duke Balthasar had, immediately after building the vast domed chapel, secured an effigy of his own person before taking thought for the monuments of his already buried ancestors, and the statue, twelve feet high, representing himself in coronation robes of green bronze brocaded with gold, holding a sceptre, and bearing on his head, of purest silver, a spiky coronet set with diamonds, was one of the curiosities which travellers admired most in Italy. But this statue was unsymmetrical, and moreover, had a dismal suggestiveness, so long as surrounded by empty niches; and the fact that only one-half of the pavement was inlaid with discs of sardonyx, jasper, and carnelian, and that the larger part of the walls were rough brick without a vestige of the mosaic pattern of lapislazuli, malachite, pearl, and coral, which had begun round the one finished tomb, rendered the chapel as poverty-stricken in one aspect as it was magnificent in another. The finishing of the chapel was therefore urgent, and two more bronze statues were actually cast, those, to wit, of the Duke's father and grandfather, and mosaic workmen called from the Medicean works in Florence.[1] But, all of a sudden, the ducal treas-

---

1 The Opificio delle pietre dure in Florence set up by Duke Ferdinando 1 de' Medici in 1588 for the production and workmanship of precious stones and mosaic work and still in existence.

ury was discovered to be empty, and the ducal credit to be exploded.

State lotteries, taxes on salt, even a sham crusade against the Dey of Algiers,[1] all failed to produce any money. The alliance, the right to pass troops through the duchy, the letting out of the ducal army to the highest bidder, had long since ceased to be a source of revenue either from the Emperor, the King of Spain, or the Most Christian One.[2] The Serene Republics of Venice and Genoa publicly warned their subjects against lending a single sequin to the Duke of Luna; the Dukes of Mantua and Modena began to worry about bad debts; the Pope himself had the atrocious taste to make complaints about suppression of church dues and interception of Peter's pence.[3] There remained to the bankrupt Duke Balthasar Maria only one hope in the world—the marriage of his grandson.

There happened to exist at that moment a sovereign of incalculable wealth, with an only daughter of marriageable age. But this potentate, although the nephew of a recent Pope, by whose confiscations his fortunes were founded, had originally been a dealer in such goods as are comprehensively known as drysalting;[4] and, rapacious as were the Princes of the Empire, each was too much ashamed of his neighbours to venture upon alliance with a family of so obtrusive an origin. Here was Balthasar Maria's opportunity: the Drysalter Prince's ducats should complete the rockery, the aqueduct, and the chapel; the drysalter's daughter should be wedded to Alberic of Luna, that was to be third of the name.

XI

Prince Alberic sternly declined. He expressed his dutiful wish that the grotto and the chapel, like all other enterprises undertaken by his grandparent, might be brought to an end worthy of

---

1 Ruling Turkish official in Algiers, leading port and capital of Algeria, North Africa.
2 The Pope.
3 Venetian gold coin in use until the fall of the Venetian republic in 1797; Peter's pence is annual tax of a penny levied on every household and paid to the papal see (also known as the see of Peter).
4 A drysalter deals in goods such as drugs, dyes, gums, oils, pickles, tinned meats, etc.

him. He declared that the aversion to drysalters was a prejudice unshared by himself. He even went so far as to suggest that the eligible princess should marry, not the heir apparent, but the reigning Duke of Luna. But, as regarded himself, he intended, as stated, to remain for many years single. Duke Balthasar had never in his life before seen a man who was determined to oppose him. He felt terrified and became speechless in the presence of young Alberic.

Direct influence having proved useless, the Duke and his counsellors, among whom the Jesuit, the Dwarf, and the Jester had been duly reinstated, looked round for means of indirect persuasion or coercion. A celebrated Venetian beauty was sent for to Luna—a lady frequently employed in diplomatic missions, which she carried through by her unparalleled grace in dancing. But Prince Alberic, having watched her for half an hour, merely remarked to his equerry that his own tame grass snakes made the same movements as the lady infinitely better and more modestly. Whereupon this means was abandoned. The Dwarf then suggested a new method of acting on the young Prince's feelings. This, which he remembered to have been employed very successfully in the case of a certain Duchess of Malfi, who had given her family much trouble some generations back, consisted in dressing a number of domestics up as ghosts and devils, hiring some genuine lunatics from a neighbouring establishment, and introducing them at dead of night into Prince Alberic's chamber.[1] But the Prince, who was busy at his orisons, merely threw a heavy stool and two candlesticks at the apparitions; and, as he did so, the tame snake rose up from the floor, growing colossal in the act, and hissed so terrifically that the whole party fled down the corridor. The most likely advice was given by the Jesuit. This truly subtle diplomatist averred that it was useless trying to act upon the Prince by means which did not already affect him; instead of clumsily constructing a lever for which

---

1 Famous as the eponymous subject of a tragic play by John Webster (1623), the historical Duchess of Amalfi, when widowed, defied her brothers' injunction not to remarry and contracted a secret marriage with her steward Antonio. When the marriage was finally discovered, she appears to have been murdered in her palace. In Act IV of Webster's play the Duchess's gaolers try to terrorise her by showing her the dead bodies of her husband and children (actually waxworks) and disturbing her with the revels of lunatics removed from a nearby hospital.

there was no fulcrum in the youth's soul, it was necessary to find out whatever leverage there might already exist.

Now, on careful enquiry, there was discovered a fact which the official spies, who always acted by precedent and pursued their inquiries according to the rules of the human heart as taught by the Secret Inquisition of the Republic of Venice, had naturally failed to perceive. This fact consisted in a rumour, very vague but very persistent, that Prince Alberic did not inhabit his wing of the palace in absolute solitude. Some of the pages attending on his person affirmed to have heard whispered conversations in the Prince's study, on entering which they had invariably found him alone; others maintained that, during the absence of the Prince from the palace, they had heard the sound of his private harpsichord, the one with the story of Orpheus and the view of Soracte on the cover,[1] although he always kept its key on his person. A footman declared that he had found in the Prince's study, and among his books and maps, a piece of embroidery certainly not belonging to the Prince's furniture and apparel, moreover, half finished, and with a needle sticking in the canvas; which piece of embroidery the Prince had thrust into his pocket. But, as none of the attendants had ever seen any visitor entering or issuing from the Prince's apartments, and the professional spies had ransacked all possible hiding-places and modes of exit in vain, these curious indications had been neglected, and the opinion had been formed that Alberic being, as every one could judge, somewhat insane, had a gift for ventriloquism, a taste for musical boxes, and a proficiency in unmanly handicrafts which he carefully secreted.

These rumours had at one time caused great delight to Duke Balthasar; but he had got tired of sitting in a dark cupboard in his grandson's chamber, and had caught a bad chill looking through his keyhole; so he had stopped all further inquiries as officious fooling on the part of impudent lacqueys.

But the Jesuit foolishly adhered to the rumour. 'Discover *her*,' he said, 'and work through her on Prince Alberic.' But Duke Balthasar, after listening twenty times to this remark with the most delighted interest, turned round on the twenty-first time and gave the Jesuit a look of Jove-like thunder. 'My father,' he said, 'I am surprised—I may say more than surprised—at a

---

1 In Greek myth a singer-poet famous for his music who journeyed to the underworld to claim his dead wife Eurydice. Mount Soracte, located in the Roman countryside, was famously praised by the Latin poet Horace (65-8 BC) in his *Odes* 1. 9.

person of your cloth descending so low as to make aspersions upon the virtue of a young prince reared in my palace and born of my blood. Never let me hear another word about ladies of light manners being secreted within these walls.' Whereupon the Jesuit retired, and was in disgrace for a fortnight, till Duke Balthasar woke up one morning with a strong apprehension of dying.

But no more was said of the mysterious female friend of Prince Alberic, still less was any attempt made to gain her intervention in the matter of the Drysalter Princess's marriage.

XII

More desperate measures were soon resorted to. It was given out that Prince Alberic was engrossed in study; and he was forbidden to leave his wing of the Red Palace, with no other view than the famous grotto with the Verde Antique Apes and the Porphyry Rhinoceros. It was published that Prince Alberic was sick; and he was confined very rigorously to a less agreeable apartment in the rear of the Palace, where he could catch sight of the plaster laurels and draperies, and the rolling plaster eyeball of one of the Twelve Cæsars under the cornice. It was judiciously hinted that the Prince had entered into religious retreat; and he was locked and bolted into the State prison, alongside of the unfinished sepulchral chapel, whence a lugubrious hammering came as the only sound of life. In each of these places the recalcitrant youth was duly argued with by some of his grandfather's familiars, and even received a visit from the old Duke in person. But threats and blandishments were all in vain, and Alberic persisted in his refusal to marry.

It was now six months since he had seen the outer world, and six weeks since he had inhabited the State prison, every stage in his confinement, almost every day thereof, having systematically deprived him of some luxury, some comfort, or some mode of passing his time. His harpsichord and foils had remained in the gala wing overlooking the grotto. His maps and books had not followed him beyond the higher story with the view of the Twelfth Cæsar. And now they had taken away from him his Virgil, his inkstand and paper, and left him only a book of hours.[1]

---

1 Richly illustrated devotional text for the wealthy laity containing set prayers for the hour of the day and time of year according to the ecclesiastical calendar.

Balthasar Maria and his counsellors felt intolerably baffled. There remained nothing further to do; for if Prince Alberic were publicly beheaded, or privately poisoned, or merely left to die of want and sadness, it was obvious Prince Alberic could no longer conclude the marriage with the Drysalter Princess, and that no money to finish the grotto and the chapel, or to carry on Court expenses, would be forthcoming.

It was a burning day of August, a Friday, thirteenth of that month, and after a long prevalence of enervating sirocco, when the old Duke determined to make one last appeal to the obedience of his grandson. The sun, setting among ominous clouds, sent a lurid orange gleam into Prince Alberic's prison chamber, at the moment that his ducal grandfather, accompanied by the Jester, the Dwarf, and the Jesuit, appeared on its threshold after prodigious clanking of keys and clattering of bolts. The unhappy youth rose as they entered, and making a profound bow, motioned his grandparent to the only chair in the place.

Balthasar Maria had never visited him before in this his worst place of confinement; and the bareness of the room, the dust and cobwebs, the excessive hardness of the chair, affected his sensitive heart; and, joined with irritation at his grandson's obstinacy and utter depression about the marriage, the grotto, and the chapel, actually caused this magnanimous sovereign to burst into tears and bitter lamentations.

'It would indeed melt the heart of a stone,' remarked the Jester sternly, while his two companions attempted to soothe the weeping Duke—'to see one of the greatest, wisest, and most valorous Princes in Europe reduced to tears by the undutifulness of his child.'

'Princes, nay kings and emperors' sons,' exclaimed the Dwarf, who was administering Melissa water[1] to the Duke, 'have perished miserably from much less.'

'Some of the most remarkable personages of sacred history are stated to have incurred eternal perdition for far slighter offences,' added the Jesuit.

Alberic had sat down on the bed. The tawny sunshine fell upon his figure. He had grown very thin, and his garments were inexpressibly threadbare. But he was spotlessly neat, his lace band was perfectly folded, his beautiful blond hair flowed in exquisite curls about his pale face, and his whole aspect was

---

1   Calming infusion made from the herb lemon balm.

serene and even cheerful. He might be twenty-two years old, and was of consummate beauty and stature.

'My Lord,' he answered slowly, 'I entreat Your Serene Highness to believe that no one could regret more deeply than I do such a spectacle as is offered me by the tears of a Duke of Luna. At the same time, I can only reiterate that I accept no responsibility ...'

A distant growling of thunder caused the old Duke to start, and interrupted Alberic's speech.

'Your obstinacy, my Lord,' exclaimed the Dwarf, who was an excessively choleric person, 'betrays the existence of a hidden conspiracy most dangerous to the state.'

'It is an indication,' added the Jester, 'of a highly deranged mind.'

'It seems to me,' whispered the Jesuit, 'to savour most undoubtedly of devilry.'

Alberic shrugged his shoulders. He had risen from the bed to close the grated window, into which a shower of hail was suddenly blowing with unparalleled violence, when the old Duke jumped on his seat, and, with eyeballs starting with terror, exclaimed, as he tottered convulsively, 'The serpent! The serpent!'

For there, in a corner, the tame grass snake was placidly coiled up, sleeping.

'The snake! The devil! Prince Alberic's pet companion!' exclaimed the three favourites, and rushed towards that corner.

Alberic threw himself forward. But he was too late. The Jester, with a blow of his harlequin's lath, had crushed the head of the startled creature; and, even while he was struggling with him and the Jesuit, the Dwarf had given it two cuts with his Turkish scimitar.

'The snake! the snake!' shrieked Duke Balthasar, heedless of the desperate struggle.

The warders and equerries waiting outside thought that Prince Alberic must be murdering his grandfather, and burst into prison and separated the combatants.

'Chain the rebel! the wizard! the madman!' cried the three favourites.

Alberic had thrown himself on the dead snake, which lay crushed and bleeding on the floor; and he moaned piteously.

But the prince was unarmed and overpowered in a moment. Three times he broke loose, but three times he was recaptured, and finally bound and gagged, and dragged away. The old Duke recovered from his fright, and was helped up from the bed on to which he had sunk. As he prepared to leave, he approached the dead snake, and looked at it for some time. He kicked its mangled head with his ribboned shoe, and turned away laughing.

'Who knows,' he said, 'whether you were not the Snake Lady? That foolish boy made a great fuss, I remember, when he was scarcely out of long clothes, about a tattered old tapestry representing that repulsive story.'

And he departed to supper.

XIII

Prince Alberic of Luna, who should have been third of his name, died a fortnight later, it was stated, insane. But those who approached him maintained that he had been in perfect possession of his faculties; and that if he refused all nourishment during his second imprisonment, it was from set purpose. He was removed at night from his apartments facing the grotto with the Verde Antique Monkeys and the Porphyry Rhinoceros, and hastily buried under a slab, which remained without any name or date, in the famous mosaic sepulchral chapel.

Duke Balthasar Maria survived him only a few months. The old Duke had plunged into excesses of debauchery with a view, apparently, to dismissing certain terrible thoughts and images which seemed to haunt him day and night, and against which no religious practices or medical prescription were of any avail. The origin of these painful delusions was probably connected with a very strange rumour, which grew to a tradition at Luna, the effect that when the prison room occupied by Prince Alberic was cleaned, after that terrible storm of the 13th August of the year 1700, the persons employed found in a corner, not the dead grass snake, which they had been ordered to cast into the palace drains, but the body of a woman, naked, and miserably disfigured with blows and sabre cuts.

Be this as it may, history records as certain that the house of Luna became extinct in 1701, the duchy lapsing to the Empire. Moreover, that the mosaic chapel remained for ever unfinished, with no statue save the green bronze and gold one of Balthasar Maria above the nameless slab covering Prince Alberic. The rockery also was never completed; only a few marble animals adorning it besides the Porphyry Rhinoceros and the Verde Antique Apes, and the water-supply being sufficient only for the greatest holidays. These things the traveller can report. Also that certain chairs and curtains in the porter's lodge of the now long-deserted Red Palace are made of the various pieces of an extremely damaged arras, having represented the story of Alberic the Blond and the Snake Lady.

A Wedding Chest[1]

To Marie Spartali Stillman 1879-1904

No. 428. A panel (five feet by two feet three inches) formerly the front of a *cassone* or coffer, intended to contain the garments and jewels of a bride.[2] *Subject*: 'The Triumph of Love.' 'Umbrian School of the Fifteenth Century.' In the right-hand corner is a half-effaced inscription: *Desider ... de Civitate Lac ... me ... ecit.*[3] This valuable painting is unfortunately much damaged by damp and mineral corrosives, owing probably to its having contained at one time buried treasure. Bequeathed in 1878 by the widow of the Rev. Lawson Stone, late Fellow of Trinity College, Cambridge.[4]

By Ascension Day, Desiderio of Castiglione del Lago had finished the front panel of the wedding chest which Messer Troilo

---

1 First published in *Pope Jacynth and Other Fantastic Tales* (London: Grant Richards, 1904). This text is taken from the second edition (London: John Lane, The Bodley Head) 115-36. The dedicatee of this story is the artist Marie Spartali Stillman (1843-1927), the daughter of the former Greek consul in London, who trained under the painter Ford Maddox Brown. A celebrated beauty, she also modelled for Dante Gabriel Rossetti and Edward Burne Jones. She married the American journalist and amateur artist W.J. Stillman in 1871 and they moved to Florence in 1878 where she became a friend of Vernon Lee. (The dates 1879-1904 presumably mark the period of their friendship up to the publication of "A Wedding Chest.") Her paintings draw on Italian literary themes, especially works by Dante and Boccaccio.

2 A *cassone* is a richly-decorated wooden coffer used as a marriage gift and intended to contain the bride's garments, linen, and valuables. The outer panels and lid are frequently painted with mythological or classical subjects. Scenes from the *Trionfi* (Triumphs), a group of celebrated poems in Latin by the great Italian poet and humanist Francesco Petrarch (1304-74) are popular subjects. The great age of *cassone* painting was from the fourteenth to the sixteenth centuries. Many Old Masters now hung in art galleries were originally *cassone* panels.

3 A translation of the half-effaced Latin inscription would seem to be "Desiderio from the city of Castiglione del Lago made me."

4 Catalogue of the Smith Museum, Leeds (Authorial note). Lee's description of a particular chest in the Smith Museum, Leeds, is invented.

Baglioni had ordered of Ser Piero Bontempi, whose shop was situated at the bottom of the steps of St. Maxentius, in that portion of the ancient city of Perugia (called by the Romans Augusta in recognition of its great glory) which takes its name from the Ivory Gate built by Theodoric, King of the Goths.[1] The said Desiderio had represented upon this panel the Triumph of Love, as described in his poem by Messer Francesco Petrarca of Arezzo, certainly, with the exception of that Dante, who saw the Vision of Hell, Purgatory, and Paradise, the only poet of recent times who can be compared to those doctissimi viri P. Virgilius, Ovidius of Sulmona, and Statius.[2] And the said Desiderio had betaken himself in this manner. He had divided the panel into four portions or regions, intended to represent the four phases

---

1 Ascension day commemorates the ascension of Jesus into heaven after his crucifixion and resurrection and takes place forty days after Easter. From the third to the first century Etruscan Perugia was the most important city of the Upper Tiber Valley. Brought under Roman subjugation in 40 BC by Octavian, the city took on the name "Augusta" and thereafter enjoyed wealth and splendour. It was invaded by the Goths at the fall of the Roman empire. The church of St. Maxentius appears to be Lee's invention. Authentic Umbrian places mentioned in this story include Castiglione del Lago, situated on the shore of Lake Trasimeno, the ancient town of Gubbio, the hilltop village of Spello and the agricultural town of Bastia. The Baglioni were one of the leading Umbrian noble families. Many of its members were fierce and skilful *condottiere* (or leaders of groups of mercenaries) who had acquired their wealth through war and who dominated Perugia between 1488-1534, constantly challenging other nobles and the papacy. There was indeed a Troilo Baglioni who in 1500 became Bishop of Perugia (in Lee's text Bishop of Spello), but Lee's protagonist, his supposed nephew, seems to be based on a combination of characteristics drawn from wilder elements of the family. Lee's chronicle bears certain similarities to Francesco Matarazzo's *Chronicles of the City of Perugia 1492-1503*, called by John Addington Symonds in his essay on Perugia (in *Sketches in Italy and Greece*, 1874), a "masterpiece of unstudied narrative." Matarazzo describes the brutal exploits of the handsome Baglioni youths with palpable admiration. As Symonds comments, "He seems unable to write about them without using the language of an adoring lover." Lee mentions Matarazzo and the Baglioni in her essay "In Umbria," first published in *Fraser's Magazine* (1881) and reprinted in *Belcaro* (1881). Lee's story seems to be set in the period covered by Matarazzo's *Chronicles*.

2 Petrarch's hometown, Arezzo, is in Tuscany. Desiderio's design for the wedding chest borrows elements from Petrarch's "The Triumph of Love," the first of his *Trionfi* (which number six in total and feature Love, Chastity, Death, Fame, Time and Eternity), and translates them

of the amorous passion: the first was a pleasant country, abundantly watered with twisting streams, of great plenty and joyousness, in which were planted many hedges of fragrant roses, both red and blue, together with elms, poplars, and other pleasant and profitable trees. The second region was somewhat mountainous, but showing large store of lordly castles and thickets of pine and oak, fit for hunting, which region, as being that of glorious love, was girt all round with groves of laurels. The third region—*aspera ac dura regio*[1]—was barren of all vegetation save huge thorns and ungrateful thistles; and in it, on rocks, was shown the pelican, who tears his own entrails to feed his young, symbolical of the cruelty of love to true lovers. Finally, the fourth region was a melancholy cypress wood, among which roosted owls and ravens and other birds of evil omen, in order to display the fact that all earthly love leads but to death. Each of these regions was surrounded by a wreath of myrtles, marvellously drawn, and with great subtlety of invention divided so as to meet the carved and gilded cornice, likewise composed of myrtles, which Ser Piero executed with singular skill with his own hand. In the middle of the panel Desiderio had represented Love, even as the poet has described:[2] a naked youth, with wings of wondrous changing colours, enthroned upon a chariot, the axle and wheels of which were red gold, and covered with a cloth of gold of such subtle device that that whole chariot seemed really to be on fire; on his back hung a bow and a quiver full of dreadful arrows, and in his hands he held the reins of four snow-white coursers, trapped with gold, and breathing fire from their nostrils. Round his eyes was bound a kerchief fringed with gold, to show that Love strikes blindly; and from his shoulders floated a scroll inscribed with the words—'Sævus Amor hominum

into his fourth "region." However the scheme of the different landscapes representing the four phases of amorous passion is his own invention. Another Tuscan, Dante Alighieri (1265-1321), is the author of the visionary poem *La Divina Commedia* (*The Divine Comedy*) which describes its speaker's journey through Hell and Purgatory to Heaven. Translation: "doctissimi viri" means "very learned men." Publius Vigilius Maro, better known as Virgil (70-19 BC), Publius Ovidius Naso, better known as Ovid (43 BC-c. AD 18), and Publius Papinius Statius (c. AD 45-96) are all famous Latin poets.

1 Translation (Latin): "harsh and hard region."
2 Desiderio's central image of Love as a naked archer youth with coloured wings standing on a chariot drawn by four white horses is taken from Part 1 of Petrarch's poem. However he has added and embellished various details such as the kerchief, the golden wheels, and cloth of gold.

deorumque deliciæ.'[1] Round his car, some before, some behind, some on horseback, some on foot, crowded those who have been famous for their love. Here you might see, on a bay horse, with an eagle on his helmet, Julius Cæsar, who loved Cleopatra, the Queen of Egypt; Sophonisba and Massinissa, in rich and strange Arabian garments; Orpheus, seeking for Eurydice, with his lute; Phædra, who died for love of Hippolytus, her stepson; Mark Antony; Rinaldo of Montalbano, who loved the beautiful Angelica; Socrates, Tibullus, Virgilius and other poets, with Messer Francesco Petrarca and Messer Giovanni Boccaccio; Tristram, who drank the love-potion, riding on a sorrel horse; and near him, Isotta, wearing a turban of cloth of gold, and these lovers of Rimini, and many more besides, the naming of whom would be too long, even as the poet has described.[2] And in the region of

1   Translation (Latin): "Savage Love the darling of men and gods." Not in Petrarch.

2   Petrarch includes all these characters in a list which totals 170 people. Gaius Julius Caesar (102/100-44 BC), Roman politician, general and statesman and former lover of Cleopatra, queen of Egypt (69-30 BC). Cleopatra killed herself to avoid being paraded as a captive by Octavian (the future Emperor Augustus), following the suicide of her lover and consort, the former Roman politician and military commander, Mark Antony (83-30 BC). Sophonisba was a Carthaginian noblewoman and daughter of Hasdrubal. Captured after the defeat of her husband Syphax in 203 BC, she took poison rather than be taken to Rome as booty. Massinissa, a former ally of Hasdrubal, who had defected to the Romans, married Sophonisba but when Scipio the Roman commander refused to ratify the marriage, sent her poison so that she could avoid the humiliation of the triumphal parade. Orpheus, legendary poet-singer who, after the death of his beloved wife Eurydice, ventured down to the Underworld to reclaim her; Phaedra, afflicted by an unreciprocated passion for her step-son Hippolytus, had him killed after claiming he had raped her; Rinaldo of Montalbana (Montalban), cousin of Orlando and suitor of Angelica in the poems *Orlando innamorata* (1495) and *Orlando furioso* (1516/1532) by Boiardo and Ariosto respectively; Socrates (469-399 BC), Greek philosopher who in Plato's *Symposium* is represented analysing love; Albius Tibullus, Latin elegiac poet (c. 55-19 BC); Virgil (see note above); Giovanni Boccaccio (1313-75), Tuscan poet famous for the *Decameron*. Tristram and Isotta (Isolde) fall in love after unwittingly drinking a love potion intended for Isotta and her future husband, King Mark of Cornwall. The lovers of Rimini are Francesca, daughter of Guido da Polenta of Ravenna and Paolo Malatesta. Francesca was married by proxy to the hunchbacked lord of Rimini, Gianciotto Malatesta, but fell in love with the proxy, his brother Paolo. The two became lovers but, when they were discovered, Gianciotto killed them.

happy love, among the laurels, he had painted his own likeness, red-haired, with a green hood falling on his shoulders, and this because he was to wed, next St. John's Eve,[1] Maddalena, the only daughter of his employer, Ser Piero. And among the unhappy lovers, he painted, at his request, Messer Troilo himself, for whom he was making this coffer. And Messer Troilo was depicted in the character of Troilus, the son of Priam, Emperor of Troy;[2] he was habited in armour, covered with a surcoat of white cloth of silver embroidered with roses; by his side was his lance, and on his head a scarlet cap; behind him were those who carried his falcon and led his hack, and men-at-arms with his banner, dressed in green and yellow parti-coloured, with a scorpion embroidered on their doublet; and from his lance floated a pennon inscribed: 'Troilus sum servus Amoris.'[3]

But Desiderio refused to paint among the procession Monna Maddalena, Piero's daughter, who was to be his wife; because he declared that it was not fit that modest damsels should lend their face to other folk; and this he said because Ser Piero had begged him not to incense Messer Troilo; for in reality he had often pourtrayed Monna Maddalena (the which was marvellously lovely), though only, it is true, in the figure of Our Lady, the Mother of God.

And the panel was ready by Ascension Day, and Ser Piero had prepared the box, and the carvings and gildings, griffins and chimæras,[4] and acanthus leaves and myrtles, with the arms of Messer Troilo Baglioni, a most beautiful work. And Mastro Cavanna of the gate of St. Peter had made a lock and a key, of marvellous worksmanship, for the same coffer. And Messer Troilo would come frequently, riding over from his castle of

---

1   St. John's Eve (23 June). St John's Day (24 June), which commemorates the birth of John the Baptist, was traditionally a time when people gathered in beautiful spots such as hilltops and by rivers to feast.
2   Troilus, son of Priam, King of Troy, brother of Hector and Paris, and the lover of Cressida who betrayed him when she agreed to be the lover of the Greek warrior Diomedes. Troilus does not feature in Petrarch's poem.
3   Translation (Latin): "I am Troilus, Love's slave."
4   Griffins are fabulous creatures with an eagle's head and wings and a lion's body; chimaeras are grotesque monsters, and the original Chimaera of Greek myth was a fire-breathing creature with a lion's head, goat's body, and serpent's tail. The griffin is the device of the Baglioni and Perugia itself.

Fratta,[1] and see the work while it was progressing, and entertain himself lengthily at the shop, speaking with benignity and wisdom wonderful in one so young, for he was only nineteen, which pleased the heart of Ser Piero; but Desiderio did not relish, for which reason he was often gruff to Messer Troilo, and had many disputes with his future father-in-law.

For Messer Troilo Baglioni, called Barbacane,[2] to distinguish him from another Troilo, his uncle, who was bishop of Spello, although a bastard, had cast his eyes on Maddalena di Ser Piero Bontempi. He had seen the damsel for the first time on the occasion of the wedding festivities of his cousin Grifone Baglioni, son of Ridolfo the elder, with Deianira degli Orsini;[3] on which occasion marvellous things were done in the city of Perugia, both by the magnificent House of Baglioni and the citizens, such as banquets, jousts, horse-races, balls in the square near the cathedral, bull-fights, allegories, both Latin and vulgar, presented with great learning and sweetness (among which was the fable of Perseus, how he freed Andromeda, written by Master Giannozzo, Belli Rector venerabilis istæ universitatis[4]), and triumphal arches and other similar devices, in which Ser Piero Bontempi made many beautiful inventions, in company with Benedetto Bonfigli, Messer Fiorenzo di Lorenzo and Piero de Castro Plebis, whom the Holiness of our Lord Pope Sixtus IV. afterwards summoned to work in his chapel in Rome.[5] On this occasion, I repeat, Messer Troilo Baglioni of Fratta, who was *unanimiter*[6] declared to be a most beautiful and courteous youth, of singular learning and prowess, and well worthy of this magnificent Baglioni family, cast his eyes on Maddalena di Ser Piero, and sent her, through his

---

1   Fratta (renamed Umbertide in 1862) is an Umbrian town but is not in the Apennines, while Fratta Terme, a spa town in the Apennines in the Forlì area, seems too far distant.

2   "Buttress" or "fortification."

3   The account of this wedding is similar to details of the ill-fated wedding celebrations of Astorre Baglione and Lavinia Orsini in 1500 as related by Matarazzo in his *Chronicles*.

4   The Latin is grammatically imperfect but indicates something like "the fine Rector of that venerable university." Giannozzo is untraced.

5   Benedetto Bonfigli, early Renaissance painter (1420-96), Fiorenzo di Lorenzo (c. 1440-1522), painter of the Umbrian school from Perugia, Piero de Castro Plebis (who often signed his name as Petrus de Castro Plebis) is better known as Perugino (c. 1445-1523), famous Perugian painter and teacher of Raphael.

6   Translation (Latin): "unanimously."

squire, the knot of ribbons off the head of a ferocious bull, whom he had killed *singulari vi ac virtute*.[1] Nor did Messer Troilo neglect other opportunities of seeing the damsel, such as at church and at her father's shop, riding over from his castle at Fratta on purpose, but always *honestis valde modibus*,[2] as the damsel showed herself very coy, and refused all presents which he sent her. Neither did Ser Piero prevent his honestly conversing with the damsel, fearing the anger of the magnificent family of Baglioni. But Desiderio di Città del Lago, the which was affianced to Monna Maddalena, often had words with Ser Piero on the subject, and one day well-nigh broke the ribs of Messer Troilo's squire, whom he charged with carrying dishonest messages.

Now it so happened that Messer Troilo, as he was the most beautiful, benign, and magnanimous of his magnificent family, was also the most cruel therof, and incapable of brooking delay or obstacles. And being, as a most beautiful youth—he was only turned nineteen, and the first down had not come to his cheeks, and his skin was astonishingly white and fair like a woman's—of a very amorous nature (of which many tales went, concerning the violence he had done to damsels and citizens' wives of Gubbio and Spello and evil deeds in the castle of Fratta in the Apennines, some of which it is more beautiful to pass in silence than to relate), being, as I say, of an amorous nature, and greatly magnanimous and ferocious of spirit, Messer Troilo was determined to possess himself of this Maddalena di Ser Piero. So, a week after, having fetched away the wedding chest from Ser Piero's workshop (paying for it duly in Florentine lilies[3]), he seized the opportunity of the festivities of St. John's Nativity, when it is the habit of the citizens to go to their gardens and vineyards to see how the country is prospering, and eat and drink in honest converse with their friends, in order to satisfy his cruel wishes. For it so happened that the said Ser Piero, who was rich and prosperous, possessing an orchard in the valley of the Tiber near San Giovanni, was entertaining his friends there, it being the eve of his daughter's wedding, peaceful and unarmed. And a serving-

---

1 Translation (Latin): "with singular strength and virtue."
2 Translation (Latin): "completely honourable in his behaviour."
3 Florentine lilies, better known as a type of iris. The dried tubers are ground down to produce a scented powder known as orris-root which is widely used in perfumery. This would have made them a valuable commodity.

wench, a Moor[1] and a slave, who had been bribed by Messer Troilo, proposed to Monna Maddalena and the damsels of her company, to refresh themselves, after picking flowers, playing with hoops, asking riddles and similar girlish games, by bathing in the Tiber, which flowed at the bottom of the orchard. To this the innocent virgin, full of joyousness, consented. Hardly had the damsels descended into the river-bed, the river being low and easy to ford on account of the summer, when behold, there swept from the opposite bank a troop of horsemen, armed and masked, who seized the astonished Maddalena, and hurried off with her, vainly screaming, like another Proserpina,[2] to her companions, who, surprised, and ashamed at being seen with no garments, screamed in return, but in vain. The horsemen galloped off through Bastia, and disappeared long before Ser Piero and his friends could come to the rescue. Thus was Monna Maddalena cruelly taken from her father and bridegroom, through the amorous passion of Messer Troilo.

Ser Piero fell upon the ground fainting for grief, and remained for several days like one dead; and when he came to he wept, and cursed wickedly, and refused to take food and sleep, and to shave his beard. But being old and prudent, and the father of other children, he conquered his grief, well knowing that it was useless to oppose providence or fight, being but a handicraftsman, with the magnificent family of Baglioni, lords of Perugia since many years, and as rich and powerful as they were magnanimous and implacable. So that when people began to say that, after all, Monna Maddalena might have fled willingly with a lover, and that there was no proof that the masked horsemen came from Messer Troilo (although those of Bastia affirmed that they had seen the green and yellow colours of Fratta, and the said Troilo came not near the town for many months after), he never contradicted such words out of prudence and fear. But Desiderio of Castiglione del Lago, hearing these words, struck the old man on the mouth till he bled.

And it came to pass, about a year after the disappearance of Monna Maddalena, and when (particularly as there had been a plague in the city, and many miracles had been performed by a

---

1 Muslim member of the mixed Berber and Arab race inhabiting North West Africa, which in the eighth century conquered Spain.
2 Proserpina is the daughter of Demeter or Ceres. She was abducted by Pluto, god of the underworld, to be his queen when he found her gathering flowers in a meadow.

holy nun of the convent of Sant'Anna, the which fasted seventy days, and Messer Ascanio Baglioni had raised a company of horse for the Florentine Signiory in their war against those of Siena) people had ceased to talk of the matter, that certain armed men, masked, but wearing the colours of Messer Troilo, and the scorpion on their doublets, rode over from Fratta, bringing with them a coffer, wrapped in black baize, which they deposited overnight on Ser Piero Bontempi's doorstep. And Ser Piero, going at daybreak to his workshop, found that coffer; and recognising it as the same which had been made, with a panel representing the Triumph of Love and many ingenious devices of sculpture and gilding, for Messer Troilo, called Barbacane, he trembled in all his limbs, and went and called Desiderio, and with him privily carried the chest into a secret chamber in his house, saying not a word to any creature. The key, a subtle piece of work of the smith Cavanna, was hanging to the lock by a green silk string, on to which was tied a piece of parchment containing these words: 'To Master Desiderio; a wedding gift from Troilo Baglioni of Fratta'—an allusion, doubtless, *ferox atque cruenta facetia*,[1] to the Triumph of Love, according to Messer Francesco Petrarca, painted upon the front of the coffer. The lid being raised, they came to a piece of red cloth, such is used for mules; *etiam*, a fold of common linen; and below it, a coverlet of green silk, which, being raised, their eyes were met (*heu! infandum patri scelaratumque donus*[2]) by the body of Monna Maddalena, naked as God had made it, dead with two stabs in the neck, the long golden hair tied with pearls but dabbed in blood; the which Maddalena was cruelly squeezed into that coffer, having on her breast the body of an infant recently born, dead like herself.

When he beheld this sight Ser Piero threw himself on the floor and wept, and uttered dreadful blasphemies. But Desiderio of Castiglione del Lago said nothing, but called a brother of Ser Piero, a priest and a prior of Saint Severus, and with his assistance carried the coffer into the garden. This garden, within the walls of the city on the side of Porta Eburnea,[3] was pleasantly situated, and abounding in flowers and trees, useful both for their fruit and their shade, and rich likewise in all herbs as thyme, marjoram, fennel and many others, that prudent housewives desire

---

1   Translation (Latin): "a harsh and cruel joke."
2   Translation (Latin): *etiam* "moreover"; *heu! infandum* ... "alas, a gift of unspeakable wickedness for the father."
3   An Etruscan arch in Perugia restored in the mediaeval era.

for their kitchen; all watered by stone canals, ingeniously constructed by Ser Piero, which were fed from a fountain where you might see a mermaid squeezing the water from her breasts, a subtle device of the same Piero, and executed in a way such as would have done honour to Phidias or Praxiteles, on hard stone from Monte Catria.[1] In this place Desiderio of Castiglione del Lago dug a deep grave under an almond-tree, the which grave he carefully lined with stones and slabs of marble which he tore up from the pavement, in order to diminish the damp, and then requested the priest, Ser Piero's brother, who had helped him in the work, to fetch his sacred vestments, and books, and all necessary for consecrating that ground. This the priest immediately did, being a holy man and sore grieved for the case of his niece. Meanwhile, with the help of Ser Piero, Desiderio tenderly lifted the body of Monna Maddalena out of the wedding chest, washed it in odorous waters, and dressed it in fine linen and bridal garments, not without much weeping over the poor damsel's sad plight, and curses upon the cruelty of her ravisher; and having embraced her tenderly, they laid her once more in the box painted with the Triumph of Love, upon folds of fine damask and brocade, her hands folded, and her head decently placed upon a pillow of silver cloth, a wreath of roses, which Desiderio himself plaited, on her hair, so that she looked like a holy saint or the damsel Julia, daughter of the Emperor Augustus Cæsar, who was discovered buried on the Appian Way, and incontinently fell into dust—a marvellous thing.[2] They filled the chest with as many

1 Famous Greek sculptors of the fourth and fifth centuries BC; Monte Catria is in the Italian Marches.

2 The most famous version of this story is told by the anti-papal humanist lawyer Stefano Infessura (1435-1500) in his racy *Diarium urbis Romae* (*Diary of the City of Rome*), a chronicle embracing the period 1294-1494. Variant versions are provided by Nantiporto and also Matarazzo in his *Chronicles*. In Infessura's narrative the beautiful Julia is the daughter of Claudius and on her discovery in 1485 becomes the object of a cult until, at the behest of Pope Innocent VII, she is secretly stolen away and buried to prevent popular deviation from Christianity. John Addington Symonds retells the story in the first chapter of his *Renaissance in Italy* (Volume 1: *The Age of Despots*, 1875). Walter Pater quoted the story in his review of Symonds in *Academy* (31 July 1875) and Oscar Wilde repeats it in his essay "The Truth of Masks," first published as "Shakespeare and Stage Costume" in *The Nineteenth Century* in May 1885. A similar-sounding story about a male corpse falling to dust is related by Lee in her essay "Ravenna and her Ghosts," first published in *Macmillan's Magazine* in September 1894, and then reprinted in *Limbo and Other Essays to Which is Now added Ariadne in Mantua* (1908).

flowers as they could find, also sweet-scented herbs, bay-leaves, orris powder, frankincense, ambergris, and a certain gum called in Syrian fizelis, and by the Jews barach, in which they say that the body of King David was kept intact from earthly corruption, and which the priest, the brother of Ser Piero, who was learned in all alchemy and astrology, had bought of certain Moors.[1] Then, with many alases! and tears, they covered the damsel's face with an embroidered veil and a fold of brocade, and closing the chest, buried it in the hole, among great store of hay and straw and sand; and closed it up, and smoothed the earth; and to mark the place Desiderio planted a tuft of fennel under the almond-tree. But not before having embraced the damsel many times, and having taken a handful of earth from her grave, and eaten it, with many imprecations upon Messer Troilo, which it were terrible to relate. Then the priest, the brother of Ser Piero, said the service for the dead, Desiderio serving him as acolyte; and they all went their way, grieving sorely. But the body of the child, which had been found in the wedding chest, they threw down a place near Saint Herculanus, where the refuse and offal and dead animals are thrown, called the *Sardegna*; because it was the bastard of Ser Troilo, *et infamiæ scelerisque partum*.[2]

Then, as this matter got abroad, and also Desiderio's imprecations against Ser Troilo, Ser Piero, who was an old man and prudent, caused him to depart privily from Perugia, for fear of the wrath of the magnificent Orazio Baglioni, uncle of Messer Troilo and lord of the town.

Desiderio of Castiglione Lago went to Rome, where he did wonderful things and beautiful, among others certain frescoes in Saints Cosmas and Damian, for the Cardinal of Ostia; and to Naples, where he entered the service of the Duke of Calabria, and followed his armies long, building fortresses and making machines and models for cannon, and other ingenious and useful things. And thus for seven years, until he heard that Ser Piero was dead at Perugia of a surfeit of eels; and that Messer Troilo was in the city, raising a company of horse with his cousin Astorre Baglioni for the Duke of Urbino; and this was before the plague, and the terrible coming to Umbria of the Spaniards and renegade Moors, under Cæsar Borgia, *Vicarius Sanctæ Ecclesiæ, seu Flagel-*

---

1 Herbs, spices and unguents used to embalm and preserve dead bodies.
2 Translation: *Sardegna*, or more usually *Sardigna*, literally means "Sardinia," and signifies a dump for carcases and putrefying meat, perhaps by way of allusion to the supposed bad air of Sardinia. Translation: "and the child of infamy and wickedness."

lum Dei et novus Attila.[1] So Desiderio came back privily to Perugia, and put up his mule at a small inn, having dyed his hair black and grown his beard, after the manner of Easterns, saying he was a Greek coming from Ancona.[2] And he went to the priest, prior of Saint Severus, and brother of Ser Piero, and discovered himself to him, who, although old, had great joy in seeing him and hearing of his intent. And Desiderio confessed all his sins to the priest and obtained absolution, and received the Body of Christ with great fervour and compunction; and the priest placed his sword on the altar, beside the gospel, as he said mass, and blessed it. And Desiderio knelt and made a vow never to touch food save the Body of Christ till he could taste of the blood of Messer Troilo.

And for three days and nights he watched him and dogged him, but Messer Troilo rarely went unaccompanied by his men, because he had offended so many honourable citizens by his amorous fury, and he knew that his kinsmen dreaded him and would gladly be rid of him, on account of his ferocity and ambition, and their desire to unite the Fief of Fratta to the other lands of the main line of the magnificent House of Baglioni, famous in arms.

But one day, towards dusk, Desiderio saw Messer Troilo coming down a steep lane near Saint Herculanus,[3] alone, for he was going to a woman of light fame called Flavia Bella, the which was very lovely. So Desiderio threw some ladders, from a neighbouring house which was being built, and sacks across the road, and hid under an arch that spanned the lane, which was greatly steep and narrow. And Messer Troilo came down, on foot, whistling and paring his nails with a small pair of scissors. And he was dressed in grey silk hose, and a doublet of red cloth and gold brocade, pleated about the skirts, and embroidered with seed pearl and laced with gold laces; and on his head he had a hat of

---

1 Cæsare Borgia (1475-1507), the illegitimate son of Pope Alexander VI, a ruthless statesman and soldier, was active in his attempts to increase the territory of the papal states. In his *Chronicles* Matarazzo tells how in October 1500 Cæsare, en route to the Romagna, came with his army of Spaniards and other foreigners into the district of Perugia where they were quartered for several days and despoiled various of the neighbouring towns. Translation: "The Vicar [or Deputy] of Holy Church, or the Whip of God and the new Attila."

2 Ancona, town and port in the Italian Marches.

3 Thirteenth-century church of St. Ercolano in Perugia.

scarlet cloth with many feathers; and his cloak and sword he carried under his left arm. And Messer Troilo was twenty-six years old, but seemed much younger, having no beard, and a face like Hyacinthus or Ganymede, whom Jove stole to be his cupbearer, on account of his beauty.[1] And he was tall and very ferocious and magnanimous of spirit. And as he went, going to Flavia the courtesan, he whistled.

And when he came near the heaped-up ladders and the sacks, Desiderio sprang upon him, and tried to run his sword through him. But although wounded, Messer Troilo grappled with him long, but he could not get at his sword, which was entangled in his cloak; and before he could free his hand and get at his dagger, Desiderio had him down, and ran his sword three times through his chest, exclaiming, 'This is from Maddalena, in return for her wedding chest!'

And Messer Troilo, seeing the blood flowing out of his chest, knew he must die, and merely said—

'Which Maddalena? Ah, I remember, old Piero's daughter. She was always a cursed difficult slut,' and died.

And Desiderio stooped over his chest, and lapped up the blood as it flowed; and it was first food he tasted since taking the Body of Christ, even as he had sworn.

Then Desiderio went stealthily to the fountain under the arch of Saint Proxedis, where the women wash linen in the daytime, and cleansed himself a little from that blood. Then he fetched his mule and hid it in some trees near Messer Piero's garden. And at night he opened the door, the priest having given him the key, and went in, and with spade and mattock he had brought dug up the wedding chest with the body of Monna Maddalena in it; the which, owing to those herbs and virtuous gums, had dried up and become much lighter. And he found the spot by looking for the fennel tuft under the almond-tree, which was then in flower, it being spring. He loaded the chest, which was mouldy and decayed, on the mule, and drove the mule before him till he got to Castiglione del Lago, where he hid. And meeting certain horsemen, who asked what he carried in that box (for they took him for a thief), he answered his sweetheart; so they laughed and

1   In classical legend beautiful young boys beloved by male gods. Hyacinthus was beloved by the god Apollo while Ganymede was abducted by Zeus, in the shape of an eagle, to be his cupbearer. In his *Chronicles* Matarazzo describes Grifonetto Baglione as "a second Ganymede."

let him pass. Thus he got safely on to the territory of Arezzo, an ancient city of Tuscany, where he stopped.

Now when they found the body of Messer Troilo, there was much astonishment and wonder. And his kinsmen were greatly wroth; but Messer Orazio and Messer Ridolfo, his uncles, said: "'Tis as well; for indeed his courage and ferocity were too great, and he would have done some evil to us all had he lived.' But they ordered him a magnificent burial. And when he lay on the street dead, many folk, particularly painters, came to look at him for his great beauty; and the women pitied him on account of his youth, and certain scholars compared him to Mars, God of War, so great was his strength and ferocity even in death.[1] And he was carried to the grave by eight men-at-arms, and twelve damsels and youths dressed in white walked behind, strewing flowers, and there was much splendour and lamentation, on account of the great power of the magnificent House of Baglioni.

As regards Desiderio of Castiglione del Lago, he remained at Arezzo till his death, preserving with him always the body of Monna Maddalena in the wedding chest painted with the Triumph of Love, because he considered she had died *odore magnæ sanctitatis*.[2]

---

1 In his *Chronicles* Matarazzo describes Astorre Baglioni as "a very Mars" and "a second Mars."
2 Translation (Latin): "in the odour of great sanctity." The holiness and blamelessness of dead saints was believed to manifest itself in a sweet fragrance given off by their bodies.

Preface to "The Virgin of the Seven Daggers" (1927)[1]

Ex-voto dans le Goût Espagnol[2]

About the third unlikely story, that of Don Juan[3] and the Madonna, I feel an apology may perhaps be owing to so good a son of the Church as you[4] nowadays show yourself.

It does seem a trifle, shall we say? *profane* to bring these two celebrated characters into such friendly relations. But if it does, allow an old agnostic adorer of true Catholicism to reply that this is new-fangled prudishness, indeed one of the results of that movement (which you never cease deploring) erroneously called *Reformation*,[5] and of the consequent necessity on the part of the

---

1 The text of the preface is taken from Vernon Lee's introduction to *For Maurice: Five Unlikely Stories* (John Lane, The Bodley Head, 1927) xvi-xxii. "The Virgin of the Seven Daggers" is the third story of five in the collection.

2 Translation (French): "a votive offering in the Spanish style." Epigraph which accompanies Charles Baudelaire's poem "A Une Madone" published in *Les Fleurs du mal* (Flowers of Evil) (1857). At the end of the poem, the speaker refers to "seven well-sharpened knives" he intends to plant in his Madonna's heart. This image resonates with the figure of the Virgin of the Seven Daggers, also known as Our Lady of Sorrows, who is often depicted with seven daggers in her breast representing the Seven Sorrows of Mary.

3 Don Juan is a fictional character famous as a heartless womanizer. The legend of Don Juan was first written down by the Spanish dramatist, Tirso de Molina, in his tragedy *The Seducer of Seville* (1630). The story was subsequently taken up by many other artists including Wolfgang Amadeus Mozart, in the opera *Don Giovanni* (1787) and Lord Byron in his long satiric poem *Don Juan* (1819–24). Another Don Juan figure appears in Lee's *Juvenilia* (1887) in the essay "Don Juan (con Stenterello)," and aspects of this early work, including an encounter with a mysterious supernatural woman, and a confrontation with a dead mirror-image, remain in the later tale.

4 The introduction is addressed to Maurice Baring (1874-1945), a member of the banking family of Baring Brothers, British diplomat, linguist, author, and Catholic convert to whom the collection *For Maurice* (1927) is dedicated. Baring met Vernon Lee in 1893 and became a lifelong friend.

5 The religious revolution that took place in the Western church in the sixteenth century. Its greatest leaders were Martin Luther and John Calvin, the latter establishing a theocracy in Geneva after his conversion to the Protestant cause. Having far-reaching political, economic, and social effects, the Reformation became the basis for the founding of Protestantism, one of the three major branches of Christianity.

one and only true Church to take occasional hints from heretical upstarts. I allude to the Counter Reformation with its sour aping of Geneva.[1] Also, alas, the more recent puritanic deprecation of whatever, throughout ages of greater faith, had survived of the antique gods and their jovial rites: gods in exile no doubt, well bred émigrés, allowed occasional visits, as Heine and Pater have shown, and as I, though unworthy, have set forth in my more authentic version of the tale of Tannhäuser.[2] All of which the Ages of Faith took as matters of course, just as they buried, whenever facility offered as at Pisa, their properly shriven bodies in carved pagan coffins, whereon, as Goethe points out: "Faunen tanzen umher, mit der Bacchantinnen Chor."[3] All which habits of mind the acrid spirit of Calvin has forbidden you, latter day papists; more's the pity in the eyes of dispassioned unbelievers, and perchance of the amused heavenly hosts. Moreover, worst of all (which brings me back to the Madonna), tries to shoo away

---

1 In Roman Catholicism, efforts in the sixteenth and early seventeenth centuries to oppose the Protestant Reformation and reform the Catholic Church.

2 Christian Johann Heinrich Heine (1797/9-1856), German poet, critic, and satirist of Jewish origin. In his essay, "The Gods in Exile" (1853), Heine suggests that due to the triumph of Christianity, the ancient Greek gods had fallen into difficulties and subsequently walked the earth in disguise; Walter Pater (1839-94), English critic, essayist, and scholar who mentions Heine's idea of "gods in exile" in *Studies in the History of the Renaissance* (1873). See Appendix B. It later becomes a central motif in Pater's fictional works; Tannhäuser (c. 1200-70), was a professional minnesinger who served noble patrons. In the German legend (popular with Romantic writers), he lives with the goddess Venus a life of pleasure but, torn by remorse, goes to Rome to seek remission of his sins. The legend is famously retold by Richard Wagner in his opera *Tannhäuser* (first produced 1845). Vernon Lee's parodic version of the story appears as the first story in *For Maurice*.

3 Quotation from *Venetian Epigrams* I, (1790), by John Wolfgang von Goethe (1749-1832). The original reads: "Sarkophagen und Urnen verzierte der Heide mit Leben:/Faunen tanzen umher, mit der Bacchantinnen Chor/Machen sie bunte Reihe; der ziegengefüssete Pausback/Zwingt den heiseren Ton wild aus dem schmetternden Horn." Translation: "Pagan burial-urns and sarcophagi, how they adorned them/With so much life! How they leap, Bacchants in chorus and fauns,/Alternating their dance, as the goatfooted satyr with cheeks puffed/Forces the harsh wild notes out of his loud braying horn!" *Johann von Goethe: Selected Poetry*, tr. and ed. David Luke (London: Libris, 1999) 86, 87.

the little children, despite Christ's own express invitation, when they play about among sacred things: have I not noticed my devout Catholic friends averting their glance from the Virgin Mary's laced petticoats, silk stockings, embroidered *fichus*[1] and pocket-handkerchiefs which dear friendly little nuns drew one by one from sacristy presses, expecting, bless them! admiration for their loving pious work? I poured it out unstintingly; but then, as my French *bien pensant*[2] cousin remarked, Vernon is only a poor materialist. Consequently, shocked only by the more prudish or gruesome forms of religion.

Which leads me, dear papist Maurice,[3] to commence my apologia (if not apology) for the tale of that Spanish Madonna and her wicked admirer by declaring that if I have anywhere in my soul a secret shrine, it is to Our Lady. Even I don't like living in places which her benignant effigy does not consecrate to sweet and noble thoughts. For is she not the divine Mother of Gods as well as God, Demeter[4] or Mary, in whom the sad and ugly things of our bodily origin and nourishment are transfigured into the grace of the immortal spirit?

Now whatever some prudish prigs of the Romanist cloth (or laity!) may be shocked by in this tale of the Madonna of the Seven Daggers, is really the outcome of my devotion to the other Madonna, Mater Gratiæ.[5] Moreover, since it all hangs together, of my detestation for all that Counter-Reformation and especially Spanish cultus of death, damnation, tears and wounds, "du sang, de la volupté et de la mort," as expounded by its devotee Barrès;[6] Asiatic *fleurs du Mal* sprung of the blood of Adonis, and taking root in the Spanish mud half and half of *auto da fés* and bull fights.[7]

---

1 Light triangular scarves that are draped over the shoulders and fastened in front or worn to fill in a low neckline.
2 Translation (French): "right-minded."
3 Maurice Baring, see note above.
4 In Greek mythology, Demeter is the goddess of fertility, of corn, grain, and the harvest.
5 Translation (Latin): "Mother of Grace."
6 Translation (French): "of blood, of pleasure, and of death." This is the title of a travel book by Auguste-Maurice Barrès (1862-1923) published in 1893. Barrès was a French writer and politician, known for his fervent nationalism.
7 Translation (French): "flowers of evil," referring to Charles Baudelaire's collection of poems of the same name (see note above); translation (Portuguese): "act of faith"—a public ceremony during which the sentences upon those brought before the Spanish Inquisition were read and after which they were executed by the secular authorities.

I dare say I may have cultivated animosity against that great Spanish art of the Catholic Revival, have lacked appreciation of its technical innovations and psychological depth. Anyhow there it is: I detest the melancholy lymphatic Hapsburgs of Velasquez, the lousy, greedy beggars of Murillo, the black and white penitents of Ribera and Zurbaran, above all the elongated ecstatics and fervent dullards of Greco.[1]

I disliked it no doubt because of having grown up among Antique and Renaissance art. I disliked it from a temperamental intuition that there is cruelty in such mournfulness, and that cruelty is obscene. All of which aversion came to a head when I found myself, for reasons of health, banished to the South of Spain in mid-winter. No doubt the nervous depression this journey was meant to cure intensified my dislike for things Spanish. And just in proportion to that natural devotion of mine to the Beloved Lady and Mother, Italian or High Dutch, who opens her scanty drapery to suckle a baby divinity, just in proportion did that aversion concentrate on those doll-madonnas in Spanish churches, all pomp and whalebone and sorrow and tears wept into Mechlin lace.[2] Feeling like this it seemed natural that the typical Spanish hero (for dear Don Quixote was at once made European by translators like Skelton), the offspring of ruthless Conquistadores, should be the conquering super-rake and super-ruffian, decoying women, murdering fathers, insulting even dead men and glorying in wickedness: Don Juan in one of his (not at all Mozartian or Byronian) legendary impersonations, like Don

---

1 Hapsburgs, royal German family, one of the principal sovereign dynasties of Europe from the fifteenth to the twentieth century; Diego Rodriguez da Silva Velásquez (1599-1660), Spanish artist who worked during the reign of the Spanish Hapsburgs. He became court painter to Philip IV of Spain; Bartolomé Esteban Murillo (1618-82), Spanish Baroque religious painter of the seventeenth century. He was the first Spanish artist to achieve fame outside the Spanish world; José de Ribera (c. 1591-1652), Spanish painter and printmaker, noted for his Baroque dramatic realism and his depictions of religious and mythological subjects; Francisco de Zurbarán (1598-1664), major painter of the Spanish Baroque, especially noted for religious subjects; Doménikos Theotokópoulos, known as "El Greco" (1541-1614), Cretan-born Spanish artist who painted in a highly individual dramatic and expressionistic style. He also worked as a sculptor and as an architect.

2 A kind of handmade lace made at, or originating in Mechlin, Belgium, defined by its distinctive mesh and particularly common during the eighteenth century.

Miguel de Mañara or Calderon's Ludovic Enio.[1] And natural, furthermore, that he and that knife-riddled Spanish Madonna should be united by common ancestry in the wickedness of man's imagination, but also by a solemn compact; that Don Juan's one and only act of faith in his career of faithlessness should be towards her, and be what deprived Hell of his distinguished presence.

So, in those icy winter afternoons when sunset put sinister crimson on the snowy mountains and on the turbid torrent beneath the Alhambra, there shaped itself in my mind what Baudelaire called an Ex-Voto dans le Goût Espagnol, the imagined story coagulating round one of the legends told me many years before by that strange friend who used to boast, in his queer Andalusian French, that "Yé suis Arave."[2] Meaning Moorish. Moorish! For there had been other folks, as terrible maybe, but far more brilliant and amiable, before the coming of Don Juan and his farthingaled madonna of the many poignards. What brought home to me this alleviating circumstance was what I chanced to witness one unforgettable winter morning. A snowstorm from the Sierra had raged all night; but now the towers of the Alhambra stood out like rose-carnations against the washed and sunny blue. And behold a miracle! the snow melting on the

---

1   Don Quixote, fictional hero created by the Spanish author, Miguel de Cervantes (1547-1616), in his novel *El Ingenioso Hidalgo Don Quijote de la Mancha* published in two parts (Part I, 1605; Part II, 1615); Thomas Shelton (not Skelton) is credited with translating Part I of Cervantes' *Don Quijote* into English in 1612, and Part II in 1620; the Conquistadores were a small group of adventurers who took part in the Spanish conquest of South and Central America in the sixteenth century; for Don Juan, see note above; Don Miguel de Mañara was a seventeenth-century nobleman on whom the legend of Don Juan is based. There are two common versions of Mañara's career. In the first he is rich and frivolous. He repents of his sins and enters the religious order, the Caridad, after meeting a funeral procession where he sees a corpse he thinks looks exactly like himself, reading this as a warning. In the second version, Mañara dedicates himself to the religious brotherhood after the death of his beloved wife in 1661. He is buried in the almshouse of the Caridad order in Seville. Vernon Lee's story seems to be based on the first version of Mañara's life; Pedro Calderón de la Barca (1600-81), Spanish dramatist and poet of the Golden Age. Among his best-known religious dramas is *El Purgatorio de San Patricio* (*The Purgatory of St. Patrick*) (1628), in which the character of Ludovico Enio appears. Enio is a villain redeemed by his ardent faith.

2   José Fernandez Gimenez, Spanish diplomat who was among the many international visitors who frequented the Paget family home at No. 12 Via Solferino, Florence, in the 1880s.

imbricated roofs and dripping into the tanks and channels, broke their long-dormant waters into wide ripples, till the whole imaged palace swayed gently, as if awakening to life. There was an Infanta, so my friend had told me, buried with all her treasure and court somewhere beneath the deserted Moorish palace.... And with the vision in those jade green waters, there wavered into my mind the suspicion that there might well have been an almost successful rival of Don Juan's gloomy Madonna, a temptation worthy of his final damnation along with a supreme renunciation worthy of his being, at last, saved.

I helped out the notion, in returning from Spain, by re-reading a book much thumbed in childhood, Lane's *Arabian Nights* with enchanting (why aren't they re-published?) illustrations by William Harvey.[1] There was also a brief glimpse of real Moors at Tangier, especially of a little Moorish bride, with blue and red triangles painted on her cheeks like my Infanta's.

So the story got drawn and coloured in my head, and was ready to write out, with scarcely a correction, the summer following on that Spanish journey, sitting on a grassy terrace above the Worcestershire Avon,[2] while my old friend John[3] (of whom more in the next chapter) tramped to and fro his easel, shouting "demons, demons!" in his struggle to paint the moving willow-reflections, the elusive, fantastic flickers on the water....

Having told you all which, and pointed out that just at that moment *you* must have been the cruelly disappointed little boy cursing my still unknown self for wasting his pocket money on that book of mine,[4] let me end this apologia of Don Juan and his Madonna, begging you, my dear Maurice, to offer up a tiny little prayer (*une toute petite prière* such as the bonne Sœur at the Beaune hospital promised me when I gave her five francs *pour ses malades*[5]), the tiniest little prayer in expiation of my (surely venial?) profanity.

---

1 Expurgated edition translated and annotated by Edward William Lane and illustrated by William Harvey which was issued in monthly parts by C. Knight & Co. between 1839-41, before being published in three-volume form by the same company.

2 The Avon is a river in the counties of Northamptonshire, Warwickshire, Worcestershire, and Gloucestershire in the midlands of England.

3 John Singer Sargent (1856-1925).

4 Lee is here referring to a story told to her by Baring, who, having been enthralled, as a child, by Lee's *The Prince of the Hundred Soups*, and having noted from the title page that the book was "by the author of *Belcaro*," saved five shillings to buy the latter only to find that it was an aesthetic treatise.

5 Translation (French): "for her patients."

The Virgin of the Seven Daggers[1]

A Moorish Ghost Story of the Seventeenth Century

Dedicated, in remembrance of the Spanish legends he was wont to tell me, to my friend of forty years back, José-Fernandez Gimenez[2]

I

IN a grass-grown square of the city of Grenada,[3] with the snows of the Sierra staring down on it all winter, and the well-nigh Africa sun glaring on its coloured tiles all summer, stands the yellow freestone Church of Our Lady of the Seven Daggers. Huge garlands of pears and melons hang, carved in stone, about the cupolas and windows; and monstrous heads with laurel wreaths and epaulets burst forth from all the arches. The roof shines barbarically, green, white and brown, above the tawny stone; and on each of the two balconied and staircased belfries, pricked up like ears above the building's monstrous front, there sways a weather-vane, figuring a heart transfixed with seven long-hilted daggers. Inside, the church presents a superb example of the pompous, pedantic and contorted Spanish architecture of the reign of the later Philips.[4] On colonnade is hoisted colonnade, pilasters climb upon pilasters, bases and capitals jut out, double and threefold, from the ground, in mid-air and near the ceiling; jagged lines everywhere as of spikes for exhibiting the heads of traitors; dizzy ledges as of mountain precipices for dashing to bits Morisco rebels;[5] line warring with line and curve with curve; a

---

1 The story was originally published in French as "La Madone aux sept glaives" in *Feuilleton du journal des débats du Samedi*, February 8, 9, 11, 12, 14, 1896. It was first published in English in two parts in the issues of January and February 1909 of *The English Review* (1908-9), 223-33; 453-65. This text is taken from *For Maurice*, pp. 95-140, dedicated to Lee's friend, Maurice Baring (see notes to the preface above).

2 See note on Gimenez above.

3 The capital of the province of Granada (not Grenada), in Andalucia, Southern Spain, situated along the Genil River, at the northwestern slope of the Sierra Nevada.

4 There were five Philips who reigned in Spain. The first, under the name of Charles I was on the throne between 1516-56, the last, Philip V, who was the first of the Bourbon dynasty, reigned between 1700-24; 1725-46.

5 "Morisco," in Spanish, means "little moor," and refers to the Spanish Muslims (or their descendants) who became baptized Christians in order to avoid persecution.

place in which the mind staggers bruised and half-stunned. But the grandeur of the church is not merely terrific; it is also gallant and ceremonious: everything on which labour can be wasted is laboured, everything on which gold can be lavished is gilded; columns and architraves curl like the curls of a periwig; walls and vaultings are flowered with precious marbles and fretted with carving and gilding like a gala dress; stone and wood are woven like lace: stucco is whipped and clotted like pastry-cooks' cream and crust; everything is crammed with flourishes like a tirade by Calderon, or a sonnet by Gongora.[1] A golden retablo[2] closes the church at the end; a black and white rood screen, of jasper and alabaster, fences it in the middle; while along each aisle hang chandeliers as for a ball; and paper flowers are stacked on every altar.

Amidst all this gloomy yet festive magnificence, and sur-rounded, in each minor chapel, by a train of waxen Christs with bloody wounds and spangled loin-cloths, and Madonnas of lesser fame weeping beady tears and carrying bewigged Infants, thrones the great Virgin of the Seven Daggers.

Is she seated or standing? 'Tis impossible to decide. She seems, beneath the gilded canopy and between the twisted columns of jasper, to be slowly rising, or slowly sinking, in a solemn court curtsey, buoyed up by her vast farthingale. Her skirts bulge out in melon-shaped folds, all damasked with minute heartsease, and brocaded with silver roses; the reddish shimmer of the gold wire, the bluish shimmer of the silver floss, blending into a strange melancholy hue without a definite name. Her body is cased like a knife in its sheath, the mysterious russet and violet of the silk made less definable still by the network of seed pearl, and the veils of delicate lace falling from head to waist. Her face, which surmounts rows upon rows of pearls, is made of wax, white with black glass eyes and a tiny coral mouth. Her head is crowned with a great jewelled crown; her slippered feet rest on a crescent moon, and in her right hand she holds a lace pocket-handker-chief. She stares steadfastly forth with a sad and ceremonious smile. In her bodice, a little clearing is made among the brocade and the seed pearl, and into this are stuck seven gold-hilted knives.

---

1 Pedro Calderón de la Barca (1600-81): see notes to preface; Luis de Góngora y Argote (1561-1627), Spanish poet known for his Baroque, convoluted style, known as Gongorism (*gongorismo*).
2 A votive picture displayed in church.

Such is Our Lady of the Seven Daggers; and such her church.

One winter afternoon, more than two hundred years ago, Charles the Melancholy being King of Spain and the New World,[1] there chanced to be kneeling in that church, already empty and dim save for the votive lamps, and more precisely on the steps before the Virgin of the Seven Daggers, a cavalier of very great birth, fortune, magnificence, and wickedness, Don Juan[2] Gusman del Pulgar, Count of Miramor. "O great Madonna, O Snow Peak untrodden of the Sierras, O Sea unnavigated of the tropics, O Gold Ore unhandled by the Spaniard, O New Minted Doubloon unpocketed by the Jew"[3]—thus prayed that devout man of quality—"look down benignly on thy knight and servant, accounted judiciously one of the greatest men of this kingdom, in wealth and honours, fearing neither the vengeance of foes, nor the rigour of laws, yet content to stand foremost among thy slaves. Consider that I have committed every crime without faltering, both murder, perjury, blasphemy, and sacrilege, yet I have always respected thy name, nor suffered any man to give greater praise to other Madonnas, neither her of Good Counsel, nor her of Swift Help, nor our Lady of Mount Carmel, nor our Lady of St. Luke of Bologna in Italy, nor our Lady of the Slipper of Famagosta in Cyprus, nor our Lady of the Pillar of Saragossa,[4] great Madonnas every one, and revered throughout the world for their

---

1 Charles II of Spain (1661-1700), the last of the Hapsburg dynasty who reigned over Spain, Naples, Sicily, and areas of the New World appropriated by the conquistadores in the sixteenth century from 1661-1700.

2 See notes to preface above.

3 Don Juan's prayer appears to be a parody of the Litany of the Virgin Mary.

4 A combination of real and fictional virgins. Our Lady of Good Counsel is also known as Our Lady of Paradise, and is said to have appeared at Genazzano, a town about twenty-five miles southeast of Rome on St. Mark's Day, 25 April, 1467, in the old church of Santa Maria; Our Lady of Swift Help does not exist, but requests for "swift help" appear in some prayers to the Virgin Mary; Our Lady of Mount Carmel is the virgin who presides over the church of Mount Carmel in Israel, a chapel erected in her honour before her Assumption into heaven. She is the patron of the Carmelite order; Our Lady of St. Luke in Bologna appears in an ancient image found in the chapel of St. Mary Major in Bologna, also venerated as Our Lady of Rome; Our Lady of the Slipper of Famagosta is fictional; Our Lady of the Pillar is the protectress of Saragossa, who is said to have descended from heaven standing on a pillar when she appeared to St. James the Apostle.

powers, and by most men preferred to thee; yet has thy servant, Juan Gusman del Pulgar, ever asserted, with words and blows, their infinite inferiority to thyself. Give me, therefore, O Great Madonna of the Seven Daggers, I pray thee, the promise that thou wilt save me ever from the clutches of Satan, as thou has wrested me ever on earth from the King's Alguazils and the Holy Officer's delators,[1] and let me never burn in eternal fire in punishment of my sins. Neither think that I ask too much, for I swear to be provided always with absolution in all rules, whether by employing my own private chaplain or using violence thereunto to any monk, priest, canon, dean, bishop, cardinal, or even the Holy Father himself. Grant me this boon, O Burning Water and Cooling Fire, O Sun that shineth at midnight, and Galaxy that resplendeth at noon—grant me this boon, and I will assert always with my tongue and my sword, in the face of His Majesty and at the feet of my latest love, that although I have been beloved of all the fairest women of the world, high and low, both Spanish, Italian, German, French, Dutch, Flemish, Jewish, Saracen, and Gipsy, to the number of many hundreds, and by seven ladies, Dolores, Fatma, Catalina, Elvira, Violante, Azahar, and Sister Seraphita, for each of whom I broke a commandment and took several lives (the last, moreover, being a cloistered nun, and therefore a case of inexpiable sacrilege), despite all this I will maintain before all men and all the Gods of Olympus that no lady was ever so fair as our Lady of the Seven Daggers of Grenada."

The church was filled with ineffable fragrance; exquisite music, among which Don Juan seemed to recognize the voice of Syphax,[2] His Majesty's own soprano singer, murmured amongst the cupolas, and the Virgin of the Seven Daggers, slowly dipped in her lace and silver brocade farthingale, rising as slowly again to her full height, and inclined her white face imperceptibly towards her jewelled bosom.

The Count of Miramor clasped his hands in ecstasy to his breast; then he arose, walked quickly down the aisle, dipped his

---

1 Algauzils are warrant or police officers; delators are informers.
2 Although not explicitly stated, Syphax, the soprano singer, is most probably a castrato as women were not permitted to sing in church. This prohibition on women's voices led the Church of Rome to import Spanish falsettists during the sixteenth century, who are now thought to have been castrati.

fingers in the black marble holy water stoop, threw a sequin[1] to the beggar who pushed open the leathern curtain, put his black hat covered with black ostrich feathers on his head, dismissed a company of bravos and guitar players who awaited him in the square, and, gathering his black cloak about him, went forth, his sword tucked under his arm, in search of Baruch, the converted Jew of the Albaycin.[2]

Don Juan Gusman del Pulgar, Count of Miramor, Grandee of the First Class, Knight of Calatrava, and of the Golden Fleece, and Prince of the Holy Roman Empire,[3] was thirty-two and a great sinner. This cavalier was tall, of large bone, his forehead low and cheekbones high, chin somewhat receding, aquiline nose, white complexion and black hair; he wore no beard, but moustachios cut short over the lip and curled upwards at the corners leaving the mouth bare; his hair flat, parted through the middle and falling nearly to his shoulders. His clothes when bent on business or pleasure, were most often of black satin, slashed with black. His portrait has been painted by Domingo Zurbaran of Seville.[4]

II

All the steeples of Grenada seemed agog with bell-ringing; the big bell on the tower of the Sail clanging irregularly into the more professional tinklings and roarings, under the vigorous, but flurried pulls of the damsels, duly accompanied by their well-ruffed duennas, who were ringing themselves a husband for the newly

---

1   Here, a gold coin used in Venice and Turkey between the sixteenth and eighteenth century.

2   The Albaycin (or Albaicin): an old quarter of the town. In the mediaeval period, the area was inhabited by both Jews and Arabs.

3   Grandee: a title of honour borne by the highest class of the Spanish nobility; a Knight of Calatrava belongs to one of Spain's major military and religious orders and a Knight of the Golden Fleece is a member of one of the highest-ranking, and most prestigious orders of the crown of Spain; as a Prince of the Holy Roman Empire, Don Juan would be one of the "electors" drawn from senior rulers of lands within the empire, who had the function of electing the king of Germany preparatory to his accession as the next emperor. The practice began in the thirteenth century and continued until the empire's end in 1806.

4   Probably Francisco de Zurbarán of Seville (1598-1662) whose dates would coincide approximately with the chronology of Lee's story.

begun year, according to the traditions of the city. Green garlands decorated the white glazed balconies, and banners with the arms of Castile and Aragon, and the pomegranate of Grenada, waved or drooped alongside of the hallowed palm-branches over the carved escutcheons on the doors.[1] From the barracks arose a practising of fifes and bugles; and from the little wineshops on the outskirts of the town a sound of guitar strumming and castagnets. The coming day was a very solemn feast for the city, being the anniversary of its liberation from the rule of the Infidels.

But although all Grenada felt festive, in anticipation of the grand bullfight of the morrow, and the grand burning of heretics and relapses in the square of Bibrambla, Don Juan Gusman del Pulgar, Count of Miramor, was fevered with intolerable impatience, not for the following day, but for the coming and tediously lagging night.

Not, however, for the reason which had made him a thousand times before upbraid the Sun God, in true poetic style, for displaying so little of the proper anxiety to hasten the happiness of one of the greatest cavaliers of Spain. The delicious heart-beating with which he had waited, sword under his cloak, for the desired rope to be lowered from a mysterious window, or the muffled figure to loom from round a corner; the fierce joy of awaiting, with a band of gallant murderers, some inconvenient father, or brother, or husband on his evening stroll; the rapture even, spiced with awful sacrilege, of stealing in amongst the lemon-trees of that cloistered court, after throwing the Sister Portress to tell-tale in the convent well—all, and even this, seemed to him trumpery and mawkish.

Don Juan sprang from the great bed, covered and curtained with dull, blood-coloured damask, on which he had been lying

---

1   Castile and Aragon is the united kingdom which came into existence by the marriage (1469) of Isabella, heiress of Castile, to Ferdinand the Catholic, King of Aragon, which in the course of history became the Kingdom of Spain, or, more precisely, of the Spains; the Castilian word for "pomegranate" is "granada" and the fruit is the heraldic device which symbolizes the city. However, the name "Granada" seems to have been bestowed by Moorish invaders in AD 711 who called the city "Gharnatah," possibly after a Jewish community known as the Gránata who helped to define the character of the region from the third century onwards. The similarity between the Moorish and the Castilian words is seemingly purely coincidental. Legend also suggests that the city may have been named after Granata, daughter of Hercules, who may have settled there.

dressed, vainly courting sleep, beneath a painted hermit, black and white in his lantern-jawedness, fondling a handsome skull. He went to the balcony, and looked out of one of its glazed windows. Below a marble goddess shimmered among the myrtle hedges and the cypresses of the tiled garden, and the pet dwarf of the house played at cards with the chaplain, the chief bravo, and a thread-bare poet who was kept to make the odes and sonnets required in the course of his master's daily courtships.

"Get out of my sight, you lazy scoundrels, all of you!" cried Don Juan, with a threat and an oath alike terrible to repeat, which sent the party, bowing and scraping as they went, scattering their cards, and pursued by his lordship's jack-boots, guitar, and missal.

Then Don Juan stood at the window rapt in contemplation of the towers of the Alhambra,[1] their tips still reddened by the departing sun, their bases already lost in the encroaching mists, on the hill yon side of the river.

He could just barely see it, that Tower of the Cypresses, where the magic hand held the key engraven on the doorway, about which, as a child, his nurse from the Morisco village of Andarax[2] had told such marvellous stories of hidden treasures and slumbering infantas. He stood long at the window, his lean white hands clasped on the rail as on the handle of his sword, gazing out with knit brows and clenched teeth, and that look which made men hug the wall and drop aside on his path.

Ah! how different from any of his other loves! the only one, decidedly, at all worthy of lineage as great as his, and a character as magnanimous. Catalina, indeed, had been exquisite when she danced, and Elvira was magnificent at a banquet, and each had long possessed his heart, and had cost him, one many thousands of doubloons for a husband, and the other the death of a favourite fencing-master, killed in a fray with her relations. Violante had been a Venetian worthy of Titian,[3] for whose sake he had been

---

1   Palace of the Moorish monarchs of Granada, Spain, built (1238–1358) on a plateau above the city. Its name (Arabic: "the red") may refer to the colour of the sun-dried bricks used in its outer walls.

2   Andarax is a village in Andalucia, Southern Spain. During the persecution of the Moriscos during the reign of Queen Isabella, Christian midwives were posted in every Morisco village. They would supervise all the pregnant women and, as soon as a baby was born, would call the priest so that the child could be baptized immediately. It seems that Don Juan's nurse might have been one of the women involved.

3   Tiziano Vecellio, known in England as "Titian" (c. 1477-1576), Italian Renaissance painter of the Venetian school.

imprisoned beneath the ducal palace, escaping only by the massacre of three gaolers; for Fatma, the Sultana of the King of Fez, he had well-nigh been impaled, and for shooting the husband of Dolores he had very nearly been broken on the wheel; Azahar, who was called so because of her cheeks like white jessamine,[1] he had carried off at the church door, out of the arms of her bridegroom; without counting that he had cut down her old father, a Grandee of the First Class. And as to Sister Seraphita—she had indeed seemed worthy of him, and Seraphita had nearly come up to his idea of an angel. But oh! what had any of these ladies cost him compared with what he was about to risk to-night? Let alone the chance of being roasted by the Holy Office (after all, he had already run that, and the risk of more serious burning hereafter also, in the case of Sister Seraphita) what if the business proved a swindle of that Jewish hound, Baruch?—Don Juan put his hand on his dagger and his black moustachios bristled up at the bare thought; let alone the possibility of imposture (though who could be so bold as to venture to impose upon him?) the adventure was full of dreadful things. It was terrible, after all, to have to blaspheme the Holy Catholic Apostolic Church, and all her saints, and inconceivably odious to have to be civil to that dog of a Mahomet of theirs; also, he had not much enjoyed a previous experience of calling up devils, who had smelt most vilely of brimstone and assafœtida,[2] besides using most uncivil language; and he really could not stomach that Jew Baruch, whose trade among others consisted in procuring for the Archbishop a batch of renegade Moors, who were solemnly dressed in white and baptized afresh every year. It was detestable that this fellow should even dream of obtaining the treasure buried under the Tower of the Cypresses. Then, there were the traditions of his family, descended in direct line from the Cid, and from that Fernan del Pulgar, who had nailed the Ave Maria to the Mosque; and half his other ancestors were painted with their foot on a Moor's decollated head, much resembling a hairdresser's block; and their very title, Miramor, was derived from a castle which had been built in full Moorish territory to stare the Moor out of countenance.[3]

---

1   Variant of jasmine.

2   The fœtid gum resin of a large umbelliferous plant (*Ferula asafoetida*) of Persia and the East Indies. It is used in medicine as an antispasmodic.

3   El Cid (Spanish, from Arabic "*al-sid*" meaning "lord") was Rodrigo Díaz de Vivar (c. 1043-99), a Castilian military leader and national hero; although Lee's Don Juan appears to be a fictional character, there

But after all, this only made it more maginificent, more deli-cious, more worthy of so magnanimous and highborn a cava-lier.... "Ah, princess ... more exquisite than Venus, more noble than Juno, and infinitely more agreeable than Minerva," ... sighed Don Juan at his window.[1] The sun had long since set, making a trail of blood along the distant river reach, among the sere spider-like poplars, turning the snows of the Mulhacen[2] a livid, bluish blood-red, and leaving all along the lower slopes of the Sierra wicked russet stains, as of the rust of blood upon marble. Dark-ness had come over the world, save where some illuminated court-yard, or window, suggested preparations for next day's revelry; the air was piercingly cold, as if filled with minute snow-flakes from the mountains. The joyful singing had ceased; and from a neighbouring church there came only a casual death toll, executed on a cracked and lugubrious bell. A shudder ran through Don Juan. "Holy Virgin of the Seven Daggers, take me under thy benign protection," he murmured mechanically.

A discreet knock aroused him.

"The Jew Baruch—I mean his worship, Señor Don Bonaven-tura," announced the page.

---

existed mediaeval Spanish noblemen bearing the names of both Gusman (spelt Guzmán), and del Pulgar. These were Fernán Pérez de Guzmán (c. 1378-1460), and Fernando del Pulgar (c. 1436-93): both were historians and writers; on the opening page of Woolf's novel, *Orlando* (1928), the eponymous hero is in the act of "slicing at the head of a Moor" decapitated and brought back to the ancestral home by Orlando's forefathers who, like those of Don Juan, appear to have fought in a war with the Moors. While Woolf was often damning about Lee's writing, and sought to distance herself from her, Lee's influence on *Orlando* and other key Woolfian texts is notable.

1 In Roman mythology, Venus was the goddess of sexual love and beauty, associated with the Greek Aphrodite; Juno was chief goddess and the female counterpart of Jupiter, closely resembling the Greek Hera, with whom she was universally identified; Minerva, the goddess of handi-crafts, the professions, the arts, and, later, war, was commonly identified with the Greek Athena, goddess of wisdom.

2 The highest peak on the Spanish mainland, situated in the Sierra Nevada, about thirty-two kilometres southeast of Granada.

III

The Tower of the Cypresses, destroyed almost in our times by the explosion of a powder magazine, formed part of the inner defences of the Alhambra. In the middle of its horse-shoe arch was engraved a huge hand holding a flag-shaped key, which was said to be that of a subterranean and enchanted palace; and the two great cypress trees, uniting in their shadows into one tapering cone of black, were said to point, under a given position of the moon, to the exact spot where the wise King Yahya, of Cordova,[1] had judiciously buried his jewels, his plate, and his favourite daughter many hundred years ago.

At the foot of this tower, and in the shade of those cypresses, Don Juan ordered his companion to spread out his magic paraphernalia. From a neatly packed basket, beneath which he had staggered up the steep hill-side in the moonlight, the learned Jew produced a book, a variety of lamps, some packets of frankincense, a pound of dead man's fat, the bones of a stillborn child who had been boiled by the witches, a live cock that had never crowed, a very ancient toad, and sundry other rarities, all of which he proceeded to dispose in the latest necromantic fashion, while the Count of Miramor mounted guard sword in hand. But when the fire was laid, the lamps lit, and the first layer of ingredients had already been placed in the cauldron; nay, when he had even borrowed Don Juan's embroidered pocket-handkerchief to envelop the cock that had never crowed, Baruch, the Jew, suddenly flung himself down before his patron, and implored him to desist from the terrible enterprise for which they had come.

"I have come hither," wailed the Jew, "lest your Lordship should possibly entertain doubts of my obligingness. I have run the risk of being burned alive in the Square of Bibrambla tomorrow morning before the bullfight; I have imperilled my eternal soul, and laid out large sums of money in the purchase of the necessary ingredients, all of which are abomination in the eyes of a true Jew—I mean of a good Christian. But now I implore your lordship to desist. You will see things so terrible that to mention them is impossible; you will be suffocated by the vilest stenches, and shaken by earthquakes and whirlwinds, besides having to listen to imprecations of the most horrid sort; you will have to blaspheme our Holy Mother Church and invoke Mahomet—may

---

1 Yahya ibn 'Ali (1024-27), penultimate Caliph of the Umayyad dynasty which ruled Cordoba between 755-1031.

he roast everlastingly in hell; you will infallibly go to hell yourself in due course; and all this for the sake of a paltry treasure of which it will be most difficult to dispose to the pawnbrokers; and of a lady, about whom, thanks to my former medical position in the harem of the Emperor of Tetuan,[1] I may assert with probability that she is fat, ill-favoured, stained with henna and most disagreeably redolent of camphor...."

"Peace, villain!" cried Don Juan, snatching him by the throat and pulling him violently on to his feet; "prepare thy messes and thy stinks, begin thy antics, and never dream of offering advice to a cavalier like me. And, remember, one other word against her Royal Highness my bride, against the Princess whom her own father has been keeping three hundred years for my benefit, and, by the Virgin of the Seven Daggers, thou shalt be hurled into yonder precipice; which, by the way, will be a very good move, in any case, when thy services are no longer wanted." So saying, he snatched from Baruch's hand the paper of responses, which the necromancer had copied out from his book of magic; and began to study it by the light of a supernumerary lamp.

"Begin!" he cried. "I am ready, and thou, great Virgin of the Seven Daggers, guard me!"

"Jab, jab, jam—Credo in Grilgroth, Astaroth et Rappatun; trish, trash, trum,"[2] began Baruch in faltering tones, as he poked a flame-tipped reed under the cauldron.

"Patapol, Valde Patapol," answered Don Juan from his paper of responses.

The flame of the cauldron leaped up with a tremendous smell of brimstone. The moon was veiled, the place was lit up crimson, and a legion of devils with the bodies of apes, the talons of eagles, and the snouts of pigs suddenly appeared in the battlements all round.

"Credo," again began Baruch; but the blasphemies he gabbled out, and which Don Juan indignantly echoed, were such as cannot possibly be recorded. A hot wind rose, whirling a desert-

---

1 Tetuán or Tétouan: city in north-central Morocco. It lies along the Wadi Martin, seven miles (eleven kilometres) from the Mediterranean Sea.
2 This appears to be a parody of the Creed, and Baruch's invocations and Don Juan's responses are constructed of mostly nonsense words.
   However, in demonology, Astaroth is a demon who governs 40 Legions. He appears as a hurtful angel riding a dragon-like beast and carries a viper in his right hand. He gives true answers, knows of past, present and future events, and can discover secrets.

ful of burning sand which stung like gnats; the bushes were on fire, each flame turned into a demon like a huge locust or scorpion, who uttered piercing shrieks and vanished, leaving a choking atmosphere of melted tallow.

"Fal lal Polychronicon Nebuzaradon,"[1] continued Baruch.

"Leviathan! Esto nobis!"[2] answered Don Juan.

The earth shook, the sound of millions of gongs filled the air, and a snowstorm enveloped everything with a shuddering cloud. A legion of demons, in the shape of white elephants, but with snakes for their trunks and tails, and the bosoms of fair women, executed a frantic dance round the cauldron, and holding hands, balanced on their hind legs.

At this moment the Jew uncovered the Black Cock who had never crowed before.

"Osiris! Apollo! Balshazar!"[3] he cried, and flung the cock with superb aim into the boiling cauldron. The cock disappeared; then, rose again, shaking his wings and clawing the air, and giving a fearful, piercing crow.

"O Sultan Yahya, Sultan Yahya," answered a terrible voice from the bowels of the earth.

Again the earth shook; streams of lava bubbled from beneath the cauldron, and a flame, like a sheet of green lightning, leaped up from the fire.

As it did so, a colossal shadow appeared on the high palace wall, and the great hand, shaped like a glover's sign, engraven on the outer arch of the tower gateway, extended its candle-shaped

---

1 The Polychronicon is a book written by the English monk and chronicler Ranulf Higden (c. 1280-1364), and Nebuzaradon may be a reference to Nebuzaradan, Nebuchadnezzar's general at the siege of Jerusalem. The words seem grouped together for sound and effect rather than for meaning.

2 In Jewish mythology, a leviathan was a primordial sea serpent. Its source is in pre-biblical Mesopotamian myth, especially that of the sea monster in the Ugaritic myth of Baal; "Esto nobis" (Latin) means "let it be for us," so in this context perhaps "exist for us."

3 Osiris: one of the gods of ancient Egypt who is often seen as both a god of fertility and the embodiment of the dead and resurrected king; Apollo, in Greek mythology, was a patron of the arts and also a god of crops and herds who became identified with Helios, the sun god; Balshazar: possibly Belshazzar, co-regent of Babylon, who, in the Bible (Daniel 5), holds a last great feast at which he sees a hand writing on a wall the Aramaic words "*mene, mene, tekel, upharsin,*" which Daniel interprets as a judgment from God foretelling the fall of Babylon.

fingers, projected a wrist, an arm to the elbow, and turned slowly in a secret lock the flag-shaped key engraven on the inside vault of the portal.

The two necromancers fell on their faces, utterly stunned.

The first to revive was Don Juan, who roughly brought the Jew back to his senses. The moon made serener daylight. There was no trace of earthquake, volcano, or simoom; and the devils had disappeared without traces; only the circle of lamps was broken through, and the cauldron upset among the embers. But the great horse-shoe portals of the tower stood open; and, at the bottom of a dark corridor, there shone a speck of dim light.

"My Lord," cried Baruch, suddenly grown bold, and plucking Don Juan by the cloak, "we must now, if you please, settle a trifling business matter. Remember that the treasure was to be mine provided the Infanta were yours. Remember also, that the smallest indiscretion on your part, such as may happen to a gay young cavalier, will result in our being burned, with the New Year batch of heretics and relapses, in Bibrambla to-morrow, immediately after high mass and just before people go to early dinner, on account of the bullfight."

"Business! Discretion! Bibrambla! Early dinner!" exclaimed the Count of Miramor; "thinkest thou I shall ever go back to Grenada and its frumpish women once I am married to my Infanta, or let thee handle my late father-in-law, King Yahya's, treasure? Execrable renegade, take the reward of thy blasphemies." And, having rapidly run him through the body, he pushed Baruch into the precipice hard by. Then, covering his left arm with his cloak, and swinging his bare sword horizontally in his right hand, he advanced into the darkness of the tower.

IV

Don Juan Gusman del Pulgar plunged down a narrow corridor, as black as the shaft of a mine, following the little speck of reddish light which seemed to advance before him. The air was icy damp and heavy with a vague choking mustiness, which Don Juan imagined to be the smell of dead bats. Hundreds of these creatures fluttered all around; and hundreds more, apparently hanging head downwards from the low roof, grazed his face with their claws, their damp furry coats and clammy leathern wings. Underfoot, the ground was slippery with innumerable little snakes, who, instead of being crushed, just wriggled under the feet. The corridor was rendered even more gruesome by the fact that it was a strongly inclined plane, and that one seemed to be walking straight into a pit.

Suddenly, a sound mingled itself with that of his footsteps, and of the drip-drop of water from the roof; or rather detached itself as a whisper from it.

"Don Juan, Don Juan!" it murmured.

"Don Juan, Don Juan!" murmured the walls and roof a few yards further; a different voice this time.

"Don Juan Gusman del Pulgar!" a third voice took up, clearer and more plaintive than the others.

The magnanimous cavalier's blood began to run cold, and icy perspiration to clot his hair. He walked on nevertheless.

"Don Juan," repeated a fourth voice, a little buzz close to his ear.

But the bats set up a dreadful shrieking which drowned it.

He shivered as he went; it seemed to him he had recognized the voice of the jasmin-cheeked Azahar, as she called on him from her death-bed.

The reddish speck had meanwhile grown large at the bottom of the shaft, and he had understood that it was not a flame, but the light of some place beyond. Might it be hell? he thought. But he strode on nevertheless, grasping his sword and brushing away the bats with his cloak.

"Don Juan! Don Juan!" cried the voices issuing faintly from the darkness. He began to understand that they were trying to detain him; and he thought he recognized the voices of Dolores and Fatma, his dead mistresses.

"Silence! you sluts!" he cried. But his knees were shaking and great drops of sweat fell from his hair on to his cheek.

The speck of light had now become quite large, and turned from red to white. He understood that it represented the exit from the gallery. But he could not understand why, as he advanced, the light, instead of being brighter, seemed filmed over and fainter.

"Juan, Juan," wailed a new voice at his ear. He stood still for a second; a sudden faintness over him.

"Seraphita!" he murmured, "it is my little nun Seraphita." But he felt that she was trying to call him back.

"Abominable witch!" he cried. "Avaunt!"

The passage had grown narrower and narrower; so narrow that now he could barely squeeze along between the clammy walls, and had to bend his head lest he should hit the ceiling with its stalactites of bats.

Suddenly there was a great rustle of wings, and a long shriek. A night bird had been startled by his tread, and had whirled on before him, tearing through the veil of vagueness which dimmed the outer light. As the bird tore open its way, a stream of dazzling light entered the corridor: it was as if a curtain had suddenly been drawn.

"Too-hoo! Too-hoo!" shrieked the bird; and Don Juan, following its flight, brushed his way through the cobwebs of four centuries, and issued, blind and dizzy, into the outer world.

V

For a long while the Count of Miramor stood dazed and dazzled, unable to see anything, save the whirling flight of the owl, which circled in what seemed a field of waving, burning red. He closed his eyes; but through the singed lids he still saw that waving red atmosphere, and the black creature whirling about him.

Then, gradually, he began to perceive and comprehend: lines and curves arose shadowy before him, and the faint plash of waters cooled his ringing ears.

He found that he was standing in a lofty colonnade, with a deep tank at his feet, surrounded by high hedges of flowering myrtles,[1] whose jade-coloured water held the reflection of Moorish porticoes, shining orange in the sunlight, of high walls covered with shimmering blue and green tiles, and of a great red tower, raising its battlements into the cloudless blue. From the tower waved two flags, a green one and one of purple with a gold pomegranate. As he stood there, a sudden breath of air shuddered through the myrtles, wafting their fragrance towards him; a fountain began to bubble; and the reflection of the porticoes and hedges and tower to vacillate in the jade-green water, furling and unfurling like the pieces of a fan; and, above, the two banners unfolded themselves slowly, and little by little began to stream in the wind.

Don Juan advanced. At the further end of the tank a peacock was standing by a myrtle hedge, immovable as if made of precious enamels; but as Don Juan went by, the short blue-green feathers of his neck began to ruffle; he moved his tail, and

---

1 Myrtle is a shrub dedicated to Venus-Aphrodite, the goddess of love.

swelling himself out, he slowly unfolded it in a dazzling wheel. As he did so, some blackbirds and thrushes in gilt cages hanging within an archway, began to twitter and to sing.

From the court of the tank, Don Juan entered another and smaller court, passing through a narrow archway. On its marble steps lay three warriors, clad in long embroidered surcoats of silk, beneath which gleamed their armour, and wearing on their heads strange helmets of steel mail, which hung loose on to their gorgets and were surmounted by gilded caps; beneath them—for they had seemingly leant on them in their slumbers—lay round targes or shields, and battleaxes of Damascus work.[1] As he passed, they began to stir and breathe heavily. He strode quickly by; but at the entrance of the smaller court, from which issued a delicious scent of full-blown Persian roses, another sentinel was leaning against a column, his hands clasped round his lance, his head bent on his breast. As Don Juan passed he slowly raised his head, and opened one eye, then the other. Don Juan rushed past, a cold sweat on his brow.

Low beams of sunlight lay upon the little inner court, in whose midst, surrounded by rose hedges, stood a great basin of alabaster, borne on four thick-set pillars; a skin, as of ice, filmed over the basin; but, as if some one should have thrown a stone on to the frozen surface, the water began to move and to trickle slowly into a second basin below.

"The waters are flowing, the nightingales are singing," murmured a figure lying by the fountain, grasping, like one just awakened, a lute which lay by his side. From the little court Don Juan entered a series of arched and domed chambers, whose roofs were hung as with icicles of gold and silver, or incrusted with mother of pearl constellations which twinkled in the darkness, while the walls shone with patterns that seemed carved of ivory and pearl and beryl[2] and amethyst where the sunbeams grazed them, or imitated some strange sea caves, filled with flitting colours, where the shadow rose fuller and higher. In these chambers Don Juan found a number of sleepers, soldiers and slaves, black and white, all of whom sprang to their feet and rubbed their eyes and made obeisance as he went. Then he entered a long passage, lined on either side by a row of sleeping eunuchs,

---

1   A type of layered steel.
2   A transparent or translucent glassy mineral. Transparent varieties in white, green, blue, yellow, or pink, are valued as gems.

dressed in robes of honour, each leaning, sword in hand, against the wall, and of slave-girls with stuff of striped silver about their loins, and sequins at the end of their long hair, and drums and timbrels in their hands. At regular intervals stood great golden cressets, in which burned sweet-smelling wood, casting a reddish light over the sleeping faces. But as Don Juan approached, the slaves inclined their bodies to the ground, touching it with their turbans, and the girls thumped on their drums and jingled the brass bells of their timbrels. Thus he passed on from chamber to chamber till he came to a great door formed of stars of cedar and ivory studded with gold nails, and bolted by a huge gold bolt, on which ran mystic inscriptions. Don Juan stopped. But, as he did so, the bolt slowly moved in its socket, retreating gradually, and the immense portals swung back, each into its carved hinge column.

Behind them was disclosed a vast circular hall, so vast that you could not possibly see where it ended, and filled with a profusion of lights, wax candles held by rows and rows of white maidens, and torches held by rows and rows of white-robed eunuchs, and cressets burning upon lofty stands, and lamps dangling from the distant vault, through which here and there entered, blending strangely with the rest, great beams of white daylight. Don Juan stopped short, blinded by this magnificence, and as he did so, the fountain in the midst of the hall arose and shivered its cypress-like crest against the topmost vault; and innumerable voices of exquisite sweetness burst forth in strange wistful chants, and instruments of all kinds, both such as are blown and such as are twanged and rubbed with a bow, and such as are shaken and thumped, united with the voices and filled the hall with sound, as it was already filled with light.

Don Juan grasped his sword and advanced. At the extremity of the hall a flight of alabaster steps led up to a daïs or raised recess, overhung by an archway whose stalactites shone like beaten gold, and whose tiled walls glistened like precious stones. And on the daïs, on a throne of sandalwood and ivory, incrusted with gems and carpeted with the work of the Chinese loom, sat the Moorish Infanta, fast asleep.

To the right and the left, but on a step beneath the princess, stood her two most intimate attendants, the Chief Duenna and the Chief Eunuch, to whom the prudent King Yahya had intrusted his only child during her sleep of four hundred years. The Chief Duenna was habited in a suit of sad-coloured violet weeds, with many modest swathings of white muslin round her yellow and wrinkled countenance. The Chief Eunuch was a portly negro, of a fine chocolate hue, with cheeks like an allegorical wind, and a complexion as shiny as a well-worn doorknocker: he was enveloped from top to toe in marigold-coloured robes, and on his head he wore a towering turban of embroidered cashmere. Both these great personages held, beside their especial insignia of office, namely, a Mecca rosary[1] in the hand of the Duenna, and a silver wand in the hand of the Eunuch, great fans of white peacocks' tails, wherewith to chase away from their royal charge any ill-advised fly. But at this moment all the flies in the place were fast asleep, and the Duenna and the Eunuch also. And between them, canopied by a parasol of white silk, on which were embroidered, in figures which moved like those in dreams, the histories of Jusuf and Zuleika, of Solomon and the Queen of Sheba,[2] and of many other famous lovers, sat the Infanta, erect, but veiled in gold-starred gauzes, as an unfinished statue is veiled in the roughness of the marble.

Don Juan walked quickly between the rows of prostrate slaves, and the singing and dancing girls, and those holding tapers and torches; and stopped only at the very foot of the throne steps.

"Awake!" he cried, "my Princess, my Bride, awake!"

A faint stir arose in the veils of the muffled form; and Don Juan felt his temples throb, and, at the same time, a deathly coldness steal over him.

"Awake!" he repeated boldly. But instead of the Infanta, it was the venerable Duenna who raised her withered countenance and looked round with a startled jerk, awakened not so much by the voices and instruments as by the tread of a masculine boot. The Chief Eunuch also awoke suddenly; but with the grace of one grown old in the antechamber of kings, he quickly suppressed a yawn, and laying his hand on his embroidered vest, he made a profound obeisance.

"Verily," he remarked, "Allah (who alone possesses the secrets of the universe) is remarkably great, since he not only ..."

"Awake, awake, Princess!" interrupted Don Juan ardently, his foot on the lowest step of the throne.

---

1   "Mecca" or "Islamic rosaries" are more commonly known as "worry-beads." The Koran gives 99 names for God and these rosaries have beads in multiples of 11 to aid meditation on these names.

2   Usually "Yusuf and Zuleika," a Sufi love story by the fifteenth-century Persian scholar, mystic, and poet Jami (1414-92); the story of Solomon and the Queen of Sheba appears in the Bible, I Kings 10. 1-14.

But the Chief Eunuch waved him back with his wand, continuing his speech—"since he not only gave unto his servant King Yahya (may his shadow never be less!) power and riches far exceeding that of any of the kings of the earth or even of Solomon the son of David ..."

"Cease, fellow!" cried Don Juan, and pushing aside the wand and the negro's dimpled chocolate hand, he rushed up the steps and flung himself at the foot of the veiled Infanta, his rapier clanging strangely as he did so.

"Unveil, my Beloved, more beautiful than Oriana, for whom Amadis wept in the Black Mountain, than Gradasilia whom Felixmarte sought on the winged dragon, than Helen of Sparta who fired the towers of Troy, than Calixto whom Jove was obliged to change into a female bear, than Venus herself on whom Paris bestowed the fatal apple.[1] Unveil and arise, like the rosy Aurora from old Tithonus' couch, and welcome the knight who has confronted every peril for thee, Juan Gusman del Pulgar, Count of Miramor, who is ready, for thee, to confront every other peril of

---

1 Oriana is a character that appears in *Amadis de Gaula,* a Spanish chivalric romance, possibly Portuguese in origin. The first known version of this work, dating from 1508, was written by Garci Ordonez (or Rodriguez) de Montalvo, who claimed to have "corrected and emended" corrupt originals. In Montalvo's version, Amadis is the most handsome, upright, and valiant of knights. The story of his incredible feats of arms, in which he is never defeated, is interwoven with that of his love for Oriana, the beautiful daughter of Lisuarte, a fictional king of England; Felixmarte is the eponymous protagonist of Melchor de Ortega's Spanish chivalric romance, *Felixmarte de Hircania,* first published in 1556, clearly based on Montalvo's paradigmatic knight, Amadis de Gaula. Both Amadis and Felixmarte are mentioned several times in Miguel de Cervantes, *El Ingenioso Hidalgo Don Quixote de la Mancha* (1605; 1615); in Greek legend, Helen of Sparta was the daughter of Zeus and Leda, Queen of Sparta. Helen became the wife of King Menelaus and was reputedly the most beautiful woman in the classical world. She eloped with, or was carried off by Paris, the Trojan Prince, thus triggering the Trojan war which lasted for ten years and was immortalized in Homer's epic poem, the *Iliad* (c. 720 BC); Callixto: possibly Callisto who, in Greek mythology, was a nymph (or, according to some sources, the daughter of Lycaon) associated with the goddess of the hunt, Artemis; in Greek mythology, Paris was the son of Priam of Troy. Zeus chose him to determine which of three goddesses was most beautiful—Hera, Athena, or Aphrodite (Venus). In the famous "Judgment of Paris," he chose Aphrodite because she offered to help him win the most beautiful woman alive, Helen of Sparta.

the world or of hell; and to fix upon thee alone his affections, more roving hitherto than those of Prince Galaor or of the many-shaped god Proteus!"[1]

A shiver ran through the veiled princess. The Chief Eunuch gave a significant nod, and waved his white wand thrice. Immediately a concert of voices and instruments, as numerous as those of the forces of the air when mustered before King Solomon, filled the vast hall. The dancing girls raised their tambourines over their heads, and poised themselves on tip-toe. A wave of fragrant essences passed through the air filled with the spray of innumerable fountains. And the Duenna, slowly advancing to the side of the throne, took in her withered fingers the top-most fold of shimmering gauze, and slowly gathering it backwards, displayed the Infanta unveiled before Don Juan's gaze.

The breast of the princess heaved deeply; her lips opened with a little sigh, and she languidly raised her long-fringed lids; then cast down her eyes on the ground, and resumed the rigidity of a statue. She was most marvellously fair. She sat on the cushions of the throne with modestly crossed legs; her hands, with nails tinged violet with henna, demurely folded in her lap. Through the thinness of her embroidered muslins shone the magnificence of purple and orange vests, stiff with gold and gems, and all subdued into a wondrous opalescent radiance. From her head there descended on either side of her person a diaphanous veil of shimmering colours, powdered over with minute glittering spangles. Her breast was covered with rows and rows of the largest pearls, a perfect network reaching from her slender throat to her waist, among which flashed diamonds embroidered in her vest. Her face was oval, with the silver pallor of the young moon; her mouth, most subtly carmined, looked like a pomegranate flower among tuberoses, for her cheeks were painted white, and the

---

1 In Greek legend, Tithonus was the son of Laomedon, king of Troy, and of Strymo, daughter of the river Scamander. Eos (Aurora) fell in love with Tithonus and requested that Zeus grant him eternal life, which he did, but Eos forgot to ask also for eternal youth, so her husband grew old and was eventually transformed into a cicada; Prince Galaor, brother of Amadis of Gaul: a gay libertine, whose adventures form a strong contrast to those of the more serious hero; in Greek mythology, Proteus was the prophetic old man of the sea who knew all things— past, present, and future—but disliked telling what he knew. Those who wanted information from him had to catch him sleeping and bind him. He would try to escape by changing his form, but if a captor held him fast he gave the wished-for answer and plunged into the sea.

orbits of her great long-fringed eyes were stained violet. In the middle of each cheek, however, was a delicate spot of pink, in which an exquisite art had painted a small pattern of pyramid shape, so naturally that you might have thought that a real piece of embroidered stuff was decorating the maiden's countenance. On her head she wore a high tiara of jewels, the ransom of many kings, which sparkled and blazed like a lit-up altar. The eyes of the princess were decorously fixed on the ground.

Don Juan stood silent in ravishment.

"Princess!" he at length began.

But the Chief Eunuch laid his wand gently on his shoulder.

"My Lord," he whispered, "it is not etiquette that your Magnificence should address her Highness in any direct fashion; let alone the fact that her Highness does not understand the Castilian tongue, nor your Magnificence the Arabic. But through the mediumship of this most respectable lady, her Discretion the Principal Duenna, and my unworthy self, a conversation can be carried on equally delicious and instructive to both parties."

"A plague upon the old brute!" thought Don Juan; but he reflected upon what had never struck him before, that they had indeed been conversing, or attempting to converse, in Spanish, and that the Castilian spoken by the Chief Eunuch was, although correct, quite obsolete, being that of the sainted King Ferdinand.[1] There was a whispered consultation between the two great dignitaries; and the Duenna approached her lips to the Infanta's ear. The princess moved her pomegranate lips in a faint smile, but without raising her eyelids, and murmured something which the ancient lady whispered to the Chief Eunuch, who bowed thrice in answer. Then turning to Don Juan with most mellifluous tones, "Her Highness the Princess," he said, bowing thrice as he mentioned her name, "is, like all princesses, but to an even more remarkable extent, endowed with the most exquisite modesty. She is curious therefore, despite the superiority of her charms—so conspicuous even to those born blind—to know whether your Magnificence does not consider her the most beautiful thing you have ever beheld."

---

1 Ferdinand II, king of Aragon, or Ferdinand the Catholic (1452–1516), king of Aragon (1479–1516), king of Castile and León (as Ferdinand V, 1474–1504), king of Sicily (1468–1516), and king of Naples (1504–16). In 1469, Ferdinand married Isabella I of Castile, and in 1474 they assumed joint rule of Castile.

Don Juan laid his hand upon his heart with an affirmative gesture more eloquent than any words.

Again an almost invisible smile hovered about the pomegranate mouth, and there was a murmur and a whispering consultation.

"Her Highness," pursued the Chief Eunuch blandly, "has been informed by the judicious instructors of her tender youth, that cavaliers are frequently fickle, and that your Lordship in particular has assured many ladies in succession that each was the most beautiful creature you have ever beheld. Without admitting for an instant the possibility of a parallel, she begs your Magnificence to satisfy her curiosity on the point. Does your Lordship consider her as infinitely more beautiful than the Lady Catalina?"

Now Catalina was one of the famous seven for whom Don Juan had committed a deadly crime.

He was taken aback by the exactness of the Infanta's information; he was rather sorry they should have told her about Catalina.

"Of course," he answered hastily, "pray do not mention such a name in her Highness's presence."

The princess bowed imperceptibly.

"Her Highness," pursued the Chief Eunuch, "still actuated by the curiosity due to her high birth and tender youth, is desirous of knowing whether your Lordship considers her far more beautiful than the Lady Violante?"

Don Juan made an impatient gesture. "Slave! never speak of Violante in my princess's presence!" he exclaimed, fixing his eyes upon the tuberose cheeks and pomegranate mouth which bloomed among that shimmer of precious stones.

"Good. And may the same be said to apply to the ladies Dolores and Elvira?"

"Dolores and Elvira and Fatma and Azahar," answered Don Juan, greatly provoked at the Chief Eunuch's want of tact, "and all the rest of womankind."

"And shall we add also, than Sister Seraphita of the Convent of Santa Isabel la Real?"

"Yes," cried Don Juan, "than Sister Seraphita, for whom I committed the greatest sin which can be committed by living man."

As he said these words, Don Juan was about to fling his arms about the princess and cut short this rather too elaborate courtship.

But again he was waved back by the white wand.

"One question more, only one, my dear Lord," whispered the Chief Eunuch; "I am most concerned at your impatience, but the laws of etiquette and the caprices of young princesses *must* go before everything, as you will readily admit. Stand back, I pray you."

Don Juan felt sorely inclined to thrust his sword through the yellow bolster of the great personage's vest; but he choked his rage, and stood quietly on the throne steps, one hand on his heart, the other on his sword-hilt, the boldest cavalier in all the kingdom of Spain.

"Speak, speak!" he begged.

The princess, without moving a muscle of her exquisite face, or unclosing her flower-like mouth, murmured some words to the Duenna, who whispered them mysteriously to the Chief Eunuch.

At this moment also the Infanta raised her heavy eyelids, stained violet with henna, and fixed upon the cavalier a glance long, dark and deep, like that of the wild antelope.

"Her Highness," resumed the Chief Eunuch, with a sweet smile, "is extremely gratified with your Lordship's answers, although of course they could not possibly have been at all different. But there remains yet another lady ..."

Don Juan shook his head impatiently.

"Another lady concerning whom the Infanta desires some information. Does your Lordship consider her more beautiful also than the Virgin of the Seven Daggers?"

The place seemed to swim about Don Juan. Before his eyes rose the throne, all vacillating in its splendour, and on the throne the Moorish Infanta with the triangular patterns painted on her tuberose cheeks, and the long look in her henna'd eyes; and the image of her was blurred, and imperceptibly it seemed to turn into the effigy, black and white in her stiff puce frock and seed-pearl stomacher, of the Virgin of the Seven Daggers staring blankly into space.

"My Lord," remarked the Chief Eunuch, "methinks that love has made you somewhat inattentive, a great blemish in a cavalier, when answering the questions of a lovely princess. I therefore venture to repeat: do you consider her more beautiful than the Virgin of the Seven Daggers?"

"Do you consider her more beautiful than the Virgin of the Seven Daggers?" repeated the Duenna, glaring at Don Juan.

"Do you consider me more beautiful than the Virgin of the Seven Daggers?" asked the princess, speaking suddenly in Spanish, or at least in language perfectly intelligible to Don Juan.

And, as she spoke the words, all the slave-girls and eunuchs and singers and players, the whole vast hall full, seemed to echo the same question.

The Count of Miramor stood silent for an instant; then raising his hand and looking round him with quiet decision, he answered in a loud voice:

"No!"

"In that case," said the Chief Eunuch with the politeness of a man desirous to cut short an embarrassing silence, "in that case I am very sorry it should be my painful duty to intimate to your Lordship that you must undergo the punishment usually allotted to cavaliers who are disobliging to young and tender princesses."

So saying, he clapped his black hands, and, as if by magic, there arose at the foot of the steps, a gigantic Berber of the Rif,[1] his brawny sunburnt limbs left bare by a scanty striped shirt, fastened round his waist by a wisp of rope, his head shaven blue except in the middle, where, encircled by a coronet of worsted rag, there flamed a top-knot of dreadful orange hair.

"Decapitate that gentleman," ordered the Chief Eunuch in his most obliging tones. Don Juan felt himself collared, dragged down the steps, and forced into a kneeling posture on the lowest landing, all in the twinkling of an eye.

From beneath the bronzed left arm of the ruffian he could see the milk-white of the alabaster steps, the gleam of an immense scimitar, the mingled blue and yellow of the cressets and tapers, the daylight filtering through the constellations in the dark cedar vault, the glitter of the Infanta's diamonds, and, of a sudden, the twinkle of the Chief Eunuch's eye.

Then all was black, and Don Juan felt himself, that is to say, his own head, rebound three times like a ball upon the alabaster steps.

VI

It had evidently all been a dream—perhaps a delusion induced by the vile fumigations of that filthy ruffian of a renegade Jew. The infidel dogs had certain abominable drugs which gave them visions of paradise and hell when smoked or chewed—nasty brutes that they were—and this was some of their devilry. But he

---

1 Member of a non-Arabic people living in North Africa. The Rif is one of the largest Berber tribes.

should pay for it, the cursed old grey-beard, the Holy Office should keep him warm, or a Miramor was not a Miramor! For Don Juan forgot, or disbelieved, not only that he himself had been beheaded by a Rif Berber the evening before, but that he had previously run poor Baruch through the body and hurled him down the rocks near the Tower of Cypresses.

This confusion of mind was excusable on the part of the cavalier. For, on opening his eyes, he had found himself lying in a most unlikely resting-place, considering the time and season, namely, a heap of old bricks and rubbish, half-hidden in withered reeds and sprouting weeds, on a ledge of the precipitous hillside which descends into the River Darro. Above him rose the dizzy red-brick straightness of the tallest tower of the Alhambra, pierced at its very top by an arched and pillared window, and scantily overgrown with the roots of a dead ivy-tree. Below, at the bottom of the precipice, dashed the little Darro, brown and swollen with melted snows, between its rows of leafless poplars; beyond it rose the roofs and balconies and orange-trees of the older part of Grenada; and above that, with the morning sunshine and mists fighting among its hovels, its square belfries and great masses of prickly pear and aloe, the Albaycin whose highest convent tower stood out already against a sky of winter blue. The Albaycin; that was the quarter of that villain Baruch, who dared to play practical jokes on grandees of Spain of the very first class!

This thought caused Don Juan to spring up, and, grasping his sword, to scramble through the sprouting elder-bushes and heaps of broken masonry, down to the bridge over the river.

It was a beautiful winter morning, sunny, blue and crisp through the white mists. And Don Juan sped along as with wings to his feet; for having remembered that it was the anniversary of the Liberation,[1] and that he, as descendant of Fernan Perez del Pulgar, would be expected to carry the banner of the city at High Mass in the cathedral, he had determined that his absence from the ceremony should raise no suspicions of his ridiculous adventure. For ridiculous it had been—and the sense of its being ridiculous filled the generous breast of the Count of Miramor with a longing to murder every man, woman or child he encountered as he sped through the streets. "Look at his Excellency the

---

1   It is likely that Don Juan is here referring to the liberation of Granada from the reign of the last Nasrid sultan, Muhammad XI, Spanish name Boabdil, who ruled from 1482 until 1492 when Granada fell to Ferdinand and Isabella, the Roman Catholic rulers of Aragon and Castile.

Count of Miramor; look at Don Juan Gusman del Pulgar! He's been made a fool of by old Baruch the renegade Jew!" he imagined everbody to be thinking.

But, on the contrary, no one took the smallest notice of him. The muleteers, driving along their beasts laden with heather and myrtle for the bakehouse ovens, allowed their loads to brush him, as if he had been the merest errand-boy; the stout black housewives, going to market with their brass braziers tucked under their cloaks, never once turned round as he pushed them rudely on the cobbles; nay, the very beggars, armless and legless and shameless, who were alighting from their go-carts and taking up their station at the church-doors, did not even extend a hand towards the passing cavalier. Before a popular barber's some citizens were waiting to have their top-knots plaited into tidy tails, discussing the while the olive harvest, the price of spart-grass and the chances of the bull-ring. This, Don Juan expected, would be a fatal spot, for from the barber's shop the news must go about that Don Juan del Pulgar, hatless and covered with mud, was hurrying home with a discomfited countenance, ill-befitting the hero of so many nocturnal adventures. But, although Don Juan had to make his way right in front of the barber's, not one of the clients did so much as turn his head, perhaps out of fear of displeasing so great a cavalier.

Suddenly, as Don Juan hurried along, he noticed for the first time, among the cobbles and the dry mud of the street, large drops of blood, growing larger as they went, becoming an almost uninterrupted line, then, in the puddles, a little red stream. Such were by no means uncommon vestiges in those days of duels and town brawls; besides, some early sportsman, a wild boar on his horse, might have been passing. But somehow or other, this track of blood exerted an odd attraction over Don Juan; and unconsciously to himself, instead of taking the short cut to his palace, he followed it along some of the chief streets of Grenada. The blood-stains, as was natural, led in the direction of the great hospital, founded by Saint John of God,[1] to which it was customary to carry the victims of accidents and street fights. Before the monumental gateway, where Saint John

---

1 Saint John of God (1495–1550). His original name was Juan Ciudad, founder of the Hospitaller Order of St. John of God (Brothers Hospitallers), a Roman Catholic religious order of nursing brothers. He was canonized in 1690.

of God knelt in effigy before the Madonna, a large crowd was collected, above whose heads oscillated the black and white banners of a mortuary confraternity, and the flame and smoke of their torches. The street was blocked with carts, and with riders rising in their stirrups to look over the crowd, and even with gaily trapped mules and gilded coaches, in which veiled ladies were anxiously questioning their lackeys and outriders. The throng of idle and curious citizens, of monks and brothers of mercy, reached up the steps and right into the cloistered court of the hospital.

"Who is it?" asked Don Juan with his usual masterful manner, pushing his way into the crowd. The man whom he addressed, a stalwart peasant with a long tail pinned under his hat, turned round vaguely, but did not answer.

"Who is it?" repeated Don Juan louder.

But no one answered, although he accompanied the question with a good push, and even a thrust with his sheathed sword.

"Cursed idiots! Are you all deaf and dumb, that you cannot answer a cavalier?" he cried angrily, and taking a portly priest by the collar, he shook him roughly.

"Jesus Maria Joseph!" exclaimed the priest; but turning round he took no notice of Don Juan, and merely rubbed his collar, muttering, "Well, if the demons are to be allowed to take respectable canons by the collar, it *is* time that we should have a good witch-burning."

Don Juan took no heed of his words, but thrust onward, knocking over, as he did so, a young woman who was lifting her child to let it see the show. The crowd parted as the woman fell, and people ran to pick her up, but no one took any notice of Don Juan. Indeed, he himself was struck by the way in which he passed through its midst, encountering no opposition from the phalanx of robust shoulders and hips.

"Who is it?" asked Don Juan again.

He had got into a clearing of the crowd. On the lowest step of the hospital gate stood a little knot of black penitents, their black linen cowls flung back on their shoulders, and of priests and monks muttering together. Some of them were beating back the crowd, others snuffing their torches against the paving-stones, and letting the wax drip off their tapers. In the midst of them, with a standard of the Virgin at its head, was a light wooden bier, set down by its bearers. It was covered with coarse black serge, on which were embroidered in yellow braid a skull and crossbones, and the monogram I.H.S.[1] Under the bier was a little red pool.

"Who is it?" asked Don Juan one last time; but instead of waiting for an answer, he stepped forward, sword in hand, and rudely pulled aside the rusty black pall.

On the bier was stretched a corpse dressed in black velvet, with lace cuffs and collar, loose boots, buff gloves, and with a blood-clotted dark matted head, lying loose half an inch above the mangled throat.

Don Juan Gusman del Pulgar stared fixedly.

It was himself.

The church into which Don Juan had fled was that of the Virgin of the Seven Daggers. It was deserted, as usual, and filled with chill morning light, in which glittered the gilded cornices and altars, and gleamed, like pools of water, the many precious marbles. A sort of mist seemed to hang about it all, and dim the splendour of the high altar.

Don Juan del Pulgar sank down in the midst of the nave; not on his knees, for (Oh horror!) he felt that he had no longer any knees, nor indeed any back, any arms, or limbs of any kind, and he dared not ask himself whether he was still in possession of a head: his only sensations were such as might be experienced by a slowly trickling pool, or a snow-wreath in process of melting, or a cloud fitting itself on to a flat surface of rock.

He was disembodied. He now understood why no one had noticed him in the crowd, why he had been able to penetrate through its thickness, and why, when he struck people and pulled them by the collar and knocked them down, they had taken no more notice of him than of a blast of wind. He was a ghost. He was dead. This must be the after life; and he was infallibly within a few minutes of hell.

"O Virgin, Virgin of the Seven Daggers!" he cried with hopeless bitterness, "is this the way you recompense my faithfulness? I have died unshriven, in the midst of mortal sin, merely because I would not say you were less beautiful than the Moorish Infanta; and this is all my reward?"

---

1 A monogram of the *nomina sacra*, or names of Jesus Christ which were sometimes shortened, particularly in Christian inscriptions: IH and XP, for Jesus and Christus, or IC and XC or IHS and XPS for *Iesous Christos*.

But even as he spoke these words an extraordinary miracle took place. The white winter light broke into wondrous iridescences; the white mist collected into shoals of dim palm-bearing angels; the cloud of stale incense, still hanging over the high altar, gathered into fleecy balls, which became the heads and backsides of chubby celestials; and Don Juan, reeling and fainting, felt himself rise, higher and higher, as if borne up on clusters of soap-bubbles. The cupola began to rise and expand; the painted clouds to move and blush a deeper pink; the painted sky to recede and turn into deep holes of real blue. As he was borne upwards, the allegorical virtues in the lunettes began to move and brandish their attributes; the colossal stucco angels on the cornices to pelt him with flowers no longer of plaster of Paris; the place was filled with delicious fragrance of incense, and with sounds of exquisitely played lutes and viols, and of voices, among which he distinctly recognized Syphax, His Majesty's chief soprano. And, as Don Juan floated upwards through the cupola of the church, his heart suddenly filled with a consciousness of extraordinary virtue; the gold transparency at the top of the dome expanded; its rays grew redder and more golden, and there burst from it at last a golden moon crescent, on which stood, in her farthingale of puce and her stomacher of seed-pearl, her big black eyes fixed mildly upon him, the Virgin of the Seven Daggers.

★ ★ ★ ★

"Your story of His Excellency the late Count of Miramor, Don Juan Gusman del Pulgar," wrote Don Pedro Calderon de la Barca, in March, 1686, to his friend, the Archpriest Morales,[1] at Grenada, "so veraciously revealed in a vision to the holy prior of Saint Nicholas, is indeed such as must touch the heart of the most stubborn. Were it presented in the shape of a play, say in the style of my *Purgatory of St. Patrick*,[2] it should outshine that humble work as much as the villainy of your late noble friend, and the marvel of his salvation, throw into the shade the villainy of my Ludovic Enio and the miracle wrought in his person. And to what better use could I dedicate whatever remains in me of the Sacred Fire than setting forth and adorning wonders so calcu-

---

1 For Calderón, see note in preface above; the "Archpriest Morales" appears to be Lee's invention.
2 *El Purgatorio de San Patricio* (1628), one of Calderón's famous religious dramas. See note on Calderón in preface above.

lated to inculcate virtue and magnify piety? But alas, my dear friend, the snows of age are as thick on my head as the snows of winter upon your Mulhacen; and who knows whether I shall ever be able to write again?"

The forecast of the illustrious dramatic poet proved, indeed, too true; and hence it is that unworthy modern hands have sought to frame the veracious and edifying history of Don Juan and the Virgin of the Seven Daggers.

Appendix A: From Algernon Charles Swinburne, "Notes on Designs of the Old Masters at Florence" (1868, 1875)[1]

[The early art criticism of the major English poet and critic Algernon Charles Swinburne (1837-1909) helped shape the "impressionistic" or "aesthetic" prose criticism of the English academic and critic Walter Pater (1839-94), extracts from whose work appear in Appendices B and C. Pater in turn was the chief influence on Lee's aesthetic writings. In this extract from his essay "Notes on Designs of the Old Masters at Florence" (first published in 1868), Swinburne describes designs by the famous Renaissance painter and sculptor Michelangelo Buonarroti (1475-1564) in the Uffizi Gallery in Florence, which he saw in the spring of 1864, and, in doing so, sets up an influential literary touchstone for the late nineteenth-century *femme fatale*. This extract has an important bearing on Lee's own treatment of the *femme fatale* in *Hauntings*, and has especial resonance in the description of Zaffirino, the ghostly androgynous *homme fatal* of "A Wicked Voice," when Magnus, the narrator, recalls "the faces of wicked, vindictive women," from his boyhood reading of Swinburne and Baudelaire.]

But in one separate head there is more tragic attraction than in these: a woman's, three times studied, with divine and subtle care; sketched and re-sketched, in youth and age, beautiful always beyond desire and cruel beyond words; fairer than heaven and more terrible than hell; pale with pride and weary with wrong-doing; a silent anger against God and man burns, white and repressed, through her clear features. In one drawing she wears a head-dress of eastern fashion rather than western, but in effect made out of the artist's mind only; plaited in the likeness of closely-welded scales as of a chrysalid serpent, raised and waved

---

1 Algernon Charles Swinburne (1837-1909), major English poet and critic, best known for *Poems and Ballads* (1866), which caused a scandal on its publication due to its sensational subject matter. His "Notes on Designs of the Old Masters at Florence" was first published in the *Fortnightly Review* in July 1868 and afterwards in *Essays and Studies* (London: Chatto & Windus, 1875), from which this extract is taken (pp. 319-21).

and rounded in the likeness of a sea-shell. In some inexplicable way all her ornaments seem to partake of her fatal nature, to bear upon them her brand of beauty fresh from hell; and this through no vulgar machinery of symbolism, no serpentine or otherwise bestial emblem: the bracelets and rings are innocent enough in shape and workmanship; but in touching her flesh they have become infected with deadly and malignant meaning. Broad bracelets divide the shapely splendour of her arms; over the nakedness of her firm and luminous breasts, just below the neck, there is passed a band as of metal. Her eyes are full of proud and passionless lust after gold and blood; her hair, close and curled, seems ready to shudder in sunder and divide into snakes. Her throat, full and fresh, round and hard to the eye as her bosom and arms, is erect and stately, the head set firm on it without any droop or lift of the chin; her mouth crueller than a tiger's, colder than a snake's, and beautiful beyond a woman's. She is the deadlier Venus incarnate;

$$\text{πολλὴ μὲν ἐν θεοῖσι κοὐκ ἀνώνυμος}$$
$$\text{θεά.}^1$$

for upon earth also many names might be found for her: Lamia re-transformed,[2] invested now with a fuller beauty, but divested of all feminine attributes not native to the snake—a Lamia loveless and unassailable by the sophist, readier to drain life out of her lover than to fade for his sake at his side; or the Persian Amestris, watching the only breasts on earth more beautiful than her own cut off from her rival's living bosom;[3] or Cleopatra, not dying but turning serpent under the serpent's bite;[4] or that queen of the extreme East who with her husband marked every day as it went by some device of a new and wonderful cruelty.[5] In one

---

1   Translation from the opening of Euripides' *Hippolytos*: "I am not a nameless goddess, but one powerful among the gods ..."

2   Swinburne alludes to Keats's poem *Lamia* (1820) which tells the story of how a young man named Lycius falls in love with Lamia, a beautiful woman, who is unmasked as a serpent by the philosopher Apollonius (Swinburne's "sophist"), who is blind to her charms.

3   Amestris, Wife of Xerxes, King of Persia (reigned 485-65 BC), described by the Greek historian Herodotus as a cruel despot.

4   Cleopatra, Queen of Egypt (68-30 BC), committed suicide by means of snakebite.

5   Ahab, King of Israel, and his wife Jezebel were by-words for cruelty and depravity. See I Kings, Chapters 16-22.

design, where the cruel and timid face of a king rises behind her, this crowned and cowering head might stand for Ahab's, and hers for that of Jezebel. Another study is in red chalk; in this the only ornaments are ear-rings. In a third, the serpentine hair is drawn up into a tuft at the crown with two ringlets hanging, heavy and deadly as small tired snakes. There is a drawing in the furthest room at the Buonarroti Palace which recalls and almost reproduces the design of these three.[1] Here also the electric hair, which looks as though it would hiss and glitter with sparks if once touched, is wound up to a tuft with serpentine plaits and involutions; all that remains of it unbound falls in one curl, shaping itself into a snake's likeness as it unwinds, right against a living snake held to the breast and throat. This is rightly registered as a study for Cleopatra; but notice has not yet been accorded to the subtle and sublime idea which transforms her death by the aspic's bite into a meeting of serpents which recognise and embrace, an encounter between the woman and the worm of Nile, almost as though this match for death were a monstrous love-match, or such a mystic marriage as that painted in the loveliest passage of "Salammbô,"[2] between the maiden body and scaly coils of the serpent and the priestess alike made sacred to the moon; so closely do the snake and the queen of snakes caress and cling. Of this idea Shakespeare also had a vague and great glimpse when he made Antony "murmur, *Where's my serpent of old Nile?*"[3] mixing a foretaste of her death with the full sweet savour of her supple and amorous "pride of life."[4] For what indeed is lovelier or more luxuriously loving than a strong and graceful snake of the nobler kind?

---

1   The Buonarroti Palace (properly the Casa Buonarroti) was the house of Michelangelo at Florence, subsequently made into a museum of his works.

2   *Salammbo* (1862), exotic novel by the French writer Gustave Flaubert (1821-80), charting the Punic Wars. Salammbo, daughter of the Carthaginian leader Hamilcar, and her pet serpent appear in a number of erotically charged scenes.

3   *Antony and Cleopatra*, I. v. 25.

4   See 1 John 2.16: "For all that *is* in the world, the lust of the flesh, and the lust of the eyes, and the pride of life, is not of the father, but is of the world."

Appendix B: From Walter Pater, "Pico della Mirandula" (1871, 1873)[1]

[Vernon Lee was a personal friend of Walter Pater (1839-94), the Oxford academic famous for his art criticism and classical studies, and was the only one of his followers acknowledged by him as a disciple. In this extract from his essay "Pico della Mirandula," first published in 1871, Pater translates from the essay "The Gods in Exile" by the German-Jewish writer Heinrich Heine (1797/9-1856), which tells the story of how the pagan deities, brought low by the triumph of Christianity, were forced to disguise themselves and go into exile, taking humble employment to support themselves. Both Pater and Lee were fascinated by the idea of the god in exile. Pater's imaginary portrait "Denys L'Auxerrois" (1886), a tale about the appearance of Dionysus-like character in the mediaeval town of Auxerre, has a determinable effect on Lee's "Dionea," a tale about a young girl cast up on the Italian shore and her impact on the local community.]

No account of the Renaissance can be complete without some notice of the attempt made by certain Italian scholars of the fifteenth century to reconcile Christianity with the religion of ancient Greece. To reconcile forms of sentiment which at first seem incompatible, to adjust the various products of the human mind to each other in one many-sided type of intellectual culture, to give the human spirit for the heart and imagination to feed upon, as much as it could possibly receive, belonged to the generous instincts of that age. An earlier and simpler generation had seen in the gods of Greece so many malignant spirits, the defeated but still living centres of the religion of darkness, strug-

---

1 Walter Pater (1839-94), art critic and classicist, noted for his influential "impressionistic" or "aesthetic" prose style. First published in the *Fortnightly Review* for 1 October 1871, "Pico della Mirandula" was subsequently collected in *Studies in the History of the Renaissance* (London: Macmillan, 1873), from which this text is taken (pp. 18-21). This text has been chosen as the one most likely to have been owned by Lee, although it is probable that she read Pater's essays before they were collected in book form.

gling, not always in vain, against the kingdom of light. Little by little, as the natural charm of pagan story reasserted itself over minds emerging out of barbarism, the religious significance which had once belonged to it was lost sight of, and it came to be regarded as the subject of a purely artistic or poetical treatment. But it was inevitable that from time to time minds should arise deeply enough impressed by its beauty and power to ask themselves whether the religion of Greece was indeed a rival of the religion of Christ; for the older gods had rehabilitated themselves, and men's allegiance was divided. And the fifteenth century was an impassioned age, so ardent and serious in its pursuit of art that it consecrated everything with which art had to do as a religious object. The restored Greek literature had made it familiar, at least in Plato, with a style of expression about the earlier gods, which had about it much of the warmth and unction of a Christian hymn. It was too familiar with such language to regard mythology as a mere story; and it was too serious to play with a religion.

'Let me briefly remind the reader,' says Heine, in the 'Gods in Exile,'[1] an essay full of that strange blending of sentiment which is characteristic of the traditions of the middle age concerning the pagan religions, 'how the gods of the older world at the time of the definite triumph of Christianity, that is, in the third century, fell into painful embarrassments which greatly resembled certain tragical situations of their earlier life. They now found themselves exposed to the same troublesome necessities to which they had once before been exposed during the primitive ages, in that revolutionary epoch when the Titans broke out of the custody of Orcus, and, piling Pelion on Ossa, scaled Olympus.[2] Unfortunate gods! They had then to take flight ignominiously, and hide themselves among us here on earth under all sorts of disguises. Most

---

1   Heinrich Heine (1797/9-1856), German-Jewish lyric poet and essayist. His essay "The Gods in Exile" appeared first as *Les Dieux en exil* in the *Revue de deux mondes* (April 1853), although Pater translates from Heine's revised shorter German version, published in Germany in 1853 and 1854. Intrigued by Heine's notion of the gods in exile, Pater refers to it many times in his writings, most signally in the stories "Denys L'Auxerrois" (1886) and "Apollo in Picardy" (1893).

2   Orcus is one of the names for the god of Hell or the Underworld. In Hell were confined the Titans, the gigantic children of Uranus and Mother Earth, and enemies of the gods, who, on their release, piled up Mt Pelion and Mt Ossa to ascend to heaven (at the top of Mt. Olympus), the home of their rivals.

of them betook themselves to Egypt, where for greater security they assumed the forms of animals, as is generally known. Just in the same way they had to take flight again, and seek entertainment in remote hiding-places, when those iconoclastic zealots, the black brood of monks, broke down all the temples, and pursued the gods with fire and curses. Many of these unfortunate emigrants, entirely deprived of shelter and ambrosia, had now to take to vulgar handicrafts as a means of earning their bread. In these circumstances many whose sacred groves had been confiscated, let themselves out for hire as wood-cutters in Germany, and had to drink beer instead of nectar. Apollo seems to have been content to take service under graziers, and as he had once kept the cows of Admetus,[1] so he lived now as a shepherd in Lower Austria. Here however, having become suspected on account of his beautiful singing, he was recognised by a learned monk as one of the old pagan gods, and handed over to the spiritual tribunal. On the rack he confessed that he was the god Apollo; and before his execution he begged that he might be suffered to play once more upon the lyre and to sing a song. And he played so touchingly, and sang with such magic, and was withal so beautiful in form and feature, that all the women wept, and many of them were so deeply impressed that they shortly afterwards fell sick. And some time afterwards the people wished to drag him from the grave again, that a stake might be driven through his body, in the belief that he had been a vampire, and that the sick women would by this means recover. But they found the grave empty.'

---

1 Banished by Zeus from Olympus for killing the Cyclops in revenge for the death of his son Aesculapius, Apollo hired himself out as a shepherd to Admetus, King of Thessaly, for nine years.

Appendix C: From Walter Pater, "Lionardo da Vinci" (1869, 1873)[1]

[In this famous passage from his essay "Lionardo da Vinci," originally published in 1869, Walter Pater describes the *Mona Lisa*, the celebrated painting by the artist and inventor Leonardo da Vinci (1452-1519). Pater's influential impressionistic description, which implies that the image of the Mona Lisa is an essential feminine archetype, a condensation of key feminine types from the past, came to epitomise the certain important characteristics of the nineteenth-century *femme fatale* and, along with Swinburne's description in Appendix A, can be seen to inform Lee's treatment of the *femme fatale* in *Hauntings*.]

'La Gioconda' is, in the truest sense, Lionardo's masterpiece, the revealing instance of his mode of thought and work. In suggestiveness, only the Melancholia of Dürer[2] is comparable to it; and no crude symbolism disturbs the effect of its subdued and graceful mystery. We all know the face and hands of the figure, set in its marble chair, in that cirque of fantastic rocks, as in some faint light under sea. Perhaps of all ancient pictures time has chilled it least.[3] As often happens with works in which invention seems to reach its limit, there is an element in it given to, not invented by, the master. In that inestimable folio of drawings, once in the

---

1   "Lionardo da Vinci" was originally published in the *Fortnightly Review* for November 1869 and afterwards in *Studies in the History of the Renaissance* (London: Macmillan & Co., 1873), from which this text is taken (pp. 116-119). This text has been chosen as the one most likely to have been owned by Lee, although it is probable that she read Pater's essays before they were collected in book form. This extract includes Pater's famous description of the *Mona Lisa*, also known as *La Gioconda*, the painting now celebrated as the best known work of Leonardo da Vinci (1452-1519), painter, sculptor, architect, and man of science.

2   Albrecht Dürer (1471-1528), German painter and engraver.

3   "Yet for Vasari there was some further magic of crimson in the lips and cheeks, lost for us" Author's Note.

possession of Vasari,[1] were certain designs by Verrocchio,[2] faces of such impressive beauty that Lionardo in his boyhood copied them many times. It is hard not to connect with these designs of the elder, by-past master, as with its germinal principle, the unfathomable smile, always with a touch of something sinister in it, which plays over all Lionardo's work. Besides, the picture is a portrait. From childhood we see this image defining itself on the fabric of his dreams; and but for express historical testimony, we might fancy this was but his ideal lady, embodied and beheld at last. What was the relationship of a living Florentine to this creature of his thought? By what strange affinities had she and the dream grown thus apart, yet so closely together? Present from the first, incorporeal in Lionardo's thought, dimly traced in the designs of Verrocchio, she is found present at last in Il Giocondo's house. That there is much of mere portraiture in the picture is attested by the legend that by artificial means, the presence of mimes and flute-players, that subtle expression was protracted on the face. Again, was it in four years and by renewed labour never really completed, or in four months and as by stroke of magic, that the image was projected?

The presence that thus so strangely rose beside the waters is expressive of what in the ways of a thousand years man had come to desire. Hers is the head upon which all 'the ends of the world are come,' and the eyelids are a little weary. It is a beauty wrought out from within upon the flesh, the deposit, little cell by cell, of strange thoughts and fantastic reveries and exquisite passions. Set it for a moment beside one of those white Greek goddesses or beautiful women of antiquity, and how would they be troubled by this beauty, into which the soul with all its maladies has passed?[3] All the thought and experience of the world have etched and moulded there in that which they have of power to refine and make expressive the outward form, the animalism of Greece, the

---

1 Giorgio Vasari (1511-74), painter, architect, and author of *Le Vite de' più eccellenti Architetti, Pittori, et Scultori Italiani*, (popularly known in English as *Lives of the Artists*), first published in 1550 and best known in the second, much enlarged, edition of 1568. *Le Vite*, one of the most important art history books ever written, is the source for many of the details in Pater's essay.

2 Andrea del Verrocchio (1435-88), Florentine painter, goldsmith, and sculptor, and the teacher of Leonardo.

3 Erroneous question mark altered to exclamation mark in subsequent editions.

lust of Rome, the reverie of the middle age with its spiritual ambition and imaginative loves, the return of the Pagan world, the sins of the Borgias.[1] She is older than the rocks among which she sits; like the vampire, she has been dead many times, and learned the secrets of the grave; and has been a diver in deep seas, and keeps their fallen day about her; and trafficked for strange webs with Eastern merchants; and, as Leda, was the mother of Helen of Troy, and, as Saint Anne, the mother of Mary;[2] and all this has been to her but as the sound of lyres and flutes, and lives only in the delicacy with which it has moulded the changing lineaments and tinged the eyelids and the hands. The fancy of a perpetual life, sweeping together ten thousand experiences, is an old one; and modern thought has conceived the idea of humanity as wrought upon by, and summing up in itself, all modes of thought and life. Certainly Lady Lisa might stand as the embodiment of the old fancy, the symbol of the modern idea.

---

1 The Borgias were an Italian noble family of Spanish descent infamous during the Renaissance for their vice and depravity.
2 Leda, wife of Tyndareus, King of Sparta, who, ravished by Zeus in the form of a swan, gave birth to the twins Castor and Pollux, and to Helen, the most beautiful woman in the world and the cause of the Trojan War; Saint Anne, the traditional name given to the mother of the Virgin Mary.

Appendix D: Vernon Lee, "Faustus and Helena: Notes on the Supernatural in Art" (1880, 1881)[1]

[In her essay "Faustus and Helena: Notes on the Supernatural in Art," first published in 1880, Vernon Lee proposes that art and the supernatural are incompatible in that art requires definition for its representations whereas the supernatural depends on suggestion and requires a lack of definite form in order to produce its effects. However, Lee's description of a sketch that does manage to communicate the supernatural implies that art can have supernatural effects if these are achieved through suggestion, and this seems to be the means used in her *Hauntings* stories where imaginative suggestion in the ephemeral and insubstantial form of memories, impressions, associations, relics, and fragments triggers ghostly occurrences.]

THERE is a story, well-known throughout the sixteenth century, which tells how Doctor Faustus of Wittenberg, having made over his soul to the fiend, employed him to raise the ghost of Helen of Sparta, in order that she might become his paramour. The story has no historic value, no scientific meaning; it lacks the hoary dignity of the tales of heroes and demi-gods, wrought, vague, and colossal forms, out of cloud and sunbeam, of those tales narrated and heard by generations of men deep hidden in the stratified ruins of lost civilisation, carried in the races from India to Hellas,[2] and to Scandinavia. Compared with them, this tale of Faustus and Helena is paltry and brand-new; it is not a myth, nay, scarcely a legend; it is a mere trifling incident added by humanistic pedantry to the ever-changing mediæval story of the man who barters his soul for knowledge, the wizard, alchemist,

---

1 "Faustus and Helena: Notes on the Supernatural in Art," first published in *Cornhill Magazine* 42 (1880), and reprinted in *Belcaro: Being Essays on Sundry Æsthetical Questions* (London: W. Satchell, 1881), pp. 70-105, from which this text is taken. *Belcaro* is dedicated to Lee's friend, the poet A. Mary. F. Robinson.
2 Ancient Greek name for Greece.

philosopher, printer, Albertus, Bacon, or Faustus.[1] It is a part, an unessential, subordinate fragment, valued in its day neither more nor less than any other part of the history of Doctor Faustus, narrated cursorily by the biographer of the wizard, overlooked by some of the ballad rhymers, alternately used and rejected by the playwrights of puppet-shows; given by Marlowe[2] himself no greater importance than the other marvellous deeds, the juggling tricks and magic journeys of his hero.

But for us, the incident of Faustus and Helena has a meaning, a fascination wholly different from any other portion of the story; the other incidents owe everything to artistic treatment: this one owes nothing. The wizard Faustus, awaiting the hour which will give him over to Hell, is the creation of Marlowe; Gretchen is even more completely the creation of Goethe;[3] the fiend of the Englishman is occasionally grand, the fiend of the German is throughout masterly; in all these cases we are in the presence of true artistic work, of stuff rendered valuable solely by the hand of the artist, of figures well defined and finite, and limited also in their power over the imagination. But the group of Faustus and Helena is different; it belongs neither to Marlowe nor to Goethe, it belongs to the legend. It does not give the complete and limited satisfaction of a work of art; it has the charm of the fantastic and fitful shapes formed by the flickering firelight or the wreathing mists; it haunts like some vague strain of music, drowsily heard in half-sleep. It fills the fancy, it oscillates and transforms itself; the artist may see it, and attempt to seize and embody it for evermore in a definite and enduring shape, but it vanishes out of his grasp, and the forms which should have inclosed it are mere empty sepulchres, haunted and charmed merely by the evoking power of our own imagination. If we are fascinated by the Lady Helen of Marlowe, walking, like some Florentine goddess, with

---

1 Albertus Magnus (c. 1193-1280), Swabian Dominican monk and noted scholastic philosopher; Roger Bacon (c. 1214-94), English Franciscan, philosopher, student of experimental science, who reputedly practiced black magic; Faustus or Faust (c. 1488-1541), wandering German astrologer and necromancer, reputed to have sold his soul to the devil and the subject of dramas by Christopher Marlowe and the leading German writer Johann Wolfgang von Goethe (1749-1832).

2 Christopher Marlowe (1564-93), English poet and playwright and author of The Tragedy of Doctor Faustus (1604, 1616).

3 Gretchen (German diminutive of Margaret) is a young girl in Goethe's play Faust (Part 1, 1808) who is seduced by Faust.

embroidered kirtle and madonna face, across the study of the old wizard of Wittenberg; if we are pleased by the stately pseudo-antique Helena of Goethe, draped in the drapery of Thorwaldsen's statues,[1] and speaking the language of Goethe's own Iphigenia,[2] as she meets the very modern Faust, gracefully masqued in mediæval costume; if we find in these attempts, the one unthinking and imperfect, the other laboured and abortive, something which delights our fancy, it is because our thoughts wander off from them and evoke a Faustus and Helena of our own, different from the creations of Marlowe and of Goethe; it is because in these definite and imperfect artistic forms, there yet remains the suggestion of the subject with all its power over the imagination. We forget Marlowe, and we forget Goethe, to follow up the infinite suggestion of the legend. We cease to see the Elizabethan and the pseudo-antique Helen; we lift our imagination from the book and see the mediæval street at Wittenberg, the gabled house of Faustus, all sculptured with quaint devices and grotesque forms of apes and cherubs and flowers; we penetrate through the low brown rooms, filled with musty books and mysterious ovens and retorts, redolent with strange scents of alchemy, to that innermost secret chamber, where the old wizard hides, in the depths of his mediæval house, the immortal woman, the god-born, the fatal, the beloved of Theseus and Paris and Achilles;[3] we are blinded by this sunshine of Antiquity pent up in the oaken-panelled chamber, such as Dürer might have etched;[4] and all around we hear circulating the mysterious rumours of the neighbours, of the burghers and students, whispering shyly of Dr.

---

1   Bertel Thorwaldsen (c. 1768-1844), famous Danish Neoclassical sculptor.
2   *Iphigenia in Tauris* (1787), play by Goethe based on one by the Greek tragedian Euripides (c. 484-406 BC) about Iphigenia, priestess of Tauris who is obliged by orders of King Thoas to sacrifice passing strangers. In Goethe's version, when her brother and cousin arrive, the noble Iphigenia manages to persuade King Thoas to let them all journey back to Greece.
3   Paris, son of King Priam of Troy, stole Helen of Sparta, the most beautiful woman in the world, from her husband Menelaus, thereby provoking the Trojan war; Theseus, a Greek hero and former suitor of Helen's, who abducted her while she was still a girl intending to marry her. Her brothers reclaimed her while he was temporarily in the Underworld. According to one tradition, the Greek hero and warrior Achilles fell in love with Helen shortly before his death and married her.
4   Albrecht Dürer (1471-1528), German Renaissance engraver and painter.

Faustus and his strange guest, in the beer cellars and in the cloisters of the old university town. And gazing thus into the fantastic intellectual mist which has risen up between us and the book we were reading, be it Marlowe or Goethe, we cease, after a while, to see Faustus or Helena, we perceive only a chaotic fluctuation of incongruous shapes; scholars in furred robes and caps pulled over their ears, burghers' wives with high sugar-loaf coif and slashed boddices, with hands demurely folded over their prayer-books, and knights in armour and immense plumes, and haggling Jews, and tonsured monks, descended out of panels of Wohlgemüth[1] and the engravings of Dürer, mingling with, changing into processions of naked athletes on foaming short-maned horses, of draped Athenian maidens carrying baskets and sickles, and priests bearing oil-jars and torches, all melting into each other, indistinct, confused, like the images in a dream; vague crowds, phantoms following in the wake of the spectre woman of Antiquity, beautiful, unimpassioned, ever young, luring to Hell the wizard of the Middle Ages.

Why does all this vanish as soon as we once more fix our eyes upon the book? Why can our fancy show us more than can the artistic genius of Marlowe and of Goethe? Why does Marlowe, believing in Helen as a satanic reality, and Goethe, striving after her as an artistic vision, equally fail to satisfy us? The question is intricate: it requires a threefold answer, dependent on the fact that this tale of Faustus and Helena is in fact a tale of the supernatural—a weird and colossal ghost-story, in which the actors are the spectre of Antiquity, ever young, beautiful, radiant, though risen from the putrescence of two thousand years; and the Middle Ages, alive, but toothless, palsied, and tottering. Why neither Marlowe nor Goethe have succeeded in giving a satisfactory artistic shape to this tale is explained by the necessary relations between art and the supernatural, between our creative power and our imaginative faculty; why Marlowe has failed in one manner and Goethe in another is explained by the fact that, as we said, for the first the tale was a supernatural reality, for the second a supernatural fiction.

What are the relations between art and the supernatural? At first sight the two appear closely allied: like the supernatural, art is born of imagination; the supernatural, like art, conjures up

---

1   Michael Wohlgemüth (1434-1519), Dürer's master, Nuremberg painter and designer of wood-cut book illustrations. His "panels" are probably triptych paintings.

unreal visions. The two have been intimately connected during the great ages of the supernatural, when instead of existing merely in a few disputed traditional dogmas, and in a little discredited traditional folklore, it constituted the whole of religion and a great part of philosophy. Gods and demons, saints and spectres, have afforded at least one-half of the subjects for art. The supernatural, in the shape of religious mythology, had art bound in its service in Antiquity and the Middle Ages; the supernatural, in the shape of spectral fancies, regained its dominion over art with the advent of romanticism. From the gods of the *Iliad* down to the Commander in *Don Giovanni*, from the sylvan divinities of Praxiteles to the fairies of Shakespeare, from the Furies of Æschylus to the Archangels of Perugino,[1] the supernatural and the artistic have constantly appeared linked together. Yet, in reality, the hostility between the supernatural and the artistic is well-nigh as great as the hostility between the supernatural and the logical. Critical reason is a solvent, it reduces the phantoms of the imagination to their most prosaic elements; artistic power, on the other hand, moulds and solidifies them into distinct and palpable forms: the synthetical definiteness of art is as sceptical as the analytical definiteness of logic. For the supernatural is necessarily essentially vague, and art is necessarily essentially distinct: give shape to the vague and it ceases to exist. The task set to the artist by the dreamer, the prophet, the priest, the ghost-seer of all times, is as difficult, though in the opposite sense, as that by which the little girl in the Venetian fairy tale sought to test the omnipotence of the emperor. She asked him for a very humble dish, quite simple and not costly, a pat of butter broiled on a gridiron. The emperor desired his cook to place the butter on the gridiron and light the fire; all was going well, when,

---

1   *Iliad*, Greek epic poem attributed to the Greek epic poet Homer (dates uncertain) describing the incidents in the last year of the Trojan war and featuring various interventions by the Greek gods. In the conclusion to the opera *Don Giovanni* (first performed in 1787), by Wolfgang Amadeus Mozart (1756-91), the statue of the Commander appears at dinner to drag the dissolute Don Giovanni off to Hell. Praxiteles (fourth century BC), Greek sculptor whose statues feature various divinities. Fairies feature notably in William Shakespeare's *A Midsummer's Night's Dream* (composed c. 1594-6). The Furies are snake-haired goddesses sent to avenge wrong and punish crime and feature prominently in the drama *The Eumenides*, third play in the trilogy, the *Oresteia* by the Greek playwright Æschylus (525-426 BC). Perugino (c. 1445-1523), famous Perugian painter and teacher of Raphael.

behold! the butter began to melt, trickled off, and vanished. The artists were asked to paint, or model, or narrate the supernatural: they set about the work in good conscience, but see, the supernatural became the natural, the gods turned into men, the madonnas into mere mothers, the angels onto armed striplings, the phantoms into mere creatures of flesh and blood.

There are in reality two sorts of supernatural, although only one really deserves the name. A great number of beliefs in all mythologies are in reality mere scientific errors—abortive attempts to explain phenomena by causes with which they have no connection—the imagination plays not more part in them than in any other sort of theorising, and the notions that unlucky accidents are due to a certain man's glance, that certain formulæ will bring rain or sunshine, that miraculous images will dispel pestilence, and kings of England cure epilepsy, must be classed under the head of mistaken generalizations, not very different in point of fact from exploded scientific theories, such as Descartes' vortices,[1] or the innate ideas of scholasticism. That there was a time when animals spoke with human voice may seem to us a piece of fairy-lore, but it was in its day a scientific hypothesis as brilliant and satisfying as Darwin's theory of evolution.[2] We must, therefore, in examining the relations between the art and the supernatural, eliminate as far as possible this species of scientific speculation, and consider only that supernatural which really deserves the name, which is beyond and outside the limits of the possible, the rational, the explicable—that supernatural which is due not to the logical faculties, arguing from wrong premises, but to the imagination wrought upon by certain kinds of physical surroundings. The divinity of the earlier races is in some measure a mistaken scientific hypothesis of the sort we have described, an attempt to explain phenomena otherwise inexplicable. But it is much more: it is the effect on the imagination of certain external impressions, it is those impressions brought to a focus, personified, but personified vaguely, in a fluctuating ever-

---

1 René Descartes (1596-1650), one of the founders of modern mathematics, and famous for his analytical geography and his theory of vortices which rests on an assumption that the matter of the universe must be in motion and that motion must result in a number of vortices. The theory was shown to be flawed by Isaac Newton (1642-1727) in his second book of the *Principia* in 1687.
2 Charles Darwin (1809-82). His theory of evolution is expounded in his *On the Origin of the Species by Means of Natural Selection* (1859).

changing manner; the personification being continually altered, reinforced, blurred out, enlarged, restricted by new series of impressions from without, even as the shape which we puzzle out of congregated cloud-masses fluctuates with their every movement—a shifting vapour now obliterates the form, now compresses it into greater distinctness: the wings of the fantastic monster seem now flapping leisurely, now extending bristling like a griffon's;[1] at one moment it has a beak and talons, at others a mane and hoofs; the breeze, the sunlight, the moonbeam, form, alter, and obliterate it. Thus is it with the supernatural: the gods, moulded out of cloud and sunlight and darkness, are for ever changing, fluctuating between a human or animal shape, god or goddess, cow, ape, or horse, and the mere phenomenon which impresses the fancy. Pan[2] is the weird, shaggy, cloven-footed shape which the goat-herd or the huntsman has seen gliding among the bushes in the grey twilight; his is the piping heard in the tangle of reeds, marsh lily, and knotted nightshade by the river side: but Pan is also the wood, with all its sights and noises, the solitude, the gloom, the infinity of rustling leaves, and cracking branches; he is the greenish-yellow light stealing in amid the boughs; he is the breeze in the foliage, the murmur of unseen waters, the mist hanging over the damp sward, the ferns and grasses which entangle the feet, and the briars which catch in the hair and garments are his grasp; and the wanderer dashes through the thickets with a sickening fear in his heart, and sinks down on the outskirts of the forest, gasping, with sweat-clotted hair, overcome by this glimpse of the great god.

In this constant renewal of the impressions on the fancy, in this unceasing shaping and reshaping of its creations, consisted the vitality of the myths of paganism, from the scorching and pestilence-bearing gods of India to the divinities shaped out of tempest and snowdrift of Scandinavia; they were constantly issuing out of the elements, renewed, changed, ever young, under the exorcism not only of the priest and of the poet, but of the village boor; and on this unceasing renovation depended the sway which they maintained, without ethical importance to help them, despite philosophy and Christianity. Christianity, born in an age of speculation and eclecticism, removed its divinities, its mystic

---

1 A griffon or griffin is a fabulous creature with an eagle's head and wings and a lion's body.
2 Pan, in form half man half goat, is the god of woods, fields and flocks. Lee echoes this passage in her story "Dionea."

figures, out of the cosmic surroundings of paganism; it forbade the imagination to touch or alter them, it regularised, defined, explained, placed the Saviour, the Virgin, the saints and angels, into a kind of supersensuous world of logic, logic adapted to Heaven, and different therefore from the logic of earth, but logic none the less. Christianity endowed them with certain definite attributes, not to be found among mortals, but analogous in a manner to mortal attributes; the Christian supernatural system belongs mainly to the category of mistaken scientific systems; its peculiarities are due, not to overwrought fancy, but to overtaxed reason. Thus the genuine supernatural was well-nigh banished by official Christianity, regulated as it was by a sort of congress of men of science, who eliminated, to the best of their powers, any vagaries of the imagination which might show themselves in their mystico-logic system. But the imagination did work nevertheless, and the supernatural did reappear, both within and without the Christian system of mythology. The Heaven of theology was too ethical, too logical, too positive, too scientific, in accordance with the science of the Middle Ages, for the minds of humanity at large; the scholars and learned clergy might study and expound it, but it was insufficient for the ignorant. The imagination reappeared once more. To the monk arose out of the silence and gloom of the damp, lichen-grown crypt, out of the fœtid emanations of the charnal-house, strange forms of horror which lurked in his steps and haunted his sleep after fasting and scourging and vigils; devils and imps, horrible and obscene, which the chisel of the stonecutter vainly attempted to reproduce, in their fluctuating abomination, on the capitals and gargoyles of cloister and cathedral. To the artisan, the weaver pent up in some dark cellar into which the daylight stole grey and faint from the narrow strip of blue sky between the overhanging eaves, for him, the hungry and toil-worn and weary of soul, there arose out of the hum of the street above, out of the half-lit dust, the winter damp and summer suffocation of the underground workshop, visions and sounds of sweetness and glory, misty clusters of white-robed angels shedding radiance around them, swaying in mystic linked dances, mingling with the sordid noises of toil seraphic harmonies, now near, now dying away into the distance, voices singing of the sunshine and flowers of Paradise. And for others, for the lean and tattered peasant, with the dull, apathetic resignation of the starved and goaded ox or horse, sleeping on the damp clay of his hut and eating strange flourless bread, and stranger carrion flesh, there came a world of the supernatural, different from that of the monk or the artisan, at once terrifying and consoling; the divinities cast out by Christianity, the divinities for ever newly begotten by nature, but begotten of a nature miserably changed, born in exile and obloquy and persecution, fostered by the wretched and the brutified; differing from the gods of antiquity as the desolate heath, barren of all save stones and prickly furze and thistle, differs from the fertile pasture-land; as the forests planted over the cornfield, whence issue wolves, and the Baron's harvest-trampling horses, differ from the forests which gave their oaks and pines to Tyrian ships;[1] divinities warped, and crippled, grown hideous and malignant and unhappy in the likeness of their miserable votaries.

This is the real supernatural, born of the imagination and its surroundings, the vital, the fluctuating, the potent; and it is this which the artist of every age, from Phidias to Giotto, from Giotto to Blake,[2] has been called upon to make known to the multitude. And there had been artistic work going on unnoticed long before the time of any painter or sculptor or poet of whom we have any record; mankind longed from the first to embody, to fix its visions of wonder, it set to work with rough unskilful fingers moulding into shape its divinities. Rude work, ugly, barbarous, blundering scratchings on walls, kneaded clay vessels, notched sticks, nonsense rhymes; but work nevertheless which already showed that art and the supernatural were at variance, the beaked and clawed figures outlined on the wall were compromises between the man and the beast, but definite compromises, so much and no more of the man, so much and no more of the beast; the goddess on the clay vessels became a mere little owl; the divinities even in the nonsense verses were presented now as very distinct cows, now as very distinct clouds, or very distinct men and women; the vague, fluctuating impressions oscillating before the imagination like the colours of a dove's wing, or the pattern of a shot silk, interwoven, unsteady, never completely united into one, never completely separated into several, were rudely seized, disentangled by art; part was taken, part thrown aside; what remained was homogeneous, definite, unchanging; it was what it was and could never be aught else.

---

1 Tyre is an ancient seaport of the Phoenicians on the Lebanon coast.

2 Phidias, Greek sculptor of the fifth century BC, famous for colossal sculptures of gold and ivory which have not survived; Giotto di Bordone (c. 1266-1337) Florentine painter and architect; William Blake (1757-1827), Romantic poet, painter, engraver, and mystic.

Goethe has remarked, with a subjective simplicity of irrever-
ence which is almost comical, that as God created man in his
image, it was only fair that man, in his turn, should create God in
his image. But the decay of pagan belief was not, as Hegel[1] imagines, due to the fact that Hellenic art was anthropomorphic. The
gods ceased to be gods not merely because they became too like
men, but because they became too like anything definite. If the
ibis on the amulet, or the owl on the terra-cotta, represents a
more vital belief in the gods than does the Venus of Milo or the
Giustiniani Minerva,[2] it is not because the idea of divinity is
more compatible with an ugly bird than with a beautiful woman,
but because whereas the beautiful woman, exquisitely wrought
by a consummate sculptor, occupied the mind of the artist and of
the beholder with the idea of her beauty, to the exclusion of all
else, the rudely-engraven ibis, or the badly-modelled owlet, on
the other hand, served merely as a symbol, as the recaller of an
idea; the mind did not pause in contemplation of the bird, but
wandered off in search of the god: the goggle eyes of the owl and
the beak of the ibis were soon forgotten in the contemplation of
the vague, ever transmuted visions of phenomena of sky and
light, of semi-human and semi-bestial shapes, of confused half-
embodied forces; in short, of the supernatural. But the human
shape did most mischief to the supernatural, merely because the
human shape was the most absolute, the most distinct of all
shapes: a god might be symbolised as a beast, but he could only
be pourtrayed as a man; and if the portrait was correct, then the
god was a man, and nothing more. Even the most fantastic
among pagan supernatural creatures, those strange monsters who
longest kept their original dual nature—the centaurs, satyrs, and
tritons[3]—became, beneath the chisel of the artist, mere aberra-

---

1 Georg Wilhem Friedrich Hegel (1770-1831), German philosopher in
   whose system of Absolute Idealism pure being is regarded as pure
   thought and the universe as its development.
2 The Venus of Milo, famous antique statue, now in the Louvre, Paris,
   discovered in 1820 on the Aegean island of Melos. The Giustiniani
   Minerva, now in the Vatican, Rome, depicts the goddess of wisdom and
   defensive war, and is a Roman copy of a Greek original, probably
   created by the sculptor Euphranor (fourth century BC), and originally
   owned by the Giustiniani family in the seventeenth century.
3 Centaur: a creature half man half horse; satyr: creature with human
   upper body and head but with goat's ears, tail, legs, and budding horns;
   triton: a sea-god in the form of a merman, often carrying a conch-shell
   trumpet.

tions from the normal, rare, and curious types like certain fair-booth phenomena, but perfectly intelligible and rational; the very Chimæra,[1] she who was to give her name to every sort of unintelligible fancy, became, in the bas-reliefs of the story of Bellerophon[2] a mere singular mixture between a lion, a dog, and a bird—a cross-breed which happens not to be possible, but which an ancient might well have conceived as adorning some distant zoological collection. How much more rationalised were not the divinities in whom only a peculiar shape of the eye, a certain structure of the leg, or a definite fashion of wearing the hair remained of their former nature. Learned men, indeed, tell us that we need only glance at Hera to see that she is at bottom a cow; at Apollo, to recognise that he is but a stag in human shape: or at Zeus,[3] to recognise that he is, in point of fact, a lion. Yet it remains true that we need only walk down the nearest street to meet ten ordinary men and women who look more like various animals than do any antique divinities, and who can yet never be said to be in reality cows, stags, or lions. The same applies to the violent efforts which are constantly being made to show in the Greek and Latin poets a distinct recollection of the cosmic nature of the gods, construing the very human movements, looks, and dress of divinities into meteorological phenomena, as has been done even by Mr. Ruskin, in his *Queen of the Air*,[4] despite his artist's sense, which should have warned him that no artistic figure, like Homer's divinities, can possibly be at the same time a woman and a whirlwind. The gods did originally partake of the character of cosmic phenomena, as they partook of the characters of beasts and birds, and of every other species of transformation, such as we may watch in dreams; but as soon as they were artistically embodied, this transformation ceased, the nature had to be specified in proportion as the form became distinct; and the drapery of Pallas, although it had inherited its purple tint from the storm-cloud, was none the less, when it clad the shoulders of

---

1   The original Chimaera of Greek myth was a fire-breathing creature with a lion's head, goat's body and serpent's tail.
2   Bellerophon, the Greek hero who slew the Chimaera with the help of the winged horse Pegasus.
3   Hera is queen of the gods and wife of Zeus, king of the gods; Apollo, son of Zeus and Leto, god of the sun, of music, poetry and prophecy.
4   John Ruskin (1819-1900), major Victorian thinker and critic. His *Queen of the Air* (1869) is a study of Athena and reflects a contemporary interest in comparative mythology.

the goddess, not a storm-cloud, but a piece of purple linen. "What do you want of me?" asks the artist. "A god," answers the believer. "What is your god to be like?" asks the artist. "My god is to be a very handsome warrior, a serene heaven, which is occasionally overcast with clouds, which clouds are sometimes very beneficial, and become (and so does the god at those moments) heavy-uddered cows; at others, they are dark, and cause annoyance, and then they capture the god, who is the light (but he is also the clouds, remember), and lock him up in a tower, and then he frees himself, and he is a neighing horse, and he is sitting on the prancing horse (which is himself, you know, and is the sky too), in the shape of two warriors, and also—" "May Cerberus[1] devour you!" cries the artist. "How can I represent all this? Do you want a warrior, or a cow, or the heavens, or a horse, or do you want a warrior with the hoofs of a horse and the horns of a cow? Explain, for, by Juno,[2] I can give you only one of these at a time."

Thus, in proportion as the gods were subjected to artistic manipulation, whether by sculptor or poet, they lost their supernatural powers. A period there doubtless was when the gods stood out quite distinct from nature, and yet remained connected with it, as the figures of a high relief stand out from the background; but gradually they were freed from the chaos of impressions which had given them birth, and then, little by little, they ceased to be gods; they were isolated from the world of the wonderful, they were respectfully shelved off into the region of the ideal, where they were contemplated, admired, discussed, but not worshipped even like their statues by Praxiteles and their pictures by Parrhasius.[3] The divinities who continued to be reverenced were the rustic divinities and the foreign gods and goddesses; the divinities which had been safe from the artistic desecration of the cities, and the divinities which were imported from hieratic, unartistic countries like Egypt and Syria; on the one hand, the gods shaped with the pruning-knife out of figwood, and stained with ochre or wine-lees, grotesque mannikins, standing like scarecrows, in orchard or corn-field, to which the peasants crowded in devout procession, leading their cleanly-dressed little

---

1 Cerberus is a fierce three-headed watch-dog who guards the entrance to the Underworld.
2 Juno, in the Roman mythological pantheon, known as Hera in the Greek pantheon, is the wife of Jupiter, king of the gods.
3 Parrhasius of Ephesus (fifth-fourth centuries BC), one of the most famous Greek painters noted for his fine lines and use of colour.

ones, and carrying gifts of fruit and milk, while the listless Tibullus,[1] fresh from sceptical Rome, looked on from his doorstep, a vague, childish veneration stealing over his mind; on the other hand, the monstrous goddesses, hundred-breasted or ibis-headed, half hidden in the Syrian and Egyptian temples, surrounded by mysterious priests, swarthy or effeminate, in mitres and tawny robes, jangling their sistra and clashing their cymbals, moving in mystic or frenzied dances, weird, obscene, and unearthly, to the melancholy drone of Phrygian or Egyptian music, sending a shudder through the atheist Catullus,[2] and filling his mind with ghastly visions of victims of the great goddess, bleeding, fainting, lashed on to madness by the wrath of the terrible divinity. These were the last survivors of paganism, and to their protection clung the old gods of Greece and Rome, reduced to human level by art, stripped naked by sculptor and poet and muffling themselves in the homely or barbaric garments of low-born or outlandish usurpers; art had been a worse enemy than scepticism: Apelles and Scopas had done more mischief than Epicurus.[3]

Christian art was, perhaps, more reverent in intention, but not less desecrating in practice; even the Giottesques[4] turned Christ, the Virgin, and the Saints, into mere Florentine men and women; even Angelico[5] himself, although a saint, was unable to show Paradise except as a flowery meadow, under a highly gilded sky, through which moved ladies and youths in most artistic but most earthly embroidered garments; and Hell except as a very hot place where men and women were being boiled and broiled and baked and fried and roasted by very comic little weasel-snouted fiends, which on a carnival car would have made Florentines roar with laughter. The real supernatural was in the cells of fever-

---

1 Albius Tibullus (c. 50-19 BC), Latin elegiac poet. Lee's description is reminiscent of his *Poems*, Book I, Poem 10.
2 Gaius Valerius Catullus (c. 84-54 BC), Roman poet. Poem 63, one of his most famous poems, is addressed to Cybele, the great eastern Mother goddess whose male priests ritually castrate themselves.
3 Apelles of Kos (c. 352-308 BC), celebrated painter; Scopas (c. 395-350 BC), sculptor and architect from the island of Paros; Epicurus (341-270 BC), Athenian philosopher who believed that human beings could gain knowledge of the world by relying on the senses and held that the highest good was pleasure (conceived of as calmness of mind).
4 The Giottesques (or Giotteschi) are Florentine and Sienese painters of the mid-fourteenth century influenced by Giotto.
5 Fra Angelico (Fra Giovanni da Fiesole, c. 1400-55), Dominican friar and major Florentine painter.

stricken, starved visionaries; it was in the contagious awe of the crowd sinking down at the sight of the stained napkin of Bolsena;[1] in that soiled piece of linen was Christ, and God, and Paradise; in that and not in the panels of Angelico and Perugino, or in the frescoes of Signorelli and Filippino.[2]

Why? Because the supernatural is nothing but ever-renewed impressions, ever-shifting fancies; and that art is the definer, the embodier, the analytic and synthetic force of form. Every artistic embodiment of impressions or fancies implies isolation of those impressions or fancies, selection, combination and balancing of them; that is to say, diminution—nay, destruction of their inherent power. As, in order to be moulded, the clay must be separated from the mound; as, in order to be carved, the wood must be cut off from the tree; as, in order to be re-shaped by art, the mass of atoms must be rudely severed; so also the mental elements of art, the mood, the fancy must be severed from the preceding and succeeding moods or fancies; artistic manipulation requires that its intellectual, like its tangible materials, cease to be vital, but the materials, mental or physical, are not only deprived of vitality and power of self-alteration; they are combined in given proportions, the action of the one on the other destroys in great part the special power of each; art is proportion, and proportion is restriction. Last of all, but most important, these isolated, no longer vital materials, neutralised by each other, are further reduced to insignificance by becoming parts of a whole conception; their separate meaning is effaced by the general meaning of the work of art; art bottles lightning to use it as white colour, and measures out thunder by the beat of the chapel-master's roll of notes. But art does not merely restrict impressions and fancies within the limits of form; in its days of maturity and independence it restricts yet closer within the limits of beauty. Partially developed art, still unconscious of its powers and aims, still in childish submission to religion, sets to work conscientiously, with no other object than to embody the supernatural; if the supernatu-

---

1   According to the Catholic Church the miracle of Bolsena which occurred in 1263 was performed to convince a sceptical priest of the reality of the transformation of the sacred elements. When, during the mass, he had consecrated the wafer, blood flowed from it and stained the napkin on which it lay. The napkin, or *corporale*, was taken to Pope Urban IV who was residing in the nearby city of Orvieto who absolved the priest and had the napkin enshrined as a holy relic in the cathedral.

2   For Angelico and Perugino, see above; Luca Signorelli (c. 1441-1523) and Filippino (Filippino Lippi 1457/8-1504), son of Fra Filippo Lippi (c. 1406-69), are both fresco painters.

ral suffers in the act of embodiment, if the fluctuating fancies which are Zeus or Pallas[1] are limited and curtailed, rendered logical and prosaic even in the wooden pre-historic idol or the roughly kneaded clay owlet, it is by no choice of the artist—his attempt is abortive, because it is thwarted by the very nature of his art. But when art is mature, things are different; the artist, conscious of his powers, instinctively recognising the futility of aiming at the embodiment of the supernatural, dragged by an irresistible longing to the display of his skill, to the imitation of the existing and to the creation of beauty, ceases to strain after the impossible and refuses to attempt anything beyond the possible. The art, which was before a mere insufficient means, is now an all-engrossing aim; unconsciously, perhaps, to himself, the artist regards the subject merely as a pretext for the treatment; and where the subject is opposed to such treatment as he desires, he sacrifices it. He may be quite as conscientious as his earliest predecessor, but his conscience has become an artistic conscience, he sees only as much as is within art's limits; the gods, or the saints, which were cloudy and supernatural to the artist of immature art, are definite and artistic to the artist of mature art; he can think, imagine, feel only in a given manner; his religious conceptions have taken the shape of his artistic creations; art has destroyed the supernatural, and the artist has swallowed up the believer. The attempts at supernatural effects are almost always limited to a sort of symbolical abbreviation, which satisfies the artist and his public respecting the subject of the work, and lends it a traditional association of the supernatural; a few spikes round the head of a young man are all that remains of the solar nature of Apollo; the little budding horns and pointed ears of the satyr must suffice to recall that he was once a mystic fusion of man and beast and forest; a gilded disc behind the head is all that shows that Giotto's figures are immortals in glory; and a pair of wings is all that explains that Perugino's St. Michael is not a mere dainty mortal warrior; the highest mysteries of Christianity are despatched with a triangle and an open book, to draw which Raphael might employ his colour-grinder, while he himself drew the finely-draped baker's daughter from Trastevere.[2]

---

1   Pallas Athena (Minerva in the Roman pantheon) is goddess of wisdom.
2   Raphael or Raffaello Sanzio (1483-1520), one of the great High Renaissance painters. According to Giorgio Vasari, he painted two intimate portraits of Margherita Luti, a baker's daughter from Trastevere, the working-class quarter of Rome, with whom he was in love: a clothed study called *La Velata* ("The Veiled Lady") and a nude study *La Fornarina* ("The Baker's Daughter").

In all these cases the artist refused to grapple with the supernatural, and dismissed it with a mere stereotyped symbol, not more artistic than the names which he might have engraved beneath each figure. Religious associations were thus awakened without the artist, whether of the time of Pericles or of the time of Leo X.,[1] giving himself further trouble; the diffusion of religious ideas and feeling spared art from being religious. Let us, therefore, in order to judge fairly of what art can or cannot do for the supernatural, seek for one of the very rare instances in which the artist has had no symbolical abbreviations at his disposal, and has been obliged, if he would awaken any idea in the mind of the spectator, to do so by means of his artistic creations. The number of such exceptional instances is extremely limited in the great art of antiquity and the Renaissance, when artistic subjects were almost always traditionally religious or plainly realistic, and consequently intelligible at first sight. There is, however, an example, and that example is a masterpiece. It is the engraving by Agostino Veneziano, after a lost drawing by Raphael, generally called "Lo Stregozzo," and representing a witch going to the Sabbath.[2] Through a swampy country, amidst rank and barren vegetation, sweeps the triumphal procession—strange, beautiful, and ghastly; a naked boy dashes headlong in front, bestriding a long-haired he-goat, and blowing a horn, little stolen children packed behind on his saddle; on he dashes, across the tufts of marsh-lily and bulrush, across stagnant pools of water, clearing the way and announcing his mistress the witch. She thrones, old, parched, lank, high on the top of an unearthly car, made of the spine and ribs of some antediluvian creature, with springs and traces of ghastly jaw and collar and thigh bones, supported on either side by galloping skeletons, skeletons made up of skeletons, of all that is strangest in the bones and beaks of beasts and birds, on which ride young fauns and satyrs. To her chariot, by a yoke of human bones, are harnessed two stalwart naked youths, and two others sustain its plough-like end; grand, magnificently moving figures,

---

1 Pericles (c. 495-429 BC), Athenian statesman and commander under whom Athens reached the summit of her power; Leo X (1475-1521; reigned 1513-21), enthusiastic patron of the arts and science, making Rome a key cultural centre.

2 Agostino Veneziano (c. 1490-1540), Italian engraver. The design known as "Lo Stregozzo" ("The Witch's Procession") engraved by Veneziano is now attributed to Giulio Romano (1492/1499-1546), painter, architect, and one of the creators of Mannerism.

bounding forward like wild horses, the unearthly carriage swinging and creaking as they go. And, as they go, brushing through the high, dry, maremma-grass,[1] the witch cowers on her chariot, clutching in one hand a heap of babies, in the other a vessel filled with fire, whose smoke, mingling with her long, dishevelled hair, floats behind, sweeping through the rank vegetation, curling and eddying into vague, strange semblances of lions, apes, chimæras. Forward dashes the outrunner on his goat, onward bound the naked litter-bearers; up gallop the fauns and satyrs on the fleshless, monstrous carcases; up and down sways the creaking, cracking chariot of bones; one moment more, and the wild, splendid, hideous triumph will have swept out of sight, leaving behind only trampled marsh-plants and a trail of fantastic, lurid smoke among the ruffled, moaning reeds and grasses.

Such is Raphael's *Stregozzo*. It is a master-piece of drawing and of pictorial fancy, it is perhaps the highest achievement of great art in the direction of the supernatural: for Dürer is often hideous, Rembrandt always obscure, and the moderns, like Blake and Doré,[2] distinctly run counter to the essential nature of art in their attempts after vagueness. When once told the subject of the print, by Agostino Veneziano, our imagination easily flies off on to the track of the supernatural; but, in so doing, it leaves the work behind, and on return to it we experience a return to the natural. If, on the other hand, we are not told the subject of the print, we very possibly see nothing supernatural in it: there are splendid figures worthy of Michael Angelo,[3] and grotesque fancies, in the shape of the skeletons and coach of bones, worthy of Leonardo;[4] as a whole, the print is striking, beautiful, and problematic, but it falls short of the effect which would be produced by the mere words "a witch riding through a marsh on a chariot of bones," if left to insinuate themselves into the imagination. Of the really supernatural, there is in it but one touch: and that is the only part

1   The Tuscan Maremma in the province of Grosseto includes a wide plain under sea level.
2   Rembrandt Harmensz van Rijn (1606-69), greatest painter of the Dutch school and also a fine etcher; Paul Gustave Doré (1832-83), famous French designer of wood-engraved book-illustrations of Dante, Milton, Balzac, and others.
3   Michelangelo Buonarroti (1475-1564), hugely influential Italian sculptor, painter, and poet, noted for his anatomically accurate, imposing, and expressive representations of the human form.
4   Leonardo da Vinci (1452-1519), celebrated Italian painter, sculptor, architect, and man of science.

of the drawing which is left vague; it is the confused shapes assumed by the eddying smoke among the rushes. All the rest is outside the region of the supernatural: it is problematic in subject, but clear, harmonious, and beautiful in treatment; the imagination may wander from it, but in its presence it must remain passive. With this masterpiece we would fain compare a picture which seems to deal with a cognate subject; a picture as suggestive as it is absolutely artistically worthless. We saw it once, many years ago, among a heap of rubbishy smudges at a picture-dealer's in Rome, and we have never forgotten it—a picture painted by some German smearer of the early sixteenth century; very ugly, stupid, and unattractive; ill drawn, ill composed, of a uniform hard, vulgar brown. It represented, with no attempt at perspective, a level country spread out like a map, dotted here and there with little spired and turretted towns, also a castle or two, a few trees and some rivers, disposed with a child's satisfaction with their mere indication, as much as to say—"here is a town, there is a castle." Some peasants were represented working in the fields, a little train of horsemen coming out of a castle, and near one of the chess-board castles a grass plot with half-a-dozen lit stakes, to which tiny figures were carrying faggots, while men-at-arms and burghers, no bigger than flies, looked on. In the foreground of the great flat expanse lay a boor, a fellow dressed like a field-labourer, in heavy sleep on the ground. Round him on the grass were marked curious circles, and in them was moving a strange figure, in cloak and helmet, with clawed wings and horns, leering horridly, moving round on tiptoe, his arms outstretched, as if gradually encircling the sleeper in order to pounce upon him; despite the complete absence of artistic skill, the gradual inevitable approach of the demon, the irresistible network of circles with which he was surrounding his prey, was perfectly indicated. Above, in the sky, two figures, half demon, half dragon, floated leisurely, like a moored boat, as if a guard of the devil below. What is the exact subject of this picture? No one can tell; but its meaning is intense for the imagination, it has the frightful suggestiveness of some old book on witchcraft, prosaic and curt; of a page opened at random of Sprenger's *Malleus Malificarum*.[1] Yes;

---

1   The *Malleus Maleficarum* or "Hammer of Witches" is an infamous 1487 textbook designed to help identify witches and advise on their interrogation and torture. It was written by two Dominicans, Heinrich Kramer and James Sprenger, who were operating as members of the Catholic Inquisition in Germany in the 1480s.

over the plain, the towns, and castles, monotonous and dull, the fiends are hovering; even over the stakes where their votaries are being burnt; and see, the peasant asleep in the field, with his spade and hoe beside him, is being surrounded by magic circles, by the invisible nets of the demon, who prowls round him like a kite ready to pounce on to its quarry.

Why is there no need to write the word *witchcraft* beneath this picture? Why can this nameless smearer succeed where Raphael has failed? Because he is content to suggest to the imagination, and lets it create for itself its world of the supernatural; because he is not an artist, and because Raphael is; because he suggests everything and shows nothing, while Raphael creates, defines, perfects, gives form to that which is by its nature formless.

If we would bring home to ourselves this action of art on the supernatural, we must examine the only species of supernatural which still retains vitality, and can still be deprived of it by art. That which remains to us of the imaginative workings of the past is traditional and well-nigh effete: we have poems and pictures, Vedic hymns,[1] Hebrew psalms, and Egyptian symbols; we have folklore and dogma; remnants of the supernatural, some labelled in our historic museums, where they are scrutinised, catalogue and eye-glass in hand; others dusty on altars and in chapels, before which we uncover our heads and cast down our eyes: relics of dead and dying faiths, of which some are daily being transferred from the church to the museum; art cannot deprive any of these of that imaginative life and power which they have long ceased to possess. We have forms of the supernatural in which we believe from acquiesence of habit, but they are not vital; we have a form of the supernatural in which, from logic and habit, we disbelieve, but which is vital; and this form of the supernatural is the ghostly. We none of us believe in ghosts as logical possibilities, but we most of us conceive them as imaginative probabilities; we can still feel the ghostly, and thence it is that a ghost is the only thing which can in any respect replace for us the divinities of old, and enable us to understand, if only for a minute, the imaginative power which they possessed, and of which they were despoiled not only by logic, but by art. By *ghost* we do not mean the vulgar apparition which is seen or heard in told or written tales; we

---

1 The Vedas are the revealed Hindu scriptures and are among the most ancient religious texts still in existence. They contain hymns, rituals, and incantations, and some of the hymns are between six to eight thousand years old.

mean the ghost which slowly rises up in our mind, the haunter not of corridors and staircases, but of our fancies. Just as the gods of primitive religions were the undulating, bright heat which made mid-day solitary and solemn as midnight; the warm damp, the sap-riser and expander of life; the sad dying away of the summer, and the leaden, suicidal sterility of winter; so the ghost, their only modern equivalent, is the damp, the darkness, the silence, the solitude; a ghost is the sound of our steps through a ruined cloister, where the ivy-berries and convolvulus growing in the fissures sway up and down among the sculptured foliage of the windows, it is the scent of mouldering plaster and mouldering bones from beneath the broken pavement; a ghost is the bright moonlight against which the cypresses stand out like black hearse-plumes, in which the blasted grey olives and gnarled fig-trees stretch their branches over the broken walls like fantastic, knotted, beckoning fingers, and the abandoned villas on the outskirts of Italian towns, with the birds flying in and out of the unglazed windows, loom forth white and ghastly; a ghost is the long-closed room of one long dead, the faint smell of withered flowers, the rustle of long-unmoved curtains, the yellow paper and faded ribbons of long-unread letters ... each and all of these things, and a hundred others besides, according to our nature, is a ghost, a vague feeling we can scarcely describe, a something pleasing and terrible which invades our whole consciousness, and which, confusedly embodied, we half dread to see behind us, we know not in what shape, if we look round.

Call we in our artist, or let us be our own artist; embody, let us see or hear this ghost, let it become visible or audible to others besides ourselves; paint us that vagueness, mould into shape that darkness, modulate into chords that silence—tell us the character and history of those vague beings.... set to work boldly or cunningly. What do we obtain? A picture, a piece of music, a story; but the ghost is gone. In its stead we get oftenest the mere image of a human being; call it a ghost if you will, it is none. And the more complete the artistic work, the less remains of the ghost. Why do those stories affect us most in which the ghost is heard but not seen? Why do those places affect us most of which we merely vaguely know that they are haunted? Why most of all those which look as if they might be haunted? Why, as soon as a figure is seen, is the charm half-lost? And why, even when there is a figure, is it kept so vague and mist-like? Would you know Hamlet's father for a ghost unless he told you he was one? and can you remember it long while he speaks in mortal words? and what would be Hamlet's father without the terrace of Elsinore, the hour, and the moonlight? Do not these embodied ghosts owe what little effect they still possess to their surroundings, and are not the surroundings the real ghost?

Throw sunshine on to them, and what remains? Thus we have wandered through the realm of the supernatural in a manner neither logical nor business-like, for logic and business-likeness are rude qualities, and scare away the ghostly; very far away do we seem to have rambled from Dr. Faustus and Helen of Sparta; but in this labyrinth of the fantastic there are sudden unexpected turns—and see, one of these has suddenly brought us back into their presence. For we have seen why the supernatural is always injured by artistic treatment, why therefore the confused images evoked in our mind by the mere threadbare tale of Faustus and Helena are superior in imaginative power to the picture carefully elaborated and shown us by Goethe. We can now understand why under his hand the infinite charm of the weird meeting of antiquity and the Middle Ages has evaporated. We can explain why the strange fancy of the classic Walpürgis-night,[1] in the second part of *Faust*, at once stimulates the imagination and gives it nothing. If we let our mind dwell on that mysterious Pharsalian plain, with its glimmering fires and flamelets alone breaking the darkness, where Faust and Mephistopheles wandering about meet the spectres of antiquity, shadowy in the gloom—the sphinxes crouching, the sirens, the dryads and oreads, the griffons and cranes flapping their unseen wings overhead;[2] where Faust springs on the back of Chiron,[3] and as he is borne along sickens

---

1 Traditionally the night of 30 April on which a witches' Sabbath took place on the Brocken, a peak of the Harz mountains. In Goethe's *Faust*, Mephistopheles takes Faust to such a gathering in the Brocken and has him revel with the witches. However, in Part 2 Goethe also introduces the idea of a "classical" Walpürgis Night in which the diabolic guide and tempter Mephistopheles transports Faustus to the Pharsalian plain, entrance to Greece and scene of a famous battle between Pompey and Caesar. On the eve of the anniversary of the battle the legendary figures of antiquity reappear and by communing with them Faust researches how to find Helen, the object of his obsession.

2 Sphinx: winged monster with a woman's head and lion's body; sirens: women or birds with women's heads living on a treacherously rocky isle to which they lure seafarers by their dangerously sweet singing; dryad: nymph inhabiting tree; oread: mountain nymph.

3 Chiron the centaur, half man half horse, teacher, and physician, carries Faust on his back while telling him tales of the legendary persons he has known including Helen whom he has also carried.

for sudden joy when the centaur tells him that Helen has been carried on that back, has clasped that neck; when we let our mind work on all this, we are charmed by the weird meetings, the mysterious shapes which elbow us; but let us take up the volume and we return to barren prose, without colour or perfume. Yet Goethe felt the supernatural as we feel it, as it can be felt only in days of disbelief, when the more logical we become in our ideas, the more we view nature as a prosaic machine constructed by no one in particular, the more poignantly, on the other hand, do we feel the delight of the transient belief in the vague and the impossible; the greater the distinctness with which we see and understand all around us, the greater the longing for a momentary half-light in which forms may appear stranger, grander, vaguer than they are. We moderns seek in the world of the supernatural a renewal of the delightful semi-obscurity of vision and keenness of fancy of our childhood; when a glimpse into fairyland was still possible, when things appeared in false lights, brighter, more important, more magnificent than now. Art indeed can afford us calm and clear enjoyment of the beautiful—enjoyment serious, self-possessed, wide-awake, such as befits mature intellects; but no picture, no symphony, no poem, can give us that delight, that delusory, imaginative pleasure which we received as children from a tawdry engraving or a hideous doll; for around that doll there was an atmosphere of glory. In certain words, in certain sights, in certain snatches of melody, words, sights, and sounds which we now recognise as trivial, commonplace, and vulgar, there was an ineffable meaning; they were spells which opened doors into realms of wonder; they were precious in proportion as they were misappreciated. We now appreciate and despise; we see, we no longer imagine. And it is to replace this uncertainty of vision, this liberty of seeing in things much more than there is, which belongs to man and to mankind in this childhood, which compensated the Middle Ages for starvation and pestilence, and compensates the child for blows and lessons, it is to replace this that we crave after the supernatural, the ghostly—no longer believed, but still felt. It was from this sickness of the prosaic, this turning away from logical certainty, that the men of the end of the eighteenth and the beginning of this century, the men who had finally destroyed belief in the religious supernatural, who were bringing light with new sciences of economy, philology, and history—Schiller, Goethe, Herder,

Coleridge[1]—left the lecture-room and the laboratory, and set gravely to work on ghostly tales and ballads. It was from this rebellion against the tyranny of the possible that Goethe was charmed with that culmination of all impossibilities, that most daring of ghost stories, the story of Faustus and Helena. He felt the seduction of the supernatural, he tried to embody it—and he failed.

The case was different with Marlowe. The bringing together of Faustus and Helena had no special meaning for the man of the sixteenth century, too far from antiquity and too near the Middle Ages to perceive as we do the strange difference between them; and the supernatural had no fascination in a time when it was all permeating and everywhere mixed with prose. The whole play of *Dr. Faustus* is conceived in a thoroughly realistic fashion; it is tragic, but not ghostly. To Marlowe's audience, and probably to Marlowe himself, despite his atheistic reputation, the story of Faustus's wonders and final damnation was quite within the realm of the possible; the intensity of the belief in the tale is shown by the total absence of any attempt to give it dignity or weirdness. Faustus evokes Lucifer with a pedantic semi-biblical Latin speech; he goes about playing the most trumpery conjuror's tricks—snatching with invisible hands the food from people's lips, clapping horns and tails on to courtiers for the Emperor's amusement, letting his legs be pulled off like boots, selling wisps of straw as horses, doing and saying things which could appear tragic and important, nay, even serious, only to people who took every second cat for a witch, who burned their neighbours for vomiting pins, who suspected devils at every turn, as the great witch-expert Sprenger shows them in his horribly matter-of-fact manual. We moderns, disbelieving in devilries, would require the most elaborately romantic and poetic accessories—a splendid lurid back-ground, a magnificent Byronian[2] invocation of the fiend. The Mephistophilis of Marlowe, in those days when devils still dwelt in people, required none of Goethe's wit or poetry; the mere fact of his being a devil, with the very real

---

1 Johann Christoph Friedrich von Schiller (1759-1805), German dramatist, lyric poet, and historian; Johann Gottfried Herder (1744-1803) German poet and critic; Samuel Taylor Coleridge (1772-1834), English Romantic poet and literary critic.
2 In the flamboyant manner of the Romantic poet George Gordon Byron (1788-1824).

association of flame and brimstone in this world and the next, was sufficient to inspire interest in him; whereas in 1800, with Voltaire's novels and Hume's treatises on the table,[1] a dull devil was no more endurable than any other sort of bore. The very superiority of Marlowe is due to this absence of weirdness, to this complete realism; the last scene of the English play is infinitely above the end of the second part of *Faust* in tragic grandeur, just because Goethe made abortive attempts, after a conscious and artificial supernatural, while Marlowe was satisfied with perfect reality of situation. The position of Faustus, when the years of his pact have expired, and he awaits midnight, which will give him over to Lucifer, is as thoroughly natural in the eyes of Marlowe as is in the eyes of Shelley the position of Beatrice Cenci[2] awaiting the moment of execution. The conversation between Faustus and the scholars, after he has made his will, is terribly life-like: they disbelieve at first, pooh-pooh his danger; then, half-convinced, beg that a priest may be fetched; but Faustus cannot deal with priests. He bids them, in agony, go pray in the next room. "Aye, pray for me, pray for me, and what noise soever you hear, come not unto me, for nothing can save me.... Gentlemen, farewell; if I live till morning, I'll visit you; if not, Faustus is gone to hell."[3] Faustus remains alone for the one hour which separates him from his doom; he clutches at the passing time, he cries to the hours to stop with no rhetorical figure of speech, but with a terrible reality of agony:

> Let this hour be but
> A year, a month, a week, a natural day,
> That Faustus may repent and save his soul.[4]

Time to repent, time to recoil from the horrible gulf into which he is being sucked; Christ, will Christ's blood not save him? He would leap up to heaven and cling fast, but Lucifer drags him

---

1 François Marie Arouet de Voltaire (1694-1778), French philosopher, historian, dramatist, and writer of satirical poems and tales; David Hume (1711-76), Scottish sceptical philosopher, author of *Treatise of Human Nature* (1739-40) and *Enquiry concerning Human Understanding* (1748).

2 Percy Bysshe Shelley (1792-1822), major Romantic poet and author of the play *The Cenci* (1819) in which his tragic heroine Beatrice Cenci is executed for the murder of her abusive father.

3 *Doctor Faustus*, V. ii. 87-9, 92-3.

4 *Doctor Faustus*, V. ii. 149-51.

down. He would seek annihilation in nature, be sucked into its senseless, feelingless mass ... and, meanwhile, the time is passing, the interval of respite is shrinking and dwindling. Would that he were a soulless brute and might perish, or that at least eternal hell were finite—a thousand, a hundred thousand years let him suffer, but not for ever and without end! Midnight begins striking. With convulsive agony he exclaims as the rain patters against the window:

> O soul, be changed into small water-drops,
> And fall into the ocean, ne'er be found.[1]

But the twelfth stroke sounds; Lucifer and his crew enter; and when next morning the students, frightened by the horrible tempest and ghastly noises of the night, enter his study, they find Faustus lying dead, torn and mangled by the demon. All this is not supernatural in our sense; such scenes as this were real for Marlowe and his audience. Such cases were surely not unfrequent; more than one man certainly watched through such a night in hopeless agony, conscious, like Faustus, of pact with the fiend—awaiting, with earth and heaven shut and bolted against him, eternal hell.

In this story of Doctor Faustus, which, to Marlowe and his contemporaries, was not a romance but a reality, the episode of the evoking of Helen is extremely secondary in interest. To raise a dead woman was not more wonderful than to turn wisps of straw into horses, and it was perhaps considered the easier of the two miracles; the sense that Helen is the ghost of a whole long-dead civilisation, that sense which is for us the whole charm of the tale, could not exist in the sixteenth century. Goethe's Faust feels for Helen as Goethe himself might have felt, as Winckelmann[2] felt for a lost antique statue, as Schiller felt for the dead Olympus: a passion intensely imaginative and poetic, born of deep appreciation of antiquity, the essentially modern, passionate, nostalgic craving for the past. In Marlowe's play, on the contrary, Faustus and the students evoke Helen from a confused pedantic impression that an ancient lady must be as much superior to a modern lady as an ancient poem, be it even by Statius

---

1 *Doctor Faustus*, V. ii. 195-96.
2 Johann Joachim Winckelmann (1717-68), German writer on Greek art and antiquities.

or Claudian,[1] must be superior to a modern poem—it is a humanistic fancy of the days of the revival of letters. But, by a strange phenomenon, Marlowe, once realising what Helen means, that she is the fairest of women, forgets the scholarly interest in her. Faustus, once in [the] presence of the wonderful woman, forgets that he had summoned her up to gratify his and his friends' pedantry; he sees her, loves her, and bursts out into the splendid tirade full of passionate fancy:

> Was this the face that launched a thousand ships,
> And burnt the topless towers of Ilium?
> Sweet Helen, make me immortal with a kiss!
> Her lips suck forth my soul! See, where it flies!
> Come, Helen, come, give me my soul again.
> Here will I dwell, for Heaven is in these lips,
> And all is dross that is not Helena.
> I will be Paris, and for love of thee,
> Instead of Troy shall Wittenberg be sacked;
> And I will combat with weak Menelaus,
> And wear thy colours on my plumed crest;
> Yea, I will wound Achilles in the heel,
> And then return to Helen for a kiss.
> Oh! thou art fairer than the evening air
> Clad in the beauty of a thousand stars;
> Brighter art thou than flaming Jupiter
> When he appeared to hapless Semele;
> More lovely than the monarch of the sky
> In wanton Arethusa's azure arms;
> And none but thou shalt be my paramour.[2]

This is real passion for a real woman, a woman very different from the splendid semi-vivified statue of Goethe, the Helen with only the cold, bloodless, intellectual life which could be infused by enthusiastic studies of ancient literature and art, gleaming bright like marble or a spectre. This Helena of Marlowe is no antique; the Elizabethan dramatist, like the painter of the fifteenth century, could not conceive the purely antique, despite all the translating of ancient writers, and all the drawing from ancient marbles. One of the prose versions of the story of

---

1 Publius Papinius Statius (c. 45-96 AD), Roman poet; Claudian or Claudius Claudianus (c. 370-404), last notable Latin classic poet.
2 *Doctor Faustus*, V. ii. 97-116.

Faustus, contains a quaint account of Helen, which sheds much light on Marlowe's conception:

> This lady appeared before them in a most riche gowne of purple velvet, costly imbrodered; her haire hanged downe loose, as faire as the beaten gold, and of such length that it reached downe to her hammes; having most amorous cole-black eyes, a sweet and pleasant round face, with lips as red as a cherry; her cheeks of a rose colour, her mouth small, her neck white like a swan; tall and slender of personage; in summe, there was no imperfect place in her; she looked around about with a rolling hawk's eye, a smiling and wanton countenance, which neerehand inflamed the hearts of all the students, but that they persuaded themselves she was a spirit, which make them lightly passe away such fancies.[1]

This fair dame in the velvet embroidered gown, with the long, hanging hair, this Helen of the original Faustus legend, is antique only in name; she belongs to the race of mediæval and modern women—the Lauras, Fiammettas, and Simonettas of Petrarch, Boccaccio, and Lorenzo dei Medici;[2] she is the sister of that slily sentimental coquette, the Monna Lisa of Leonardo. The strong and simple women of Homer, and even of Euripides, majestic and matronly even in shame, would repudiate this slender, smiling, ogling beauty; Briseis,[3] though the captive of Achilles' spear, would turn with scorn from her. The antique woman has a dignity due to her very inferiority and restrictedness of position; she has the simplicity, the completeness, the absence of everything suggestive of degradation, like that of some stately animal, pure in its animal nature. The modern woman, with more freedom and more ideal, rarely approaches to this character; she is too complex to be perfect, she is frail because she has an ideal,

---

1 This seems to be a slightly altered version of an extract from Chapter 45 of the English translation of *The Faust Book* originally published in Frankfurt in 1587. See *The Historie of the damnable life, and the deserved death of Doctor Iohn Faustus*, translated from the German by P.F. Gent (London, 1592).

2 Respectively the inspiring admired or beloved women addressed or described in verse by the poets Francesco Petrarch (c. 1304-74), Giovanni Boccaccio (1313-75), and Lorenzo de' Medici (1449-92), also ruler of Florence and patron of the arts.

3 Briseis, the wife of King Mynes of Lymessus, an ally of Troy, was won as a war prize by the hero Achilles who fell in love with her.

she is dubious because she is free, she may fall because she may rise. Helen deserted Menelaus[1] and brought ruin upon Troy, therefore, in the eyes of Antiquity, she was the victim of fate, she might be unruffled, spotless, majestic; but to the man of the sixteenth century she was merely frail and false. The rolling hawk's eye and the wanton smile of the old legend-monger would have perplexed Homer, but they were necessary for Marlowe; his Helen was essentially modern, he had probably no inkling that an antique Helen as distinguished from a modern could exist. In the paramour of Faustus he saw merely the most beautiful woman, some fair and wanton creature, dressed not in chaste and majestic antique drapery, but in fantastic garments of lawn, like those of Hero[2] in his own poem:

> The lining purple silk, with gilt stars drawn;
> Her wide sleeves green, and bordered with a grove
> Where Venus, in her naked glory strove
> To please the careless and disdainful eyes
> Of proud Adonis, that before her lies;
> Her kirtle blue....
> Upon her head she wore a myrtle wreath
> From whence her veil reached to the ground beneath;
> Her veil was artificial flowers and leaves
> Whose workmanship both man and beast deceives.[3]

Some slim and dainty goddess of Botticelli,[4] very mortal withal, long and sinuous, tightly clad in brocaded garments and clinging cobweb veils, beautiful with the delicate, diaphanous beauty, rather emaciated and hectic, of high rank, and the conscious, elaborate fascination of a woman of fashion—a creature whom, like the Gioconda, Leonardo might have spent years in decking and painting, ever changing the ornaments and ever altering the portrait; to whom courtly poets like Bembo and Castiglione[5]

---

1   Menelaus, husband of Helen of Sparta. Her abduction by Paris provoked the Trojan war.
2   Hero, eponymous female character in Christopher Marlowe's epic poem *Hero and Leander* (1598).
3   *Hero and Leander*, I. 10-20.
4   Sandro Botticelli (c. 1445-1510), Florentine Renaissance painter, creator of *The Birth of Venus*.
5   Pietro Bembo (1470-1547), cardinal, poet, and famous humanist scholar; Baldassare Castiglione (1478-1529), Italian humanist, diplomat, courtier, and poet, most famous for his *The Book of the Courtier* (1528).

might have written scores of sonnets and canzoni to her hands, her eyes, her hair, her lips, a fanciful inventory to which she listened languidly under the cypresses of Florentine gardens. Some such being, even rarer and more dubious for being an exotic in the England of Elizabeth, was Marlowe's Helen; such, and not a ghostly figure, descended from a pedestal, white and marble-like in her unruffled drapery, walking with solid step and unswerving, placid glance through the study, crammed with books, and vials, and strange instruments, of the mediæval wizard of Wittenberg. Marlowe deluded himself as well as Faustus, and palmed off on to him a mere modern lady. To raise a real spectre of the antique is a craving of our own century; Goethe attempted to do it and failed, for what reasons we have seen; but we have all of us the charm wherewith to evoke for ourselves a real Helena, on condition that, unlike Faustus and unlike Goethe, we seek not to show her to others, and remain satisfied if the weird and glorious figure haunt only our own imagination.

Appendix E: A. Mary F. Robinson, "Before a Bust of Venus (Found in a Greek Vineyard, A.D. 900)" (1881)[1]

[In this poem from *The Crowned Hippolytus, Translated from Euripides, with New Poems* (1881), Vernon Lee's intimate friend, the poet and scholar Agnes Mary Frances Robinson (1857-1944), shows that she shared in the passion for classical sculpture and mythology that so absorbed Lee and her half-brother, the poet Eugene Lee-Hamilton. Like Lee in her story "Dionea" and like Lee-Hamilton in his sonnets on a recovered antique torso (Appendix H), she singles out Venus-Aphrodite, goddess of Love, for special attention in "Before a Bust of Venus," a poem that explores the impact made by a Greek statue of the goddess on an early mediaeval monastic community.]

AH! God, how beautiful!
                    Gaze, gaze, mine eyes,
And learn by heart this wonder of surprise.
Yet 'tis a snare, some old Greek friend, alas!
What's this? Is Aphrodite on the plinth?
Why did I never hear how fair she was?
Yet 'tis a vanity; the straight white brow
Set in thick hair curled like a hyacinth.
Our saints have no such foreheads, wide and low,

---

1 Agnes Mary Frances Robinson (1857-1944), literary scholar, author, poet, biographer, and intimate friend of Vernon Lee, known after her first marriage (1888) as Darmesteter and after her second (1894) as Duclaux, wrote on a wide range of subjects which reflected her interest in European literature and culture. Among her respected early poetry are the collections *A Handful of Honeysuckle* (1878) and *The Crowned Hippolytus, Translated from Euripides, with New Poems* (1881). Her *Collected Poems* appeared in 1902. She wrote thirty books including biographies such as *La Vie de Emile Duclaux* (1907), *Emily Brontë* in the *Eminent Women* series (1883), *Victor Hugo* (1921), and *Life of Racine* (1925). 1883 saw the publication of her first work of fiction: *Arden: A Novel. The End of the Middle Ages: Essays and Questions in History* (1888) is among her scholarly works. The text of "Before a Bust of Venus" is taken from *The Crowned Hippolytus, Translated from Euripides, with New Poems* (London: C. Kegan Paul & Co., 1881), 134-38.

Nor such clear wondering eyes of amethyst.
Not bent down, gravewards, like the eyes of a nun,
Nor lifted like Our Lady's, as though nought
Should stand 'twixt them and her enthronèd Son;
These eyes look forward, claiming as they list
Homage or fear from all men, North or South,
Unless they share it with the perfect mouth
Which (Heaven assoil me for so foul a thought!)
It were enough of Heaven to have kissed.
And ah! the shapely shoulder broken short
Where my spade struck as though mere stone were there!
The grace of neck and throat and snow-white breast
Shown through dark earth-stains how divinely rare!
Women enough I have seen, yet never guessed
Beneath their scapulars they are so fair!
O lovely rounded throat and parted lips
Still sweet with some unuttered speech or song!
To think the word that you have kept so long,
Should you now speak it, were my soul's eclipse!
To think your beauty is but the slave of Dis,[1]
But a rich garment for a fiend to wear,
Tempting the gazer to unholy bliss!
Our black Madonna[2] no one longs to kiss,
Nor ever praised, alas! as I praise this
Most beautiful white devil, Satan's snare!

And yet, since heaven is beautiful, they say,
In the other world, and hell sheer ugliness,
Why is the beauty round us night and day
Only a sense to shame us, not to bless?
O Maker of Beauty, who yet madest me
And gave me sense all lovely things to see,
Why must Thy creature, whom Thou callest good,
By men be vilified, misunderstood?

Once to the cloister garden, long ago,
Our monks sent me to fetch the herbs they eat;

---

1   Dis, Hades, or Pluto are all names for the pagan god who rules the
    Underworld, and by extension are synonyms for the Underworld itself.
    Here the name is associated with the Devil and the Hell of Christianity.
2   One of the paintings or statues which date from the mediaeval period
    and which portray the Virgin Mary with dark or black skin.

But when I came there, 'mid the lowly roots
I saw a tall sweet-smelling bramble grow,
With open-hearted blossoms, red and sweet,
Set in green leaves and dainty rosy shoots;
Then home, forgetting radish roots, I ran.
But when I reached the cloister, rose in hand,
The hungry monks were angered to a man;
Only old Father Ambrose made a stand
Against their wrath, and thus admonished me:
"Child, thou art right," he said, "the rose is fair.
Though worldly beauties are but fleeting shows,
And of small worth the painted blossoms be,
Saving as types of beauty otherwhere;
Still, God made roses red, not grey or black,
To light for a moment's space the upward track.
But if our Father makes His weeds so rare,
What must His flowers be?
                                        Child, thou art God's rose,
Whom yet thy will can change to briar or tare,
Or make more sweet than any flower that grows.
Hadst thou this morning done thy duty right
Thou wert beyond all roses in God's sight."

He was no judge of beauty; yet again,
After so many years, his voice comes back
With the break and shake in it and sharp thin strain:
"God made His roses red, not grey or black,
To light for a moment's space the upward track."
Like them this face, soulless and sweetly vain,
Was made to yield a transient delight,
Not more, lest satisfied with finite gain
We lose perception of the infinite.
This is no fiend's face surely; sweet and round
'Tis, of its kind, complete in womanhood,
Youthful and fair; but once the ideal found,
The comely mask shows something missed or lost.
Its mere perfection of accomplishment
Shows the worst failure of the soul: content.
That artist felt no fire of Pentecost![1]

---

1   Jewish harvest festival and the time when, according to the New Testa-
    ment (Acts 2. 1-43), the Holy Spirit descended on Christ's apostles,
    allowing them to perform miracles through Divine agency.

Yet, O fair face, I will gaze on thee now;
In time to come I shall have no delight
From those sweet eyes and that low, placid brow.
Let us enjoy the starshine through the night;
At daybreak we shall look for it no more.
So when my soul, that I send on before,
Finds God, my body, left a while on earth,
Shall deem mere worldly things of little worth.
O Thou, true Light, true Beauty, that I adore!
O everlasting Music, heavenly Dew
My parched soul sighs for till my lips sigh too!
Come down and fill me, thy poor chalice cup,
That nothing but Thy glory shall fill up.

And when at last, her earthly service done,
With all her senses pure and unabused,
My singing soul shall find her wings and fly
Beyond the stars and higher and yet more high,
Beyond the holy moon, beyond the sun,
Through worlds in heaven with sound and light suffused—
Then all the souls I shall have saved shall meet me
And with exceeding gladness greet me;
Then we will wander to and fro
Where the living waters glow,
And watch the angels come and go
Through all the fields of that fair land,
And all together we shall stand
In shining ranks at God's right hand.
For in a dream I saw the same.
Towards me the singing spirits leant,
All bowing when they spoke His name,
And with their heads their haloes bent.
With them shall I stand side by side,
And hear their music evermore;
I shall behold my God, my guide,
And see His face that I adore.
    I shall be satisfied.

Think, O my soul, in that diviner bliss,
How wouldst thou sorrow to have stayed at this!

And yet—O heaven, how beautiful she is!

Appendix F: Eugene Lee-Hamilton, "The Mandolin" (A.D. 1559) (1882)[1]

[Vernon Lee much admired this dramatic monologue by her older half-brother, the poet Eugene Lee-Hamilton (1845-1907), which appears in his collection *The New Medusa and Other Poems* (1882). Like Lee's story "A Wicked Voice," which it probably influenced, the poem features a narrator whose sanity is threatened by oppressive phantasmal music. In both story and poem this haunting seems to be the result of an earlier slight or wrongdoing committed against a singer or musician.]

SIT nearer to my bed.
Have I been rambling? I can ill command
The sequence of my thoughts, though words come fast.
    A fire is in my head
And in my veins, like hell's own flame fast fanned.
No sleep for eighty nights. It cannot last.
    The Pope ere long, perhaps ere close of day,
    Will have a scarlet hat to give away.[2]

    Good priest, dost hear a sound,
A faint far sound as of a mandolin?
Thou hearest nought? Well, well; it matters not.

---

1 Eugene Lee-Hamilton (1845-1907), English poet and older half-brother to Vernon Lee. Invalided out of the Diplomatic Service in 1873, Lee-Hamilton was confined to his bed in a semi-paralysed condition (probably psycho-somatic in origin) for the next twenty years and cared for by his mother and half-sister. Vernon Lee was key in helping secure publication of his poems. He began to recover in 1894 and subsequently travelled, married, and had a daughter who unfortunately died in infancy. Lee-Hamilton showed particular proficiency in his dramatic monologues and sonnets. The text of "The Mandolin," is taken from *The New Medusa and Other Poems* (London: Elliot Stock, 1882), 86-97. This collection was dedicated to Lee's friend, the poet A. Mary F. Robinson.

2 The speaker, a cardinal, imagines either that if he dies, the Pope will have to replace him with a new cardinal or that, on his imminent election to the papacy, he will be in a position to give away his red cardinal's hat.

I, who was to be crowned
At the next Conclave![1] I was safe to win;
And t'will be soon: Caraffa's step has got
    So tottering.[2] O God, that I should miss
    The prize within my grasp and end like this!

    'Three little months ago
What Cardinal was so robust as I?
And now the rings drop off my fingers lean!
    I have a deadly foe
Who steals away my life till I shall die,
A foe whom well I know, though all unseen,
    Unseizable, unstrikable; he lurks
    Ever at hand, and my destruction works.

    Thou thinkest I am mad?
Not mad, no, no; but kept awake to death,
And sent by daily inches into hell.
    Slow starving were less bad
Or measured poison, or the hard-drawn breath
And shrivelling muscles of a wasting spell.
    I tell thee, Father, I've been months awake,
    Spent with the thirst that sleep alone can slake.

    O holy, holy Sleep,
Thou sweet but over-frightenable power!
Thou, whom a tinkle scares or whispered word;
    Return, return and creep
Over my sense, and in this final hour
Lay on my lids the kiss so long deferred.
    But ah, it may not be; and I shall die
    Awake, I know; the foe is hovering nigh.

    Attend; I'll tell thee all:
I tried to steal his life; and in return,
Night after night he steals my sleep away.
    Oh, I would slowly maul
His body with the pincers, or would burn

---

[1] Meeting-place or assembly of cardinals for the election of a new pope.
[2] Giampietro Caraffa (b.1476) became Pope Paul IV in 1555 and died on
    18 August 1559 aged 83.

His limbs upon red embers, or would flay
    The skin from off him slowly, if he fell
    Into my hands, though I should sicken hell.

     The mischief all began
With Claudia, whom thou knewest, my own niece,[1]
My dowered ward brought up in my own home.
     I had an old pet plan
That she should wed Duke Philip, and increase
The number of my partisans in Rome.
    Oh they were matched; for he had rank and power,
    And she rare beauty and a princely dower.

     With infinite delight
I saw her beauty come, and watched its growth
With greater rapture than a miser knows,
     Who in the silent night
Counts up his growing treasure, and is loth
To close the lid, and seek his lone repose.
    And long before her beauty was full-blown
    Men called her worthy of a ducal crown.

     But as her beauty grew
Her lip would often curl, her brow contract,
With ominous impatience of control;
     The least compulsion drew
Rebellious answers; all respect she lacked;
The spirit of resistance filled her soul:
    She took not to Duke Philip, as the year
    For marriage neared; and I began to fear.

     Give me again to drink:
There is a fierce excitement in my brain,
And speech relieves me; but my strength sinks fast,
     The end is near, I think.
And I would tell thee all, that not in vain
May be thy absolution at the last.
    Where was it I had got? I lose the thread
    Of thought at times, and know not what I've said.

---

1   "Niece" may be a possible cover for "illegitimate daughter." Cardinals, like all Catholic priests, take a vow of chastity.

Ay, now I recollect.
There was a man who hung about me ever,
One Hannibal Petroni, bastard born,
    Whom I did half suspect
Of making love to Claudia. He was clever,
And had the arts and ways which should adorn
    A better birth; but from the first I hated
    His very sight, and hatred ne'er abated.

        He played with rare, rare skill
Upon the mandolin; his wrist was stronger
Than that of any player I have known;
        And with his quivering quill
He could sustain the thrilling high notes longer
Than others could; and drew a voice-like tone
    Of unexampled clearness from the wire,
    Which often made me, while I loathed, admire.

        For 'tis a wondrous thing
The mandolin, when played with cunning hand,
And charms the nerves till pleasure grows too sharp;
        Now mimicking the string
Of a guitar, now aping at command
The viol or the weird Æolian harp,[1]
    The sound now tinkles, now vibrates, now comes
    Faint, thin, and threadlike; 'tis a gnat that hums.

        And he would often come
On breezeless, moonlit nights of May and June,
And play beneath these windows, or quite near,
        When every sound in Rome
Had died away; and I abhorred his tune,
For well I knew it was for Claudia's ear;
    And I would pace my chamber while he played
    And, in my heart, curse moon and serenade.

        How came this thing about?
My mind grows hazy and my temples swell.
Give me more drink! Oh, I remember now.
        One morning I found out

---

1 Musical instrument designed to produce sound as the wind passes
    across its strings.

That they were corresponding—letters fell
Into my hands. It was a crushing blow;
    My plans were crumbling. In my fear and wrath
    I said, "Why wait? Remove him from thy path."

    It's easy here in Rome,
Provided you are liberal with the price;
The willing Tiber[1] sweeps all trace away.
    Yet ere I sent him home
To heaven or hell, I think I warned him twice
To go his way; but he preferred to stay.
    He braved me in his rashness, and I said,
    "Let the destruction be on his own head."

    When Claudia learnt his death,
What a young tigress! I can see her now,
With eyes illumined by a haggard flame,
    And feel her withering breath,
As in a hissing, never-ending flow
She poured her awful curses on my name.
    'Twas well I kept her close; for she had proofs
    And would have howled them from the very roofs.

    It is an ugly tale,
And must be told; but what was I to do?
I wanted peace not war; but one by one
    I saw my efforts fail.
She was unmanageable, and she drew
Her fate upon herself—aye, she alone.
    I placed her in a convent, where they tried
    All means in vain. She spurned her food and died.

    But he, the cause of all,
I know not how, has risen from the dead,
And takes my life by stealing sleep away.
    No sooner do I fall
Asleep each night, than, creeping light of tread
Beneath my window, he begins to play.
    How well I know his touch! It takes my life
    Less quickly but more surely than the knife.

---

1 River of central Italy flowing through Rome to the Mediterranean sea.

Now 'tis a rapid burst
Of high and brilliant melody, which ceases
As soon as it has waked me with a leap.
        And now a sound, at first
As faint as a gnat's humming, which increases
And creeps between the folded thoughts of sleep,
        Tickling the brain, and keeping in suspense
        Through night's long hours the o'er-excited sense.

        Oh! I have placed my spies
All round the house, and offered huge rewards
To any that may see him; but in vain.
        The cunning rogue defies
The best-laid plan, and fears nor troops nor swords;
But, scarce my eyes are closed, begins again
        His artful serenade. Oh, he is sly!
        And loves to fool the watchman and the spy.

        But I should find a way
To catch him yet, if my retainers had
A little faith and helped me as they ought.
        I overheard one say
"Mark me, the cardinal is going mad;
He hears a mandolin where there is nought."
        Ay, that's Petroni's skill. He sends the sound
        Straight to my ear, unheard by those around!

        Once, on a moonlit night,
I caught a glimpse of him, the villain sat
Beneath my window on the garden-wall;
        And, in the silvery light,
I saw his mandolin. Then, like a cat,
I crept downstairs, with fierce intent to fall
        Upon and throttle him. I made a rush
        And seized him by the throat. It was a bush.

        But I have talked o'ermuch;
And something like a drowsiness descends
Upon my eyelids with a languid weight.
        Oh, would it were the touch
Of sweet, returning sleep, to make amends
For long desertion, ere it be too late!
        My fevered pulse grows calm; my heated brow
        Aches less and less, and throbs no longer now.

O sleep, gentle sleep!
I feel thee near; thou hast returned at last.
It was that draught of soothing hellebore.
     I feel sweet slumber creep
Across each aching sense, as in the past,
And consciousness is fading more and more.
     I care not to awake again; let death,
     Whenever sleep shall leave me, take my breath.

     Give ear! give ear! give ear!
I hear him; he is coming; it is he!
He plays triumphant strains, faint, far away.
     Ye fools, do ye not hear?
Oh, we shall catch him yet, and you shall see
A year of hell compressed into a day.
     Bring me my clothes, and help me out of bed.
     Oh, I can stand; I'm weak, but not yet dead.

     Bring me my scarlet cloak
And scarlet stockings.[1] No, they're dyed with blood.
Oh, you may laugh! But it's beyond a doubt
     The dyer's let them soak,
In every street, in murder-reddened mud;
It is the only dye which won't wash out.
     The Pope is dead; Caraffa's dead at last.
     I'm wanted at the conclave: dress me fast.

     Who dares to hold me down?
I'm papable.[2] By noon we must convene;
Bring me my clothes, and help me quick to rise.
     When I've the triple crown
Safe on my head, I'll sweep the cesspool clean.
What's all that muttering? Speak out loud, ye spies!
     There's a conspiracy at work, I know,
     To keep me from the conclave—but I'll go,

     The Papacy is lost.
Lost, wholly lost! The Papal keys, all black

---

1 Official garb of a cardinal.
2 Fit for election to the papacy.

With rust and dirt, won't turn the lock of heaven.[1]
      What's that? what's that? The Host?[2]
There's poison in the wafer—take it back!
I'll spit it out! I'll rather die unshriven!
      Help, Claudia, help! Where's Claudia? Where's she fled?
      They're smothering me with pillows in my bed.

---

1 Papal keys, insignia of the papacy, representing all authority in heaven
   and earth and symbolically passed from one pope to the next.
2 Consecrated wafer believed by Catholics to be the body of Christ.

Appendix G: A. Mary F. Robinson, "The Ladies of Milan" (1889)[1]

[This extract is taken from a chapter in A. Mary F. Robinson, *The End of the Middle Ages: Essays and Questions in History* (1889). A close personal friend of Vernon Lee, Robinson was equally fascinated by European history and art (see Appendix E). Robinson's depiction of the beautiful Beatrice d'Este (1475-97) and the tensions between powerful Italian families such as the Viscontis and the Sforzas resonates interestingly with Lee's fictional account of Urbania's past in "Armour Dure: Passages from the Diary of Spiridion Trepka," originally published in *Murray's Magazine* 1 (1887) and reprinted in *Hauntings* (1890).]

"Cherchez la femme"[2]

Last year I was in Lombardy, and, as a faithful adherent of the Viscontis,[3] I stayed a little in Pavia.[4] I found it a rather gloomy little Lombard town, whitewashed and paven. Here and there a wine-coloured wall or tower broke the pallid monotony of the streets. The famous fortress, where Isabel of Arragon[5] eat her

---

1   A. Mary F. Robinson, *The End of the Middle Ages: Essays and Questions in History* (London: T. Fisher Unwin, 1889), pp. 300-13. Robinson dedicated her book to John Addington Symonds (1840-1893), author of *Renaissance in Italy* which appeared in seven volumes at intervals between 1875 and 1886. Like Walter Pater, Symonds was an important influence on Vernon Lee's own writings on the Renaissance in works such as *Euphorion* (1884).

2   Translation (French): "look for the woman." Common saying, implying that, where there is trouble or intrigue, a woman is always responsible.

3   Milanese family that dominated the history of northern Italy in the fourteenth and fifteenth centuries. By 1349, the Viscontis ruled many of the cities in the area, including Pavia.

4   Capital of Pavia Province, Lombardy, northern Italy, on the River Tiano near its confluence with the Po. It was the last Lombard city to fall to the Visconti family (1359) who built the cathedral and started the construction of the Certosa di Pavia, a Carthusian monastery, in 1396.

5   Isabel of Arragon (1470-1524) married her cousin, Giangaleazzo Sforza, Duke of Milan, in 1488, becoming duchess of a state under the control of Lodovico il Moro, son of Francesca Sforza and Bianca Maria Visconti. Lodovico later expelled Duke Giangaleazzo and his wife from the Dukedom of Milan and banished them to Pavia.

heart in bitterness so many years, still exists, much rebuilt and altered indeed, but always a mass of fine red colour. In Pavia, however, there was nothing so interesting to me as those phantoms of vanished Viscontis and long-supplanted Sforzas[1] that seemed so strangely out of place in this sad little sordid university town. And among these ranks of tragic shadows, the least forgiven, the least beloved, was always the Duchess Beatrice.[2]

I had known her too long, the youthful and charming Lady Macbeth of Lombardy. I knew her as well as one can know a person, familiar through the gossip of acquaintance, although unseen and distant. I had heard of her as a haughty and ambitious woman, accepting with a smile the crimes that placed the crown of Milan on her head. She appeared as some Herodias of Luini's,[3] exquisite and sinister. And yet I knew she had been dearly worshipped in her lifetime and long lamented in her tomb. There are such Sirens, heartless and chill themselves, but capable of seizing an honest love with the same hands that grasp at a blood-stained treasure. Such, in my eyes, was the adored and evil wife of Lodovico il Moro.

It was Christmas-time and cold; with difficulty I roused myself to visit the Certosa. It is six miles, I suppose, from Pavia. The wretched carriage slowly dragged along through the muddy country; and from the whitened window one felt rather than saw the immense desolation of the view. On either hand of the raised road, a sluggish canal, and beyond a monotonous landscape of brown marshy pastures and bright green rice fields flecked with water, across which the scant snow drifted. The road seemed to extend for ever in front, unbroken, unturning. Suddenly in the middle of the country the carriage stopped; I walked a few steps up a muddy lane. To the right over a wall there appeared a great dome, with rose-red minarets, with spires of pale red, ivory and

---

1 Italian family that ruled the Duchy of Milan 1450-99.
2 Beatrice d'Este (1475-97), cousin of Isabel of Aragon, who married Lodovico il Moro and supplanted Isabel as Duchess of Milan in 1494 when Duke Giangaleazzo died, ostensibly from tuberculosis, but possibly poisoned by il Moro. The Duchess Beatrice is credited with bringing Coreggio, Castiglione, and Leonardo da Vinci to the court of Milan, and being responsible for the beauty of the Certosa at Pavia where she and Lodovico are buried.
3 Bernardino Luini (1480-1532), Italian artist of the Lombardian school, mostly known for his paintings of religious subjects. His "Herodias" hangs in the Galleria degli Uffizi, Florence.

marble, among innumerable shaft-like towers tipped with cream-white columns. It is the Certosa.

At another season and in better health I should have found much to linger over in the great façade of the Certosa, fantastic, incoherent as a Midsummer Night's Dream. Every inch of the front is covered thickly with ornament in high relief—Roman emperors and paladins of chivalry, eagles with praying angels on their outspread pinions, exquisite maidens floating full-length on a dolphin's back, Sirens suckling their unearthly babes, hippogriffs,[1] Prophets of Israel: strange, unexpected as the visions of delirium, they are assembled there. But, alone, in the bitter wind, I glanced at it all for a moment and entered the vast foundation of Giangaleazzo Visconti. Great halls, enormous, cold, spoiled as much as may be by the seventeenth century; a few good pictures by Borgognone,[2] many bad ones; posthumous portraits of the great Viscontis: it was not so interesting as I had supposed.

Still I wandered on, making reflections on the difference of type in the Sforza and Visconti heads: the older tyrants keen-faced, refined with delicate, bone-less oval faces, and thin firm lips ridged out in a narrow line. There is something wolf-like in the long pointed noses, the pointed chins, low foreheads, as well as in the keen eyes, narrow and high in the head; altogether an interesting type, subtle, cruel, intellectual, and fierce. The Sforzas with their Wellington noses, their strongly marked eyebrows, prim-pursed lips and rounded chins, seem a square-faced kindly race of captains. Lodovico il Moro himself is there, with the fat face and fine chin of the elderly Napoleon, the delicate beak-like nose of Wellington; a small querulous neat-lipped mouth, and immense eyebrows, stretched like the talons of an eagle across the low forehead, complete the odd, refined physiognomy of the man. I looked at him with interest for a moment. But there, straight before me, stood the tomb of the wife he lost so young, the Duchess Beatrice.

To think that she is dead, and to think she was a woman! Impossible. She is a lively child, fallen asleep in playtime: motionless, but

---

1 A winged horse with the head and claws of an eagle, often found in ancient Greek art, and appearing in mediaeval legends.
2 Ambrogio Borgognone, also Bergognone (c. 1450/60-1523), originally Ambrogio di Stefano da Fossano, Italian painter of the Lombard school whose use of subdued and subtle colours led Bernard Berenson to refer to him as the "Whistler of the Renaissance." He painted an altarpiece and frescoes for the Certosa (1514).

full of a contained vivacity. Her tumbled curls hang loosely round her shoulders, and stand up in a little frizz above the rounded childish forehead. As she lies there, a look of infantine candour is diffused over the soft, adorable, irregular features. She has straight, brief eyebrows like a little girl, but her closed eyelids are rounded like the petals of a thick white flower, and richly fringed with lashes. The little nose is of no particular shape—not quite a straight nose, but certainly not a snub; it is the prettiest nose at Court, with a rounded end like a child's. The cheeks, too, are round apple-cheeks, not in the least like the Herodias of Luini; and round is the neat bewitching chin. But her chief beauty is her mouth—a mouth with the soft-closed lips of a dear child pretending to be asleep, yet smiling as if to say, "Soon I shall jump up and throw my arms around your neck, and you will be so surprised!"

The round head rises from a long plump throat. The small figure too is slender and plump at once, and very small, full of life still, it seems, under the pretty tight silk dress, with the slashed and purfled sleeves, and the long train of brocade, so lovingly, so carefully arranged not to encumber nor hide those little pattened feet, that were so fain of dancing and seem so ready to awake and dance again. This, then, is the famous Beatrice!—I looked and looked, at last I understood not only her, but the love of Lodovico: "And so, dear child, thou canst not live without a crown?—Ah well! What shouldst thou know of murder, dishonour, and the ruin of great states? Thou wilt never understand these gloomy things, and I shall pay the price—Ah God in heaven, I thank Thee for the gift of an immortal soul, since I may lose it for the pleasure of this child!"

Perhaps it was in this way that Lodovico reasoned; or perhaps it may be that at heart Macbeth is no less ambitious than his wife. Who knows? The wife, at least, must stand for something. At least, some share in the ruin of their country must be accorded to these three women—Bonne,[1] who recalled Lodovico to Milan; Isabel, who inspired the war of Arragon and Sforza; and Beatrice, whose ambition urged her to invite the French to Italy.

---

1 Bonne de Savoie (1449-1503) became the second wife of Galeazzo Maria Sforza, Duke of Milan, in 1468 and, later, the mother-in-law of Isabel of Aragon. After the Duke's death Bonne took a lover, Antonio Tassino, at whose suggestion she requested her brother-in-law Lodovico il Moro's presence in Milan. Il Moro subsequently imprisoned his nephews and exiled Bonne "for immorality"; she was forced to seek asylum at the court of her brother-in-law, Louis XI of France, while il Moro took control of the Duchy of Milan.

Appendix H: Eugene Lee-Hamilton, "On a Surf-Rolled Torso of Venus" (1884, 1894)

[The following sonnet by the poet Eugene Lee-Hamilton (1845-1907), given in two versions, shows the interest in antique statuary and the legends of Venus-Aphrodite, shared by Lee and her older half-brother. Lee suggested the subject for the sonnet to Lee-Hamilton, who, housebound by a severe illness for many years, had little opportunity to seek out new sights for inspiration. His treatment of the subject, based on his sister's description, shows the great creative sympathy that existed between the siblings. The theme of Venus washed up on the shore is central to Lee's story "Dionea," in which the enigmatic female protagonist is the model for a sculpture of Aphrodite.]

Version 1.

"On a Surf-Rolled Torso of Venus, Found at Tripoli Vecchio, and Now in the Louvre"[1]

ONE day in the world's youth, long, long ago,
    Before the golden hair of Time grew grey,
    The bright warm sea, scarce stirred by the dolphins' play,
Was swept by sudden music soft and low;
And rippling, as 'neath kisses, parted slow,
    And gave a new and dripping goddess birth,

---

1   Text taken from *Apollo and Marsyas, and Other Poems* (London: Elliot Stock, 1884) 133. After a trip to the Louvre in 1883, Lee suggested a sculpture she had seen there as a possible subject for her brother: "I saw at the Louvre a very beautiful & singular thing, which I recommend to Eugène as a possible sonnet subject. It is a torso, half draped, of a Venus, found on the seashore at a place in Africa called Tripoli Vecchio—somewhere near Carthage, I presume. It has evidently been rolled for years & years in the surf, for it is all worn away, every line & curve softened, so it looks exquisitely soft & strange & creamy, hand, breasts & drapery all indicated clearly but washed by the sea into something soft, vague & lovely." Letter of Saturday 23 June 1893 to her mother, Matilda Paget, in *Vernon Lee's Letters* (1937) 117. Tripoli is an historic Libyan city on the Mediterranean coast.

Who brought transcendent loveliness on earth,
With limbs more pure than sunset-tinted snow.
And lo, that self-same sea has now upthrown
    A mutilated Venus, rolled and rolled
For ages by the surf, and that has grown
    More soft, more chaste, more lovely than of old,
With every line made vague, so that the stone
    Seems seen as through a veil which ages hold.

Version 2.

"On a Surf-Rolled Torso of Venus. Discovered at Tripoli
Vecchio"[1]

ONE day, in the world's youth, long, long ago,
    Before the golden hair of Time grew gray,
    The bright warm sea, scarce stirred by dolphins' play,
Was swept by sudden music strange and low;

And rippling with the kisses Zephyrs blow,[2]
    Gave forth a dripping goddess, whose strong sway
    All earth, all air, all wave, was to obey,
Throned on a shell more rosy than dawn's glow.[3]

And, lo, that self-same sea has now upthrown
    A mutilated Venus, roll'd and roll'd
For centuries in surf, and who has grown

More soft, more chaste, more lovely than of old,
    With every line made vague, so that the stone
Seems seen as through a veil which Ages hold.

---

1 Text taken from *Sonnets of the Wingless Hours* (London: Eliot Stock, 1894) 44.
2 Gentle westerly breezes personified as deities.
3 Lines 5-8 evoke the famous painting *The Birth of Venus* (c. 1485-6) in the Uffizi Gallery, Florence, by the Renaissance Italian painter Sandro Botticelli (1445-1510).

Appendix I: Vernon Lee, "Out of Venice at Last" (1925)[1]

[This brief impressionistic essay by Vernon Lee is characteristic of the many essays on travel she was to write throughout her career and shows her sensitivity to the historic atmosphere of a particular place—in this instance Venice with its many literary and musical associations. Although published in 1925, a good while after *Hauntings* (1890), the essay is nonetheless effective in conveying the claustrophobia of Venice, that sense of being overwhelmed by the past as experienced by Magnus, the narrator of "A Wicked Voice."]

OUT of Venice at last, and back once more in these most friendly Paduan hills. A north breeze after heavy rain; the clouds are turning these hill-tops into Alps. Between them are great, flat, green meadows, little bays and coves of the withdrawn Adriatic among its volcanic islands; and on them white cattle are browsing in the October freshness. Out of Venice at last! The wind stirs the sunburnt thistles on the rocks; the moving sunshine lights the first flame of yellow and russet on poplars and hedgerows; from unseen yards rise kindly farm noises. And the mists and languors and regrets and dreams of Venice are swept, are cleansed away, as by rain and wind, out of my soul! Alert thoughts begin to arise, binding the distant and future and me to them in orderly patterns, bringing me back into the life of other things, after those days of moody isolation of my self, a self fluctuating and shifting in stagnation like the shallow and stagnant Venetian waters: those shallow waters of Venice, wherein the brooding sirocco vapours[2] and the stormy sunsets put shifting iridescences and sanguine splendours and scales of unclutchable gold; all the dead greatness and the happiness which has never really been, and the crumble of endless neglect and the creepy life of obscure baseness, seem all to be in their ooze, never thoroughly rinsed by the storms and

---

1   The text of "Out of Venice at Last" is taken from *The Golden Keys and Other Essays on the Genius Loci* (John Lane, The Bodley Head: London, 1925) 73-77.
2   Hot oppressive wind which blows from the North coast of Africa over the Mediterranean and parts of southern Europe.

the tides and sending up faint miasmas in which the soul fevers and dissolves, as it rocks to and fro, vaguely queasy with the faint lurch of the gondola and its inhumanly slow progress.

Is it that such conditions of feeling exclude all remembrance of sounder life; or that there is really, to people like myself, a kind of poison of body and soul in Venice? For it seems to me that I have rarely been healthily happy in Venice, never quite free from regrets and from longings, or the delusive happiness which is streaked with them. The very beauty and poetry of Venice, its shimmering colours and sliding forms, as of a past whose heroism is overlaid by suspicion and pleasure-seeking (the builders of St. Mark's succeeded by the *Ridotto* masquerade of Longhi[1]), the things which Venice offers to the eye and the fancy conspire to melt and mar our soul like some music of ungraspable *timbres* and unstable rhythms and modulations, with the enervation also of "too much": more sequences of colours on the waters, more palaces, more canals, more romance, and more magnificence and squalor. In Venice I catch myself trying to *isolate*, if I may use such an expression, *the enough*. I have to realize the charm of one detail, to live through one suggestion (the rigging and mirrored keel of a single boat, or the grace of a single house, or the perfection, say, of one piece of stone lattice-work or framed marble slab in the narthex of St. Mark's), before I can live it into my own life and keep it as mine. The virtue of paucity, the stimulus of the insufficient and the unfinished, the spell of the fragment forcing us to furnish what it lacks out of our own heart and mind, these enhancements of the world and of us are not called forth by Venice. Venice is always too much and too much so. I cannot cope with it, it submerges me. It does not seem a mere association of fortuitous coincidences that Venice should make me understand what Wagner's music is to some other folk: Wagner was right to die there, and Browning should have died in the Euganean Hills or at Asolo.[2] Instead of the bracing effects of

---

1 St. Mark's Basilica, the much-admired Byzantine-style cathedral church of Venice; Pietro Longhi (1702-85), Venetian genre painter. The *ridotto* was an often rather disreputable space behind theatres where visitors from all parts of society mingled and engaged in conversation, gambling, and other forms of lively entertainment. Nearly all visitors were obliged to wear a mask. Longhi and other artists depicted dark-lit *ridotti* in their paintings.
2 Wilhem Richard Wagner (1813-83), German composer of operas, died at Venice as did the English Victorian poet Robert Browning (1812-89).

the other arts (its own earlier painting and its own Byzantine and Gothic carving), Venice, taken all in all, has the effect rather of music when music is least like them and most viciously itself. It brings up, with each dip of the oar, the past, or rather the might-have-been; it dissolves my energies like its own moist and shifting skies; it brings a knot into my throat and almost tears into my eyes, like a languorous waltz or a distant accordion, and into my mind the ignominious sadness of lovers' quarrels, like Musset's and George Sand's, of the going to bits of Byron,[1] and of its own long, shameful crumble, ending in sale of shrines and heirlooms, and dead women's fans and dead babies' shoes at the curiosity dealers.

And now, thank heaven, I am out of it all. On the top of the hill the oaks come to an end, and the scrub of Venetian sumach;[2] there is only thin grass and broken volcanic stone. Opposite are faintly outlined Alps, and at the end of the misty twilit plain one knows that there is Venice.

But I am out of it, and safe. That marvellous, more than Wagnerian symphony of sights and fancies, with its lapsing rhythms and insidious *timbres* and modulations, is out of earshot of my spirit. All I can hear is Alpine wind among the grasses, dimmed farmyard sounds, and the note of a cricket, delicate in the stillness. And in myself a certain melody of Beethoven's,[3] one of a quartet, the words of which are ... well, *Out of Venice at last*, or much to that effect.

The Euganean Hills, in the centre of the Veneto region, were famously praised by the Romantic poet Percy Bysshe Shelley, while Asolo, a beautiful little town in the Treviso province of the Veneto, was much loved by Browning and commemorated in his last volume *Asolando*, published on his death day.

1   Alfred de Musset (1810-57), French Romantic poet and lover of Armandine Aurore Dudevant, better known as the woman novelist George Sand (1804-76). The couple moved to Venice in December 1833 but the relationship quickly deteriorated and ended in 1834; George Gordon Byron (1788-1824), major English Romantic poet, was mostly resident in Venice from 1816 to 1819 writing poetry and leading a life of pleasure.

2   Venetian sumach or *Rhus cotinus* is an attractive shrub or small tree better known as the "smoke tree" or "smoke bush."

3   Ludvig van Beethoven (1770-1827), famous German composer of Flemish descent and here cited as an antithesis to Wagner.

Bibliography

Primary Texts (For details of Lee's many articles, see the bibliography by Phyllis F. Mannocchi listed below.)

Studies of the Eighteenth Century in Italy. London: W. Satchell, 1880.

Studies of the Eighteenth Century in Italy. 2nd edition, with a Retrospective Chapter. London: T. Fisher Unwin, 1907.

Tuscan Fairy Tales. London: W. Satchell, 1880.

Belcaro: Being Essays on Sundry Æsthetical Questions. London: W. Satchell, 1881.

Ottilie: An Eighteenth Century Idyll. London: T. Fisher Unwin, 1883.

The Prince of the Hundred Soups. London: T. Fisher Unwin, 1883.

The Countess of Albany. Eminent Women Series. London: W.H. Allen, 1884.

Euphorion: Being Studies of the Antique and the Mediæval in the Renaissance. London: T. Fisher Unwin, 1884.

Miss Brown. 3 vols. Edinburgh: W. Blackwood, 1884.

A Phantom Lover: A Fantastic Story. Edinburgh: W. Blackwood, 1886.

Baldwin: Being Dialogues on Views and Aspirations. London: T. Fisher Unwin, 1886.

Juvenilia: Being a Second Series of Essays on Sundry Æsthetical Questions. London: T. Fisher Unwin, 1887.

Hauntings: Fantastic Stories. London: W. Heinemann, 1890.

Vanitas: Polite Stories. London: W. Heinemann, 1892.

Vanitas: Polite Stories Including the Hitherto Unpublished Story "A Frivolous Conversation." 2nd ed. London: John Lane, 1911.

Althea: A Second Book of Dialogues on Aspirations and Duties. London: Osgood, McIlvaine & Co., 1894.

Renaissance Fancies and Studies: Being a Sequel to Euphorion. London: Smith, Elder & Co., 1895.

Limbo, and Other Essays. London: Grant Richards, 1897.

Genius Loci: Notes on Places. London: Grant Richards, 1899.

Ariadne in Mantua: A Romance in Five Acts. Oxford: Basil Blackwell, 1903.

Penelope Brandling: A Tale of the Welsh Coast in the Eighteenth Century. London: T. Fisher Unwin, 1903.

Hortus Vitae: Essays on the Gardening of Life. London: John Lane, 1904.

Pope Jacynth and Other Fantastic Tales. London: Grant Richards, 1904.

The Enchanted Woods and Other Essays. London: John Lane, 1905.

Sister Benvenuta and the Christ Child: An Eighteenth Century Legend. New York: Mitchell Kennerley, 1905; London: Grant Richards, 1906.

The Spirit of Rome: Leaves from a Diary. London: John Lane, 1906.

Gospels of Anarchy, and Other Contemporary Studies. London: T. Fisher Unwin, 1908.

Laurus Nobilis: Chapters on Art and Life. London: John Lane, 1908.

Limbo and Other Essays to Which is Now Added Ariadne in Mantua. London: John Lane, 1908.

The Sentimental Traveller: Notes on Places. London: John Lane, 1908.

Beauty and Ugliness, and Other Studies in Psychological Aesthetics. With Clementina Anstruther-Thomson. London: John Lane, 1912.

Vital Lies: Studies of Some Varieties of Recent Obscurantism. 2 vols. London: John Lane, 1912.

The Beautiful: An Introduction to Psychological Aesthetics. Cambridge: Cambridge UP, 1913.

Louis Norbert: A Two-fold Romance. London: John Lane, 1914.

The Tower of Mirrors and Other Essays on the Spirit of Places. London: John Lane, 1914.

The Ballet of the Nations: A Present-day Morality. London: Chatto & Windus, 1915.

Satan the Waster: A Philosophical War Trilogy. London: John Lane, 1920; Reissued, with a new Preface by the author. London: John Lane, 1930.

The Handling of Words and Other Studies in Literary Psychology. London: John Lane, 1923.

Art and Man: Essays and Fragments. By Clementina Anstruther-Thomson. Edited and with an introduction by Vernon Lee. London: John Lane, 1924.

The Golden Keys and Other Essays on the Genius Loci. London: John Lane, 1925.

Proteus: Or the Future of Intelligence. London: Kegan Paul, Trench, Trübner and Co., 1925.

The Poet's Eye: Notes on some Differences between Verse and Prose.
The Hogarth Essays Series. London: L. and V. Woolf,
Hogarth Press, 1926.
For Maurice: Five Unlikely Stories. London: John Lane, 1927.
*A Vernon Lee Anthology: Selections from the Earlier works by Irene
Cooper Willis.* Explanatory Notice by Vernon Lee. London:
John Lane, 1929.
*Music and Its Lovers: An Empirical Study of Emotional and Imagi-
native Responses to Music.* London: G. Allen & Unwin, 1932.
Vernon Lee's Letters, edited with an Introduction by Irene
Cooper Willis. London: Privately Printed, 1937.

Selections (Stories)

The Snake Lady and Other Stories, ed. Horace Gregory. New
York: Grove Press, 1954.
Supernatural Tales: Excursions into Fantasy, ed. Irene Cooper
Willis. London: Peter Owen, 1955; Reprinted 1987.
Pope Jacynth and More Supernatural Tales. London: Peter Owen,
1956.
Vernon Lee: Hauntings: The Supernatural Stories, ed. David G.
Rowlands. Ashcroft, British Columbia: Ash-Tree Press,
2002.
Hauntings: Fantastic Stories. Doylestone, PA: Wildside Press,
Print on demand.

Bibliographies

Mannocchi, Phyllis F. "Vernon Lee: A Reintroduction and
Primary Bibliography." *English Literature in Transition 1880-
1920* 26: 4 (1983): 231-267.
Markgraf, Carl. "Vernon Lee: A Commentary and Annotated
Bibliography." *English Literature in Transition 1880-1920* 26: 4
(1983): 268-312.

Biography and Background

Colby, Vineta. "The Puritan Aesthete: Vernon Lee." *The Singu-
lar Anomaly: Women Novelists of the Nineteenth Century.* New
York and London: New York UP and U of London P, 1970.
235-304.
———. *Vernon Lee: A Literary Biography.* Charlottesville and
London: U of Virginia P, 2003.

Gunn, Peter. *Vernon Lee: Violet Paget, 1856-1935*. London: Oxford University Press, 1964.

Mannocchi, Phyllis F. "Vernon Lee and Kit Anstruther-Thompson: A Study of Love and Collaboration between Romantic Friends." *Women's Studies* 12 (1986): 129-48.

Secondary Criticism

Agnew, Lois. "Vernon Lee and the Victorian Aesthetic Movement: Feminine Souls and Shifting Sites of Contest." *Nineteenth-Century Prose* 26: 2 (1999): 127-42.

Basham, Diana. Ch 5: "Life after Spiritualism: Victorian Women's Ghost Stories." *The Trial of Woman: Feminism and the Occult Sciences in Victorian Literature and Society*. London and Basingstoke: Macmillan, 1992. 151-177.

Beer, Gillian. "The Dissidence of Vernon Lee: Satan the Waster and the Will to Believe." In *Women's Fiction and the Great War*, eds. Suzanne Raitt and Trudi Tate. Oxford: Clarendon Press, 1997. 107-31.

Bizzotto, Elisa. "I discepoli pateriani: Vernon Lee e Oscar Wilde." *La Mano e l'anima: Il ritratto immaginario fin de siècle*. Milan: Cisalpino, 2001. 97-128.

——. "Pater's Reception in Italy: A General View." In *The Reception of Walter Pater in Europe*, ed. Stephen Bann. London and New York: Athlone Press, 2004. 62-86.

Block, Jr., Edwin F. "The Classical Mirror: Violet Paget's 'Amour Dure' (1890)." *Rituals of Disintegration: Romance and Madness in the Victorian Psychomythic Tale*. New York and London: Garland Publishing Inc., 1993. 61-88.

Brown, Alison. "Vernon Lee and the Renaissance: From Burckhardt to Berenson." In *Victorian and Edwardian Responses to the Italian Renaissance, c. 1800-c.1900*, ed. J. Law and L. Østermark-Johansen. Aldershot and Burlington VT: Ashgate, 2005.

Caballero, Carlo. "'A Wicked Voice': On Vernon Lee, Wagner and the Effects of Music." *Victorian Studies* 35: 4 (1992): 385-408.

Cary, Richard. "Vernon Lee's Vignettes of Literary Acquaintances." *Colby Library Quarterly* 9 (1970): 179-99.

Christensen, Peter. "The Burden of History in Vernon Lee's Ghost Story 'Amour Dure'." *Studies in the Humanities* 16: 1 (1989): 33-43.

——. "'A Wicked Voice': Vernon Lee's Artist Parable." *Lamar Journal of the Humanities* 15: 2 (1989): 3-15.

Denisoff, Dennis. "Vernon Lee." In *Nineteenth-Century British Women Writers: A Biobibliographical Sourcebook*, ed. Abigail Burnham Bloom. New York: Greenwood, 2000. 249-51.

——. "The Forest Beyond the Frame: Picturing Women's Desires in Vernon Lee and Virginia Woolf." In *Women and British Aestheticism*, eds. Talia Schaffer and Kathy Alexis Psomiades. Charlottesville: University of Virginia Press, 2000. 251-69.

——. "Vernon Lee's Sapphic Aestheticisms." *Aestheticism and Sexual Parody: 1840-1940.* Cambridge: Cambridge University Press, 2001. 42-55.

——. "The Forest Beyond the Frame: Women's Desires in Vernon Lee and Virginia Woolf." *Sexual Visuality from Literature to Film, 1850-1950.* London: Palgrave, 2004. 98-120. (Revised version.)

——. "Nasty Business: Vernon Lee and the Decadence of Stability." *Maschillità decadenti: La Lunga fin de siècle*, eds. Marco Pustianaz and Luisa Villa. Bergamo: Sestante/Bergamo University Press, 2004. 281-300.

Edel, Leon. "Henry James and Vernon Lee." *PMLA* 69 (1954): 677-8.

Fraser, Hilary. "Women and the Ends of Art History: Vision and Corporeality in Nineteenth-Century Discourse." *Victorian Studies* 42: 1 (1999): 77-100.

——. "Vernon Lee: England, Italy and Identity Politics." In *Britannia Italia Germania: Taste and Travel in the Nineteenth Century*, eds. Carol Richardson and Graham Smith. Edinburgh, VARIE, at the University of Edinburgh, 2001. 175-91.

——. "Regarding the Eighteenth Century: Vernon Lee and Emilia Dilke Construct a Period." In *The Victorians and the Eighteenth Century*, eds. Francis O'Gorman, and Kathleen Turner. Aldershot and Burlington VT: Ashgate, 2004. 223-49.

——. "Interstitial Identities: Vernon Lee and the spaces in-between." In *Marketing the Author: Authorial Personae, Narrative Selves and Self Fashioning 1880-1930*, ed. Marysa Demoor. Houndmills, Basingstoke: Palgrave, 2004. 114-33.

Gardner, Burdett. "An Apology for Henry James's 'Tiger Cat'." *PMLA* 68 (1953): 688-95.

——. *The Lesbian Imagination (Victorian Style): A Psychological and Critical Study of Vernon Lee* (Dissertation 1954). Published New York: Garland, 1987.

Geffroy-Menoux, Sophie. "Celebrations in the Texts of Vernon Lee: The Disruption of the Carnivalesque." *Alizés* 13: *Celebrations, CAPES & Other Essays* (January 1997):157-75.

———. "Le fantastique de Vernon Lee au tournant du siècle: entre baroque et grotesque." In *La littérature fantastique en Grande-Bretagne au tournant du siècle*, ed. Max Duperray. Presses Universitaires de Provence, 1997. 147-70.

———. "L'imaginaire du souterrain/souterrain de l'imaginaire: Vernon Lee." In *Le souterrain*, ed. Aurelia Gaillard. Paris: L'Harmattan, 1998. 185-195.

———. "L'enfant dans les textes de Vernon Lee." *Cahiers Victoriens & Edouardiens* 47 (April 1998): 251-63.

———. "La musique dans les textes de Vernon Lee." *Cahiers Victoriens & Edouardiens* 49: "La musique" (April 1999): 57-70.

———. *La voix maudite: Trois nouvelles fantastiques de Vernon Lee.* Traduction, préface, postface, notes et une nouvelle inédite de S. Geoffroy-Menoux. Rennes: Terre de Brume, 2001.

———. "Triste cire, cendres ardentes: la 'poupée' de Vernon Lee." In *Le Visage Vert* 10, ed. Legrand Ferronnière. Paris: Joëlle Losfeld, 2001. 83-91.

———. "Les voix maudites de Vernon Lee: du bel canto a *mal'aria* dans 'Winthrop's Adventure' (1881), 'La voix maudite' (1887), 'The Virgin of the Seven Daggers'." *Alizés* 22 (June 2002): 113-34.

———. "L'esthétique trans-artistique picturo-musico-littéraire de Vernon Lee." Forthcoming in *Cahiers de Narratologie* 6 (June 2003) CNA, Presses Universitaires de Nice.

Hotchkiss, Jane. "(P)revising Freud: Vernon Lee's Castration Phantasy." In *Seeing Double: Revisioning Edwardian and Modernist Literature*, eds. Karla M. Kaplan and Anne B. Simpson. London and Basingstoke: Macmillan, 1996. 21-38.

Kane, Mary Patricia. *Spurious Ghosts: The Fantastic Tales of Vernon Lee.* Rome: Carocci, 2004.

Leighton, Angela. "Ghosts, Aestheticism, and Vernon Lee." *Victorian Literature and Culture* 28: 1 (2000): 1-14.

———. "Resurrections of the Body: Women Writers and the Idea of the Renaissance." In *Unfolding the South: Nineteenth-century British Women Writers and Artists in Italy 1789-1900*, eds. Alison Chapman and Jane Stabler. Manchester: Manchester U P, 2003. 222-38.

Licht, Merete. "Henry James's Portrait of a Lady: Vernon Lee in *The Princess Casamassima*." In *A Literary Miscellany Presented to Eric Jacobsen*, eds. Graham D. Caie and Holger Nørgaard. Copenhagen: Publications of the Department of the English Department of Copenhagen, 1988. 285-303.

Maltz, Diana. "Engaging 'Delicate Brains': From Working-Class Enculturation to Upper-Class Lesbian Liberation in Vernon Lee and Kit Anstruther-Thomson's Psychological Aesthetics." In *Women and British Aestheticism*, eds. Talia Schaffer and Kathy Alexis Psomiades. Charlottesville: U of Virginia P, 2000. 211-29.

Maxwell, Catherine. "From Dionysus to 'Dionea': Vernon Lee's Portraits." *Word & Image* 13, 3 (July-Sept 1997): 253-69.

———. "Vernon Lee and the Ghosts of Italy." In *Unfolding the South: Nineteenth-century British Women Writers and Artists in Italy 1789-1900*, eds. Alison Chapman and Jane Stabler. Manchester: Manchester UP, 2003. 201-21.

Melani, Sandro, "I ritratti fatali di Vernon Lee." *Rivista di Studi Vittoriani* 1 (1996): 125-41.

Navarette, Susan. "Articulating the Dead: Vernon Lee, Decadence and 'The Doll'." In *The Shape of Fear: Horror and the Fin de Siècle Culture of Decadence*. Kentucky: UP of Kentucky, 1998. 140-76.

O'Gorman, Francis, and Kathleen Turner, eds. *The Victorians and the Eighteenth Century Reassessing the Tradition*. Aldershot and Burlington VT: Ashgate, 2004. 223-49

Ormond, Leonée. "Vernon Lee as a Critic of Aestheticism in *Miss Brown*." *Colby Library Quarterly* 9 (1970): 131-54.

Ormond, Richard. "John Singer Sargent and Vernon Lee." *Colby Library Quarterly* 9 (1970): 154-78.

Palacio, Jean de. "Y a-t-il une écriture féminine de la Décadence? (à propos d'une nouvelle de Vernon Lee)." *Romantisme: Revue du Dix-Neuvième Siècle* 42 (1983): 177-86.

Pireddu, Nicoletta. *Antropologi all corte della bellezza. Decadenza ed economia simbolica nell Europa fin de siècle*. Verona: Edizioni Fiorini, 2002.

———. "Vernon Lee: Aesthetic Expenditure, *Noblesse Oblige*." In *Athena's Shuttle: Myth, Religion, Ideology from Romanticism to Modernism*, eds. Franco Marucci and Emma Sdegno. Milan: Cisalpino, 2000. 175-94.

Pulham, Patricia. "Vernon Lee: A Forgotten Voice." *The Hun-*

garian Journal of English and American Studies 5: 2 (Spring 1999): 51-62.

——. "The Castrato and the Cry in Vernon Lee's Wicked Voices." *Victorian Literature and Culture* 30: 2 (2002): 421-37.

——. "A Transatlantic Alliance: Charlotte Perkins Gilman and Vernon Lee." In *Feminist Forerunners: (New) Womanism and Feminism in the Early Twentieth Century,* ed. Ann Heilmann. London: Pandora Press, 2003. 34-43.

Psomiades, Kathy Alexis. *Beauty's Body: Femininity and Representation in British Aestheticism.* Stanford: Stanford UP, 1997. 165-77.

——. "'Still Burning from This Strangling Embrace': Vernon Lee on Desire and Aesthetics." In *Victorian Sexual Dissidence,* ed. Richard Dellamora. Chicago and London: U of Chicago P, 1999. 21-41.

Robbins, Ruth. "Vernon Lee: Decadent Woman?" In *Fears and Fantasies of the Late Nineteenth Century,* ed. John Stokes. London and Birmingham: Macmillan, 1992. 139-61.

Severi, Rita. ed. *Ariadne in Mantua/Arianna in Mantova.* Verona: Edizioni Postumia–Cierre, 1996.

——. "Vernon Lee and Mantua." *Journal of Anglo-Italian Studies* 5 (1998): 179-200.

——. "Vernon Lee a Bologna: La scrittrice ricorda i suoi viaggi." *Il Carrobbio* (2002): 217-26.

Tintner, Adeline R. "Fiction is the Best Revenge: Portraits of Henry James by Four Women Writers." *Turn of the Century Women* 2: 2 (Winter 1985): 42-9.

——. "Vernon Lee's 'Oke of Okehurst; Or the Phantom-Lover' and James's 'The Way It Came'." *Studies in Short Fiction* 28: 3 (Summer 1991): 355-62.

——. "Bronzino's *Lucrezia Panciatichi* in *The Wings of the Dove* via Vernon Lee." *Henry James and the Lust of the Eyes: Thirteen Artists in His Work.* Baton Rouge and London: Louisiana State UP, 1993. 95-104.

Vicinus, Martha. "The Adolescent Boy: Fin-de-Siècle Femme Fatale?" *Journal of the History of Homosexuality* 5, (1994): 90-114. Reprinted in *Victorian Sexual Dissidence,* ed. Richard Dellamora. Chicago and London: U of Chicago P, 1999. 83-106.

——. "'Singed by Love': Vernon Lee." In *Intimate Friends: Women Who Loved Women, 1778-1928.* Chicago and London: U of Chicago P, 2004. 152-165.

Weber, Carl J. "Henry James and His Tiger-Cat." *PMLA* 68 (1953): 672-87.

Zorn, Christa. "Aesthetic Intertextuality as Cultural Critique: Vernon Lee Rewrites History through Walter Pater's 'La Gioconda'." *The Victorian Newsletter* (Spring 1997): 4-10.

———. *Vernon Lee: Aesthetics, History and the Victorian Female Intellectual*. Athens, Ohio: Ohio UP, 2003.

Other texts

Lee-Hamilton, Eugene. *Selected Poems of Eugene Lee-Hamilton (1845-1907): A Victorian Craftsman Rediscovered*, ed. MacDonald P. Jackson. Studies in British Literature, Volume 63. Lewiston, Queenston and Lampeter: The Edwin Mellen Press, 2002.

Matarazzo, Francesco. *Chronicles of the City of Perugia*. Translated by Edward Strachan Morgan. London: J. M. Dent & Co., 1905.

Robinson, A. Mary F. *The Collected Poems, Lyrical and Narrative of A. Mary F. Robinson*. London: T. Fisher Unwin: London, 1902.

Symonds, John Addington. *Sketches in Italy and Greece*. London: Smith, Elder, & Co., 1874.

Symonds, John Addington. *Renaissance in Italy*. 7 vols. London: Smith, Elder & Co., 1875-1886.

The interior of this book is printed on 100% recycled paper.